Her
Fr
Se

BOOKS BY ANNA MANSELL

How to Mend a Broken Heart
The Lost Wife
I Wanted to Tell You

anna
mansell

Her Best Friend's Secret

Bookouture

Published by Bookouture in 2019

An imprint of StoryFire Ltd.

Carmelite House
50 Victoria Embankment
London EC4Y 0DZ

www.bookouture.com

ISBN: 978-1-78681-953-6
eBook ISBN: 978-1-78681-952-9

For Victoria

Prologue

Emily gazed out of the train window at Dawlish. The English Channel, rough as it was today, crashed against the sea wall, spraying the carriages with salty droplets. The last time she'd done this journey, it had been the other way, leaving Cornwall for a new life in L.A., at the behest of her father's legal career some twenty-four years ago. She'd been back several times in the last few years, pretty much whenever Jackson afforded her the time, but never on the train. Public transport? Jackson wouldn't hear of it. Things like that had been exciting in the early days, the way he cared for her, took control, she felt loved, she felt special, she felt like a princess... a feeling she now knew she'd grown more and more uncomfortable with. Suffocated. Controlled.

Another wave crashed against her window, the water like tiny pebbles smashing against the carriage. There was something she loved about trains: the romance, the possibility, the chance to daydream as the world whizzed by. Only daydreaming this time felt dangerous. She didn't want to think. She didn't want to let her mind wander into the what-ifs and maybes. She especially didn't want to revisit the last text Jackson sent to her because she couldn't allow anything to make her think twice about this return journey. She had lied to him and he had no idea. She shook off a flicker of guilt; she'd made the right decision, it was time to make a change. Besides, it was too late to go back now. And irrespective of what she had – or hadn't – done, New York wasn't home any more. Her old life wasn't right. She was forty. A new life beckoned, albeit out of the blue. A life as far away from her old one as she could possibly imagine. And if she was going to make it work, there was only one place she could be: Cornwall. Home. The only place anything had ever made sense.

Amanda

It was Amanda's third shower of the day. Thursdays could be like that. Thursdays at the end of the month, particularly so. She got it; she'd be the same. Except when she used to get her pay cheque it was a gorgeously unusual pair of Irregular Choice shoes that she'd spend the surplus on, not sex. Still, she wasn't judging, she had bills to pay. And she desperately wanted to invite her daughter Zennor on holiday. She missed the bones of her, the way she used to laugh at Amanda's jokes, or complain at her when she moved a stray hair from her face. Amanda missed showing her teenage daughter tenderness because long before she moved out, Zennor didn't want to see it, or feel it any more. Amanda had always hoped it was a phase, just hormones getting in the way of being open to signs of love and affection from her mother. But then she moved to live with her dad and things got progressively worse. She rarely picked the phone up to Amanda now, never mind allowed her to show her love. Could they get that back? With a week in the sun? She had to at least try so the extra cash from all these clients might just make the pipe dream a reality.

Amanda perched on the edge of the bath, drying herself, leaning into the memory of her last holiday: Tenerife, the warmth of the sun on her back; two weeks of lounging by the pool with a good book. Admittedly, her last trip away had been paid for by a client, the kind of client who genuinely just wanted her company. An escort in the truest sense. The kind of escort job she'd signed up to do when this business was first offered as a viable alternative to cleaning holiday lets down in St Agnes. She hated cleaning. She was crap at it. And at £10 an hour – on a good day – it was a tenth of what she could earn an hour doing what she did now; and she'd never once had an orgasm whilst cleaning the grout on a fishing loft conversion.

Not that she got them with Mr Tenerife. The physical side of their relationship didn't progress beyond escorting, but they'd become good friends. He'd tell her how he felt less lonely when with her. That she had been one of the things to turn his life around after his wife passed away. Companionship on his terms. They read books side by side, put the world to rights over dinner, she'd listen to him reminisce over his life and times, she'd hold his hand as he spoke of regrets: the lack of children being his biggest. When he grew too ill to visit her, she popped in to see him, first at home, then at the hospice. When he passed, she hadn't expected the grief that followed. She still missed Mr Tenerife.

There was a knock at the door, loud and purposeful. She could tell a lot by a door knock. She could tell if she'd be the one guiding them in, taking it slowly, settling their nerves. Or if she'd open the door and be suffocated by some bloke's desire to get his end away. This was definitely an end away kind of guy. Today that suited her though, not least because she'd promised George next door that she'd pop round and re-programme his heating.

She unhooked the silk negligee from her bathroom door, looking longingly at the hoody and lounge pants she was desperate to get in to today. She slicked on lip gloss, ruffled her hair to life, then headed for the front door.

She could see his reflection through the glass. Tall. She liked them tall. He shifted weight from one foot to another. He was broad too. Broad and tall. Broad, tall and knocking again. Broad, tall and eager then. This might actually be fun.

'Hi,' she said, smile wide, hair flicked, cleavage gently accentuated as she coquettishly leaned against the door. 'I've been waiting, oh!—' God. Was that…? Was Sixth Form Trev stood in her doorway? Imaginatively titled because he was in the year above Amanda at school and his surname was Trevelly. 'Well, hi!' she said as he pushed through the door, giving her a grin and a wink. She clicked it shut behind her, wondering why the hottest boy from school was now standing in her hallway, all grown up and about to pay for her services, some twenty plus years later. 'Well… I didn't expect to see you… I mean… wow.'

He took off his jacket, slinging it on the bannister. 'Is that okay there?' he asked, his come-to-bed eyes apparently seeing past her fluster.

'Yeah, of course. No problem. Uhm, so… again, wow.'

'What?' He took a step towards her, groin first.

Amanda recomposed herself. 'Sixth Form Trev!' she said, because that was definitely not the name he'd booked under, she might have neatened up her shave had she known. 'Is that really you?'

'I'm no longer in the sixth form and most people use my proper name these days, but yes, it's me.'

Christ. The number of times she'd thought about shagging Sixth Form Trev, back in the day. 'Do you… remember me?' she asked, resisting letting her own groin touch his because probably they needed to sort out the housekeeping first.

His face didn't flinch but he let out a low laugh. 'Amanda Kenwyn. If I'm not very much mistaken.'

'Perhaps I've not aged that much,' she purred.

'No more than me.' He took another step towards her. She shifted her weight as he leaned closer, she could feel him ready to go.

'And you're okay about that?'

Trev fixed her with a look that suggested he was more than okay with that. She swallowed. He leaned in, brushing his lips against hers at first before kissing with an urgency she rarely got from first-time clients. His breath was heavy, his kisses hot. 'Where do you want me?' he asked, looking around her hallway.

'Eager?'

'It's been a while…'

She bit down on her lip, resisting the suggestion that they could start off in the lounge, then work through every room in her modest Truro town house. At no additional cost.

'Through here,' she said, moving past him and down the hallway to her back room. He followed, his clothes rustling as he dropped them to the floor. 'The money goes on the side. Do you need a shower first?'

A black ginger and neroli candle burned, the scent welcoming her as she opened the door to her work room, the inviting clean bed sheets turned her on even more and as he dropped two £50 notes on the side, she knew she just had to pretend she was doing him a service, and very much not the other way around…

Emily

Emily looked down at her iPhone. Three thirty. Eighteen exhausting hours ago she'd checked in at JFK Airport. The flight home hadn't been delayed but every single part of her journey since arriving back on UK soil had taken forever. She'd made it as far as Truro but the branch line was down so she had no choice but to get a bus back, her heart – and spirit – deflated on realising there was anything up to two more hours before she'd finally make it home. It was only ever at times like this that she considered whether buying a house in the remote, tiny Cornish village of Gorran Haven had been a mistake. Not that she'd let on to her father when she finally called her parents to explain why she'd not be visiting them in the Hamptons this weekend. She knew that whatever he thought of her buying a sixteenth century farm cottage in a village with barely any phone signal, she would feel peace the second she walked through the stable door. And if Jenny from down the lane had done the shopping as she promised she would, Emily would have no cause to leave the house for days. After the last few weeks… months… jeez, it was probably longer, Emily could not be happier about that. Home. Somewhere nobody gave a shit about who she was, who she'd worked with, what awards she had or hadn't won. Somewhere she could dress how she liked, eat what she wanted, be the person she wanted to be without criticism or judgement. Nobody remotely cared and that was everything she needed right now.

Making her way across the glossy pavements, wet in the Cornish mizzle, she headed from Truro train station, down through town, over to the bus stop. She passed Mannings, the hotel Jackson always made them stop at if they ever visited Cornwall. She always wanted to be by the sea but he felt being in the city was better, even though he'd complain at how quiet it was compared to New York. There was no comparison she'd say. That's why she liked it. He never got the point of Cornwall and couldn't understand why she had wanted to buy a place there. He'd taken no interest in it and had never even bothered to visit. He wanted her in New York. He wanted her on hand for auditions, for networking, for smiling and being pretty whenever he needed her to be. She looked down at the clothes she had left their apartment in, twenty-four hours earlier. Elasticated waistbands just as advised. A loose-fitting shirt. Comfortable clothes for an uncomfortable appointment.

Her phone dinged with a message, her Apple Watch replicating the announcement. His name came up and she scrolled down to get rid of yet another desperate text. What was it now? Thirty? One just before the appointment she had ignored because she'd already started having doubts, then every hour after the fact. Thirty texts. Roughly the same number in emails. God knows how many phone calls, initially from his assistant before Emily's absence was escalated to him calling directly himself. He'd probably also been the one to get the theatre company manager to call on the pretence of checking she was okay after the run had finished. The curtain had come down; the applause dissolved; when she could no longer hear the ringing in her ears, Emily could hear herself think. And whilst she didn't know what she did want, she was pretty certain of what she didn't want. Now, with an ocean between them, however long this journey had been, it was only a matter of time before she'd stop looking backwards and start feeling better. She hoped.

Head up. The statue of The Drummer in Lemon Quay in sight, Emily headed back towards the bus station. She marvelled at the drummer's nakedness, the controversy having made it over to NY via social media, though now it seemed seagull poo pretty much protected his modesty. There was a new Primark open and some kind of food market set up in white tents across the pedestrian precinct. There was a big sign for ostrich burgers and Emily wondered when things had got so artisan.

'Emily?'

She pulled up sharp at the sound of her name. 'Emily Nance... is that you?'

In true professional style, Emily painted on the smile that went with signing autographs and taking selfies. The village might not give a damn who she was but she supposed it might be different in Truro, or maybe Falmouth. She spun round, ready to greet her fan. 'Of course it's me, hi!' She tried to hide the American drawl she'd picked up, it had no place now she was home.

'Oh my god! You haven't changed a bit!'

Emily peered at the woman before her. She was pretty, a neatly cut bob. Her eyes sparkled and her smile was friendly. She didn't have a camera phone or a pad and pen for signing. She had a white tunic on, a name badge pinned. Lauren. Lauren?

'God, it's been bloody years, hasn't it! How many? Twenty? Actually, it must be more, what year did you go? Ninety-seven? Ninety-six? Jesus, how are we so old? Though you look amazing. How *are* you? How's life? I heard you were in New York now! Did L.A. get a bit much? You're still acting though, right? I couldn't believe it when I heard you were doing it, though I don't know why, you always said you'd be an actress.' The woman pulled her into a hug. It wasn't one of those actor type hugs that don't feel like the person actually wanted to touch you, no, this was like a meant hug, with added squeeze and real-life affection. 'How the bloody hell are you?'

And as the woman released Emily, her smile grew familiar, her blonde hair was shorter now, but it was the same colour. It was as fine as it ever was. Her mouth was painted with the same shade of frosted pink lipstick she used to wear back when they were teenagers. Emily's heart leaped. 'Bloody hell, Lolly? *Lolly*! It never is... Lolly Teague?'

'Yes,' she said, 'that's me!'

'Lolly.' Emily took a moment, unsure how to feel about such familiarity standing before her. It was what she'd come home for but now it was in front of her...

'I know I've said it, but, god you look amazing. I saw that film, the one about the woman who climbed Everest on her own, which by the way was incredible! Did you actually have to climb Everest or was it all CGI? I said to my husband, "Surely she can't have had to climb it." We watched it at the Regal. It was amazing. HD and everything, your skin looked phenomenal and I was like, "Can that possibly be real, we are all so old now," and look at you, here in Truro. Stood right before me in real life definition and,' she peered at Emily's skin, 'yes, it bloody well is real.'

Emily coloured slightly. Mostly because she'd spent quite a lot of money on a dermabrasion before the Everest film and it felt a little unfair for Lolly to think that she'd still look like this without spending thousands on facial routines and not living on a cliff top in Cornwall any more. 'Thanks, though... I've had a bit of help. Perks of the job, you know?'

'Right.'

Lolly stepped back, her body posture suddenly shifting from excited kid to slightly worn down... nurse? Is that what she is now? Emily wasn't sure and felt bad that she had no idea. How had someone so important become such a stranger? A stranger. That's effectively what she was. Time has changed. Life has moved on. So, probably, has she. 'Lolly, it's so lovely to see you. I…' she glanced over at the bus stop and down at her watch '… I have to get a bus though,' she said, apologetically. 'I'm on the last leg of a horrendous journey – I bought a place in Gorran Haven a while back, it's time to settle back home.' She paused and felt her feet throbbing. 'But if I have to be in these trainers for any longer than is absolutely necessary I think my feet might implode.'

'Oh, of course. Sorry. Go on. Wow, though. How lovely to see you, I'm—' She stopped, as if thinking twice about what she was going to say before coming out with it anyway. 'I'm a big fan. You know, just like I was back in the day. Well done, you made it. You're doing it. I never doubted you.'

Emily pulled her in for a squeeze, basically to buy herself time to blink back the tears that such sentiment invited. It seemed odd to feel so distant from the woman standing before her, the woman who, when they were teenage girls, pretty much fuelled Emily's self-belief. Would she ever have made it in life were it not for Lolly's enthusiastic encouragement? Probably not… a fact that placed Emily even further away from a zone in which compliments were welcome. 'Thanks,' she said, squeezing her eyes tightly shut. 'It's lovely to see you.' She released Lolly. 'I'd better be going…'

'Sure. Of course. Well… see you…'

'Yeah… bye.'

Emily moved to cross the road to the bus terminus but a hand caught her arm. 'Hey, this is my number. In case you wanna catch up. It'd be lovely to chat, you know… I mean, I'm sure you've got loads of friends now, you're probably overrun by people.' Emily looked down at the scrap of paper Lolly was scribbling her number on. 'And not cause you're famous or anything, it's not that. I just remember how much we'd laugh, when we were kids. And, I feel like I've a whole load to tell you and a whole lot of listening to do. If you wanna. No pressure. Just… you know… if you like.'

'That'd be cool, Lolly. At some point. Yes. Thanks.'

The women stared at each other, each considering the other and their past and the lives they'd not shared and the stories they could tell. And Emily felt her heart drop to her stinky trainers at the prospect of having to tell anybody about the reality of what appeared to be such a life. She buried every part of her that wanted to drag Lolly to the nearest pub and tell her everything, stuffing the number in her jeans pocket instead.

Lolly

'Hey, babes, you won't believe who I saw today!' Lolly kicked her clogs off, threw her bag in the understairs cupboard and went off in search of Kitt, her husband of fifteen years. She found him at his desk, hunched over his laptop. 'I swear to god, you won't guess!'

Lolly still hadn't got used to his new glasses so peered for a moment from his office doorway. She didn't look at him much these days, she realised that as she stared. They just milled around one another normally, getting on with life as husband and wife, parents, employees. Did that change when the kids came along? That sense of the other one being almost invisible? Not in a bad way, just in a… life carries on and they were comfortable way. He was starting to look a bit like his dad and she wondered if she looked much like her mum, except that Lolly was now older than her mum, the last time she saw her.

Kitt peered up from the laptop, adjusting the bridge down his nose so he could focus on her.

'Come on, try and guess!'

'Guess what?'

'Who I saw today.'

'God, I don't know!'

'You'll not believe it.'

Kitt fixed her with an exasperated look, before throwing his glasses on the desk and leaning back in his chair. 'If I'll not believe it then I'll never guess so why don't we cut out the middle man?'

'Because that's not as much fun!' Lolly narrowed her eyes. 'If you guess it, we can have sex,' she purred.

'Wow, we're gaming for favours now, are we?' He didn't sound as turned on by the idea as she had hoped.

'Come on, the kids won't be back until six. I make that forty-five minutes.' She lowered her voice. 'We could do it right here, on your desk.' She stepped inside his office, ruffling her hair so it fell across her face in a way he'd once said he found really sexy. She'd laughed because she could barely see out, but at this point in time, she would do anything to get laid and he definitely seemed to need more provocation than once upon a time. 'You don't have to do anything. Just sit there, let me—'

'I have to get this finished, Lolly. I'm late, it should have been in by lunchtime. If I don't get it done they won't trust me to work from home again.'

'Maybe I can help?' Lolly stepped across to his desk, laying it on thick: a fixed look, open lips, a bend at the hips to see what he was doing so there'd be just enough gap down her top for him to perve. Which he did, just as she knew he would. Some things don't change. 'If time is a problem, I can be quick.'

'Quick?' he said, moving his glasses from the desk as she straddled him.

'Really quick.'

She kissed his ear, which always made him groan. 'It's the perfect time, babe. I just need your sperm. You don't have to do a thing.'

Kitt got hold of Lolly's hands, just as she was about to unbuckle his jeans. 'It's the perfect time?' he said, coldly.

'Well, I mean, you know…' Shit. She knew she should have stuck to the come on and not mentioned the fact that her phone app had told her she had a three-hour window to maximise their chances of conceiving, hence practically running home from the bus.

'You just need my sperm,' he said, moving her from his knee. She rubbed her wrist where he'd held too tight.

'I don't mean it like that, I want *you* too.' He shrugged, disbelieving. 'Of course I want you too, I love you.' She leant back in to kiss him but as was the case so often of late, he didn't respond.

'Lolly, I can't keep doing this. It doesn't feel… I don't know. It's all so…'

'What?' She was pushing him now. The last time they'd had this discussion, he'd said she was desperate and that caused a fair and proper row. They didn't speak for days after that until she decided to apologise because he'd made it clear how much she'd hurt him and, if she was totally honest, she'd hit the final window in that ovulation cycle and couldn't bear the idea of another month not being pregnant when she took her next test.

Kitt sighed. 'We need to take our time, Lolly. I can't just… perform. You know? I want to feel like you want *me*, not just my sperm.'

'I want both.'

'And the doctor said it might not work. It can take a year or so after the reversal before things are back to normal. We can keep doing this, but maybe it's just not going to happen. And we're not getting any younger. I don't know… maybe…' Lolly bit down hard on her bottom lip because she knew what was coming next and it wasn't going to be her. 'Why can't you be happy with the two we've got?' he said, quietly.

Her bottom lip wobbled. Her eyes stung. No matter how hard she looked up to the ceiling, she knew she was going to cry and she was even more annoyed that her tears weren't a result of raging hormones. Not the pregnancy kind, at any rate.

'Come here.' He pulled her back onto his lap, holding her tight. 'I know, I know you want another, but I think you have to be realistic. And besides, I've had a full-on day. I'm behind on this, the kids are going to be back soon. Can you imagine the years of therapy if they walked in on us fucking by the fish tank?'

Lolly let out one of those teary sad laughs. She looked over at the fish tank, just able to make out her reflection, refracted by a skull and one of those sunken pirate ship things. 'I suppose so.'

'Look, let's make some time this weekend. Ted's got a sleep over and Stan won't hear a thing when he's asleep. We can take our time. Make love. Be together because we want to be, not just because your temperature is right and you need my sperm.' He kissed her, gently. 'I love you.'

He hadn't been this affectionate for months. She couldn't remember the last time he looked her in the eye like he was doing now. Was he still inside? The man she fell for all those years ago? The man who rescued her? Who promised her everything so long as they were side by side?

'I love you too,' she said.

'Then let me finish this,' he said, with a half-smile, before moving her out of his way. 'Come on. It's nearly five thirty and you've not got your PJs on yet. The world could very possibly end.'

Lolly nodded because it was true, she had been in the house for more than five minutes and hadn't yet taken off her bra. If she hadn't been desperate to get pregnant this would basically be unheard of. 'Okay. Okay. Sorry.'

'I know you are. It's fine. I get it.'

Lolly wasn't sure that he did. Not really. Partly because she'd never said that actually, she was desperate to have another child on the basis that the odds had to work in her favour. She wanted a girl. And she knew it was selfish and she knew it wasn't right to have a preference and she knew she was a bad person and if she told anyone she wouldn't blame them for judging her, but it was how it was. She wanted a girl. She wanted what her sister, Joanna, and their mum had had. What she had never experienced because her mum passed away when Lolly was small. She wanted to fix the past with a new future. She wanted that bond. That connection between mother and daughter. She loved her sons, of course she did. They were... everything. She just really, really wanted a daughter too. No matter how guilty that made her feel.

Jess

'You off home?' Jess asked from behind her laptop.

'Yeah, got a date with that bloke from last week,' said one of the juniors, Vicky.

'Wow, really? The one who squeaked?'

'Thought I'd see if it was a one-off. Or if he could mimic any other animals during intercourse.'

'So it's research.'

'Right.'

'And not at all because he knows how to find your G spot without using Google.'

'Definitely not that.'

'Well, have fun. Perhaps don't text me straight after this time. I couldn't get back to sleep, every time I closed my eyes I had visions and audio that I just don't need.' Jess went back to her laptop, making a few more notes on the pitch she'd been working up all day, distractions, distractions. 'Oh, Vic!'

Vicky popped her head back round the door. 'Yeah?'

'Top job today, really good. I reckon they're gonna be your first new client.'

'Fingers crossed!' Vicky beamed.

'And the new guy, Jay, he should be good to work with on it. He knows his stuff, so… you'll make a good team.'

'Do you think? I'm nervous. New job, new boss. I liked working with you. I don't like change. And what if he's a dick?'

'He's not a dick.'

'How do you know?'

'I know him,' she said, because there was no point hiding that fact at least. 'I've known him for years. Not… closely, you know. I guess I know of him, more than know, know him. But he's good. He's great. You'll be fine.'

'Yeah, and I can still talk to you if needs be, right?'

'Of course you can. Always!'

'Cheers, Jess.' She went to leave, then paused. 'You'll be a tough act to follow. As bosses go.' Vicky smiled, then left, leaving Jess alone in the office. Again.

Normally, she didn't mind this time of night. She'd always got most of her work done between six and eight of an evening. It was rare she had company, unless there was a really big project that all the team were involved in. And since she would start later than most, mornings not really being her thing, it suited her. The office would shut down, phones would go quiet. Lights in corners of the open plan would automatically sense a lack of motion, sending corners into darkness. Which was fine until one randomly came on and Jess shit herself thinking someone had come back in to spook her… or worse. Her imagination totally made her great at her job. Advertising, marketing, it all needed wild thinking and a creative brain. It's just that the same brain was also capable of making her think she was about to be cut down by the water cooler, despite the treble locks and Dave the security guard downstairs.

Dave the security guard. Bless him. He'd asked her out again this lunchtime, just quietly, on the down low. Keen not to embarrass her but keen for her to realise he was serious. That he had been for months now. She felt bad for him, she'd known about unrequited love and she knew it could take a while to get over it, but he would. She had. At least, she thought she had. Until the focus of her unrequited affections appeared on the stairwell, heading to her place for an interview with the directors. The man she thought she'd moved on from stood before her on the third floor. Did he move as if to give her a hug or was that her imagination too? He said he was thrilled to see her after 'all this time', but she wasn't sure he could be. She'd broken his heart, hadn't she? Or maybe not, since he'd moved on… Either way, it was a lifetime ago and the grown-up in her told her it didn't need to matter. She smiled. She wished him luck. Then she hid in the toilet from him for something like forty-five minutes… only coming out in the end because she was desperate for a cigarette.

Jay Trewellan. Unlike what she'd told Vicky, Jess knew Jay well. From the way his eyes crinkled when he laughed to the tiny, heart-shaped freckle on his chest. Despite all the years that had passed, she could still imagine the feel of his lips against hers, or how safe she felt in his arms. Safe. Something she'd so needed to feel when they first met.

The first thing she looked for was a ring on his wedding finger and the thump in her heart when she saw it spoke volumes. Still there after all these years. Jealousy. It hurt to know Jay and his wife Niamh were still together, no doubt perfect, happy, in love. And it hurt that she couldn't let them have that, without feeling such deep-seated, unattractive, jealousy. What a hateful emotion. What kind of person was she? Why couldn't she just let them be together, why couldn't she be happy for them? She'd been the one to walk away, after all. She'd been the one to tell him she was going travelling, that she needed to be free and he couldn't keep her from that. She'd been the one to tell him she was happy for them when she was in New Zealand, eighteen months later, and he'd emailed to tell her about their relationship. It stung, she remembered that, but she wasn't ready to go home. She was trying her very best to live the young life she thought she was supposed to. One that drowned out anything that went before it with drink and drugs and meaningless sex with strangers. She certainly wasn't ready to settle down. Jay and Niamh were. She just hadn't anticipated how much that fact would hurt her when she finally came home. Or how real she'd feel the loss when she went on dates with different blokes and realised that Jay was the only man to ever make her feel like it was her he wanted to be with. Her, not just her body. Not her bum or her boobs or her curves. He was the only man to ever make her feel like she was sexy because she was smart and funny and had spirit. She had never before, or since for that matter, been with a man that did not simply objectify her for his own sexual gain. She got attraction, she did, she'd seen Tom Hardy, she knew about lust, but Jay? Jay was a whole different ball game. How could she have walked away from someone who'd made everything better?

Emily

Emily wrapped herself up in the freshly laundered terry towelling dressing gown that Jenny had left by the bed. Jenny had also lit the fire, filled the fridge, put the hot water on and made sure the bedding was clean, ready for Emily's return. Jenny was basically Emily's hero. She'd left a note listing all the things she'd sorted and apologising for the bits she'd not managed to get off Emily's last-minute list: avocado, Baker Tom's bread, oil for the tank – which was coming tomorrow, according to the note. Emily had always been able to rely on Jenny to look after the house and get things ready for her return, but the dressing gown was an extra bonus this time. It came with a note, *For you to lounge around in. Enjoy! X*

She padded down the wonky stairs, ducking beneath the beam and into the kitchen. She paused, moving her feet about the warm tiles, the underfloor heating giving a moment's bliss. Getting a glass out, she reached for a bottle of Argentinian Malbec off the rack and went into the lounge, dropping into the Duresta sofa she'd bought the last time she was back. She glugged the wine into her glass. She tucked her feet beneath the many, many cushions. Her heart began to thaw with the sound of the birds in the garden and the sheep on the hill, and though she couldn't quite hear it today, the ocean was no more than a few minutes' walk away. This was life suddenly, but perfectly, starting anew. On her terms. In her home country.

She sipped at the wine and let out a deep sigh of joy. God, she'd been desperate for this. The space, more than the wine. The solitude. She'd probably longed for it from the moment she went back to Jackson after the last time she tried to leave, two and a half years ago. It was a half-hearted attempt. She'd not been ready, she wasn't strong enough. She went to a friend's apartment round the corner from theirs and it didn't take him long to track her down. He told her she needed him. He took her in his arms and laughed, gently, at just how silly she'd been. He promised things would be different and she'd been so desperate to believe him because to be alone was terrifying. Jackson was her US agent and her boyfriend of almost ten years. He was the guy that saw her on Broadway, and promptly wooed her with flowers and expensive meals. He'd lavished her with gifts and told her everything she wanted to hear: that she was an Oscar winner in the making; that she could have everything her heart desired, both in work and in love; that she was smart as well as beautiful. Her father instantly approved and when Emily moved in with him, her dad somehow stopped giving his opinion on every facet of her life, he stopped judging. Instead of sarcasm about her latest job, he'd ask about Jackson: what was he working on next? Who was he working with? He'd tell Emily how glad he was that she had finally met someone who could keep her in line.

Keep her in line!

When she thought about that now, she couldn't help wonder what sort of line she was supposed to be kept in? What sort of life did her father think she deserved? Apparently she was too opinionated, though Emily couldn't help feel that version of her had long gone. Maybe that's why it didn't work out when she tried leaving before, her dad said she was making a mistake and she believed him. He reminded her she had it all and she felt bad for being so ungrateful.

But she knew now it wasn't that she was ungrateful. It just wasn't the life she wanted. It didn't feel right. She felt trapped and judged and small. For too long it was a life she couldn't escape because apparently the expensive apartment relied on her income as well as Jackson's, despite the fact he'd lived there long before her arrival. A life in which the wine and the meals and the parties were essential whether she was in the mood or not, and all funded as business investments. One in which she was supposed to be grateful she still had her looks, without Jackson realising that if she did, it was because she spent a fortune on keeping her face looking as young and ageless as possible.

She took a sip of wine, it trickled down her throat and into her belly. She took another sip, then a third and before she knew it, almost a full glass had gone and she felt sick, and guilty, and full of regret. Jackson always said she thought of nobody but herself and she was proving him right... She stared at her glass, then ran a hand over her delicately swollen belly. Was she starting to show? Would those sips of wine damage her unborn child? Had she just put it and herself at risk? Jackson's words, when she told him she was pregnant, echoed in her mind. *You're not a natural mother*, he'd said. And whilst she was still confused about the tiny life growing inside of her, she knew she had to work out what she really felt, without the noise of anybody else's opinion or agenda. She needed to do that quickly, before anybody found out where she was, not least Jackson. He'd booked the termination; he'd been the one to encourage her it wasn't the right time to have a child. That he had a hotline straight through to the clinic shouldn't have been the only reason she questioned what they were doing. That he booked women in for this left, right, and centre when a baby threatened to interrupt her career, or perhaps the girlfriend, partner or one-night stand of a male client who'd not taken enough care, these were different.

Vile, yet different, but this was her body, their child. Surely she had to be certain about what she wanted to do before making a decision she could never go back on. Maybe she could be a natural mother. If she just gave herself the chance…

She placed her glass on the coffee table, pushing that and the bottle out of reach. Her eyes fell to the photo she'd been inspired to dig out after bumping into Lolly. A photo sent over in a shipment of things from the past, sent to her little cottage when she first bought it and wanted to create a home from home. A photo of four girls, not yet sixteen; a whole life ahead of them; carefree; unified. Emily, Lolly, Amanda and Jess. Lolly… Lolly. Seeing her today had thrown Emily, she hadn't changed a bit. Or maybe she had, maybe they all had, and yet, Emily still yearned to reconnect. If anyone could understand what she was going through right now, surely it would be those girls. Wouldn't it? They were friends forever, they'd made that promise before she moved away back in 1996. Was it too late to ask for help?

Lolly

'You never said who you saw today,' said Kitt, who'd been tiptoeing around Lolly since their earlier discussion.

Lolly rubbed dots of moisturiser across her forehead and cheeks, the rich smell of frankincense spelling bedtime. She wasn't enjoying the small talk but married life was all about letting things go sometimes.

'Come on, who did you see?' he asked again, simultaneously climbing into bed and plugging in his iPad to charge.

Lolly sighed, climbing in beside him. 'Emily, I saw Emily.' She tried not to sound totally pissed off with him. Her mood probably wasn't his fault.

'Emily?'

'Nance! Emily Nance.' She cringed at her impatience.

'Nance! Blimey, what's she doing in Cornwall? I thought it was New York, New York for her. Or L.A. or something.'

'She said she had a place out Gorran way. Gorran Haven. Said she was coming home.' Lolly picked up her book, re-reading the blurb because she'd tried to read it so many times and somehow couldn't focus. 'Surprised she didn't go to her parents' place up in Rock. Dunno if they've still got it. They did keep it on to begin with, didn't they? Do you remember it? The little path from their garden to the beach.' He'd remember it. That's where he and Lolly first kissed, aged about fifteen or sixteen. They'd just listened to that song from the Coca-Cola ad, 'First Kiss'. He'd asked her if she'd ever kissed anyone before and they snuck away from Emily's party and snogged on the beach. He tasted of pizza. Probably why they didn't do it again until twelve years later. 'Lovely house, that.'

'So, did you talk to her?' Kitt asked, sounding bored as he flicked through boats he couldn't afford on eBay.

'Briefly. She was running for the bus.'

'The bus!' He paused to look up. 'How the mighty fall!'

'Kitt! That's not nice. Maybe she's aware of her carbon footprint or something.'

'Yes, I always got that about Emily Nance.' He returned to his iPad. 'Her interest in her carbon footprint, that's her all over.'

'You barely knew her,' said Lolly, irritated. She turned her bedside lamp up, cracking the spine as she opened the book where she'd saved the page. Her phone had just alerted her to the fact that she had about three hours of peak ovulation left before her temperature dropped and their chances of conceiving dissolved for another month. She was not going to beg. 'I gave her my number, in case she wanted to catch up. It'd be nice to see her. I miss the girls.'

'Which girls?'

'Us girls. Emily, Amanda and Jess.'

Kitt turned to look at her. 'Didn't you fall out?'

'No! Not exactly, it was… Emily left. Didn't stay in touch. Then, I don't know, I went to college, made new mates there.' Lolly thought. 'Actually, Jess went travelling, she'd sort of pulled away from us all before that anyway, then her going away finished it off. It was strange, she changed. Sort of closed off. I hated that, I missed her.'

'You always miss people.'

'Oh god, then Amanda got pregnant, then married. I tried to stay in touch, in case she needed help with Zennor or something but, I don't know, she didn't seem to want to. I guess we all must have just drifted...' Lolly stared at the page, words not really making sense. Losing touch with the girls had always been a source of pain for her, something hadn't felt right about it but she'd never really known what. 'You must have schoolmates you don't talk to any more.'

'I do. And that's fine. No need to drag up the past.'

'Maybe for you.' Kitt raised his eyebrows as if she was being ridiculous and she tried to ignore the feeling that he was right. 'Maybe it's 'cause I'm getting older. I suppose seeing her made them all come back to mind and I wanna check they're okay, you know?' Kitt was erratically scrolling now. 'It's easy to think you don't care when you drift apart, but that's not true. We were good friends, Christ, I wouldn't have survived most of my teens if it wasn't for those girls.'

'Did you know there is an actual Flat Earth Society.' Kitt turned the iPad to face Lolly, clearly no longer interested in boats or hearing about her old school friends. 'A group of people who genuinely believe the earth is flat. Like... images from space have been made up... it's all a conspiracy.'

Lolly shuffled down into their bed, pretending to read her book. 'I just think it'd be nice to reunite,' she said, quietly.

'Apparently flat earthers have members "all over the globe"... I mean... can they not see the irony?'

'Maybe I'll message one of them.'

Kitt put his iPad down. 'Message who?'

'Jess, maybe I'll message Jess. We connected on Facebook years ago. Maybe we should just get over it all and meet up. She might still be in touch with Amanda.'

'Are we still talking about this? Come here…' He pulled her towards him, running his hand down her side, letting it rest on her thigh. 'Forget them. You've got me…' He moved in closer, fixing his eyes on her. 'Maybe we should pick up where we left off earlier?' he said, kissing her neck, running his hand through her hair. 'See if we can't make that baby you so desperately want,' he said, moving on top of her, his knee parting her legs until he lay between her thighs, his hand on the small of her back. 'Lovely, Lolly,' he said, his breath hot on her face. 'Come here…'

Amanda

Amanda had been enjoying the comforts of PJs and *Queer Eye* on Netflix, but when her mate Karenza knocked on her door on the way to Vertigo, it whet her appetite for a few impromptu Thursday night drinks. So now she was enjoying every beat of the DJ's music and howling with laughter at some bloke who'd taken a shine to her. She always liked this bit, the flirtation, the banter, the casual resting of a hand on a thigh so she could lean in to talk over the music. Whilst she wasn't in the market for a boyfriend, it was a reminder of how thrilling the chase could be. And this guy was definitely chasing her, which was flattering given the fact he couldn't have been older than twenty-five. He was hot, young, chatty. He worked at ShelterBox and was definitely interested in her. She wondered how long for, if she fessed up to her day job, it usually put them off hence her invariably telling people she was a cleaner when asked. Which wasn't untrue. She did still do the odd shift here and there. Mainly because George next door needed a bit of help around the house and it meant she didn't have to lie to her daughter Zennor if she kept it up.

'Pretty good nails for a cleaner,' said the guy, whose name Amanda had overlooked. Detail unimportant.

'I like to look after myself,' she said. Just as she treated him to a gentle scratch of her nails down his thigh, there was a voice from behind her.

'Mum!'

The guy looked startled and no amount of gin could swallow the thud of Amanda's heart to her knees. 'Zennor! Hi, love.' Amanda spun round on her stool, hoping to find a much happier, brighter face than the one she actually saw. She couldn't blame her daughter. There's probably few things worse than walking in on your mum flirting like that.

'And you!' she said, staring at the guy as Amanda retracted her hand. 'What the hell are you doing?'

'Zennor,' said the guy, and Amanda's heart dropped the final distance from knees to boots. 'Fancy seeing you... I was just, this is...'

'My mother!'

'So it seems...'

Amanda closed her eyes. Shit. How well did these two know each other?

'Mum, Billy. Billy... my mum.'

Amanda's heart seeped out of her boots as Zennor emphasised the introduction. She reached for her glass, knocking back the remains of her drink. 'I think maybe I should leave.'

'Yes. You probably should,' said Zennor, stonily.

Amanda grabbed her jacket from the back of her chair, looking to see if she could catch Karenza's eye, but she was nowhere to be seen. 'Well, anyway, Billy, nice chatting.' Zennor crossed her arms, waiting. Amanda went to leave then turned back. 'Oh, love, I texted earlier, did you get my message? I wondered what you were up to on Sunday, maybe we could have dinner?'

'I'm busy. With Dad.'

'Right, fine, no problem. Just... well, anyway, maybe another time then. It's just that it's been a while...' Amanda leant in to kiss Zennor's cheek, making her flinch. 'I miss you...' Zennor looked to the ground. 'Okay, well, maybe another time. Have fun.'

With a cocktail of guilt and disappointment flooding her veins, Amanda weaved through the crowd, desperate to turn back and plead with Zennor not to be angry, to give them some time to get this fractured relationship back on track. Knowing better than to try that when Zennor was embarrassed and angry, she stepped out into the night sky, taking a lungful of fresh air before heading off in the direction of home.

'I can't believe you!' Came Zennor's angry voice into the street. Amanda stopped short, taking a deep breath. 'You're so embarrassing, Mum.'

'Zennor, please.'

She marched towards her, teenage anger raging. 'No! Mum! Please nothing! We've talked about this, about you, here. This is where I come, with my mates, to hang out. What would have happened if I hadn't turned up?'

'What do you mean, what would have happened?'

'With Billy? What would have happened? I know what he's like and *everyone* knows what you're like, Mum.'

Zennor didn't know anything, but statements like that sometimes made Amanda wonder. 'What's that supposed to mean?'

'Interested in anything with a pulse. Well, anything except Dad!'

'That's not fair.'

'He could basically be your son!'

'You're overreacting!'

'Am I?'

'We were just talking.'

'Billy never just talks. That's the reason we broke up.' Shit. 'If I hadn't turned up you would definitely have ended up having sex.'

'Zennor! I don't sleep with every man I talk to!'

Zennor paused, a sadness washing over her. 'He's very persuasive...'

Amanda wanted to reach out to her not so little girl. She'd met boys like that when she was Zennor's age. Nineteen. A time when some girls just need a boy to make them feel like the sexiest girl alive, until they practically ignore them once they've got what they wanted, pushing the girl right back to the lack of self-confidence they started with.

'I'm a grown woman, love. Billy couldn't have persuaded me to do anything I didn't want to.' That much was true. Zennor stared at Amanda and though Amanda knew her daughter was a little bit broken right now, she also knew that now wasn't the time to try and fix things. Drunk and angry Zennor was not open to reason. 'Go on, love. Go back. Here,' Amanda pulled a tenner out of her purse. 'Take this, get yourself some food. Avoid boys like Billy. I am sorry if I embarrassed you.'

'Dad would never do this to me,' was Zennor's parting gift. Amanda knew it was pointless chasing after her, despite the fact that every time she lorded her dad up, putting him on a pedestal, Amanda was desperate to remind her that he hadn't been around for them for most of her life. That he had caused all sorts of drama when Amanda found out she was pregnant. That they had got married in a rush because his mum made him even though neither of them really wanted to and it had been no surprise when he eventually slept with someone else, causing Amanda to invite him to leave. Which he did. Without so much as a backward glance until fifteen years later when he came back, cap in hand, suddenly becoming the saviour of Zennor's entire life. It wasn't just unfair, it was the most hurtful thing he could have done to Amanda, however unintended the outcome might have been. But Zennor was nineteen. She was angry. She had just walked in on her mother in a bar, talking to some bloke she has either had sex with or would like to have sex with and Amanda knew what the anger that comes from disappointment felt like.

Jess

Jess tucked her duvet under her knees, laptop in front of her. *This Morning* was on the TV that sat on her chest of drawers. Wallpaper really, she wasn't paying much attention. She preferred Holly and Phil but it was Friday so what could she do. Still, working from home had its perks and making her bed into a temporary desk was definitely one of them. Vaping over her laptop was another. Jess took a lungful of the strawberry flavoured aerosol, blowing it out again, always astonished by the amount of 'smoke' she'd release. Tonight Matthew, I'm going to be that girl from Transvision Vamp with the platinum hair… Wendy James! That was her. She was amazing but Jess was always deeply jealous of her because Nathan Brader, from two years above at school, totally fancied Wendy James and Jess totally fancied him. Jess caught sight of herself in the dresser mirror before hiding back behind her laptop screen. She was definitely not looking like Wendy James right now. Nathan Brader still wouldn't look twice.

She went back to her presentation. A bid for a new client, a dairy farm selling straight from cow to consumer. She wanted their business, and not just because visits to a hamlet in West Cornwall were a great escape from the office. If she could get a few more meetings outside of the office, and a few more days working from home like this, she could probably get away with not having to see Jay much at all.

A notification came up on her Mac, a message from Lolly Teague. Christ, they'd had the occasional 'hey, how are you' chat on Facebook in past years, but Jess had always kept it to a minimum, not sure she could cope with a full-on reconnection. It was funny really. She'd only thought about Lolly and Amanda these last few days when Jay reappeared. They'd encouraged her to go out with him in the first place. She'd always been the one to ignore male attention, aggressively so in some cases, though they never understood why. But he'd been so gentle, and they'd been so encouraging. Which had made her angry with them later on because if it hadn't been for them, she would never have allowed herself to fall for him.

Maybe she hadn't been fair. It wasn't their fault she pushed people away. It wasn't even hers, she'd recently begun to accept.

Hey! How are you? Guess who I saw yesterday? I just had to message you!

She just *had* to message. That was Lolly of old, always the one with all the gossip in the group. Another reason Jess had pulled back, they'd always told each other everything…

Jess paused, her heart racing. Matt, her brother, kept telling her to stop hiding, to embrace life's offerings. What would he do in this situation? He'd guess, for sure. She typed back. *Aidan Turner?* Matt hated Aidan Turner but as he was back filming *Poldark*, it would have been his first go to. Besides, most locals – whilst never watching the TV show because there are only so many episodes of his torso you can watch and ignore the bad Cornish accents and limp storyline – had a *Poldark* story. If it wasn't that they'd bumped into him in Tesco, it was that they'd climbed into his dirty bed sheets after he vacated his room and therefore all but had sex with him in some kind of tenuous six (sex?) degrees of separation thing.

Nope. Not Aidan Turner. Better!

Better? Jess waited, looking for the bubbles to suggest Lolly was typing another clue. None came. Jess thought. *Dawn French? Sue Perkins? Kate Winslet? George Clooney? Liza Tarbuck? Paul Weller? That one from Bananarama that was married to Andrew Ridgeley? Andrew Ridgeley?* Before clicking send, Jess checked she hadn't missed off any other famous people who either lived or were often seen down in Cornwall… confused as to why she'd be messaging her about it anyway. She resisted adding David Cameron. Nobody who knew her would brag about seeing David Cameron.

Emily Nance!

Emily Nance? Jess's heart stopped. Emily Nance? Wasn't she some kind of sitcom superstar now?

She's back in Cornwall. Oh my god, she looked amazing. X

Jess swallowed. Conflicted.

She was in a hurry. We didn't really get a chance to talk but I gave her my number, in case she wants to meet up. And now I keep thinking about it, I mean, it'd be cool, wouldn't it? The old crew back together? I'd love to know what you're all up to. What we've all done in life. There must be LOADS to catch up on!

That couldn't happen. It wouldn't work. Jess hadn't seen Emily since she moved away. She'd barely seen her since the night of Emily's 16th birthday party just before the family unexpectedly left town. She cleared her throat, the way she always did when memories of that night threatened to surface. Yes, she missed Emily when she left. As much as she missed the rest of the girls since, but there was good reason for keeping them in her past. She hovered over the keyboard, wondering how to phrase it. She could say she was too busy, she was working, she was going away. Yet, knowing she was probably on her phone, awaiting Jess's response, reminded her how much she loved Lolly… and Amanda and Emily, for that matter. She really loved them, always had. Even though time had passed. Their friendship was deep, it was significant. It was the kind of friendship she'd never found again, even now, as a fully-fledged grown-up. Maybe enough time had passed. Maybe it would be okay.

What do you say? Say yes! Even if Emily doesn't call, I'd love to see you, and Amanda. Pleeeeaaaase say yes!!! I really miss you all. Pleeeeeaaaaasssseeeee!

Jess typed excuses, deleted them. She stared out of her bedroom window. She typed more excuses and deleted them. She imagined Lolly waiting her response like a giddy puppy and she was overwhelmed by a nostalgic love for her. She imagined what her brother Matt would say if she told him she'd rejected the invite and she suddenly realised how tired she was of hiding.

That sounds great. Let me know when. x

Emily

Walking down the hill to the village shop, Emily released a deep breath into the gentle spring air. The sun was out just enough to take the edge off the temperature when you got out of the shade. She paused for a moment, lifting her face skyward like a sunflower, bathing in a gentle warmth that bled into her bones. It was good to be back. She'd popped in to Jenny's to say thank you for getting things sorted. She'd wandered down the lane enjoying the sound of the gulls and the smell of the sea air. Pregnant or not, it was good to be back. She was almost living one of those clichéd Cornish lives that she read about in books, except that usually they weren't up the duff with an ex-boyfriend's baby… or running away from an industry that had taken her youth and her life and her confidence and her—

'Morning, it's a bleddy goodun!'

Emily opened her eyes to the sound of Bill, one of the village's oldest residents. He'd lived here since he was a boy, in the same house he was born in. He was usually to be found making withy pots down by the harbour and selling daffodils by the bunch. His car would play classical music as he weaved the willow into shape, selling his pots to holidaymakers since the fishermen tended to stick to the modern versions these days.

'I sawee was back. You need anything? Bill Jnr is out on the boat now, if you want some fish when he's back. Fresh mackerel?'

'Oooh, Bill. I love mackerel. Yes, that would be amazing.'

'Righton.'

'How are you anyway?'

'Me? Oh, yeah, good. Same. Yeah. Junior's still fishing. Betty's alright too.'

'Still making cakes for the village store?'

'Yeah, still down Cakebreads. Pop in and say hello if you get chance. She'd love to see you.'

'I'm on my way now, will be great to see her too.'

'Onwards.'

'See you later, Bill.'

'See you later.'

Bill shuffled on and Emily smiled widely, her heart full of home. This is where she was supposed to be. All those years she'd been touring or holed up on Broadway. The six months she made that horrendous straight to DVD film and the US sitcom that fizzled out after its second series. Even the stuff that went well, the blockbuster films or the theatre runs playing characters she adored or was inspired by. Good, bad or indifferent, she kept telling herself she was happy. She'd kid herself that the parties and the money and the free clothes were all worth it. That the tax-deductible hair appointments and the facial treatments that kept the years away were all to her benefit and something she couldn't possibly get if she'd stayed in Cornwall. And she was right, there wasn't much call for Botox down Gorran Haven, though she was aware of a few places up in Truro that she could go if needs be. Somehow though, she wasn't sure she needed to any more. She needed to feel the wind on her face. She needed to walk along the cliff tops. She needed to lie on the fine shingle of Vault Beach. She needed to potter in the garden and get the barbecue going to cook Bill Jnr's mackerel. She needed not to be mourning the loss of her old life because there was nothing to mourn. It had been lonely when she lived it, surrounded by people and noise. Now that she was here, alone in her home, no one to talk to or perform for, she didn't feel lonely any more.

The shop bell dinged as she walked in. 'Morning!' she called, seeking out Betty's cheery face. A young girl behind the counter looked up from pricing with a wide smile. 'Oh, hi, is Betty in?'

'She's had to pop out. She'll be back in later,' said the girl.

'Ahhh, right. Shame.' Disappointed, but reassured that she could come back any time, Emily pottered around the shop. She picked things up off the shelves, dropping them into her basket. At the back of the store, a selection of Betty's cakes, freshly baked, lured Emily to take a closer look. She crouched down to smell the cakes, uncertain which to choose.

The shop door dinged again. 'Hi. Morning. Can you help me?'

Emily's heart stopped. She recognised that voice. That accent. She scuttled away from the cakes and out of view.

'I'm looking for someone, I think she might be here.'

Emily held her breath.

'Okay…' said the girl.

'Yeah, Emily. Emily Nance? She's got a place here. I think she might have just got back to the UK after being away for a while. Do you know her?'

Emily wondered when Jackson had organised for his intern to fly in. She wondered if he'd given her the heads up on any of those voicemails she'd not listened to. *Hi, just to let you know that I can't be bothered to fight for you, but my minimum wage P.A. will be there in a shot.* For a moment she panicked that somehow Jackson had found out she was still pregnant and this was his attempt to get her back, feeble as it was. But he didn't want children, did he? Else why would he have made the appointment?

'Emily who?'

'Nance. She's an actress. Nothing major, you probably won't have heard of her actually.'

Emily wanted to point out that she'd been in more things than the intern who was jobbing until he got his big break, but staying out of view was vital until she knew what she was going to do with her life and this baby. She crouched behind a rack of toilet rolls and tampons, hoping that Mason, or whatever this one was called, wouldn't look round the shop and catch her reflection in the security mirror above.

'Uhm, no. I don't know her, but I've only just moved here. Has she lived here long?' asked the girl.

'Well, she's not been here for years, by all accounts. I understand she bought somewhere a while back. Apparently she's Cornish. This is her home or something, I'm not altogether sure. I'm just here for my boss.'

Here for his boss. Unbelievable. Emily's knees began to ache from crouching but she daren't move to resist the burn.

'Right.'

A delicate smell of shea butter seemed to come from the posh toilet rolls on the very bottom shelf and Emily turned her nose away, nausea rising. What's that about? She always liked shea butter.

'So… you don't know her.'

'I'm sorry. No. I don't.'

'Okay then.' Mason let out a deep sigh that covered up the squeak of Emily's shoe as her knee forced her to adjust, despite having tried to resist moving. 'Well…' he drawled.

'The lady who owns the shop will be in later,' offered the girl. 'She might know her. If you wanted to pop back?'

'Oh. Okay. What time?'

'Erm… maybe two thirty? Three.'

'Two thirty or three?' Interns were always particular about time. It was their job to be. Jackson would have liked that about this one.

'Well, somewhere around then. You know. When she's ready.'

'Right.' Emily knew that her own attitude to time – being inspired by the Cornish sense of dreckly: she'd get to it, just as soon as – used to drive Jackson insane. If Mason, or Jackson for that matter, thought he could pin Betty down to a time, they were kidding themselves.

'Shall I take your name? Let Betty know you might pop in.'

Mason sighed again. 'Don't worry, she erm… she won't know me, thanks. I'll just… I'll come back.' He turned to leave, looking at his phone, then paused by the door. 'Can you tell me where I might get a signal? This thing's stopped working, I'm not sure if it's the phone or what? I can't seem to find a UK carrier that my service will allow.'

'Oh yeah, no. You won't get a signal down here. Gorran maybe, if you're lucky.'

'Gorran? Aren't I in Gorran?'

'No, this is Gorran Haven. Gorran is the next village up. That sometimes has a signal, failing that I think by the time you get up towards Heligan it's pretty good, so maybe just head back there.'

'Heligan.'

'Yeah…'

'Right.'

Emily bit down on her lip, desperate to stand up, desperate for Mason to leave. As the shop doorbell dinged and the door clicked shut again, she let out a massive sigh and pushed herself up with a groan. 'Shit, my knees,' she said, propping herself up against the Always Extra with wings, straining to peer out of the front door. She could just about see the back of Mason's head before he climbed into a large, black 4x4 and drove off up the hill. Jackson had really pulled out the stops for this one, wonder if he flew in first class too.

'Jesus, thank god for that,' she said as the sound of the car's engine disappeared, replaced by the cawing of a gull. The girl looked at her, wide-eyed. 'Sorry, sorry. Shit though, I didn't think I'd be able to get back up again. My knees are buggered.' The girl continued to stare blankly. 'Okay, erm… I heard you just say to that chap that Betty's back in later, but do you know where she is? I could really do with a quick chat.'

'She's at home. Sorry.'

'Right. Right. Okay…' Emily looked around. She'd have to get what she needed then head home via Betty's. She could dodge out of the shop and up the alleyway out of view. There was no way she could risk Jackson finding her here. It wasn't an option. Not yet, at least.

Amanda

Amanda rolled off Trev. Back again, two days in a row. He'd only arrived fifteen minutes ago but now lay practically comatose on her bed, a ridiculous smile on his face. If yesterday's form had anything to go by, this was merely a pit stop, not the end of proceedings. Amanda was quite happy to relax into the warmth of the bed sheets until she was required again. She traced a fingernail from his chest down to his navel, enjoying his slight flinch as she circled it before placing her hand on his belly.

Usually, at this point, she'd lie there wondering when the client was going to leave. Sometimes she'd have some shopping to pick up for George next door, other days she'd be on a tight turnaround from one client to the next and liked to shower and change the sheets first. Maybe even grab a cuppa. Her online Asda order was likely to timeout in the next ten minutes but for this particular client, she didn't really mind.

Eventually, he opened his eyes, rubbing them with the heel of his hands before turning to grin at her and, for a moment, she was back at school aged fourteen, maybe fifteen. He was on the school fields, showing off. Handstands. Back flips. Anything to impress the girls. He'd been held back a year, having failed most of his GCSEs. He was older than the rest of his year and though only the school year above, several actual years older than Amanda. It meant that he was the first guy in school to have a car. An Escort. Burgundy, if memory served her. He'd wait in the car park for his on/off girlfriend, usually leant against the car with the same grin he'd just given Amanda now. Or sat in it, listening to Bon Jovi on full volume. Probably showing off. None of the girls minded him showing off. He was fit, they knew it. He probably knew it. One of the teachers had mentioned something so she probably knew it too. That wouldn't happen nowadays.

He let out a contented sigh.

'So, Mr Trevelly. What brings you here? Especially two days in a row,' asked Amanda, shifting to lie on her side, resting her head on her hand. 'Are you satisfying a long-held fantasy to have sex with me? One you've nurtured since we were at school. Could you just not stop thinking about me and finally had to track me down so you could see if I was as good as your fantasy?'

'Erm…' He looked at her, half cocky smirk, half terror in his eyes.

'I'm teasing. I don't think for a moment that you've given me a second thought since school. But, seriously, what brings a guy like you to see a woman like me?' She reached for his hand. 'I'm guessing you're married or do you just like the wedding ring look?'

'I'm married.'

Amanda didn't normally ask questions like this. Some married men came to see her because they were dicks who couldn't control themselves and though Amanda hated that part of her job, she'd reason it was better they saw her than have drunken, unprotected sex down town, or worse, an affair. Then there were others, for whom it was the only way they ever had sex. She'd long stopped judging on the basis she could never really know which were which. On this occasion, however, curiosity was getting the better of her. 'So how come you're here?'

'Ahhh, I dunno. It's complicated.'

'It always is.'

'Probably. And I'm not sure I should be talking to you about it even if it weren't.'

'You'd be surprised what people talk about when they see me. Some of them, that's all they want to do. I'm not about to share your secrets, I can assure you of that!'

'People don't know what you do?'

'Some do. Some don't. It doesn't generally come up in conversation.'

'What do they think?'

Amanda smiled, wryly. 'Some don't care, some are shocked but fine, some stop talking to me altogether.'

'Does it bother you?'

'Sometimes, I don't like the judgement, the pitying looks, like I must be doing this because I'm either a nymphomaniac or feeding a drug habit or being pimped out.'

'Are you?'

'No! I mean, I like sex, I love it, but I can live without it. If I had to. And I categorically don't do drugs.'

'Have you got a pimp?'

'What! Share my takings with some bloke who does nothing, not bloody likely!'

'So why do you do it?'

'I thought we were talking about you and your complicated marriage.'

'I'll tell you about me if you tell me about you.'

'Like I said. I like sex. And I'm single so why the hell not. My daughter lives with her dad, there's just me at home. Bills need paying. I've a mortgage. I brought my daughter up in this house, I don't want to move. Besides, it's good money and I can work the hours I want to work. I like my job.'

'You did seem to be having a good time?'

Amanda fixed him with an intense look. 'Sometimes it's particularly satisfying.'

Trev moved to his side, his breath on her face. 'Ever fake it?'

'Why bother? You're not here for me, you're here for you. That's fine. You don't care if I have a good time. It just so happens that on some occasions... I do too.'

'Right.' His pupils dilated.

'So you have kids, you've been together for years...'

Trev moved closer to her. 'I don't think I want to talk about me any more.' He reached his hand to her hip, pulling her into him. 'I've still got twenty minutes, haven't I?'

Emily

Emily knocked on the old green painted door at Betty and Bill's. A breeze whipped up some baking smells, making Emily's belly rumble. She'd not been able to stop eating since she got home, she was permanently hungry. Another baby related thing, she assumed. Or the not having to be on film or stage thing... nobody looking over her shoulder, tutting whenever she put anything other than fresh air in her mouth.

She could hear Radio Four coming through the single glaze of the cottage windows. She knocked again, louder. 'Come in!' came a voice.

Pushing the door open, Emily shouted out. 'Betty? Are you in? It's Emily. Emily Nance.'

'Well, bugger me, Emily Nance! We've not seen you in an age.' Betty came out from the kitchen, pulling a flour-covered apron over her head. 'How are you? You're looking well.' She pulled Emily into a hug and, like Lolly's yesterday, it was just the kind of hug she needed. All maternal and warm. 'Tea? Cake? I've saffron buns coming out in a minute.'

'Oh my god, that would be amazing,' gushed Emily, who would have shipped Betty's saffron buns out to the US were it not frowned upon with the air miles and whatnot. 'Your saffron buns are the best, Betty.'

'Well, that's kind of you to say.'

Betty milled about in the kitchen, putting the kettle on. Reaching for a teapot. Getting plates and knives out, placing them on the oilcloth-covered table. 'Sit down, love, go on,' instructed Betty.

Emily took a seat at the head of the table by the window. A rambling rose covered part of the glaze, emerging green and with a promise of buds in June. The kitchen was full of pots and recipe books. Several mismatched chairs surrounded the table as well as an old wingback in the corner with a crocheted throw over it.

'Now tell me, what brings you back from the bright lights?' asked Betty, tipping the saffron buns out onto a rack. She put her oven-gloved hand on the stainless-steel kettle that was warming up on the range cooker. 'How long you here for this time?'

Emily sighed. 'Forever?'

'Forever? That's a long old time.'

'Yeah. Would be nice though, to think I could stay here forever.'

'What about all your adventures though? Eh? I thought you loved it in America. I thought Bill said you were living the dream or something, isn't that what you said the last time you were here?'

Emily cringed. 'That probably is what I said, yes. I don't know, maybe I was trying to sell it to myself more than Bill.'

Betty nodded, wisely. 'We've all done it. I tried living up Fowey once, but it just wasn't me.'

'I guess.' Emily took the plate that Betty offered. She poured milk into her tea. She waited for Betty to officially offer her a saffron bun, salivating at the smell, just knowing that the butter would melt and the bun would be warm and the comfort would be off the actual scale.

'Go on. Don't be polite!' said Betty, which was all the encouragement Emily needed. She reached for a bun and the butter, cutting it open and watching the steam rise. 'So, what have you dropped in for? Not that it isn't entirely lovely to see you, of course!'

Emily took a bite of the saffron bun, closing her eyes to savour it. 'Oh. My. God,' she said, mouth full. 'That is sooooo good!'

Betty looked pleased.

A few more mouthfuls, Emily regained control of her belly and thoughts. 'So… this is a bit awkward, and I feel awful asking you to get involved in any way, but I need help.'

'What can I do?' asked Betty, pulling a chair up at the table too.

'Somebody came into Cakebreads just now, asking after me. The girl said she didn't know me and that the person should come back later to ask you.'

'Aye, I'm in at around two.'

'Yes, that's what she said. The thing is…' Emily paused. She bit down on her lip because she didn't want to let on that she felt like she could cry. 'The thing is, I don't want the person asking for me to know where I am. He knows that I have a place here, but he doesn't know exactly where and I can't have him find me.'

'Right…'

'And I know it's awkward for you, I don't like to think you have to get involved in my life like this, but I really need some time.'

'Has he hurt you? Is he…'

'No! No, it's nothing like that. Well, not exactly, no. It's just that… I need to get my head straight before I see him. Well, his boss Jackson, actually. Who has no doubt sent him on the strict instruction to find me at all costs.'

'Right…'

'Jackson is my ex. I left… under difficult circumstances. I need to make sure that I work out what I want to say before I see either of them. He'll try to get me to go back with him, it'll be the only reason Jackson sent him.'

'And you don't want to go back with him?'

'I don't, Betty. I really don't. I don't think it's good for me. I don't think it's… well… I need to be here. At home. In Cornwall.'

'Okay. So this chap, what does he look like?'

'He's tallish. Maybe six foot. Dark hair. Well-groomed, immaculate, in fact. Suited and booted.' Jackson always insisted on all his interns looking the part. It was all to do with his brand, apparently. 'You'll recognise him. He doesn't look like a local. And he's driving a big black car.'

'Oh, that's his Range Rover I saw earlier.'

'Yeah, that's him.'

'Right.'

'Would you mind?'

Betty poured herself a tea, reaching for a bun. 'Of course not, my bewtie. You don't want to be found, we won't say where you are. I'll get the message out. You know this village will look after you.'

Emily relaxed a little, that was one of the best things about getting a place here. Nobody cared about her. In as much as nobody cared who she was in America. Or who she used to be here in the UK. Nobody was interested in her glossy parties and free designer gear. Did she contribute to the village? Did she buy local? Did she lord it up, or did she just get on with her life and let the village get on with theirs, that's all they were bothered about.

'Don't you worry, love. Bill and I will sort it. Let Jenny know too. I'll get a message to the rest of the village. It'll be *Emily who*, until you tell us different.'

'Thanks, Betty, I really appreciate it.'

'No problem. Now, let me pack up some of these buns for you to take back to your place. If you're going in to hiding, you're going to need sustenance. Junior can bring you some mackerel up later and I'll get Jenny to bring you some more bread up tomorrow. And milk. Okay. Hey, there's a new pizza van that visits now. Every Wednesday outside the shop. Wood fired. Very posh. One of us can bring you some up if needs be.'

'Thanks, Betty, thanks so much.'

'Now, go on. Get yourself back before this Jackson character returns. Nip up the ope, he'll never find you.'

Jess

Jess flicked through her phone, waiting for the kettle to boil. Facebook was full of RIPs for some celebrity Jess had never heard of. Quote after quote after quote of not looking at your feet but up at the stars. Jess knew the quotes were right, she'd lived many years of her life afraid to look up, but right now she could feel circumstances forcing her head back down again.

Lolly hadn't been back in touch since last week, so perhaps the idea of them meeting up would go away now. Except that the more Jess thought about it, the less worried she'd become, and the more excited at the prospect of reconnecting with girls who knew her better than anyone, despite how much time had passed. Once upon a time, she needed them, their support, their love. She needed them just to be able to breathe. And it wasn't that she didn't have friends: she knew people, she had mates, she enjoyed socials with her colleagues. It was more that the prospect of meeting up with them had whet her appetite for the kind of connection she'd had with them before life got in the way and ruined it all. Besides, if Jay Trewellan was going to be around, she'd want to be avoiding those nights out anyway.

She saw him this morning. He looked… actually she didn't want to think about how he looked. Or how he'd smiled at her. Or how he'd asked for a meeting with her later on this afternoon. He specified just the two of them. He wanted to work out the best way to manage the company's main accounts. Was she wrong to wonder if he had an ulterior motive? Would that even have crossed his mind? He was a professional, surely. It was a sensible course of action. Why then was she overanalysing? She had to get a grip. He was here to do a job. Her feelings would pass. She just needed to remember that any feelings were a result of nostalgia, not real, living emotion.

'Jess.'

Jay stood at the archway to the kitchen, leaning against it with a mug in his hand, smiling.

'Jay…' She had never wished so hard for the ground to swallow her whole.

'I wasn't sure if we ask around for coffee or just make our own?'

The kettle boiled and Jess poured steaming water onto her peppermint teabag. 'We make our own. We used to ask around but as the team got bigger so did the drinks orders and then some people didn't bother making them and others would make them every two minutes for an excuse to hide in the kitchen.' Which clearly wasn't a safe place to hide any more. 'So it's each to their own now. You might have to boil more water, there's not much left.'

'Right.' He took the kettle from her, faffing with the taps and spraying himself with cold water as it caught on the kettle lid. 'Shit.' Jess threw a tea towel for him. 'Cheers.'

She remembered back when they first met, down at the Hub in St Ives. She was there for a summer season and he'd been there for a few years. He'd hang a tea towel from the hook in his jeans and, as they got closer, she'd pull it from him as he walked past, flicking him with it before throwing it back for him to catch. The first time they kissed was in the backroom. It was closing time. Just the two of them there to lock up. She'd nicked his tea towel again and he chased after her, pinning her to the wall with it. She'd panicked at first, frightened she couldn't escape and worried about what he'd do. Jay sensed something, eased back on his grip, apologised, asked her if she was okay and as she looked into his eyes – the way you do when you're eighteen and think life is like the movies – she'd felt herself relax into him, all fear gone. He wasn't threatening, he wasn't intimidating. He made her feel safe somehow. She'd told him she was okay, barely able to breathe. He leaned in to kiss her, the first time she'd kissed anyone since the party at Emily's house and she wasn't frightened. It was slow and gentle and caring and she lost track of all time and space and reality and the world fizzed and she melted and, shit, how could she have walked away from that all those years ago?

'So we're meeting at three?' he asked as she took her tea and went to leave.

'Yes. Three. If that's okay with you.'

'That's great. I'm looking forward to it. See you then.'

'Great.'

But it wasn't great. It wasn't great all afternoon. Jess sent off her pitch to the dairy farm, talked to a few clients about some new work they wanted doing. Looked through some creative proposals that the designers had come up with for a restaurant rebrand. They were good, but there was something missing. Normally, Jess would know how to fix it and they all looked at her, waiting for her steer when she told them it wasn't quite right. But she had nothing except memories and regret.

Three o'clock approached. She went to put the kettle on again, taking out a cafetière for two. She nipped to the loo then came back via his desk. 'Coffee?'

'Please.'

'See you in the meeting room.'

'Great.'

So there she was, laptop under her arm. Tray with two cups, a full cafetière, and some biscuits she found at the back of the cupboard. 'Don't expect this treatment every time we sit down to a meeting,' she said, her hand shaking as she pushed them towards him. 'It's a one-off, 'cause you're new. God knows how long they've been in the cupboard for.'

'Wow, thanks. You really know how to welcome a guy.' He grinned at her, his eyes sparkling.

In silence, she poured them coffee. She passed him the sugar, she sat herself down. She tried to get her heart to calm by breathing in through her nose and out through her mouth – as inconspicuously as she could. She took up a seat opposite him, crossing her legs beneath the table, taking extra care for them not to touch. She thought she'd prepared herself for this, for being in the same office as him. In the same room. The only man she'd ever truly loved, something that terrified her at the time, something that still terrified her. And as she looked up to him to start the meeting and their eyes met, it was like she was back in the Hub's back office again and she knew she was probably going to have to resign.

So,' she began. 'How's your first day going?'

'It's good,' he said, stirring his coffee. 'The team seems bright.'

'They're young. They have brightness in abundance.'

'I'll try not to hold that against them,' he said, with a laugh. 'And you? How's your day?' he asked.

'Me? It's fine. Thanks, yeah. Great. A couple of bits of art direction to sort out, but for the most part, it's good. Okay, so maybe we should go through client by client and we can make a plan about who's going to be the best main point of contact.'

'We could do that.' He paused, sipping at his coffee. Eyes still fixed firmly on her. 'Or we could catch up,' he said, gently. 'Find out what we've each been up to for all these years.'

Fuck.

Jay put his cup down. 'I never stopped thinking about you. Wondering how you were doing, how life was treating you, wondering if you were happy…'

Jess shifted in her seat. Her heart raced. He should stop talking.

'Wondering if you ever met anybody? Settled down?'

'I haven't met anyone,' she said, wishing she didn't want to know how he felt about that. 'I'm fine. I mean, I'm happy. Life is good.'

'Don't you get lonely?'

Yes! All the time! And now you're back that's got a whole lot worse! 'No. Not really. I'm fine on my own.'

'You always were happy to be on your own, weren't you? You never seemed to need anyone. I think that was part of the attraction, it was like you were with me 'cause you wanted to be, not because you needed to be. It was…' He paused, and Jess hoped he wouldn't finish the sentence. 'It was very sexy.'

'Jay, please.'

'What?'

'Don't do this. We're at work. You're married.'

'I know, and it's good. I'm happy, but I guess your first loves never fully go away, do they?'

'We were kids.'

'Doesn't mean we weren't in love.'

'I can't have been that much in love, I walked away,' she said. 'And you got together with Niamh, so even if you were, you got over it pretty quickly.'

'It was eighteen months later.'

'Still. You met someone else, and you're happily married. And I'm… happily single. So there we are. No stress. No complications. Just me and my job. Happy days.'

'Fair enough, I guess.' Jay took a sip of coffee. 'If that's what you want, I mean.'

'Yeah. It is. It means I can focus on work.' Jess tapped her laptop to reinforce the point. 'Which we should do now.'

'Jess.'

She slammed her pen down, an act of frustration making him raise his eyebrows, which frustrated her even more. 'What, Jay? What?'

'Jess, I'm sorry. I didn't mean to make it awkward. I just think there is some housekeeping to do so we can get things out of the way, focus on work like you say. I'm not here to cause a problem, Jess.' He paused, letting out a sigh as he moved bits of paper around. 'Look, I took this job because it was a great opportunity. A rare offer in Cornwall. Something I could do to push myself. Something to get the money coming in so that Niamh could take a step back, be with the kids, retrain maybe. I didn't do it to piss you off.'

Hearing Niamh's name again pinched at Jess's mood. 'I'm not pissed off.'

'But you're not okay.'

Jess paused. She had two options. Be honest – *I'm not okay, turns out I probably still love you, I've probably always loved you. I probably only walked away because I couldn't handle the intensity of our relationship, it was too much, too young, I had baggage.* Or she could lie. 'I am fine. I am more than fine. I am great. Like I say, happy in my life, happy in my work. I love this job. I love the people. I love the challenge too. I know exactly what you mean about there not being many offers like this down in Cornwall and I totally understand you wanting to progress and make the most of the opportunity. You didn't need to think twice about taking the job, this is for you. You're going to be great. Let's just get on with what we have to discuss, shall we? I have quite a bit to do after our meeting.'

'Okay... if you're sure—'

'I'm sure! Jay!' She fixed him with a look that she hoped would prove just how sure she was. He gave a shallow, injured bird nod. Jess focussed on the files before her wondering how long it would be until she stopped feeling sick. Until her heart returned to its normal pace. Until the tremble in her hands subsided. 'So, hotels. They are our biggest clients, they make up sixty per cent of our annual income and, with some of our bigger, more exclusive clients, it's lucrative work. What's your experience with hotels?'

She held her hands together tightly, willing the strength of her grasp to steady them. And she looked at him. That was that. Except it wasn't, not really. Because what he said and how he looked at her, didn't somehow correlate. She felt gagged because there was so much she wanted to say but there was no way she could, or would – he was a married man. She was right before, she was definitely going to have to leave.

Lolly

'One, two, three.' Lolly and her colleague, Beth, lifted today's physio client. 'Come on, Rhona, you need to sit up for a while. When you've got your breath back, we'll come do some exercises, okay? You fancy a little walk?'

'Not really,' grumbled Rhona. 'Everything hurts.'

'I know, it will. But if you want to get back home again, you need to do these. How's the breath exercises going?' Beth passed Lolly the lung capacity measure. 'Can you reach that little happy face yet?'

'Oh, that I can do,' said Rhona, breathing into the plastic contraption until the little yellow ball reached the level Lolly had set it to the day before. 'There you go.'

'Brilliant.' Lolly adjusted the marker point. 'This is your next target.'

Rhona groaned. 'You're a hard taskmaster.'

'I am. Because I want you to get better. Now, give me ten minutes then we'll come back and take a walk down the ward. You reckon you can get all the way down the corridor today?'

'If it means I'm closer to getting out of this place, I'll do anything.'

'Brilliant.' Lolly winked at her patient then ushered Beth out of the room.

'Right, let's go sort that paperwork out before we come back.' Beth followed Lolly back to their office just off the ward. Well, it was described as an office but it was really more of a cupboard. There was just about enough room for two desks, facing each other, no window. The strip lighting above was pretty brutal and if they closed the door for too long, it just got hot and airless. Still, it was their sanctuary. Beth closed the door behind them.

'Come on then, Lol, what's up?'

Lolly picked through some paperwork on her desk, filing a few bits in the tray to her right. Signing something then dropping it into a manila folder and placing it in a separate tray. 'What do you mean, what's up? I'm fine.'

'I can see that. I could see that since you arrived this morning. It's hard to tell if it's the lack of smile or the distracted look in your eye, either way, you are definitely fine. I'd like to be as fine as you, it's an inspiring level of—'

'Alright!' Lolly put her hands up in submission. 'Yes, okay, I'm not entirely alright. But I'm also not up for picking apart all the reasons why, especially not whilst sat here in the office.'

'Oh, but this is such a place of comfort and joy. Why not explore your deepest feelings in this safe space? Mind the cactus. And the shredder.'

Lolly smiled, in spite of herself. She and Beth had worked together for about a year, not long and yet they got on really well. They chatted about life outside of work with openness. Apart from today. Lolly wasn't up for chatting about it today. Not least because Beth had no children and was desperate for them and hearing Lolly pining for a third might seem a little insensitive. 'It's fine, it's nothing. Kitt's being a pain in the arse and I'm knackered, that's all.'

'Ahhh. I get that. I've decided I'm not going to talk to Si any more.'

'That might impact on baby making.'

'Yeah, well, I don't have to talk to him to have sex. At least that way he can't piss me off. It's a win-win.'

'What's he done now?'

'Oh, you know, just suggesting that maybe part of the problem is my age.'

'Woah… that's a bold statement from a man kissing forty.'

'I know, right. I pointed out that I am ten years his junior and most definitely not out of my prime and then he mentioned something about Kirstie Allsopp banging on about women who wait to have children and I decided I'd quite like to smash him in the face.'

'Kirstie Allsopp? I thought she was houses?'

'Yes, she is. Also wombs. And women who leave them to ferment.'

'Ferment?'

'Maybe that's not the word she used. The point is, she has an opinion and Si thinks it's gospel.'

'Is that because he'd like to have sex with her?'

'More than likely. Men are so shallow.'

'Says the woman with a picture of Idris Elba on her laptop.'

'That is not shallow, that is…' peering at it '… yeah… totally justified.'

Lolly's phone pinged a message. 'Oh!'

'What?' Beth reached into her top drawer for a few stashed away mini eggs. 'You want one?' she offered.

'No, ta. Well. That's a nice surprise.'

'What is?'

Lolly read the message again. *It was so nice to see you the other day. How about that coffee? And what about the other girls? Are you still in touch with Jess or Amanda? We should all get together!*

'Come on, Lol, what's nice?'

'This. A blast from the past.'

'Oh?' Beth shoved another three mini eggs in before shutting the drawer. 'Don't let me have any more of those today.'

'Ah, shut your face. Eat what you want. Have you heard of Emily Nance?'

'Uhm... no... I don't think so...'

'She's done a few films and a bit of TV in America mainly, I think. I grew up with her. There were four of us who basically travelled through most of our teens together. Well, except that she moved away when we were about sixteen, I suppose. Pretty much cut all ties. It upset us at the time, but probably wasn't her fault. No social media back then. Anyway, I bumped into her in Truro the other day.'

'Cool. God, I'd love to see some of my old schoolmates. Not all of them... some of them were dicks, but some of them... Oh, it's been more than five minutes, we need to get back to Rhona.'

'Yeah. Come on, I'll message her later. It'd be nice though, to catch up. See what we're all up to.'

'Unless you quickly realise why you all lost touch,' pointed out Beth. 'What if they're all psycho, or this actor one is a total luvvy? What if one of them is a serial killer?'

'I do not have serial killer ex-friends.'

'Well, they're hardly going to tell you that, *are* they?'

'Beth, you're an idiot. Come on.' Lolly shut the office door behind them. 'No, it'd be great. What can possibly go wrong?'

Emily

That would be amazing, I'd love to catch up with you all. Coffee sounds good, unless you fancy something a little stronger?

Emily was quick to type back. *Coffee's good.* She paused over the keyboard, should she explain why? What if she decided not to keep it, which was still a possibility? Would Lolly judge? Would any of them. Shit, what was she thinking? Meeting up could be a terrible idea. What if they all hated each other and it got awkward? Or hated her? She'd gone so quickly. Totally failed to keep in touch. It didn't seem as if Lolly was upset with her the other day, but what if the others were? Would an apology be enough to get them back in her life? *I'm off the drink. Bit of a detox. I'll have decaf and avoid the cake.* She read it back, Christ, she sounded like all of the fun. *Unless they have biscotti. I love biscotti.* She wasn't sure this addition made her much more appealing, but she'd clicked send before she could think twice and at the end of the day, she didn't actually have to have decaf. Or biscotti. She slammed the laptop shut, then yelped at the sight of a face peering in at the window. 'Shit!'

'Sorry,' said the man, nose to glass. 'I tried knocking, I don't know if you heard? Mum said you would defo be in... sorry...!' His face was turning a gentle shade of pink and Emily felt bad for the drama. She hopped off the stool and jogged over to the door.

'I was just bringing you some of this,' he said, flustered.

'Come in, come in.' Emily ushered him in quickly, before carefully peering to check if anyone had seen him arrive, contradicting her fear of paparazzi by inviting in a stranger. 'Quickly.'

'Oh, right. Okay. I'm in, I'm in.' The man stood in her hallway, now more bright red then gentle pink. He stared at the film and theatre posters on her walls, then back to Emily before offering up the box. 'Mackerel.'

'Pardon?'

'Erm… Dad said you wanted mackerel. Sorry it's taken so long, I didn't get back out on the boat 'til this morning.'

'Oh, yes. Fish. Mackerel. Oh! Junior. You're Bill Junior.'

'Yes.'

'Lovely.'

They paused, looking at each other.

'So… do you want some of the fish…?'

'Oh! Yes. Right. Of course. Thank you.' Emily went to take the box off him.

'No, no. I'll put it down for you. Where do you want it?'

'Right, okay, sure. Down here?' She jogged down the steps to the kitchen. 'Mind your head.'

'Shit.' Bill Junior dropped the box on the table and rubbed his head where he'd obviously cracked it on the low beam.

'Shit, sorry. Are you okay? I've got ice…' The poor bloke was now basically purple. 'Oh god, shall we start again?'

He rubbed at his head and laughed good-naturedly. 'That sounds like a plan.' They paused, awkwardly. 'I'm Bill Junior, but most people call me Mac.'

'Of course they do.'

'Because of the fish.'

'The fish?'

'The... *mackerel*...' he said, as if having to spell it out, pointing at the box of fish.

Emily laughed this time. 'Jesus. Starting again didn't really help, did it?'

'I guess not.' Mac rubbed at his head again. 'How big is the bump?'

Emily's hands flew to her stomach before she realised he was talking about the bump on his forehead. She peered at the perfect egg shape that was forming beneath his thick black curls. 'Yeah... that's...'

'Like a comedy bump to the head?'

'Pretty much.'

'Good. Good. Look, I'd better go. Where do you want these?'

Mac opened the box up to show beautiful, silvery fish with crystal clear eyes and stripy, marble markings along their backs.

'Oh!'

'What?'

'They're... whole?'

'Erm... yes. Fresh. Caught this morning.'

'Right.' Emily had never gutted fish before. Fish gutting was a job for the men in the house, not for Emily or her mum. That's what her dad always said. Not that he did much fishing to bring the fresh stuff back. It was usually to show off to his London lawyer friends, rather than a regular occurrence because he actually liked fishing. He'd take them on a boat he'd bought but barely used. They'd go out all day, back when the tide returned. They'd gut the fish down in the boat shed before bringing them up for her mother to cook.

'You do know what to do with them, right?'

It was Emily's turn to colour up now. 'Well, no… actually. I've never had to do it before.'

'Oh, okay. I just assumed. Never mind… shall I…?' He looked at his watch.

'Oh no, no. Don't worry. I can probably find it on YouTube or something.'

'Nah… I'll do it, YouTube tutorials are all well and good but… well, I've got time.' Mac smiled at Emily. His eyes crinkled at the edge. They made him look warm and friendly. He didn't have a beard as such, but he'd definitely not shaved for several days. He had a thick blue cable knit jumper with a hole on one elbow and a leather patch on the other. There was the faint aroma of fish about him… it wasn't the most attractive smell but Emily assumed he must have been on the boat, come back and been delivering, and perhaps not had time to shower yet. 'Too good to gut wrong.'

'Right.'

'So, I need a wooden chopping board and a sharp knife.'

Emily spun round, looking at her kitchen. Wondering where either of those things might be. She opened a few drawers, pushing them closed again. 'I've been away. I'm not sure… any over there?' Mac started opening drawers himself, eventually finding the knives before Emily got to them. 'Oh, great, there you go,' she said, then spotting a chopping board down the side by the microwave. 'Here's the board.'

'Brilliant. Okay. So, the tip is, let the knife do the work. Don't force it or you'll butcher the fish. Take the knife just behind the gills first, on either side, until it won't go any further. Then you snap and pull the head so it takes most of the guts with it.' Emily's mouth started to water and not in a good way. She reached to open a window. 'Then you feel for the spine, taking the tip of your knife on one side, letting it run down the back until… Emily?'

Emily had disappeared. Emily had her head down her downstairs toilet. It seemed Emily's baby was not a fan of filleting fish.

Jess

Jess topped up her wine. She'd been reworking her CV, something she'd not had to do for about eight years. She'd written paragraphs. Deleted them. She'd written more paragraphs, then deleted them again. She'd tried bullet points but couldn't sum all her experience up in single sentences. She'd gone back to paragraphs before opening the Rioja and staring at her laptop screen. Facebook was still full of dead celebrities which kept sending her down internet rabbit holes that included old episodes of *Bullseye* and the joy of satin pink jump-suits and enormous eighties hair. She wondered if anyone had ever won a speedboat and, if so, where the hell had they put it since most contestants appeared to live on the poverty line. Her daydream was interrupted by Lolly.

Emily messaged!

Shit.

So we were thinking we'd go for drinks at The Old Grammar School. Unless you can think of anywhere else? Maybe Sunday? Did I ask if you're in touch with Amanda? I think she's still down here but don't know where she lives. Can you get a message to her or shall I track her down?

Jess hadn't seen Amanda since their early twenties, after she'd got back from travelling. They'd met up a few times back then. Amanda had always had Zennor in tow though and Jess got frustrated at being unable to talk to her, which, looking back, she felt bad about now. Somehow, at the time, it felt as if Amanda was judging her. As if becoming a mother had catapulted her superiority. Jess didn't like the scrutiny and Amanda seemed to have put up a barrier. She thought back to the last time they saw each other. They'd gone for coffee at the garden centre and the whole conversation was stilted, interrupted by Zennor's needs. She must have been about two, walking, jabbering, running off all the time.

Would it have been different if Lolly had been there? She'd have kept things flowing, she'd have asked all about Jess's travels and Amanda's new life as a mum, she had no filter, she always asked the questions nobody else dared. But she'd been working full-time up at Treliske by then. Her career just beginning. Jess was envious of how grown up it seemed to go out to work each day, to get a monthly pay packet. Apparently Lolly had a little flat in Truro, a share with some other girls so Amanda said. Amanda too, lived in her own place. They were both being grown-ups and Jess remembered how it appealed. It was the catapult to push her to take her first job in marketing, up in Manchester. An ad agency. Feeling out of place in Cornwall, she'd been drawn by the adventure of a big city, shops and money. Though now she realised that perhaps she'd used it as an opportunity to run away. Again. She had a habit of doing that. Was it time to stop?

She reread Lolly's message. Tapping out a response.

I'm not in touch but let me see if I can find her.

She poured herself another glass of wine. She didn't usually drink on a weekday but tonight was an exception. She was three days into working full-time with Jay and it was proving hard. Too hard. He was smart and funny, just like he'd always been. The team loved him. They'd had a meeting with one of Jess's clients today, handing them over to Jay. The client loved him too, he'd had some great ideas, really innovative. He'd got them to agree to increase their advertising spend and, in turn, generated an uplift in income for the business. It was thrilling for Jess to see him settle in and be so great at his job but it hurt too. He was chatty with her, friendly, they'd catch each other's eye from time to time and though she always turned away, she wasn't sure if he did the same. She couldn't work out if him being attentive to her every word was because he wanted to learn, or something else. She hung onto his phone calls to Niamh, waiting to hear him tell her he loved her, something to remind Jess that he was happily married, and felt conflicted when the words didn't come because perhaps he still had feelings for her. She built a taller, thicker wall.

Would the girls understand? Would time apart freshen up their friendship? Could she confide in them about this? What advice would they give?

She typed Amanda's full name into Facebook's search function. Several came up, but the one at the top was undoubtedly her. Flame-red hair, full curls and a face of make-up and mischief. Jess clicked on her picture. Her Facebook account was full of call-outs for charity, links to petitions for causes she seemed to believe in, a few photos of her with her cat, with friends of all ages. A busy life, full of love and positivity.

Hey, Amanda! I was thinking about you and wondered if you were on here and look, here you are.

Jess paused. What if Amanda didn't want to hear from her? She couldn't remember who was supposed to call who next, as they left each other at the garden centre car park. Had they both known it would be the last time or had Amanda waited for her to call? And, if so, why hadn't she reached out? Maybe Jess had been right all along, maybe Amanda did judge her. Maybe Amanda's life was now a million miles away from the four girls. What if this would just be ignored, an embarrassing reach out from someone desperate... Lolly's giddy face came to mind, the feel of the kind of squeeze hug only Lolly was able to give. And Emily, how vulnerable she used to be, how protective Jess had always felt over her, and Amanda, how strong she was, how much Jess had needed her when they were kids, how much they'd needed each other.

So Lolly has been in touch, she bumped into Emily. They'd like us all to meet up for coffee and I know it's been forever, but I'd love to know how you are, what you're up to! Hope you get this message... x

Amanda

What are you up to... That's just one of the many reasons Amanda had avoided reigniting friendships with people from back in the day. Life moved on, she had enough people in her world, those she cared for, those who looked out for her. The last time she saw Jess it had been awful. Amanda was exhausted from life with a small child and felt cut off from everyone she knew. She was also embarrassed about the state of her marriage with Pete because everyone had told her it wouldn't work and, much as she'd tried to hide it and make out that she was winning at life, she had often wondered if that really came across. She had said something about how she'd get in touch soon, that maybe they'd go out for coffee or something but she'd known, as she'd walked back to the bus stop that day, that she'd not be making contact with Jess or any of the girls. Life had changed. She had changed. It hurt to see them be the girls they'd always been, exploring all that life had to offer when she was exploring nothing more than dirty nappies and an empty bed. Did she want to open up that can of pain again, the loss of losing friends who she had adored? And did she have the energy to cover up the life she led now? Would they judge if she shared all? Would they understand how it came about? The photos and videos back in the early days when she was a single mum with bills to pay. She wanted to keep their house. It was Zennor's home. She had to survive, even if initially she'd felt as though she'd left her dignity at the spare room door. She never did it when Zennor was in the house.

I'd love to know how you are.

Would she? Would she really? Or would they all ask the question about what she did for a living, because people never asked interesting questions? Nobody wanted to know what great thing you did today, or what made you laugh, or sad, what made you think differently about something. No, it was all what do you do and where do you live? And whatever your answer, you'd be ranked by social importance. You'd be defined by it. The thing was, Amanda loved her job, she really loved it: the money, the freedom, the hours, she loved the sex, she had always loved sex, but her job didn't define her. It was not all that she was. It wasn't her sum total. People didn't get that. Not just about escorts, about anything. Doctors, teachers, stay at home mothers, lawyers, shop assistants, cleaners – that was it, that's all they were. They were interesting or not, based wholly on their CV. Would Jess, Lolly and Emily judge in the same way?

Or could they get back to where they were, the four of them, inseparable? Determined. There for one another. Amanda's guiding lights. The reason she survived when her parents split up. The reason she just about made it through her GCSEs. The reason she waited to lose her virginity with someone who gave a shit as opposed to some seventeen-year-old she met at a party when they were all no more than sixteen. They had been everything to Amanda.

I know it's been forever. It has. Forever. Years. A lifetime ago. Things had moved on. People change. For any brief, romantic notion Amanda might have about reconnecting with girls she once loved back when she was a kid, there was nothing to say they'd get on now, just 'cause they did once upon a time. More likely, they'd realise why they'd drifted apart.

And yet, so often, she'd wondered herself: about how they all were. How America was for Emily, how nursing was for Lolly, how Manchester had been for Jess... how life had been for Jess, she'd changed, long before they parted ways. Something had shifted, before she went travelling even, Amanda remembered. Emily left, which devastated them all, and something in Jess appeared to fracture.

Amanda stared at the message, nostalgia flicking her heart. She had friends, plenty, good ones, but none that knew her from back then. None that understood her past. There was something comforting about the idea of people who'd seen you evolve from child to young adult. And they'd had a laugh, back then. She couldn't remember belly laughing with anyone the way she had with those girls, back in the day.

She flicked the kettle on, yawning. It was her first day off in months and she had planned to spend it lounging around in her pyjamas watching *Jeremy Kyle* and reading, not second-guessing a social situation. Jess said that they wanted to go to The Old Grammar School on Sunday. Amanda had hoped Zennor would change her mind about lunch on Sunday. She'd called a few times, and texted. She left a message on one occasion but had no idea if she'd listened to it. She'd read the messages, Amanda could tell. Yet still she ignored her. Amanda hated not knowing what she was doing. She hated the ice between them and now the silence. It was too much. Zennor might legally be a grown-up, but she'd never stop being Amanda's baby. It had been the two of them against the world for so long, they were each other's everything and this fracture in their relationship tore Amanda apart.

And suddenly, the only people Amanda wanted to share that pain with was Emily, Lolly and Jess.

Emily

Emily braced herself by the worktop. If she was going to overcome the nausea, she probably needed to eat something. By the time she'd made it back out of the bathroom, Mac had filleted the catch, cleaned up the mess and put the fish in the fridge. He'd checked she was okay, asking through the locked bathroom door. She'd managed to mumble a response and after hearing him hover outside the door for a second, presumably uncertain what to do under the circumstances, eventually the front door closed and the house fell silent. Well, apart from the delicate sound of one final gip before she managed to escape the bathroom. So this was morning sickness. She'd been hoping that she might avoid this bit. That the universe would help her adjust to this potential new life course by letting her skip this stage. Ease her in gently. She'd been dreading the prospect after remembering a colleague on a film set who'd begged her to keep her own sickness quiet for fear of losing the job. Emily covered up by telling the producer she was bulimic, which felt shitty at the time, but it was a fact that bulimia was far more forgivable than pregnancy when it came to Hollywood.

Hollywood. Film and television. Theatre wasn't much better. Most of them in it for themselves, egos, the producers all vying for position at any cost. Which is exactly why she couldn't tell Jackson that she was still pregnant. His career was everything to him, it was his priority. Could he ever be excited about the prospect of becoming a father? It didn't appear so, he'd been pretty quick to arrange a termination for her. It was a business call, like all the other times. Why hadn't her pregnancy been different for him? Instead, they barely discussed it and she went along with his plan because she thought that's what she was supposed to do. Which was what she always did, do what she was supposed to do. Any excitement had gone, fast replaced with shock. She didn't feel how she imagined other women must feel, how she always imagined she'd feel, any time she'd daydreamed about parenthood before. So that was a good enough reason to terminate, wasn't it?

That's what she'd allowed herself to believe. Jackson had never wanted kids. He'd made that abundantly clear from the outset. It was why he split up with his first wife, and his second for that matter. Emily had briefly thought she might be different. Not just about the baby, but their relationship. That she might be the one to get him to settle, to enjoy being with someone as much as he enjoyed his work. He'd tell her that he loved her, that he wasn't the same without her. If they ever quarrelled, on the rare occasions she'd bother disagreeing with him, things would escalate, he'd shout. He'd tell her she was wrong and give her every reason why. Then if she cried, he'd buy lavish gifts to make her feel better. Don't cry, here, take this handbag or necklace or weekend away to a five-star hotel. She had all the finest designer gowns to choose from when attending an event. She'd recount the name of the designer with a wide, privileged smile. She was good at making out she was happy. Mostly because she wasn't certain she wasn't, perhaps until now. It was false. Everything was smoke and mirrors for the sake of his reputation. The things she'd told herself were simply because he cared, started to look much more like things to control her, to keep her in place. To keep her in line, just as her father always wanted. Which was no doubt why Daddy liked him. Was it right that his acceptance brought about her relief? Her mum thought Jackson was sweet. He seemed to patchwork their relationship too, something she'd been longing for since she was fifteen or sixteen, when pending adulthood seemed to push them all apart. And yet, she missed him. Maybe he'd just needed time too, to get used to the idea of becoming a dad. Had she been too quick to leave?

Her tummy rumbled. She peered at the plate of mackerel in the fridge. Good oils. Vitamins. Probably exactly what her body needed right now, irrespective of the fact she had no idea what to do with it. The phone rang.

'Emily? Junior said you weren't very well, are you okay? Do you need anything?' Betty's voice was concern rather than nosiness. Emily was glad she could tell the difference.

'Junior?' Emily asked and then she remembered. 'Oh, Mac. Yes, no. Don't worry. I'm fine, I just came over a bit… queasy, that's all.' Part of her wanted to tell Betty why, it was likely she'd have some remedy to pass over, some pearl of maternal wisdom. 'I'm fine, honestly. In fact, I was just going to cook some of the fish that Mac left. Bless him, he sorted it all out for me, all I've got to do is cook it.' Emily realised she'd said it in a way that suggested she had the first idea how to cook it. Was it too late to ask for help?

'Oh, bless him, he's a good lad. Makes us very proud.'

'I should think so.'

'But you're okay? 'Cause I can come up and help out if you need anything?'

'I'm fine, truly.' Emily looked down at the mackerel and around her kitchen. 'Just need to find the right pan for the fish. And some butter… yes? Butter?'

'Yes, a little bit of butter, just fry them off a little, will be lovely. You don't need to add anything to it.'

'Right.'

'Lovely, it'll make your hair shine. Perfect.'

Emily swallowed back a vague wash of nausea.

'Erm, whilst I've got you, Emily. That young man came back, the one you warned me about.'

'Oh, right. Yes.'

'Yes, I didn't tell him anything, obviously. I mean, I told him I had a rough idea who you were but no clue where you lived.'

'Thanks, Betty.'

'It's fine. No problem. I told the girls at the Women's Group too.' Emily had once called the Women's Group the Women's Institute when she first moved in and thought she should acquaint herself with the neighbours. Betty made it very clear they were not the same thing. *We do not make jam,* she'd said. 'They understand. We once did a similar thing for Frances O'Connor. Not shielding her from a movie mogul, just from her ex-husband, but still, I think you're pretty well covered.'

'Amazing, thanks, Betty. I was wondering how long I'd have to hide for.'

'Oh, you've no need to hide now. He's gone back apparently, boss's orders. They have a meeting for something, I can't remember. He did tell me, I wasn't really interested. Anyway, he left a note for you, from Jackson, I think. He asked me to pass it on if you came into the shop. It's down on the till, unless you want me to get Mac to drop it up?'

Emily paled at the idea of Mac coming back to her house having embarrassed herself utterly the first time. 'No, no. It's fine. If Mason's definitely gone, I'll come down to the shop. Probably tomorrow now.'

'Right on.'

'Thanks, Betty.'

'You're very welcome, my bird. Glad to help. See you later.'

Emily powered up her laptop whilst the mackerel cooked in butter. She scrolled through updates from friends, a few pictures from a young company manager she'd worked with who'd gone off and had a baby. She watched some viral film from a group of mums and their Down Syndrome children, they were all singing a song in a car about how they wouldn't change a thing, all ahead of World Down Syndrome Day and Emily couldn't help but cry. She put her hand to her belly and wondered briefly. She was forty. She'd be classed as an older mum. Were older mums more at risk? Should it factor into her thinking? They wouldn't change a thing… She scrolled on, and there was his face. Jackson. His arm draped over some young actress he'd been courting for a new Broadway show he was producing. A job Emily would actually have quite liked but he'd told her she was too old. Which is what he said about parenthood. That they were both too old.

Amanda

Amanda sat down at the breakfast bar, a cheese toastie under the grill, and reread the message from Jess. She'd thought about it off and on throughout *Jeremy Kyle* and *This Morning*. Now *Loose Women* were on and the four of them on stage together made Amanda wonder if they were really friends in real life, as they appeared on screen. And if not, who were these women's real friends? And were they people from a million years ago who knew them before they were famous? Like friends she had, who knew her before she was an escort.

Jaffa the cat purred and stretched on the kitchen worktop, inviting her to rub his belly. 'What do you think, Jaffa? Should I go meet them for coffee?' He let her rub his tummy for three seconds before changing his mind about her affection, giving her a warning swipe with claws extended, then darted out the cat flap. 'Thanks for the advice,' she called after him.

She turned the toastie over, turning her attention to a pair of trainers under the stairs, taking the Stilton out of them to check how they smelled. They were almost ready for the client who'd gifted them on the basis that she returned them after several sweaty wears. That she didn't have smelly feet was not something she was going to let stand in the way of payment, so she'd keep them where they were until the cheese honk had really set in. These were the sort of things she couldn't talk about to just anyone, but the sort of things that – with the right people – would make them howl with laughter, protagonist's anonymity protected. Could she chat to the girls about that sort of thing? Would they find the humour in it? She'd never tell anyone that she was having incredible sex with Trev, obviously, that wasn't okay, he paid her for her modesty as much as her sex game… but she could totally tell them she was shagging a fitty from school and leave them all guessing.

The Magic 8-Ball caught her eye. Zennor had bought it for her a few Christmases ago and it's true to say she'd used it more than once since then. She reached up to the shelf, taking it in her hands. How best to ask the question? If she was going to put her faith in a plastic chance ball, she really needed to channel the right mood.

She closed her eyes and centred herself. *Magic 8, Magic 8, should I reconnect with my mates?* Amanda shook the ball, holding it tightly in her hands, looking up to the ceiling and concentrating on her question. *Come on Magic 8, give a girl a sign…* Slowly, nervously, she turned it over in her hand, revealing the answer: Ask again later. Amanda threw the ball across the sofa. She picked up her phone. Jess said Sunday. The Old Grammar School. The four of them, back together, reunited, a lifetime behind them, they couldn't possibly run out of things to say. She was going to go. She was doing it. She was definitely not going to stress about this. They were her girls, her tribe.

Oh my god, hi! How lovely to hear from you! Meeting up would be brilliant, yes! Sunday, at The Old Grammar School. I will definitely be there, woohoo!!! Xxxx

Emily

Emily dropped her bag down on the shingle and, rolling a towel out, lowered herself gently to sit cross-legged, facing out to sea, hands on her knees, back straight. She gazed at the clear blue water. Small, clean waves rolled in from as far as she could see. There were no clouds, just miles and miles of crisp blue sky. A gull caught a thermal, letting the warmth lift it before it ducked out, gliding back down. Beyond the gull, cormorants dove for fish and if she wasn't mistaken, a seal was playing in the waves too. The scene lifted her heart, it filled her with contentment. She looked towards the sun, closing her eyes to feel its gentle warmth. Today's sickness had subsided, leaving utter exhaustion, but a strange sense of peace. Maybe she could do this alone, maybe she didn't need to tell Jackson. Maybe this baby would be the making of her, give her new focus. Women did it all the time, why couldn't she? Who was he to say she wasn't a natural mother; maybe she was the most natural mother in the world?

She clasped her hands together, stretching them above her head, letting the knots and clicks unpick themselves as she leant from one side to the other. Shaking out the stretch, she looked to her bag. She'd been down to Cakebreads and picked up the letter. She had considered ripping it up. Putting it in the bin. Ignoring it completely, and yet, part of her was curious.

He'd made Mason come all this way, he'd flown him to London, he'd no doubt hired him that massive Range Rover to drive from Heathrow to Cornwall. These were big things, expensive, maybe he did care, maybe he was beginning to realise… But she had left for good reason, hadn't she? She couldn't just give in, she'd gone back once before.

The letter shook in her hands.

Dear Emily

I wish I could have come to see you, you must feel so distressed right now, to have run away like this. I guess the clinic was harder than you expected? I understand. If I could have been there to hold your hand through it, baby, you know I would have. And now, all the way in England, I don't know what made you go so far, we could have talked. I wish I had time to come see you. I sent Mason because I love you. I need you to come home. You need to be at home.

He says the village you bought that place in is beautiful. He says he can see why you'd love it. He says the village shop is like Walmart wrapped in a tiny 4 square meter package. If they don't have it, you probably don't need it.

That was true, Emily had never struggled to get what she needed and if she did, it was usually possible to order it in.

So I get it, I really do. But Emily, you can't work out there. You were born to be on the stage, to be on screen. You are destined for brilliant things. Brilliant things can't come your way in Cornwall. There's another job come up, it's a film. Schwimmer is directing. You'd be incredible in it and he agrees. It could be your big break, Emily. He said he'd keep it open for this week, hence my writing.

Emily paused, looking out to sea. A ship passed slowly on the horizon. At the other end of the beach, someone walked a Labrador, throwing a stick and waiting as the dog jumped after it, leaping in and out of the waves to collect it, then shaking off its coat before dropping the stick for its owner to repeat the process. Simple things. Emily thought and wondered about getting a dog, Jackson had always said no.

The lady in the shop said she'd give you this. So here it is, my letter to you. Come home, baby, please. Let's talk. We've always been able to get through things before. We did the right thing. I miss you. Schwimmer needs you. You need us, let's make it work.

Love, J x

Emily let out a sigh, falling back onto the towel. The letter clutched in her hand. It was all about work. About her career. Her future. And, as her agent, that effectively meant his work, career and future too. We did the right thing. That's all he could say. Maybe he's not the natural parent, maybe he's the one that shouldn't have kids. That didn't mean she couldn't. If she was ready. If she really wanted to. She could do it alone, couldn't she? Could she? But was she ready to think about someone else as well as her? Did she even have that in her?

Lolly

Lolly stuck her head around the lounge door. 'Ted! Leave your brother alone! Stan, stop tormenting him. For god's sake you two, why can't you just get on?'

She'd been ignoring the bickering that had escalated to a full-on nuclear fall-out because the dishwasher needed emptying and the washing machine was beeping at her and the dog had done a wee by the kitchen door because neither of the boys had taken her out, despite Lolly asking them to because she needed a wee of her own. And because Kitt was supposed to be here, not her. She grabbed at the remote, choosing something for them to both watch together, ignoring the groans of disgust when she settled on *The Worst Witch*. 'It's good! I used to love this as a kid. I had a cat called Tabby and everything. Now watch this or play nicely together.'

Passing through the hallway to the kitchen, she picked her phone up, dialling Kitt again, his phone going straight through to voicemail. *'Where are you? Are you okay? Call me!'* She hung up then checked again to see if he'd read her text message. He hadn't, and she had no idea where he was. Was he okay? Lolly couldn't help but think the worst when he went off radar like this. The first time, about three months ago, it was all out meltdown: he had definitely been in an accident and if he wasn't dead, he was at the very least being treated for life changing injuries at Royal Cornwall Hospital. Every time a car went past she paused, waiting for the knock on the door from the police, wondering if she'd instinctively know he was dead, or invite them in for them to break the bad news in serial drama fashion; kids playing in the background, her stifling heartbroken, disbelieving sobs. When he finally walked back in the house she had to pretend she'd not just daydreamed burying him six feet under.

This time though she knew it would be one of his usual reasons. Getting distracted down the pub, or held up at work, or leaving his phone at home/in the car/down at the Blue Bar in Porthtowan. Though irritating, each one was easier to digest than the drama she used to construct. And the smell of stale ale settled any worries she had about affairs. Besides, why do men go off and have an affair? Because they're not getting any at home and she could categorically say that was not a problem for them at the moment. In fact, he was usually the one to turn her down so it definitely wasn't going to be that.

Even still, she was pissed off. It had to stop. She was supposed to be at work and it was his turn to cook tea tonight. He'd promised. Thank god one of the girls could take over her shift when she was called by the After School Club because he hadn't turned up to collect the kids. Maybe she should try Facebook messenger. *Are you coming home!?* she typed, clicking send as she walked into the kitchen to find the water for the pasta about to boil over and the dog eating something suspect beneath the fridge.

Right! I am not doing this alone. 'Stan! Come and unload the dishwasher, please.' There was a groan, just audible from the lounge. 'Ted, can you take the toilet paper up to the bathroom, hang your uniform up, then come back down and set the table, please?' There was another audible groan and the two of them came plodding through like the teenagers they were a long way off being. God help her when that came to pass. The boys set about their chores and Lolly stirred the pasta pan for a moment, using that as an excuse to gaze out of the window.

Had Jess heard back from Amanda yet? That's what she wanted to know. Because what she needed at this point in her life was some women to talk to. Women who might have a small chance of understanding what it was like to be a mother to two children with a husband who wasn't pulling his weight, and her having to keep things fresh and sexy despite wanting to confront him about his absenteeism, because if she was confrontational in any way, there'd be no possibility that they could keep up the sex life she'd been nurturing. They'd managed it twice over the weekend, it wasn't her optimum time, but it had to all help. Nine months, they'd been trying and nothing. The doctor told them it might take a while, something about turning over his sperm after the reversal, she couldn't remember the detail, but nine months? That was the longest ever! She'd been pretty quick to catch with the boys, both times thinking they'd have to wait ages and both times falling pregnant pretty much straight away. She knew she was lucky for that and thanked the gods at the time, but still… she just wanted one more. That's all she wanted. Just one more.

Outside in the garden, the magnolia tree they planted when they first moved in after getting married. It was a gift from her grandparents, something for them to nurture in their new life together. They'd almost killed it the first few years, but it seemed to be doing well now. In fact, it seemed to be thriving like the children, which Lolly was fairly sure had little to do with her, or Kitt for that matter. Nature versus nurture and all that.

The phone rang and she jumped to answer it.

'Hey, Lol, it's me.' Joanna, Lolly's older sister. 'Just checking in, is now a bad time?' Joanna had no idea about good times and bad times because she jetted between the UK and the US and her body clock was buggered. That fact, and her lack of children, meant Joanna often called at entirely the wrong time but Lolly was always so pleased to hear from her that she really didn't mind. 'I had a moment and it's been forever since we spoke so I thought I'd give it a go. How are you?'

'Ah, hey. So nice to hear from you, I'm good thanks!' Lolly had never been entirely honest with her sister. She'd always put that down to the age gap, eleven years is a lot. And given that their mother passed away when Lolly was just months old, Joanna ended up more mother figure than big sister, something they both disliked but had never found a way to change.

'So, Lolly, I've got a ton of holiday owed and I was thinking, when I'm back in London in a few weeks, I'd extend my stay, come down to see you. Have you room for me? I can always get in at a B&B if not, I wouldn't want to put you out.'

'No! Kitt and I wouldn't hear of it, you must come here.' Lolly scrunched her eyes up because she knew the boys would hear her and complain about having to share a bedroom again, just to accommodate a visitor. Something else Lolly hadn't really thought about in terms of having another child. Bedrooms. Kitt kept saying the house wasn't big enough. 'How long were you thinking you'd stay?'

'Well, I don't want to be a burden, but it'd be lovely to catch up with a few people, chill out a bit, so I don't know… maybe two weeks?'

Two weeks! Christ, Kitt would go mad. The boys would kick off. She reached for the pesto from the fridge. 'Two weeks would be amazing. We'd love that.'

'Are you sure, if you're sure you're sure.'

'Of course I'm sure. Like you say, you want to spend proper time, meet up with people. Hey, speaking of which, I'm hoping to catch up with the girls this weekend.'

'What girls?

'THE girls? Amanda, Emily and Jess.' Lolly poured the pasta into a colander just as Ted came in to start laying the table. 'I'm talking to your Aunty JoJo, she's coming over to visit. Won't that be nice!' She widened her eyes in warning to both boys so they were clear that moaning was not an option.

'I thought Emily was over here?'

'She came back. Says she's back for good.' Lolly leaned over to change the knives and forks to the right way around, then felt bad because Ted had tried his best.

'Oh! Right. Lovely, gosh, it must have been years since you last saw them.'

'About twenty, I reckon. More or less. Even more since Emily went.'

'Amazing, I hope it goes well. Let me know, won't you? Look, someone's just come in, I need to go. I'll get the dates emailed, okay. And thanks, Lolly, I can't wait.'

'Us too,' she said, hanging up and dropping her phone on the side.

The kitchen door opened. 'Who was that?' asked Kitt, wandering in as if he'd never meant to pick the kids up or cook them tea.

'Joanna. Where the hell have you been?' Lolly dumped pasta pesto on each plate, all but throwing them down on the table. 'Hungry?'

'Urm, yes, please. Thanks. I've been at work. Are you okay?'

'No, Kitt. I'm not okay. I am supposed to be at work. You were due to be at home with the kids.'

Kitt opened and closed his mouth.

'This has got to stop! Where the hell is your head?'

'Sorry, sorry! I thought that was tomorrow. I've been… shit!' He pulled her into a hug. 'I am SO sorry, it's been one of those weeks.'

Lolly pulled away as he leaned in to give her a kiss. It had been one of those weeks for months now and she didn't know how to make it stop.

Jess

Jess stretched out, her desk full of paperwork. The only people left were Jay, Vicky and Jess, everyone else having packed up an hour or so ago. Jay looked up and around. 'Where'd everyone go?' he asked.

'Home! It's nearly half six.'

'Shit, really? Christ, I was reading through these old presentations, totally lost track of time. They're good, better than good.' He paused, looking at Jess, who went back to her paperwork, busily sifting through things. 'You're really great at your job, Jess. I mean, I never doubted it, obviously, but this, it's seriously impressive.'

'We've got a great team, in fact, that one you're looking at was mostly Vicky's work.'

Vicky looked up, beaming. 'Ahhh, thanks, Jess. I seem to think you held my hand on it though.'

'Nah, you do yourself a disservice.'

'Well, whoever, however, it's great. I'm excited. The more I learn, the more I'm chuffed to be part of the team. You'll have to teach me some of your magic,' he said and Jess wondered if there was a hint of flirtation in his tone. He checked his watch. 'Well, I'd better go. My turn to cook tonight.'

'Oooh, what you having?' Vicky loved to talk about food. It was one of the reasons the firm were expanding into the restaurant sector.

'Actually, I'm cheating tonight. Bought some Homity pie from Archie Browns.'

'Oh, I love Homity pie. Now I need Homity pie.' Vicky drifted off as if remembering the last time she ate it.

Jay gathered his bags. Vicky slammed her laptop shut. 'Yeah, think that's me done too. You fancy a quick drink, Jess?'

Jess let out a groan. 'No, I'm okay ta. Gonna finish up on some of this then head off. You there with your Homity goodness, I have a tin of stag chilli with my name on it.' Jess ignored Vicky's physical repulsion. 'It's that or tinned ravioli.'

'You need to go food shopping,' said Vicky. 'And stop buying tinned food.'

'You need to stop worrying about my kitchen habits. See you tomorrow.'

Vicky slung her bag on her back. 'Yeah, alright. See you tomorrow.'

'See you tomorrow, Jess.' Jay popped his head through the hoodie he was putting on. 'Don't work too late.'

'Yeah. Thanks.'

Jess waited 'til she heard the doors click shut. She waited for that peace to fall around the office, the corner lights to dim, the whir of Vicky's laptop to stop. Within minutes, the only sound was a printer somewhere round the other side of the office, set to print some big file and left until the morning. She moved her mouse to wake up her computer. The message from Amanda was awaiting her response, she'd somehow been having second thoughts about the meet up. Jay was really knocking her mood and a quick look on Facebook was enough to see that the others appeared to have life well and truly sorted, with partners and careers and children and lives. Actual lives. Lives that operated outside of their chosen jobs.

The FaceTime sound kicked out around the silence. It was her brother, Matt.

'Yo, fartface. How are you?' he said.

Jess laughed. 'I think it's the way you greet me that I love the most.'

'Well, you know. We have to set the tone.'

'I guess so.' She stared at the screen, her brother had his iPad leant up against something so he could keep on working whilst they talked. They did that from time to time, when they were both working late. He looked his usual self, he was the walking epitome of a graphic designer. A geek chic tee, messy hair and skin that said I survive on coffee and pork products alone. She was just about to ask him what he was working on when a message from Lolly popped up. *Did you hear back from Amanda, are we on for Sunday?* And before she realised, Jess had let out a sigh that turned into a groan.

'Oh dear, that sounded painful.'

'Mmmm.'

He poured coffee from a cafetière into the *Doctor Who* mug she'd bought him last Christmas. 'What's up?'

'You drink too much coffee. You won't sleep tonight.'

'How do you know it's not decaf?'

'Because you're not dead, and that is the only way you'd allow such filth to pass your lips.'

'Yes, well, that's true. But I wasn't the one to let out a sigh. You sounded like Mum in those days when she knew Dad was still eating a full English at Smokey Joe's despite the doctor's specific instruction to stop and them paying for weekly Weight Watchers classes.'

'Yes, well, it's not quite that bad.'

'So what's up then?'

'Do you remember Amanda, Lolly and Emily?' He would remember them. He was obsessed with Emily for many more years than was healthy. She was like the Rachel to his Ross. Only he didn't stalk her in later life and then control her every move. 'Well, Lolly got in touch to say that she'd bumped into Emily and that Emily wanted to catch up and would I message Amanda, which I did, and Amanda wants to meet up too and now it seems I've agreed to have coffee with them all on Sunday morning.'

'Shit.'

'I know.'

'No! No! I mean, Shit! You're going to have to go out and meet with real life people that have probably forgotten you're a dickhead.' Jess raised her eyebrows at Matt in the same way their mum used to when one of them was in trouble. 'And looking at me like that is not going to help.'

'Ahhhh, what am I going to do, Matt? I don't want to see people. I don't want to talk to people. Eurgh! People are horrible.'

'Those people knew you when you were a hormonal dickhead. At least you're just a dickhead now.'

'Matt!'

'Come on, you do this all the time.'

'What?'

'You avoid shit. You talk yourself out of things that might be good for you. You decide you won't like it and then you end up being forty years old with few friends, no husband or boyfriend or significant other. Christ, you've not even got a cat, Jess. At least get yourself a cat!'

'I don't like cats.'

'And I judge you for that.'

'I know. Look, I can't explain it. I'm just… I don't want stuff that takes work, you know? I like my life as it is. I'm okay.'

'Okay or happy?'

Jess looked over to Jay's desk. 'I was happy…'

'What's changed?' Matt peered at her over his mug as he drank.

'Ha! Well… oh god…'

'Come on, spill it. Have you met someone? You've met someone! Finally, maybe a shag would loosen you up a bit!'

'Who says I've not been getting any, just 'cause I'm single.'

'Eurgh, yes, well, whatever, I don't want to think about that. So let's, for the purposes of the court, suggest you're not short on sex. You love your job. You don't have a cat. You have friends who want to meet up with you and you should be happy about that. I promise you, you won't regret it. So what else has gone wrong?'

'Jay.'

'What about him?' Matt knew everything about Jay. He'd known all about Jay before Jess went travelling and was there to pick up the pieces when Jess got back. 'What's up?'

'I have a new work colleague.'

Matt's mouth fell open.

'He started this week.'

'No.'

'Yes.'

'Oh.'

'Exactly. He is the new Head of Advertising. We are supposed to be working alongside one another.'

Matt paused, studying his little sister's face. 'Which I guess is going to be totally fine because you are well and truly over him, yes?'

'You'd think right, after all this time. Yes, totally fine. Or maybe no. Not fine at all. In fact, awful, horrendous. It's a whole new level of torture that I entirely did not see coming.' Matt's eyes widened. 'I have to share an office with the man I thought I wasn't in love with any more, Matt. I have to share clients with the man I thought I'd stopped dreaming about having children with. I effectively sit next to the man I thought I'd got over wanting to spend the rest of my life with, all the while knowing he has a beautiful, positively lovely wife and two utterly gorgeous children.'

'Jess—'

'Not only is it horrendous, it is possibly the end of my career because how on earth can I possibly spend—'

'Jess—'

'—every day of my working life beside the only man I've ever truly loved. A man I am nowhere near as over as I thought I was. It's been forever, how can this still *be*?'

'Jess!' Matt had his head in his hands. When he looked back up, Jess had paled in the knowledge she was probably not alone. Matt took on the look of pity, the one where you wish you could fix something for someone you love but you know that there is literally nothing you can do. And Jess wondered just how long Jay had been standing behind her.

Emily

With her eyes shut, the setting sun glowed orange behind her eyelids. She let her hand fall open, loosening her grip on Jackson's letter. But as she did, something cold and wet thrust into her hand. 'What the!' She jumped up, terrified.

'Colin, come here!' said a voice. 'Sorry, he's very friendly!'

'Mac! Hi!' Emily crossed her arms and wished she didn't feel her skin prickle with embarrassment. She bent down to fuss the dog. He was wet and sandy and it took all her resolve not to recoil at the wet dog hair that left its mark on her hand where she'd fussed him. And was he really called *Colin*?

'You feeling better?' he asked, grabbing hold of Colin's collar, stooping slightly as he talked to her. 'You look better than the other day.'

'Thanks.'

'Oh, I didn't mean you looked terrible… Though you did look sort of green. Sorry, I should probably just have brought you the fillets. I didn't think.'

'No, no. It's fine. I don't know what came over me. I was just… it's fine. I'm loads better.'

Mac turned to stand beside her, throwing a stick for Colin to chase into the sea. 'How beautiful is this,' he said.

'Stunning. It's so nice to be back.'

'Where were you before?'

'New York.' Mac didn't look at her, but she saw him raise his eyebrows. 'I'd been there a few years. L.A. before that.'

'Right.'

Emily smiled to herself, usually when she told people that, they wanted to know everything. Where had she lived, what had she done out there. What was it like? Or they'd tell her stories of when they'd visited and places they'd been, shows they'd seen, food they'd eaten. Mac had nothing to say. She liked his disinterest.

'I bought the cottage years ago, from some money I got for a show that flopped. Before it flopped… when they thought it would be a big hit and were investing in its future.' Mac nodded. 'I wanted to know that I could pop back whenever I had time, that I'd have somewhere to go. A home from home.'

'Nice for those who can.' Second homes were a sore subject for the locals, Emily knew and understood why. 'I know, I know. It's alright for me, etcetera. But I'm here now, ready to work… well, not work straight away but I will. When I decide what I want to do.'

'Yeah?'

'Yeah. Definitely. I guess I can do anything, right?'

'If you can do anything anywhere, Cornwall is the place to do it.'

Emily smiled. The sea sparkled. 'I think you're right. I feel like I'm home now. Like I belong.'

Mac took a few steps forward, meeting Colin who'd brought the stick back and was waiting excitedly for him to throw it again. 'I know what you mean,' he said, launching the stick back into the sea. 'Wouldn't be anywhere else.' He turned to face her, the breeze whipped up his hair and he had to move it aside to see her.

'Have you ever lived anywhere else?'

Mac shook his head. 'Nope. No need. I have all I want here, on the doorstep. Gorran Haven born and bred and quite happy to keep it that way.'

Once upon a time, Emily thought that unambitious. When her Cornish friends had no aspiration to leave, no dreams. At least, not the kind of dreams that her dad thought she should have. The dreams to be a lawyer or an accountant. Something solid and important in the world. A job you could get work anywhere doing.

'I have all I need here, and all I'll ever need.'

'Which is?'

'The sea. My family. My friends. Enough work to put food on the table and enough free time to enjoy life.'

'I'm realising that's probably all any of us need.'

Mac stuffed his hands in his pockets. 'It's a shame more people don't see it.'

'I didn't, for a long time. Upbringing, the world I worked in, I don't know. I think it's time I broke the cycle,' she said.

'The cycle?'

'Living to work. Needing all of the money. The stuff. You know? I left New York because all that wasn't right any more… well, that's not the only reason I left, but it was one of them and I guess…' She looked down at the letter, still in her hand. She ripped it up, stuffing it in her bag. 'I guess it's time to make some changes.'

Mac nodded, beginning to move on. 'Well, I'd better leave you to it. I've a few jobs to do. Get the dog back.'

'Right.'

'Oh, by the way, I noticed some of the tiles had come off your roof. Just a few, but they've loosened some others, and it might be worth sorting them before it gets worse.'

'Oh, right. I didn't...' Emily had no idea.

'I can always pop up and do it.'

'Oh, no. There's no need.'

Mac took the stick and threw it again. 'It's fine, it wouldn't take me long. Unless you'd rather get someone else?'

'What? No! That's... I mean, if you're sure! I'd pay you for it.'

'No, no. It's fine. Won't take two minutes.'

'Maybe I can cook something for you, I don't know, pay back some other way.' Emily wondered if Mac looked at her as if he didn't believe she could cook. Which wasn't entirely off the mark.

'Don't worry, I'll sort it. It's fine.'

'Okay, thanks. Thank you.'

'Glad you're feeling better.'

'Thanks!' Emily said to his retreating back, but she wasn't sure he heard her. Or cared whether she answered or not. And that was strangely comforting.

Jess

'Shit! Shit! Shit, shit, shit!' Jess was stood, hands on head, stamping her foot and spinning on her heels, none of which changed the situation whatsoever.

'There's nothing you could have done, Jess,' said Matt, his face up close to the screen. 'Calm down, breathe.'

'How can I breathe? For god's sake, Matt! What the hell? I thought he'd gone. He HAD gone. He left with Vicky.'

'You weren't to know he'd come back.'

'I should never have mentioned it. I should have kept it to myself.'

'Yes, because keeping things bottled up always works out well. Jess, you didn't know. It's not your fault.'

Jess dropped down into her chair, her hands in her hair. 'I know it's not my fault, Matt, but fucking hell, he clearly heard every word and I have to work with him! I have to face him tomorrow, and the day after, and the day after that and even if I hand my notice in, I still have to work with him for another three months and all the while he knows. He just looked at me, Matt. He just stared.'

Matt grabbed hold of his iPad. 'If I could grab hold of you right now, I would. I'd grab hold of you by your shoulders and say for god's sake, you've got to calm down because nothing good can come of the drama.'

'The drama!' she shrieked. 'The fucking drama! He just walked in to find out that I am hook, line, and sinker still in love with him, despite the fact that we have to work together. What was I thinking? I'm just going to have to leave.'

'Why should you?'

'Why shouldn't I!'

'Because that's your job. Your career. You love that job, you've worked hard at it. You've built up that client list, you've supported that team. You're the reason he has a job at all, from what you've said to me. If you weren't doing what you do, there'd be no job for him. Walking away is not an option. If anyone has to go, he should.'

'He can't leave, he's only just got here!'

'Then it won't matter if he goes. He can just get another job.'

'Yes, because there are a million jobs like this, paying this salary, in Cornwall. It's literally as easy as walking out of here today and into a new office tomorrow. He'll be fine.'

'He's not your concern.'

'It's not his fault.'

'It's not your fault either, Jess. Do not fall on your sword over something like this. Do not let a man ruin your career!'

Jess groaned, leaning back in her chair. Panic and fear taking over.

'Oh, sis. No! Don't cry! You're too far away from me to do that! Please, I hate it when you cry.' That was true. Matt had always hated it when Jess cried, right from her being born, apparently. She'd cry as a baby and he'd run to her, stroking her cheek until she calmed down. If she fell over, when she was little, he'd be there before their mum or dad, taking her hand and pulling her up. When she had her heart broken aged twelve, he was the one to hold her until she stopped sobbing.

He hated her crying but he was always there when she did. Until he moved away. 'Right, I'm coming down.'

'No, no! You can't, don't be silly.'

Matt looked at his laptop, she knew he'd be googling train times. 'I could be there tomorrow.'

'What about 'Chelle? She won't want you up and leaving to come to me!'

'She won't mind, if I told her—'

'No! You can't tell her anything.' Matt knew everything about Jess and Jay, even from before tonight. But only on the basis that he swore he'd never tell his long-term girlfriend Michelle and Jess was positive that he hadn't told her. She couldn't bear the idea of her knowing anything about this. It wasn't that Michelle would judge or sneer, it's just that she was so bloody successful at everything… 'Don't worry. I'm fine. I'll work something out.'

'You need to talk to him. If he won't leave and you can't leave, you need to talk to him and clear the air.'

'I can't do that, Matt.'

'Jess, you have to. You're a grown-up. This is shit, but you can deal with it. I know you can. You've just got to tackle it, then move on. And for god's sake, go see the girls on Sunday. It'll do you good. Get some focus in your life, something that's not work or Jay Trewellan. Okay? Seriously, before it becomes a real problem. You were fine, you've been fine for ages. You'd moved on.'

'Apparently not.'

'Okay, if not moved on exactly, you were at least doing fine. You need to continue doing fine. This is a blip, a minor interruption to doing fine. Get back to that place and get yourself out there. Meet somebody!'

'Maybe I don't want to meet somebody.' She sniffed.

'I'd believe that if I didn't think it was because you were frightened of getting hurt. He moved on. He met somebody. You left them to it. That he is back in your life changes nothing. It's time for you now, Jess. You're forty. It's time to take stock. Make some life changes. Start with the girls, see where it takes you. You are stronger and more brilliant than you seem to realise. It's time to live that.' Jess sniffed again, half nodding. She loved her big brother. 'Look, I'm going. You should go home too. Call me this weekend. When you've had time to breathe and realised I'm right. Tell me how you're going to spin things around. Be strong. Stand your ground. You can't help how you feel, but you can totally help how you act.'

'Love you.'

'Love you too. Call me, okay.'

'I will.'

'Make sure you do.'

Amanda

Amanda jumped at the sound of a knock on her front door. Since sending the message back to Jess, she'd been panicking. Maybe it was best that they left things in the past, something lovely to look back on. What if their conversation was a car crash or they'd all grown so far apart that it made Amanda feel like she'd epically failed in life? *Had* she epically failed in life? She didn't feel it, but she wasn't exactly living the kind of life most people enjoyed. Enjoyed or endured? Sometimes it was hard to tell. The doorbell rang out, urgently.

'Coming, I'm coming. Sorry!' She jogged down the hall and opened the door. 'Oh.' She turned and walked back down the hall, leaving the door open. 'It's you.'

Pete, Amanda's ex-husband, followed her into the house. 'Lovely to see you too.'

'Shut the door behind you.'

'I did.'

'I meant with you on the other side of it.'

Pete let out a laugh. 'God, you're a spiteful cow. It's no wonder I left.'

'I kicked you out. Because you had sex with that girl.'

'That girl had a name. We were together fifteen years, Amanda, it was hardly a fling.'

Amanda had never worked out if that fact made it hurt more. 'Yeah, I'm not interested. Now what do you want and do you need a drink?'

'If it's red and in a glass, I will have one. Though it will have to be quick.' Pete pulled out a stool to the breakfast bar, perching, relaxed.

'Some things never change,' she said, eyebrows raised.

'You're not funny.'

Amanda reached for a bottle of red from the shelf. 'This is all I have so don't get snobby about it.'

'As if I would.'

Amanda poured two glasses, clinking Pete's before he'd had the chance to pick it up. 'What do you want?'

Pete sipped at his drink. He made a noise that suggested he wasn't sure where to start and Amanda could feel her hackles rise even further than they already were. She was always on edge when he rocked up. Her mate Karenza told her it was a defence mechanism, because she still loved him, that the edge and spite she portrayed whenever she saw him was to ensure that they never rekindled their relationship and she didn't have to get hurt again. Amanda had never been entirely convinced but was aware that however she felt about him leaving her, and the rows they'd had since, he was the father of her child. She did, on some level, still have feelings for him. Not that she'd let that on to him.

'Zennor told me she saw you out the other night.'

'And you're here to tell me off for being out on a school night.'

'I'm not here to tell you off for anything. It's just that she was pretty upset when she got home. I found her sobbing in the lounge at two in the morning.' Amanda's heart ached. 'She said you were talking to Billy Harvey.'

'And?'

'And? Seriously?'

'Pete, I was out having a few drinks. I was chatting to some bloke who started chatting to me. I am allowed to go out, you know. I'm allowed a life.'

'Of course you are, but not with Billy Harvey!' Amanda looked at him, confused. 'Billy Harvey is Zennor's…' He paused, searching for the right description. 'Zennor and Billy, they're like… you and me…'

'Shit, she's pregnant?'

'No! No, she's not pregnant.' He took a sip of wine. 'Christ, I hope not anyway. No, I mean, she loves him.'

'I never loved you.'

Pete looked at her. 'Right. And I never loved you either.' They stared at each other for a moment. 'She's a bit broken, right now. She's hurting. He's been a shit to her, made her feel all special and important and like the only girl in the world and then, as she fell head over heels for him, he decided he wasn't sure any more and shagged one of her mates.'

'Hardly a mate.'

'Well, no, we know that, but she's…'

'Broken.'

'Like I said.'

Amanda let out a sigh. 'Shitting hell, I really didn't mean to… I was just having a drink. I should have realised something was really up from her reaction.'

Pete shook his head and it made Amanda want to smash him in the face. He used to do it when they were together, shaking his head like he knew better than she did about something, usually something to do with herself, like *sure, you're really sorry about x* or, *of course you're not going to kick off about y*. God, he was irritating. Especially when he'd do that shake of his head to himself, then flex his jaw muscle straight after and he knew fine well that Amanda always found that a total turn on.

She never knew why… maybe it took her back to the days he'd walk her home from babysitting and they'd stand beneath the streetlight, her hand held in his, all youthful and carefree. He'd tease her, he'd act all aloof, like he wasn't really interested, before leaning in to kiss her and it was always the most intense kiss. The most enveloping moment.

'Amanda.'

'What? Sorry, I…' She hopped off her stool and hid her head in the cupboard, searching out a bag of crisps or something to focus her mind on. 'So what do you think I should do? I've texted her. I wanted to take her out on Sunday. She just doesn't seem to want anything to do with me. I don't know what to do.'

'I know. I've told her she's being unfair.'

'You have?' Amanda did hate him, but she did also like him. He had his moments.

'Of course I have. I've said she's only got one of you and however much of a douche you can be, you're basically a good human being and she could do a lot worse.'

'Wow, you really know how to big a girl up.'

'They weren't my exact words. I was paraphrasing.'

'And what did she say.'

'Not a lot.'

'Right.'

He knocked his wine back. 'I guess, really, I was just dropping by to let you know that she is fine. To not worry. To give her some space. I think this has less to do with you and more to do with Billy Harvey.'

'Billy Harvey is a shit.'

'He is.'

Pete moved around to Amanda. 'Come here, dickhead. Give us a cuddle.'

'I hate it when you do this,' she said, totally allowing herself to be wrapped up in his strong arms. 'And don't call me a dickhead.'

'It takes one to know one.' He kissed the top of her head.

'You know you didn't have to come round to tell me all of this, you could have called. Or texted.'

He looked at her as he let her go and walked ahead of her back down the hallway. With his hand on the door latch, he said, 'I could have. But it's been ages since I saw you so…' Opening the door, he turned to face Amanda. 'Give Zennor some space, she will come round. I'll keep on at her.'

'Promise.'

'Promise.' He jogged down the path, pausing at the gate. 'I did love you, for the record.' Then he turned and left, waving over his shoulder as he went and Amanda was irritated by his assumption that she'd still be watching.

Lolly

Exhausted, Lolly pulled the bedroom door closed, child number two now fast asleep, and she could practically hear the gin and tonic calling. She was a walking maternal cliché and she very much did not care.

Downstairs, Kitt lay on the sofa, his long legs stretched out so she couldn't sit down anywhere except on them or in the rocker in the corner. She nudged his feet, making him snore then jump awake. 'Tired?' she asked, aware of the disdain in her tone.

'Knackered! I don't know what's up with me. I've just been full on these last few weeks.'

Yes, full on, thought Lolly. *It's tough juggling… work and work and, basically, just work.* 'Mmmm,' was all that she said.

'You okay?' He moved up to give her space.

'Yup.' She hated that she just answered yes when actually she was supremely pissed off with him, but she couldn't quite work out how to say what she wanted to say, or what was wrong, over and above the fact that she was alone in juggling work and home and kids and had had enough. It's not that he wouldn't do things if she asked for help, she just sometimes got fed up of asking.

'You wanna watch *Breaking Bad*?'

'Yup.' Her clipped response was probably disguised by her picking up the gin and tonic, ice clinking against the glass. She took a long sip, feeling the ice-cold liquid trickle down her chest and into her legs. That was the thing she liked best about gin, the fuzz it gave her. The way it knocked off the edges of her day. It was like being wrapped in cotton wool and right now, as bruised as she felt by the state of their lives, she needed cotton wool. Kitt navigated Netflix, picking out the latest episode for them to watch. Did he not realise she was pissed off, or was he ignoring it? Was he avoiding it, like he so often did, because he didn't want a row? Were they not worth the fight any more?

'God, I can't remember any of that last episode,' he said as the catch-up played out before the new episode.

'No. You fell asleep.'

'You sound pissed off.'

She took another sip of gin. 'No. No.' *Yes! Yes!*

Kitt paused the telly and sighed. He shifted again, this time to cross his legs beneath himself. 'What's the matter?'

Lolly's eyes stung.

'Why are you pissed off with me?'

'You were supposed to pick the kids up, Kitt. I was working. You were supposed to be there.'

'I know, I know. And I'm sorry, I don't know how it happened. I just totally lost track of the days, I'm sorry.' He leant forward, reaching out for her hand but she kept them firmly grasped around her glass. 'It's more than that though, isn't it?'

She bit the inside of her mouth, then took another sip of drink.

'Talk to me.' He searched out eye contact.

'I just... I don't know... I feel... I can't explain how I feel, actually. I keep trying to work it out and I don't know. Things aren't right. We're not right. I want another baby and you don't seem to care, even though I thought we'd agreed to it. I thought we'd signed up for it? Together!'

'You signed up for it,' he said, dropping eye contact.

'You agreed! You had your vasectomy reversed!'

'Because you wanted a baby so desperately. Because you *want* one so desperately.'

'What, so you're not remotely bothered?'

'I want you to be happy.'

If that were true, it didn't sound much like it. It sounded as if he thought the very thing was an impossibility. As if her happiness were so unlikely, he didn't know why he bothered trying. Was that fair, she wondered? Was she impossible to please at the moment? She didn't think so… she thought they were on the same page. Instead, he was sat in front of her, all folded in on himself. Crossed arms and legs. Defensive. She sort of knew she was being obstinate with her response, but she felt obstinate. She didn't feel like letting him off the hook entirely. 'So, you don't actually want another baby.'

'I didn't, no. But you explained why you do and I support that, I mean… I can't promise it'll be the girl you seem to have your heart set on, but I can try. I can do my bit.'

'That requires you to actually do your bit.'

'Is this about last Thursday? I was tired, Lolly. Does it really matter when it happens?'

'Yes! It does! That's the point! The whole thing for us is that with your reversal and my age, we have the odds stacked against us, so yes! It does matter when it happens, to give us any chance whatsoever, it has to be when my temperature is right.'

'Which is the least sexy thing in the world. I'm not a performing monkey, Lolly. Christ!'

'You're a bloke! How difficult can it be?'

'Well…' He looked at her. Did she see an element of hurt in his eyes? Any guilt she felt, if she did, was quickly replaced with the feeling of tough because he'd said he wanted another child and he knew what it meant to her and she didn't want to be made to feel guilty about something they'd both signed up for. 'It's not difficult getting it up, per se,' he said. 'It's difficult when… it feels so perfunctory. So…'

'What, so I'm shit in bed?'

'That's not what I said. Oh my god, Lolly, this isn't about you being crap in bed or even about us and our sex life. This is about the fact that I feel used and you feel let down. This is about us hitting a rocky patch in our marriage and you are blaming me for it all and it's not fair.'

'A rocky patch?' Since when did he think they'd hit a rocky patch? At what point in the last few months had it been difficult? They'd been married fifteen years, she knew about rocky patches. She remembered when they'd just had their first and wondered if she even loved him any more. She remembered the time a colleague made a pass at her and she had that feeling in her pants that she'd not had with him for bloody ages. She remembered the way he flirted with one of her friends because he thought she wasn't looking. Of all the times they might be in a rocky patch, now did not feel like a rocky patch. 'I just want another baby, Kitt. I didn't realise that forced us into a rocky patch. I want a daughter. I want what Joanna had with Mum. That fierce connection between mother and daughter, that sense that she is a tiny part of you and you are helping to shape her future.'

'That's what you do with the boys.'

'But…' Lolly felt her eyes sting again because every time they talked about this she felt like she just hadn't found the way to articulate what mattered. Because in truth, she didn't really know. Except that

Joanna had got the best of their mum's years. Joanna grew up in their mum's care, she saw her as a woman to look up to and be inspired by. Their mum saw Joanna as the tiny version of her, learning, growing, the bits of her that were feisty and powerful were Mum. The bits of her that were strong and funny, they were Mum. The bits of her that could survive anything that life threw at them, they were Mum. Lolly didn't have that because their mum passed away before she even got to walk. To talk. To tell her mum that she loved her and hear it said in return, rather than imagined, whispered on a falling white feather, or the chirp of a robin. Lolly loved her boys, that wasn't in question, she just wanted to love a girl too, then be around for that girl until she was fully grown. To be there for the important moments in life. There for all the things that Lolly wished her own mother had been there for. She looked over at the photo of herself, a babe in her mum's arms. She wanted that, there, captured on an old Polaroid. They were at a street party. Lolly was a tiny, days-old baby, wrapped in a white shawl and yellow knitted baby clothes. Her mum was in a stripy jumper and had permed hair. She didn't want the hair... or the stripy jumper, but she wanted the babe in arms.

Jess

Friday night. Jay had been avoiding Jess since walking in on her chat with Matt on Wednesday. When she arrived on Thursday morning he was in the meeting room. They caught sight of each other, she smiled, he seemed to stare for just a minute longer before going back to the discussion he was having. He joked in the office with everyone, he wasn't rude to her. In fact, she didn't imagine anyone had noticed the frost between them, but she knew it. She felt it. Her muscles were tight from the stress. Her shoulders ached. Her head ached. She would join conversations and avoid his eye. She presented her usual in charge, in control, on top of her game self. Until she sat back at her desk. There, despite being in full view to the team, she would stare at the screen. She'd read files, make notes that were nothing but doodles on the pad. She'd go to the filing cabinet, she'd go back to her desk. She'd wait until he'd made a drink before she went to the kitchen.

And at night, when the team had left, she brought up her CV and worked on it. She browsed job sites. She looked at houses in Exeter and Bristol. She worked out how much she had in savings and her bank account to see if she could move away. It was all doable. She could sell her house, the market in Cornwall was still moving. Maybe it would sell quickly and then she'd have no other reason to stay. She looked at the files on her desk, the pile of work she'd not achieved these last few days. She piled them into a bag to take home and catch up on over the weekend, then she dropped into her chair, exhausted. 'Fuck!' she shouted out. 'Fucking fuck!'

'You always were a potty mouth.'

Jess held her breath. She didn't want to turn around this time. She didn't want to see him there. She didn't want to have this conversation, whatever conversation he'd come back to have, she wanted to avoid it. She wanted to just pretend nothing had happened and hand her notice in and move on. She wanted to run away. She always ran away.

Running away was what lost her Jay in the first place…

'Should we talk?' he said.

'No. We shouldn't talk. You should go home. I should move on.'

Jay moved to stand beside her desk. 'Don't be stupid.'

Jess could hear her heart and wondered if he could hear it too.

'Moving on is crazy. This is your team, your career. Why would you throw that all away?'

'Because I can't bear the idea of working here, with you. That's why. Especially not now, now you know. God, I can't even—'

'Look at me.'

'No.' Her eyes stung.

'Look at me, Jess. Please.'

'If I don't look at you, I don't have to see the pity in your eyes. I don't need that. I don't need to be patronised.'

Jay turned to face her, in her peripheral vision she could see him look at her. What did he think? What did he see? Was it a pitiful sight? Was she old and stupid? Did she look like a woman who'd wasted her life pining for a man she walked away from? Did he see how vulnerable she was?

'I miss you, Jess. I've always missed you.'

'Don't, Jay. Don't do this. Whatever you're thinking, whatever your plan is. Just go. Leave.'

'I thought we could make it work. I thought we could be friends.'

'I thought I'd come back from travelling and you and I would pick up where we left off. Sometimes things don't work out.'

Jay perched on the edge of her desk. 'We were kids, Jess. That was never going to happen, was it? Surely you knew that when you left?'

'If I knew it, I wouldn't have…' She paused. She gathered herself. She began again, quieter. 'If I knew it, I wouldn't have gone.' She turned to face him this time, his smile glassy through her tears. 'I wouldn't have gone Jay, I just…'

Jay nodded, looking down at the floor.

'I was a kid, I was just… stupid. I needed to go. I needed to get away from here. I needed to work out who I was and what I wanted out of life. I needed to escape. I thought you'd be there when I got back. Fuck!' She laughed. 'The arrogance.'

'I probably thought I'd be there when you got back too.'

'And yet…'

'And yet you made it clear you were doing your thing. Travelling. Experiencing life. Living it. You made it clear you weren't coming home until you had seen and done all of the things you wanted to and you…' Jay's words dried up. He moved to perch on the desk in front of Jess's.

'And I, what?'

'You changed, you weren't you. You all but said you thought I was wasting my life by working and waiting, you said my lack of ambition wasn't attractive. You said I was lame.' Jay fixed her with a look that suggested she wasn't the only one who'd been hurt by the turn of events. It was a look that didn't apologise for reminding her that she had said all of those things. It wasn't a look of anger or hatred, but it was a look that said the damage was done, long before she finally made it home from her travels. 'You told me to move on.'

'I didn't mean it.'

'I didn't know that.'

'I… I was an idiot. Drunk, probably. Especially if I said all those things whilst I was in New Zealand. I drank A LOT in New Zealand.'

'What? You don't remember saying those things?'

Jess sighed. She could feel her cheeks colour up. 'Of course I remember,' she whispered. She remembered saying all of those things because she very definitely wasn't drunk when she said them. She'd spent the day sobbing on the bed of her bedsit, wondering how to climb out of herself, how to heal the pain, how to escape. She hurt and she wanted him to hurt. She wanted to go home but she wanted to hide. She wanted to drink and smoke and have casual sex and skinny dip and jump from the highest cliff into the deepest blue pools. And yet, none of those things made her feel better. And that day, the last time she spoke to Jay, she couldn't bring herself to confess that really, she hated travelling and being away from home and being without Jay by her side, but the intensity of their feelings was too much. It fought with the fear that lived in her stomach since the night of Emily's party. It scared her. She didn't want to feel anything. She wanted invisibility, she craved numbness.

'You moved on, Jess,' he said. 'We were naive to think it could have ended any other way. We were kids.'

Jess bit down on her lip because she knew it wasn't okay to tell him that she may have been a kid but she knew that she loved him.

'I always wondered what might have been,' he said, standing to move beside her.

'Don't, Jay.'

'I'll never not wonder…'

Jess steeled herself. 'Go home, Jay. Go home to your wife.'

The room fell silent for just a second before Jess heard Jay's footsteps walking away.

She'd had time to work it out now. It had been twenty years of hiding from her feelings. Him arriving in her office was a shock, but nothing like the shock she felt to realise she'd been avoiding relationships all these years, avoiding the chance to meet somebody new, it had all been because her heart hadn't healed. She'd carried as much fear of her feelings as she had this love for him. But Matt was right, she didn't deserve to feel like this, she had as much right as the next person to be happy. To love and be loved. Maybe it was time to let go, she just didn't know how. Would seeing Emily help? If she didn't, she might never fully move on.

Lolly

Lolly stacked the bowls in the dishwasher, singing along to Saturday morning Radio Two. The sun shone through their patio doors and the boys were wrapped up, making the most of the weather, out in the garden. They chased each other with foam swords, Stan running up the steps of their climbing frame, before turning on Ted with the tip of his sword digging menacingly into his scarf.

'Careful!' Lolly shouted.

The boys carried on regardless. She wondered if any of the other girls had children. She guessed not for Emily, she'd not read anything anywhere to suggest otherwise. She knew about Amanda's Zennor but didn't know if she'd had any more. Jess didn't seem interested in anything other than work, if her Facebook page was anything to go by. And that's when it hit Lolly. The butterflies at the prospect of meeting up with them tomorrow. She hadn't been expecting it, having effectively instigated the meet up in the first place. Had she not bumped into Emily and given her her number, would any of this be happening? And now that it is, what will it actually be like? Did they have anything in common any more? Could she function in a group of women that were not her colleagues or other mums from school? What would she talk about? Who even was she? Apart from wife, mother and physio. Was that enough?

'Another coffee?' Kitt said, flicking the kettle on.

It had always been enough before. 'Please,' she said, absentmindedly. Recently, she'd started to question everything. Was it approaching her forties that did that? The whole baby thing? The state of her and Kitt's marriage… which was possibly overstating the last couple of days' worth of frost, but still… things weren't on an even keel and Lolly didn't like it.

'I've put a wash on.'

She looked up sharply. 'Have you?' He never put a wash on.

'A few shirts, some odds and sods.'

'Right.' Of course, his own stuff mostly then. She tried not to be irritated.

'Anything else you need doing?'

She wanted to tell him to look around the house and see what he could find for himself but having pissed him off by turning him down for sex this morning, mainly because she didn't like him very much at the moment, and she wasn't ovulating, and she didn't really feel up to it whilst the kids snaffled Honey Nut Loops in the room below, she didn't want to say anything that might bring about more bickering. 'The bathrooms need a going over. I was going to run the hoover round downstairs too.'

'Right.' He made up a coffee, flicking through the papers whilst it stewed. There was a heavy quiet between them. A loaded one. 'So what do you fancy doing this weekend?' he said, eventually.

'I thought we could go out later, make the most of the sunshine. Maybe take the bikes along the Camel Trail? Have you remembered I'm out tomorrow?'

'Eh?' He looked up sharply from the paper.

'Tomorrow, I'm out.'

'Where?'

'The Old Grammar School.'

'Truro? On a Sunday.'

Once upon a time, Truro on a Sunday wouldn't have seemed such a shocking thing. Before kids, Truro on a Sunday, for a roast and a catch up with mates, could happen quite often.

'I'm meeting the girls.'

'Which girls?'

'Jess, Amanda and Emily. I told you.'

Kitt looked surprised. 'No, you told me that you were *thinking* of meeting up, that you'd seen Emily in town. You never said you were *actually* meeting up.' Lolly couldn't be sure if that was the case. 'I don't understand why you would. I mean…' He shut the paper, pushing it away. He faffed with the coffee cups, spilling coffee on the side. 'Shit!'

'I really bloody missed Emily when she left. I can't wait to see her and talk, properly talk. Why wouldn't we meet up?' she said, instinctively rushing to get a cloth.

'I dunno, I guess I'm just surprised, that's all. I thought you were one for looking forward not into the past.' Lolly stared at him. 'That's what you always said to me. I can do that!'

Kitt took the cloth from her, wiping down the spilt coffee, knocking what was left of the milk over the floor. 'Christ!' Lolly threw him a load of kitchen roll then went to the utility room for the mop. 'What are you going to talk about?' he shouted through to her. 'What if you just all sit there with nothing to say?'

Lolly came back through, handing him the mop before taking over coffee making duties. 'Why wouldn't I have anything to say?' Did she sound defensive? She felt like she sounded defensive. 'You might not find me very interesting any more, but I have plenty to talk about. It'll be nice to see them.'

Kitt mopped at the milk, pushing it around the floor.

'Come here, for god's sake.' She took over, pushing him out of the way. 'Take the boys out for the day, then you'll not even notice I've gone.' Her phone pinged in her pocket as she wrung out the mop. It was Joanna. Lolly groaned.

'What?'

'Nothing, just Joanna sending me the dates she wants to stay.'

'What!' His tone wasn't exactly a surprise and, in the past, she might have shared his horror but today he'd pissed her off.

'For a week. Maybe two.'

'How long?'

'It'll be nice. I haven't seen her for ages and it'll be good for the boys.'

'They hate sharing a room.'

'Yeah, well, it doesn't happen very often and, forgive me, but I'd like to see what remaining family I have, so it'll be fine. Don't worry, I'll plan loads of stuff to do with her. You'll barely have to see her.'

'Of course I'll have to see her. I can hardly move out for the week, can I?'

Lolly resisted the urge to tell him he'd be welcome to because she knew that they were words of frustration and she just needed to let go. She just needed to get over what he said the other night about not wanting another child, despite this morning happily snuggling into her in search of a quickie. And she needed to get over the fact that sex had become something to fertilise her not keep them close. 'It'll be fine. It'll be nice.'

'I'll remind you of that when you're complaining about her taking over the house.' He picked up his wallet. 'I'll get some more milk.'

'We can get some in a bit, when we go out.'

'I want coffee!' he said, frustrated.

He disappeared down the hallway, slamming the door behind him and Lolly wondered how long the frost would last and if she was really to blame. They'd been in an okay place before she decided she wanted another baby, that was one of the reasons she felt the time was right. And she had assumed he wouldn't have gone for a reversal if he'd had any concerns. But looking at it now, there was a tilt in their connection, a shift that she couldn't quite grasp like she had in days gone by.

Joanna coming would be good for her. They could talk. Same with meeting the girls tomorrow. It was time Lolly paid a bit more attention to who she was. It was time she became more than the sum of wife, mother and employee.

Jess

Matt had, by the time he'd finished his brotherly lecture, managed to convince Jess not to jump to any decisions. She'd called him on the taxi ride over, much to his irritation because her signal kept dropping out in the dips between Falmouth and Truro, but they'd managed to speak for long enough for her to update him on the conversation with Jay and for him to tell her all the reasons she should stay and all the reasons she should not walk away from her job. And she should absolutely not read too much into Jay's choice of words. That he missed her did not mean he wanted to leave his wife and start afresh with her. Not that she wanted him to... necessarily.

'You need to open up your world, Jess. Embrace friendships, find something to occupy your time,' Matt had said. 'You've been all work for too long, where is the fun in your life?'

She'd tried to convince him that work *was* fun for her. That she got all the fun she needed from the variety in her client list. From a young team who were brimming with energy and enthusiasm and ideas. That she didn't need anything else. To which he'd pointed out that she was about to meet up with the girls from school and if she really did have all the fun in the world, she wouldn't have needed the reunion.

The reunion. She did need this reunion. If Matt was right about her life and the things she needed to do, there were some ghosts to lay to rest. Matt had no idea about her motivation for meeting the girls. Matt knew every last bit of her life, except the truth about what happened at that party when she was sixteen. A secret that she could now see had shaped the rest of her life. That she pushed those she loved away. That, apart from her brother, she avoided close friendships, relationships, that she threw herself into work, it all pointed to that one night at Emily's house. A night she had buried so deeply, she wasn't even sure what was true and what her confused, sixteen year old brain had made up any more.

She paused over the road, staring at The Old Grammar School. It had a classic, Cornish, granite exterior, with a tiny, no longer used, school bell on the top; each side flanked by giant umbrellas for the brave diners who wanted to sit outside in the cold. The last time she'd been here, she'd been one of those brave diners sat outside, smoking. Though now she realised she hadn't been brave that night, she'd just been wishing she could go home early. She'd been out on a works do and by the time they'd all eaten burgers the size of their heads, she'd been ready to head home to the quiet of her own space. Away from people and noise.

Would she feel the same amongst the girls? A need to escape? Once upon a time, with these three, she was just Jess. Jess who was gregarious and silly and loud. Jess who could recite sketches from *French and Saunders* or *Vic Reeves Big Night Out*. Jess who loved Blur over Oasis. Jess who sobbed during *Four Weddings and a Funeral*, embarrassing the rest of them in the cinema. Jess who hid copies of Jilly Cooper's *Riders* in her schoolbooks so teachers wouldn't see what she was reading. They didn't really know the Jess who'd gone off travelling when she didn't really want to. They didn't really know the Jess whose broken heart fractured further when she finally came home. They didn't really know the Jess who had convinced herself that she was happy with her life. Would they bring out that old Jess? Did they have that power? Or was there a new Jess to be invented? And if so, what role did these girls… these women, have to play?

She walked slowly up to the front door. She checked her watch, she was early. She hadn't wanted to be the first person there, yet she always had been, back in the day. She'd always been the first person to arrive anywhere… some things never change.

Emily

Emily woke with butterflies in her stomach. At first she thought it was nausea but ginger biscuits and full fat Coke, which it turned out was totally her pregnancy tonic, had sorted that out. Full fat or no, it seemed that all the sugar in the world could not arrest the butterflies though. And as she walked back across Lemon Quay, the place she'd first bumped into Lolly, less than two weeks ago, the butterflies were no longer doing a gentle dance, more a booted stamp. Why was she so nervous? They were ordinary women, women who knew her. The real her. The her that she was before the standing ovations and celebrity friends took over. A few of her newer friends had reached out in the last few days. The odd message on Facebook or WhatsApp. She felt bad ignoring them, they didn't really deserve her silence, she just couldn't face the prospect of lying to them. She knew people would think she was crazy for coming home now, they'd all want to know why, how she could walk away from her career, her apartment, Jackson... Jackson was popular. He had people on his side. Everybody loved Jackson.

But she'd always known she wasn't like most people. She'd always felt like she faked it. Not loving Jackson, that bit had been true ... to begin with. But living with what seemed like the perfect life was hard. Constantly having to think about how she looked and what she wore, it drained her. Before coming home, she'd been running on empty and it didn't feel like that now. Already. The longer she sat on the beaches, read in the bath, sang to herself as she pottered in the garden, the fuller she felt. The stronger. She was recharging. She'd even begun to imagine what it might be like to share it all with a small person.

She crossed over by a jewellers, the window packed full of vintage rings and trinkets. She took the wide cobbled street over to Cathedral Lane. The clothes in the Accessorize window included a tiny baby mannequin with something floral and sparkly and the butterflies made way for her heart to flip at the sight. Was she carrying a boy or a girl? What might it look like? She pulled her coat around her, letting her hand momentarily rest on her stomach before shaking off the thoughts, which made way for the butterflies to return. Just as she turned the corner by the cathedral, The Old Grammar School came into view. A woman paused by the doorway, checking her watch before heading inside. Was that Jess? It had been so long but it would be hard to mistake the confident stride, the time check. Even as a teenager, she'd been sorted, on her game. She was the one they all wished they could be more like which made Emily pause, she faltered, she considered turning back around because suddenly, this all seemed too much. Who was she and could she fake whoever that was to the rest of them? Maybe being on her own was fine for a bit longer. She'd only just got back. She didn't have to rush into anything; friendships, decisions, none of it, she could take her time, they'd understand, wouldn't they?

'Emily! Hey!' Lolly appeared from nowhere, pulling Emily in for a kiss. Her eyes were bright, her smile friendly and assured. 'I am SO glad you messaged in the end, I can't wait to hear all about how things are for you. And the other two, it has been way too long!'

She slipped her arm through Emily's with a familiarity that would, on any other day, with any other person, have felt entirely alien and inappropriate. But Emily remembered Lolly had always walked, arm hooked through the crook of someone else's. She moved in the direction of the bar, chattering away about how excited she was, how nice it was to get out of the house and how cheeky it felt to do it on a Sunday when she should be at home with the kids and her husband…

Lolly

'I mean, Sundays are supposed to be a family day, aren't they? That's what Kitt said this morning. Oh my god, he's SO grumpy at the moment.' Lolly checked up the one-way street before hopping down the kerb to cross over. She clasped her hands together, her arm still looped through Emily's because once she'd put it there, she wasn't sure how to remove it again without feeling like she'd been over familiar or made things awkward. She was kicking herself for being an idiot, letting her nerves get the better of her chat, relieved that Emily appeared totally cool with it all. She was probably used to over friendliness, they're all like that in her industry. 'Bets on Jess is here already!' she said, opening the door to let Emily in.

'Right there,' said Emily, her smile suddenly widening at the sight of Jess waiting at the table to the right of the door.

'I didn't order any drinks yet, I wasn't sure what to get in.' Jess looked up at the blackboard above the bar. 'I had considered a massive jug of some kind of cocktail but wasn't sure that was appropriate for a Sunday lunchtime.'

'Haha, probably not,' said Emily. 'Oh my god, come here, how are you? You've not changed a bit. How is that fair?' she said, sidling onto the bench seat beside Jess, pulling her in for a hug.

Jess held her back by her shoulders, studying her face. 'I haven't changed! Christ, that's sum bleddy rich coming from you!' she said.

She turned to Lolly, who was wondering if either of them would notice if she did in fact get the large cocktail pitcher because it may not be appropriate for a Sunday lunchtime but if she went home pissed, at least she could just fall asleep on the sofa, rather than pick up the row she had had with Kitt before she left the house. And also she was terrified.

'Lolly, how are you?' Jess tried to ease herself out of the side of the table to give Lolly a hug.

'I'm good, thank you. Really good. Oh my god, it's so nice to see you!' Lolly gave her an awkward over the table hug. 'How mad is this?' she said, battling to escape the cross-body bag, which had tangled with her coat and hair. She eventually extricated herself, dropping onto the bench seat opposite Emily and Jess, exhausted.

'Christ, what the hell have you got in that bag?' asked Jess, peering at what was probably more a weekend bag to those without children.

'What haven't I?' she said, reaching into it. 'Wipes. A toy car. A packet of raisins. A book. A pack of physio bands. A diary…' She looked closer at the bottom of her bag, having laid all previous items in a line down the table. 'And possibly enough crumbs to make up a packet of digestives at the bottom. Oh my god, that's gross!' She took out a wipe to wipe her hands clear of whatever aged food stuff she'd managed to stick her finger into. 'Eurgh!'

Emily looked stunned at the collection on the table.

'There are many benefits to not having children,' said Jess, holding up a tiny bag that can't have stored more than a purse, phone and keys in it. 'But handbag size is definitely one of them.'

'There are more. Many more. Two cocktails and I'll tell you them all.' Lolly always did that, when she was out with friends. She was always self-deprecating, and always complaining about having kids. She never knew why she did it, especially knowing how desperate she was for another, and yet, she couldn't help it. It was an attempt to be funny, to connect with those around her. Would the girls find stuff like that funny any more? Had they ever? This was going to be harder than she thought.

Amanda

Amanda threw her work phone in the basket, ignoring the several voicemails she'd received in the last twenty-four hours. Her ad made it abundantly clear that they were to ring back if she didn't pick up. No text messages, no voicemails. And she was not inclined to call them back if they couldn't follow simple instructions, as invariably those were the ones who didn't play by the rules anyway. Besides, she was too busy shitting herself at the prospect of meeting up with the girls. She couldn't do it. She'd lain awake all night last night, going over the last twenty years and the life she had led, wondering how on earth she could tell them about the car crash that was her life. Nothing had turned out the way she planned and, whilst she knew it wasn't her fault, she had never really stopped feeling guilty about kicking Pete out, or embarrassed about the fact that Zennor was so quick to move in with her dad when he came back. Had she been that bad a mother? Had Zennor hated her that much? She'd tried calling her again this morning, still nothing. Why couldn't she be the kind of mum that Zennor wanted?

No. She couldn't do it. It had been a mistake to think she could. She didn't have the energy to hide who she really was, she didn't have the words to explain what was going off with Zennor and she had no idea what else to talk about. Besides, George next door needed some shopping doing, after the community nurse had gone. Maybe she could do some of his washing too. She'd noticed he seemed to be wearing the same shirt and trousers for days now, if not longer. Then maybe she could come back, clean the house, cook a roast. Karenza might like to come round and share it with her, she loved a roast dinner.

Amanda poured another coffee from the machine, turning Madonna's *Immaculate Collection* up on her stereo, skipping round the kitchen like a 1980s, big-haired Madge. Without the big hair. Or the bank balance. Her personal phone pinged this time so she turned the music up a notch. 'Borderline': a song she was not entirely surprised to realise she still knew all the words to. The knot in her dressing gown loosened as she danced, and by the time 'Papa Don't Preach' came on she'd theatrically dropped it to the floor, pleading with her 'papa' that she was going to keep her baby. Her phone pinged out again so she danced into the lounge, leaving phone, dressing gown and dignity behind.

Jess

'She's not read the text,' said Jess, checking her phone again. 'It's delivered but not seen. And it is only twelve. By Amanda standards, that's not that late. How long do we wait to call her, make sure she's okay?' Jess looked down at her phone as the girls placed an order with the skinny-jeaned, bearded waiter.

'Nah, don't worry yet,' said Lolly. 'Like you say, it's not late by her standards. She was always late. Do you remember when she nearly missed Maths GCSE because she was binge watching videos of *Friends* and totally lost track of time?'

'Oh, god, yes! She loved that show, didn't she? Do you remember she tried to give herself a Rachel haircut?' said Emily.

'Oh my god! I'd forgotten that,' screeched Lolly. 'She wore a hat for weeks after that, didn't she?'

The girls, laughed. Jess relaxed a little.

'It was never that bad, but she was mortified, wasn't she? Oh, god, it all seems so bloody long ago.'

'It was. But clearly not long enough for her to have learned the art of timekeeping,' said Jess, with a smile.

'Nah, she's still got at least another half hour before I'd start to worry,' said Lolly.

The waiter placed their drinks order down before them. 'So don't judge me, but I'm starting with a tea. That said, I can't promise I'm staying dry, ladies.'

'It's like that, is it?' said Jess, realising how nice it was to see Lolly's smiling face.

'If you'd heard my husband this morning, you too would be on the bottle.'

'Mine's the peppermint, thank you,' said Emily, taking it from the waiter then smiling politely, placing her hands on her knees. Jess wondered if Emily had always been like this and she'd forgotten, or if life had buttoned her up.

'So, ladies. Where do we begin?' asked Lolly.

'Tell us about your kids,' said Emily.

Lolly flicked through photos on her phone, chatting happily about her two boys. How Ted was the feisty one and Stan was more like her. How she adores them though they drive her crazy.

'And what about your husband?' Emily asked, sipping at her tea.

'Do you remember Andrew Trevelly? From school?'

'Andrew Trevelly?' pondered Emily.

'As in Trev, Andrew Trevelly,' said Jess. 'Cheeky grin and sparkling eyes.'

'Ha! Yes, that's him. Though I call him Kitt, long story to do with *Knight Rider*, anyway, yeah, well, we've been together… sixteen years. Ish.'

Jess watched as Lolly talked about her husband. There was a fondness when she talked about him, but she was less animated than when she talked about the boys. That's motherhood, Jess supposed.

'Didn't you two snog down by the river at my 16th that time?' asked Emily.

Jess stiffened. 'Yes, we did. I wasn't at all impressed. In fact, it took a lot of flirting on his part before I gave him another crack at this apple. We've had our ups and downs, like anyone does, I guess. I mean he drives me to distraction, but I love him. Which, you know, is handy.'

'Very handy. Considering he's your husband.' Emily sounded surprised.

'Oh, you must know what men can be like though. Surely! Come on, Emily, tell us about your life, the jobs—'

'The men,' interjected Jess, clumsily joining in because as awkward as this felt, Matt's words rang through her mind.

'Oooh, yes, the men. I bet you've met some gorgeous ones in your line of work. Are you with anyone? Did you get married? Have kids?'

Was Emily squirming, or protecting the privacy of an A-lister? It was hard to tell from her mumbled response to Lolly's question.

'And what about you, Jess? What have you been up to?' Lolly's voice spiked suddenly. 'Oh my goodness, it's so nice to see you both. I just want to hear about everything since we all last met.'

'We should keep some of this for Amanda,' said Emily. 'We're going to have to repeat ourselves if she doesn't hurry.' She looked at her watch, then over to the door.

'Agh! I can hardly bear the anticipation,' said Lolly, clapping her hands in glee.

Emily smiled, then sipped at her tea. 'It's nice in here, isn't it,' she said, reaching for the menu. 'Food looks good too. Have you eaten here?'

'Not for years, it was always yummy, but eating out is bloody expensive with kids too. And on my wage… it would definitely be a treat.'

'What is it you do?' Emily absentmindedly dunked the teabag that floated in the glass teapot the waiter had set down before her. 'Didn't you want to be a nurse?'

'I did. I'm in physio now. Mostly post-operative care.'

'Wow, amazing.'

'I like it. I feel like I'm helping, making a difference, you know.'

'Of course.'

The conversation stalled. Emily topped up her tea. Lolly blew across the top of hers. Jess remembered that Amanda had always been the one to fizz things up between them. She was like Zebedee, or Tigger, all jumpy and giddy and full of stories. If Jess was going to do what Matt said, and reconnect with these women, they needed the old dynamic. They needed all four of them together. 'This isn't right, without Amanda. Hang on, I'm calling her.'

Amanda

Madonna stopped singing and Amanda's personal phone rang in the kitchen. She was now feeling guilty… and a bit like she was missing out. They'd loved each other, was that it? The first kind of true love for someone outside the family. Someone that wasn't a love interest. Just real, true love without the strings and the complications. Once upon a time, she wasn't sure she could have breathed without them by her side.

She padded through to the kitchen. There was a voicemail. They were allowed on her personal phone. *'Hey, Amanda. It's Jess. We're all here. We're desperate to see you, to catch up. Is everything okay? Are you on your way? Text me what drink you want and I'll get it in. I'm guessing you've probably moved off snakebite now?'*

Snakebite. Lager, cider and blackcurrant cordial. It had been so cheap to drink and so great at getting her smashed, she had regularly taken pints of that when they were out. It was so nice that Jess remembered. What else would she remember? The time they nicked a bottle of Mad Dog 20/20 and hid down by the viaduct to drink it? Amanda had been so consumed by guilt at lifting from their local shop that she went back the next day and left the right change for the bottle, just casually round by the postcards and the pasty-shaped soft toys. Did Jess remember the time they sat in her bedroom listening to Boy George and Soul II Soul? Did Jess and Lolly remember Monday nights in The

Loft drinking Smirnoff Ice, a few years after Emily had gone and before Jess went travelling? Actually, could anybody remember those nights?

Amanda missed them. She actually physically missed them. They'd been her heart and soul when it mattered. She could deflect the questions; she'd been doing so for years. These were her friends. If she left now and ran, she could be there in five. They'd never know she'd had second thoughts.

Emily

Having left Amanda a message, the women had picked up the small talk. Discussions about how Truro had changed. How they hadn't been to the Masked Ball in years. How the new roads up at Temple were making all the difference. It was polite, middle-aged chat. Touching on subjects, but not really getting into opinions. Were Jess and Lolly as nervous as Emily? She had really hoped it wouldn't feel like this. She'd really wanted to meet up with them and for it be like old times. People talk about that happening, about real friends not needing to stay in touch because you pick up where you left off. Today had always been about reconnecting. About building her friendships and putting down roots. She'd been nervous, she'd worried it might have been a bad move, but her gut had told her not to panic. Instinct had said she should meet them. Yet somehow, now she was sat in front of them, she felt unable to let go. She kept catching herself, arms folded, mouth tight – even in a smile. She listened to Lolly talk about her husband and kids and all she wanted to ask was, how was it really? Could she do it on her own if she had to? What was being a mum like? Lolly seemed so happy, so settled in life. And Jess, in charge, on it, the epitome of a career woman. Her destiny in her sights. She was so strong and in control, it seemed to Emily. Yet how could she be intimidated by the person she had once confided in – about everything. Jess had been the one they'd all talk to. She was the steady, stable one. The one that made stuff happen. She knew everything about the girls before the rest of them and so often offered up some good advice and a calming influence. What about Emily had changed to make Jess's demeanour so intimidating?

There was a ding of a text and Jess jumped on it. 'Amanda says she'll be here in a minute,' she said, putting her phone back down. Was she relieved too?

'Have you seen much of her, Jess?' asked Lolly, which made Emily feel bad at the fact that she'd lost touch with all of them. She'd left them all behind when she went to L.A. She'd promised to write letters, but never did. She wasn't allowed to call them because of the cost, even though money wasn't really a problem to her dad. She'd never got the chance to come back when she was young, not until work started picking up and she could pay for the trip herself. That she'd never made contact on her visits back; did it make her a bad person? Did they think she didn't care? Had they talked about her after she left? Did they judge?

Had she judged when they all stayed put? Maybe, she thought, if she was honest. They chatted and she listened and she wished she knew how to open up, even just a little bit.

Ten minutes passed before the door flung open with a gust of air. 'Now come on you lot! What's this? *Tea*?' a familiar voice boomed. 'Because, as far as I'm concerned, the yardarm has passed in some country somewhere and I therefore see no reason not to get on it.'

Amanda stood proudly before them, her face brimming with mischief. She'd changed, got older maybe, wiser in the eyes perhaps, but it was still so obviously her.

'You're here!' Lolly squealed like she always could, jumped up and flung her arms around her. Amanda grinned over her shoulder at Emily.

Emily shifted in her seat. This was it. This was the four of them. Back together again.

'Come on, get up, give us a hug,' she instructed Jess, who dutifully complied.

Emily knew she'd not get away with staying where she was so shuffled around the table to give Amanda a hug too. She felt warm, her hug was strong and full of love. Had she always been a hugger? Emily couldn't remember.

'Sorry I'm late ladies. I was dancing to Madonna in my kitchen and totally lost track of time.'

'You hated Madonna!' said Jess, sitting back down.

'Nah, I think I just thought it was cool to hate Madonna. She's incredible! I wanted to go see her a few years back but it would have meant leaving Cornwall and who wants to do that voluntarily?' Emily dropped her eyes to her drink, fiddling with her nails. 'Apart from you, Lady Emily of The Emmys.'

'I don't know if my leaving was voluntary…'

'Well, whatever it was, you're back here now. How the bloody hell are you? What brings you here? Has the career nosedived?'

There was a pause in the banter. Jess looked wide-eyed at Amanda, Emily opened her mouth, not sure how to respond. Of them all, Amanda had always been the one to call a spade a shovel if it made for a gag. There was silence, then a snort, followed by a belly laugh from Lolly, 'Oh my god, Amanda! Rude! You kill me!'

'I always killed you,' Amanda replied, with a grin.

'You did.' Lolly nodded, taking a drink. 'You did.'

'I'll have a large Sauvignon Blanc, please,' Amanda shouted to the waiter behind the bar. 'Anyone else?' she asked.

'Yes! I'll have one. Why the hell not,' said Lolly.

'Maybe in a bit,' said Jess.

'Not for me,' Emily said, wishing more than anything else in the world for a long, cold drink of wine or gin or a cosmo. Or maybe a Martini. On the rocks. Anything to take away the nerves.

'Come on then, what have I missed? I was joking about your career, obviously, Emily, but how come you're back? What's going on? What's going on for you all?'

Jess

Jess was relieved to see Amanda. Whilst Lolly had always been the talker, she was now reminded Amanda had always been the one to lift them all. She always had something to say or a story to tell. Jess could remember the times she'd defer to Amanda when it came to making small talk with boys. It wasn't that she couldn't talk to them, more that Amanda was so vibrant with it. Was she still like that? It would appear so from the energy that followed her in just now. She fizzed and sparked, always had. Jess remembered feeling envy at that, back when they were kids. Would she feel that now? Would Amanda's energy brighten her own light, like it had once upon a time, or could it dim it now? She remembered what Matt had said about her reconnecting, finding ways to diversify her life. Were these women the ones to help her to do that? They were familiar strangers at the moment, maybe too much time had passed.

'Come on then, Amanda,' said Lolly. 'What are you up to these days? How's Zennor?'

'Ahhh, she's okay. Yeah. Good. She lives with her dad.'

'No way! He came back?' Lolly looked open-mouthed at Jess and Jess raised her eyebrows conspiratorially, just like they always used to.

Amanda laughed to herself. 'He did. Yeah. Like some saviour, he returned and Zennor, like so many of us before, was wrapped up in his charm within seconds.'

'Pete was many things, charming being just one of them,' said Lolly, with a hint of lust in her tone.

'Which one was Pete?' asked Emily, to Amanda's relief. Faking the chat was harder if she didn't know who she was talking about.

'Pete. Pete Lennon. Tall. Dark.'

'Handsome?' Emily smiled.

'If you like that sort of thing,' said Amanda. 'You won't remember him, Em. We met him after you'd gone. On the morning after the night we celebrated my eighteenth.'

Lolly had a sudden jolt of memory. 'Yes, we called him Chapel Porth Pete. We went down for a breakfast baguette and he chatted you up over the cheesy mushrooms.' They'd gone to mop up their hangover with one of the beach cafe's infamous breakfast baguettes and some surfer charmed the pants off Amanda within seconds. 'He was hot, I remember that.'

'As I say, if you like that sort of thing.'

'If I remember right, you very much did like that sort of thing!' Jess raised her eyebrows in Amanda's direction.

'If you remember right, I very much did like that sort of thing with pretty much anyone who had a pulse.'

'God, I was always so jealous of you!' said Lolly, saying out loud what Jess had already been thinking.

'*Jealous*? Of me? Whatever for?' Amanda slugged her wine back. 'Ahh, that's better.'

'I don't know, you were always so confident in that department. So comfortable in your own skin. I loved that about you.'

Amanda took another large gulp of her drink. 'What's the point of being anything else? I'm fabulous, darling.' She grinned at Lolly who shook her head in admiration. 'We all are! Aren't we?'

Jess couldn't remember the last time she actually felt 'fabulous, darling'.

Lolly sighed, wistfully. 'I like to think I am fabulous sometimes and then I catch sight of myself in a mirror and realise my mother is staring back.'

'No! Don't do that!' said Amanda. 'Don't bail out like that. You're gorgeous. We're just all getting older. We should be embracing it, not picking fault. Christ, it's not gonna get better, we might as well love it all regardless.'

As they talked, Jess realised there *was* a time and place she felt 'fabulous, darling'. It was at work. When she was on top of her game. When she had a client in the palm of her hand, or one of the team was confiding in her, or succeeding at something she knew she'd taught them. Matt was right, Jess was getting everything from work. Where was her balance?

'So,' said Lolly. 'What about you, Jess? What have you been up to since we were last together?'

Jess thought for a moment. 'I don't know, life's pretty quiet. Mostly work, if I'm honest. Which is fine, I enjoy that.' Or she had, until Jay had turned up. 'When I got back from travelling, I went up to Manchester for a bit, worked for an ad agency up there, really learned the business, then came back down here when a young agency were starting up and have been around ever since. I mean, I guess that was about ten years ago.'

'Same place?' asked Amanda, incredulous.

'Yeah, I like it. Well, liked it. It's probably time to move on again now.'

'I keep wondering that,' chipped in Lolly, much to Jess's relief. 'But I don't know what I'd do if I didn't do physio. I think that's it for me, that's my lot.'

'You don't have to sound so down about it,' said Amanda.

'I'm not, I just… I don't know. Do you ever get to thinking about your life and what it is now versus what you thought it was going to be?'

If she'd have asked that of Jess even two weeks ago, she wouldn't have automatically thought about Jay, that much she did know.

'Christ, you haven't changed a bit.' Amanda laughed.

'What?' Lolly looked up, surprised.

'You think too much, always did.'

'Do I? I don't know if that's true, I mean, I just like to pick things apart a bit, work out the best options. Reflection is good, isn't it?' The girls looked at her, grinning. 'Kitt says I think too much too.'

'Surely we all think,' said Jess. 'We're grown-ups, we have to think about stuff. We have to work things out.'

'*Grown-ups*? Speak for yourself,' said Amanda. And Jess wondered if that was part of her problem, she was pretty much all grown up these days.

Amanda

Amanda couldn't believe how relaxed she was. How great it was to be sat amongst these women. How could she have considered not coming? She still wasn't sure she'd tell them everything, but maybe it didn't matter. Just having them in reach was reassuring. Familiar. 'So what did I miss, whilst you were waiting for me?'

'I tell you what you did miss, that our little Lolly only went and bagged the hottest guy at school!'

Lolly flushed with something akin to pride. 'Hey, try being married to him, he may have been hot, but he's still a pain in the arse.'

'So who did you marry?' asked Amanda.

'Only Andrew Trevelley,' said Jess. 'Do you remember, he of the inexplicably short shorts and the legs to actually die for!'

Amanda froze.

'Yes, I did marry him. Except I call him Kitt. We've been together for about sixteen years now. Two boys. It's… well, it's okay. It's nice.'

Amanda's mouth ran dry.

'Okay? Nice?' asked Jess.

'Well, good. It's good,' said Lolly.

Heart in her mouth, Amanda stood. 'Wow, that's… blimey. He was… shit, excuse me, I need to…' She looked around, she couldn't just leave. However much she wanted to, that would make things worse. 'I need the bathroom, terrible pelvic floor, do you get that? Old age…'

She excused herself from the table, making her way across the room to the toilets, willing herself not to pass out or crumble. She couldn't let them know anything was wrong. Her choice of work had been a consideration in not joining the girls today, but not for this reason. Not because she thought for a single moment that the world was so incredibly small that she'd have been sleeping with one of the girl's husbands. She wanted to run away and yet, she wanted to know Lolly's side of things. She wanted to hear about Trev, Andrew, Kitt… whatever he wanted to be called, she wanted to know everything about him from his wife's point of view. From the moment she sat down, she remembered how much she had adored Lolly. Her giddiness. Her lightness. She had been the baby of the group in so many ways, she'd always been vulnerable. She still had that edge, even now, and Amanda wanted to protect her, just like she had back in the day. How could it be that she was married to Andrew Trevelley? And how could Andrew Trevelley be doing this to Lolly?

Amanda stared at herself in the mirror. She felt old. She felt stupid. She felt pretty vulnerable herself. She felt like the worst woman in the world and she'd never felt like that because of her job before. She didn't relish the fact that some of her clients were married, but she'd long since made a choice not to judge because nobody knows what's going on behind closed doors. But Lolly? Surely Lolly wasn't a bad person to be married to. How could he be anything other than wildly smug? She's smart and funny and gorgeous.

Shit.

She pulled her phone out, dialling Karenza. She'd know what to do. Except her phone rang out and Amanda wanted to cry. Maybe she could get Pete to call her, give her an excuse to leave. Maybe she could just tell them she felt unwell.

But she didn't, well, she felt sick, sick to her bones, but she wasn't unwell. And whatever was going on here, she could not just pretend it wasn't happening. Nor could she let on. She was going to have to pretend. She was going to have to see this through. She was going to have to speak to Trev later, when she was alone.

She looked down at her hands, old and dry. She looked back up to the mirror, her eyes dark and afraid. Would they notice if she never left the bathroom? Someone tried the door, making her jump. She flushed the loo as if to prove she'd just used it, then washed her hands, splashing her face with lukewarm water. She had to stick this out. However much she was desperate to run away, she couldn't just leave. She loved Lolly and she was not about to break her heart. Amanda shook off the fear and fair strutted back through the room to their table, her heart thumping.

Jess

'God knows *what* my husband thinks about half the time,' said Lolly as Amanda sat down, looking white as a sheet. Was she okay? Lolly chirruped on. 'I mean, we've been married forever, we have kids. Our conversations are usually built around who's picking who up and what to have for tea.'

'Ahhh, don't you do date nights?' asked Amanda, which made Jess shudder, she hated date nights. She hated it even more when people tagged them on Facebook. Did that mean the two concerned were going home to have sex that night and did she really want that mental image of Mick and Sally from three doors down?

'*Date nights*? Christ, we should be so lucky!'

Amanda raised her eyebrows.

'This is why I never got married,' said Jess.

'I mean, we do okay. We manage. In between the kids and work and arguing about whose turn it is to take the bin out.'

'Sexy,' said Jess.

'I guess you don't live with anyone then, Jess?' asked Emily.

'Nah.' Jess shook her head. 'I just… never found anyone I wanted to move in with, you know? I like my independence too much. I like my life.' She paused, looking down at her drink. 'I never fancied making compromises.'

Emily laughed to herself. 'Why do you think I'm back in Cornwall?' she said, uncharacteristically.

Amanda took a sip of her wine, and Jess noticed her hand shook. Was she nervous? She didn't appear it when she arrived. Amanda didn't used to be the nervous type, far from it. Was she as suddenly overwhelmed as Jess felt, now they sat together like this?

'Was it good to get away from Cornwall? When you first left, I mean. It happened so suddenly, I don't think any of us saw it coming,' said Lolly, making Jess look up sharply.

'It was sudden to me too. Dad just came home one day to say he had this opportunity in L.A. and we had to go. Within two weeks, we'd left home. We'd left everything I knew and we were in this new, stiflingly hot country, and I was in a new school without any friends. I hated it.'

'Ahhh, Emily!' said Lolly, reaching out to hold her hand.

'It took a while to settle in,' Emily went on. 'I think I pretty much hated it until I joined a theatre group, outside of school. I felt like I made friends there, not friends like you lot, but people I could at least hang out with. Have fun with. And that's when the work opportunities started opening up, so then it got exciting. Working on stage, meeting brilliant, creative people. I think, after a while, I stopped giving home a second thought.'

'So what's changed?' asked Lolly.

'I don't know… I've done it for so long. It's been fun. A lot of fun. It's been glamorous at times. The parties, you know. The dresses. The travel. I just…' Emily's voice faltered. 'I think maybe I'm done with it.'

'I guess the high life grows tiresome,' said Jess, keeping her feelings in check.

'It looks so glamorous though.' Lolly looked off dreamily. 'Where were you living?'

'New York, by the time I left. We had this amazing apartment in Manhattan. I loved it. I miss the apartment, that much I can say.'

'We?' asked Lolly.

Emily shifted in her seat. 'We. I was living with someone.'

The girls went quiet. Once upon a time they'd have jumped on this, Amanda often first up, she'd have dragged out every last detail with lascivious joy but seemed distracted. Not entirely with the group. Had someone said something to upset her? 'It's complicated.'

'Life's complicated,' said Jess.

'You don't have to talk about it, if you don't want to,' said Lolly. 'Sorry, I shouldn't have said anything.'

Emily looked into her tea. Amanda gazed, glassy-eyed. Lolly's cheeks flushed and Jess wondered if this had all been a terrible mistake.

Emily

'Do you want to talk about it?' said Lolly, carefully.

She did. She realised. She actually did. But what if this catch up was a one-off? Did any of them remember their pact to be friends for life on the last day she saw them? A pact she couldn't uphold because she'd been so far away, so lonely, so jealous of what she imagined they'd all be doing without her. She felt like they could help her get her head straight. With Jess's stability and Lolly's care and Amanda's fire, they were the perfect combination of brilliant women and she wanted to tell them every last detail. It didn't matter that they'd spent so long out of touch, suddenly they were everything that had the potential to be right in her life and she needed them, now more than ever.

'I do, though I don't know if I can put any of it into words.'

So far, nobody had really asked about why she'd come home. Even Betty hadn't asked. Mac didn't seem too interested. Yet these three, sat, eyes wide, waiting. Lolly sipped her drink.

'Jackson was my agent. To begin with. I signed with him when I was about twenty-one, I think, we didn't get together until years later, on my thirtieth birthday. But professionally, we'd been together for years. It worked, we were a team. He got the work, I delivered it. We were inseparable for a long time before it got personal. By the time it happened, everybody said they'd been waiting. That we were destined to be together. We were really good together, strong.'

'A New York power couple, I just knew it.' Lolly sighed, dreamily.

'I don't know about that, but we were doing okay.'

'So what changed?' asked Amanda.

Emily reached her hand down to her belly. 'Everything.' She paused. 'Nothing,' she reasoned. 'Him... maybe me,' she added. Emily noticed Jess smile to herself. 'What?'

'I remember you always had that ability to sum everything up yet say nothing at all.' Amanda nodded agreement, which made Emily feel exposed. 'It's not a criticism,' Jess said, reaching her hand out to Emily's for just a moment. 'It just made me smile. It makes me wonder if we're all still basically the same. I wonder if circumstances have changed, but we haven't.'

Emily thought about just how much she had changed from being a kid to an actor to now, back here. Her thoughts were no longer consumed with career and numbers and being seen in the right place at the right time in the right gown. She wasn't even sure if they were her thoughts or Jackson's. All she knew was that her current thoughts were all about the moment, the now. The now that led to a new tomorrow for which she wasn't sure she was entirely prepared for. But was it that everything had changed? Or was it that everything had gone back to the way it had been before life intervened?

She looked at the women sat around her, brilliant and fierce and waiting for her to speak. 'What were all your dreams?' she asked. 'When we were kids. What did you want to do?'

'I wanted to marry Tom Cruise,' said Jess. Amanda recoiled. 'Yeah, that was before I realised the whole Scientology thing.'

'And the not living to get married thing!' said Amanda.

'Yeah, that too.'

'Is it bad that that's exactly what I wanted to do?' asked Lolly.

'What? Marry Tom Cruise?'

'No, no. I was more a Leonardo DiCaprio kind of girl. But get married, that's what I wanted to do. Get married and have children.'

Jess shook her head. 'That's not bad. If it's what you wanted,' she said. 'As opposed to you thinking that was all you were good for.'

Lolly looked thoughtful.

'And you've done that, right?' As the words came out, Emily felt a pang of envy that she wasn't expecting.

'I have. Yes.'

'How's that working out for you?' asked Amanda.

'It's… it's fine. It's okay. It's good.'

'You're really selling it to us,' said Jess.

'Well, you know. It's hard.'

Emily watched Lolly carefully. 'What bit's hard?'

'All of it. Sometimes!' Lolly joked. 'I don't know, being married is hard sometimes. Being a mum is the hardest.' Amanda nodded her agreement. 'And yet I'd do it all over again,' she said, quietly.

Amanda took a sip of wine. 'Would you?'

'Yes. God. A million per cent, yes.'

'Do you want more kids then?' asked Jess.

Lolly looked down into her glass before draining it of the wine. 'You girls always could unpick me,' she said, with a half laugh. Jess noticed the empty glass and motioned to the waiter for another. 'I'd love more. I really would. Just…' she paused, pushing the empty glass away from her. She looked at the girls, her eyes falling on Emily last and Emily wondered if she could sense something. If she knew. Her voice lowered, 'I feel bad saying it. I have children. This shouldn't even be a thing, but…' Lolly fiddled with the stem on her empty wine glass. 'I just really want a girl.'

There was a beat. A moment for them to hear what she said. Before Amanda reached out her hand to Lolly's. Emily kept hers on her belly. It felt unfamiliar. Swollen. It felt loaded.

'I hate myself for saying it,' said Lolly, apologetically. 'I mean, people just want healthy babies, right? They don't care. Some people are desperate. Some babies need homes. I know all that, and I get it, but I can't help it…' She sighed, looking out of the window. Emily followed her gaze to the grey sky above them. 'I do want another baby. But only if it's a girl.'

The waiter delivered the wine.

'Why a girl specifically?' asked Emily.

'I want what Jo and Mum had. What I missed out on.' Emily noticed Lolly shifting in her seat, biting down on her bottom lip, her eyes glistening. 'I want what they had. I want it for me. I want the bond of mother and daughter. I want to watch a mini me grow up into her own person. I want to help her become her best self.'

The girls had rarely talked about Lolly's mum not being there when they were kids. None of them really having the emotional strength to know what to say, or when. Emily wasn't sure she was any better equipped now.

Lolly

Lolly sat back, taking a moment to see these women before her. These women who had meant so much to her, to each other, back when they were kids. Women she'd been so out of touch with. Women with their own stories, their own lives, their own history. Did they all see the same thing – a group of friends who'd drifted? Had they thought about her as she'd so often thought about them? And was it fair of her to suddenly have this overwhelming feeling that she needed these women in her life? They'd barely been back together five minutes, she wanted to give a good impression, she wanted them to like her. She wanted to pretend she wasn't ultimately a flawed human being, but she also wanted to tell them everything; which would contradict the 'she' she was presenting. Did everyone do that? Present the person they wanted others to see? She couldn't imagine it of Emily, who sat there so composed. Or Amanda, all life and mischief, she hadn't changed a bit.

'I felt it, when I had the boys. I felt that joy of new parenthood, I did. But I felt loss too,' said Lolly. 'Is that awful?' The girls all rallied with nos. It's not awful. You can't help how you feel, but their words did nothing to appease her. She'd never said it outright to anyone, not even Kitt. She hadn't dared because she didn't want to be judged. She knew she was being selfish… at least, that's what she felt. Did the girls think it of her? Despite what they said? Would they go back to their friends or partners and tell them what she said? Would they pick apart the morality of it all? 'And it's silly, because parenting without your mum on hand, that's the worst, the hardest thing.'

'I don't know what I'd have done without my mum there,' agreed Amanda.

Lolly smiled, sadly. 'I miss her,' she said. 'Which is stupid, impossible even. I was a baby. I barely remember her, never mind remember what she ever did for me as a mother.'

'It's not impossible,' said Jess, nudging her gently.

'Maybe I miss the person I thought she would be with me, you know? The person Jo has told me all about. Maybe I miss the fantasy. Whatever it is that I miss… it's big. It's in my heart. It's…'

'It's totally understandable,' said Jess, and the girls agreed.

'I feel her absence,' said Lolly, sadly.

The girls fell silent. Lolly felt a sense of shame in her belly. It was Amanda who came to her rescue in the end, something Lolly remembered she'd often done in the past. When things had got awkward, Amanda could always be relied upon to shift gears.

'So I bet you're at it like rabbits then!' she said suddenly, eyes wide.

Jess rolled her eyes, a wry smile on her face. 'Typical.'

'What? It's necessary. And aren't we supposed to be hitting our peak now? Isn't that what they say?'

'Christ, I feel sorry for the men of Cornwall if you're only just hitting your peak.'

'They bloody love it,' Amanda purred.

'We're supposed to be trying.'

Amanda finished her wine off and Jess topped her up.

'Kitt had a vasectomy after the boys. It was a joint decision, we just thought it would be simpler. Yet from the moment he got back from the clinic, I couldn't work out how I'd agreed. I was terrified. It brought it all crashing back. I was never going to have a daughter. I was never going to close that circle, you know? Does that make sense?'

'Hey, look, I have a daughter, you might have done yourself a favour,' said Amanda, still trying to lighten the mood.

'I tried not to worry about it for ages. I thought time would heal it all. I thought I'd get over that need, you know?' Emily cocked her head to one side. 'The need to have a baby, have you never had it? It's like biology takes over and you have to have one, you have to have a baby.'

'Sounds horrendous,' said Jess, with a sympathetic smile.

'It's all-consuming is what it is. So we've been trying. Kitt had the reversal months ago and we've just got to keep fingers crossed now.'

'And have sex,' added Amanda.

Lolly laughed to herself. 'Yeah… well… that could be better too.'

Amanda took another slug of wine. Lolly followed suit, wiping her mouth with her sleeve afterwards. 'I think perhaps I'm being a little too demanding. Or he has gone cold on the idea of having another one.' She groaned. 'Or maybe he's gone cold on me. Shit, girls, this is not what you want from a reunion, is it? Sorry, Emily. You make it all the way back here, bother to text, and I've just done a right Debbie Downer.'

Emily looked from Lolly to Amanda and Jess. 'When did life get complicated?' she asked.

'When you left for the U.S.,' said Lolly. 'Not that we're blaming you, Emily, obviously.'

'I didn't want to go!'

'We know, we know.' Lolly patted her hand.

Jess sat up, thoughtfully. 'Things were different after that though, weren't they? I mean… we changed…' Lolly turned to look at Jess, who ran a finger round the rim of her glass. 'Or maybe I just changed. I don't know. The dynamics were different though. Our lives were different. Suddenly things were happening that were out of our control... just at a point when we thought we should be making our own decisions, decisions were being made for us. And big ones too, it felt like. Do you know what I mean?'

'What, 'cause we were teenagers. We were planning our future lives, our careers.'

'Exactly, I dunno about you three, but I felt like I knew what I wanted in life.'

'Are we going back to Tom Cruise?' asked Amanda.

'Please god, no,' Emily answered, with a laugh.

'And then a grown-up came along and took away our choice,' said Jess, quietly.

'Sometimes I think I preferred it when were kids,' said Lolly. 'When we didn't have the complexities of relationships to deal with, or demons to face up to. When we could go out and get pissed up and not have to be adult the next day on a raging hangover.'

Amanda

Amanda sat there, listening to them all, conflicted. Being with them all again was like getting in your PJs on a winter's night. It was like putting the fire on and drinking hot chocolate, or a really expensive rum. It was like being wrapped up safe and warm and protected from life's cold hard truths. Except that life's cold hard truths were sitting across from her in the form of a woman she totally loved. Always had. She'd adored Lolly from the moment they first met, back in the junior school one sunny September day. They must have been about eight, maybe seven. Lolly had moved to the area from somewhere up country, Sheffield maybe, Amanda couldn't now remember. But she did remember seeing this girl in the playground. Clinging to her dad's leg, smiling shyly at anyone who might look in her direction. Amanda had been buddied up with her, and she'd been taken with Lolly's accent, the way she said bath with a hard 'a' instead of her own Cornish, elongated vowels. The way she would smile at a joke but be too scared to join in until she was invited. Amanda remembered how she'd taken her by the hand at the end of the day, introducing her to her own mum and dad as her new best friend. She remembered how Lolly had beamed and Amanda had loved how she could make her smile and laugh.

When they were just turned twelve, Lolly had started her periods and didn't know who to talk to. She felt embarrassed, she felt she couldn't talk to her dad. By then, her big sister Joanna had stayed in London after finishing uni. Amanda had taken Lolly to the shop to help her buy what she needed before walking her home, giving a pep talk about how it was okay to tell her dad. That all girls had periods. That she had nothing to be ashamed of.

Amanda remembered all of the things they used to do together, the two of them and as a four with Emily and Jess. And now, after all these years, they were back in touch and it was brilliant, and glorious. It was, after some initial nerves, really lovely to see them.

So how could she tell Lolly that she had slept with her husband? And how could he do that to her when she was so desperate for a baby? It can't be like he wasn't getting any at home.

'Come on then,' Emily said, sitting up to face Amanda. 'What's life been like for you? How old is Zennor now? What's it like? Do you work? What do you do?'

Amanda swallowed. She wanted to reach out and tell them everything, but knew she couldn't say anything at all. Not now, at least. Not here.

'Zennor is nineteen.'

'Ouch!' said Jess. 'How did that happen?'

'I know, right. Nineteen, knows everything and dislikes me. Hence her living with daddy dearest.'

'How can anyone dislike you?' shrieked Lolly, who it would now appear was rather enjoying the Sunday afternoon drinking.

Amanda laughed to herself. 'I think I'm probably a disappointment to her.'

Jess shook her head. 'Isn't it supposed to be the other way around?'

'I know, right. But, amongst other things, the hair, the clothes, the penchant for daytime drinking.' She raised her glass by way of proof. 'I've never walked in on her talking to someone I thought I was seeing.'

'Eh?'

Amanda buried her head in her hands. 'Oh god, the other night, she came into a bar to find me getting chatted up by a bloke she has history with. I mean, I wasn't doing anything, we were just chatting, but shit, it must have been awful for her and is another example of my not conforming. I'm probably a pretty crap mum.'

'No! I refuse to believe that,' said Lolly. 'If my mum was an independent woman, out and about, living her life, I'd be so proud. I'd rather have had that than someone who stayed at home knitting and watching *Morse*,' said Lolly.

'I love *Morse*,' pointed out Jess. 'In fact, I started watching *Endeavour* recently, anyone seen that? Oh my god, I love it. It's the character Morse, but from the early years. It's bloody brilliant... I plan to go back to *Morse* from episode one when I've finished all the *Endeavours*...' Jess trailed off as the girls all stared. 'It's possible I need to get out more.' The women giggled. 'What about work then, Amanda, what do you do?'

Amanda picked up the menu. 'Oh, you know what it's like down here. A bit of this, a bit of that. Cleaning. Mostly.'

'I'd be shit at that,' said Lolly. 'I can barely keep on top of my own house, never mind somebody else's.'

'Same,' said Emily. 'We had someone in back in New York. I keep thinking I should get someone here.'

Amanda looked at Emily with a smirk. 'How the other half live, eh.'

Emily paused. 'Well, I was going to ask if you would do it but since you put it like that... maybe it'd be weird.'

'Little bit,' agreed Amanda, not entirely sure if Emily was joking or not.

There was a pause in the conversation. The women looked at each other.

'It's good to see you all, you know. I was worried, that this would be awkward,' said Emily.

'Well, apart from you suggesting I become your cleaner, I'd say it's not been too bad.'

Emily coloured. 'I was kidding.' She grinned.

Amanda agreed, it was good to see them all. It was good to hear how they were, to get an insight into how life had treated them and see if the hopes and dreams they had had come to life. She just didn't know if she could do this again. The thought of hurting Lolly, if she ever found out what she'd done, well that was more than she could take.

A rush of cold air came through the door and it made the girls shiver. But as Jess looked up, her face dropped.

Jess

Jay and Niamh stood in the entrance to the bar. For a moment, it looked like Jay was going to turn around and leave but thought better of it, much to Jess's frustration.

'Jess, hi. I erm…' Jay looked from Jess to Niamh. 'This is Jess. From work.' But it seemed to Jess that he needn't have explained which Jess she was given that Niamh stared at her. Hard.

'Hi! Wow. Fancy seeing you here.' It was every clichéd hello in the book but Jess had nothing else to offer.

'Yeah.' He hovered, and Jess wished he'd just walk on by. 'Mum's got the kids, so we could do some shopping and then we thought we might as well take advantage of the moment to be grown-ups. Niamh wants a cocktail, don't you, love?' Niamh nodded but if looks could kill, Jess would be six feet under.

'Nice. I'm just catching up with this lot. Old schoolmates.'

'Nice.'

'Well, enjoy your cocktails,' said Jess, smiling brightly.

Niamh gave a shallow nod, looking Jess up and down.

'Thanks. We will. Right, oh look, love. There's a table free over by the window. Let's…' Jay ushered Niamh away from Jess and though she didn't want to watch, Jess couldn't help but notice the two exchange words. Did Niamh know about Jess? About the other night? About twenty years ago? How much do you tell your wife about past loves?

'Jess,' said Lolly, gently.

'Hmmm?'

'Are you okay?'

'Yes! Of course!' She looked back over to see Niamh staring at her as Jay walked over to the bar. She swallowed.

'Was that... Jay as in Jay, Jay?' asked Amanda.

'No...!' Lolly looked back over at them. 'No way! Is it? Oh my god, it is!'

'Jay who?' asked Emily.

'The Jay who Jess fell for back in the day, before she went off travelling.'

'I never understood why you walked away from him,' said Amanda, distractedly.

'Jay *who*?' repeated Emily.

'He was the love of her life,' said Lolly. 'Wasn't he, Jess? After you left, Emily, she went a bit weird. Sorry, Jess, but you did a bit. Do you remember? Then she met Jay.' She motioned towards him. 'And Amanda and I were worried about her, she talked about him all the time but wouldn't seem to do anything about it.'

'We made her,' said Amanda. 'Not in a bad way, just in a "come on, he is fit" way. Which he was.'

'Still is!' said Lolly.

Jess looked down at her watch. 'You know what, girls, I'm sorry, but I think I need to... I should probably...' She looked around for her bag, dropping her phone and purse into it.

'You can't go!' screeched Lolly.

'Yeah! Please don't go!' Emily looked from Jess to Jay and Niamh, she reached out to Jess which made her all the more conflicted. 'I want to know ALL about this weird phase and how he fixed it for you!'

Jess couldn't bear it. She loved Emily, she'd missed her when she moved away but she could never tell her why she'd gone weird. She could never admit her dark secrets, or why she'd really ended up leaving Jay. Maybe it would be better to leave these friendships in the past, whatever Matt thought.

'Look, I'm sorry, I just need to… I hadn't realised what time it was. I have a bit of work to catch up on, big week at work…' She leaned across to kiss Emily and Lolly. She gave a squeeze to Amanda. 'Let's do this again. Soon. I'd love it. I miss you all. You're bloody lovely. Let's stay in touch this time, okay?'

The girls stared, open-mouthed. She blew them a kiss then headed out the door. She got as far as the pavement before realising she was cold because she'd left her coat behind. And she hadn't left any money for drinks. And Jay and Niamh were sat in the window, chatting to one another, him looking over Niamh's shoulder to watch her. This wasn't right, Jess could only imagine what Matt would say if she told him how it all ground to a sudden ending like this. And bloody hell it was cold without her coat. Shit. Reluctantly, she turned on her heel and went back inside.

As she pushed the door open, Amanda held up her coat. Lolly gave her a smile like she did that time she failed her driving test and didn't want to admit how devastated she was. Emily shuffled round the table towards her. 'Let's go somewhere else,' she said, pulling her stuff together. 'I'll get these, you lot sort out where we're headed next.'

Lolly discreetly got hold of Jess's hand, holding it tight and close in to her hip, eyes fixed on Amanda.

'More drinks somewhere or do you all want to come to mine?' Amanda asked.

'I think I just want to go home,' said Jess. 'I don't know, it's complicated.'

'All the more reason for you to come to mine then. Come on, I have wine and tea and crisps and *Immaculate Collection* on repeat.'

And the part of Jess that didn't want to open up to the girls was suffocated by the part of Jess that wondered how she'd survived the last twenty years of her life without them. They were a four, ready to take on the world.

'Get your coat,' said Amanda as she hooked her arm through Jess's. 'You've pulled.'

Amanda

'Come in, come in. Don't bother about your shoes, I can't remember the last time I mopped or hoovered. Mind the cat.' Amanda picked Jaffa up, kissed his head and shooed him off upstairs. 'Coats on the bannister if you want.' She turned the heating dial up until it clicked, noticing her hands shaking as she did. She didn't do nerves. Not for years. It just wasn't her way. 'Kitchen's this way. I'm not waiting on you hand and foot. Open cupboards, find food and drink, I need a wee.'

Emily, Jess and Lolly stood looking round Amanda's kitchen. 'Glasses in that cupboard, kettle's over there,' said Amanda as she dived out of the room.

She scanned the downstairs to make sure there was nothing that could give her away. She shut the door on her workroom before retreating to the downstairs loo. The house felt full of familiarity, which terrified her. Lolly was right there, right out in the kitchen. Steps away from the room that her husband was in just days ago. It was clear they had to leave the bar, that bit was fine, but it was so obvious Jess wasn't okay, they couldn't have parted ways yet. She'd done the right thing, inviting them to hers, but guilt still spiked.

'What are you drinking?' Lolly shouted.

'Red, please,' she answered, making her way back to the kitchen. 'Is anyone hungry? I've a chicken in the fridge. I could roast it and shove some potatoes on too. Not exactly a Sunday dinner, but something to look forward to whilst we chat.'

'I don't know that I should be out for dinner too, it was my turn to cook.' Lolly's phone pinged with a message. She took a cursory glance before fiddling with it and dropping it back in her bag. 'You know what? I'm on silent, girls. Radio silence. He can fend for himself for a bit! You sticking to tea, Emily?' she asked, finding teabags and dropping one into a mug when Emily nodded.

Amanda got out wine and glasses, filling up a glass each for Jess and Lolly.

'Let's go into the lounge, I'll get the fire on.' Amanda knelt before the open fire, making a teepee out of sticks and paper, before shoving a load of firelighters in the base and holding a flame to them.

'So, ladies, I propose a toast,' she said as the teepee began raging behind her. 'Here's to old friends.' The girls clinked, murmured and drank, then fell silent.

It was Emily who broke it. 'So, Jess, what's going on? Why do you look like your world has crashed around you?'

Jess squirmed. 'I don't think I want to talk about it, about him.'

'Come on!' said Amanda, 'this is us. You can talk to us about anything. She knew him years back, Em. After you'd gone, before she went off travelling. What were we? Seventeen?'

'Yes,' agreed Lolly. 'Seventeen, eighteen. He was gorgeous and SO into you.'

Jess let out a groan. She buried her head in her hands before peeking through her hair to see the three of them, patiently waiting. 'Gah! It was a lifetime ago. It's in the past. It's stupid.'

'What's stupid?' asked Emily.

'This. Him. Me. He's just a work colleague, I need to get a grip,' said Jess.

'You still have feelings for him then.' Lolly tucked her feet beneath her, pulling a throw down from the sofa and covering her knees. 'Which have caught you by surprise?'

Jess nodded.

'The one that got away?' asked Emily and Jess bit down on her bottom lip.

'I don't know if he got away or I pushed him away. I wasn't in the right place, I was...' Her eyes flicked up at Emily. 'It's complicated. He was... special. He made me feel like nobody ever has before or since. I couldn't cope. I was going away anyway, travelling, do you remember?' Lolly and Amanda nodded. 'I ended it. I've no right to feel sad about any of it.' Jess buried her head again, then stared out of the window.

'You're allowed to feel how you feel,' said Amanda, gently. 'Nobody can tell you otherwise.'

'I guess.'

'Was it just the travelling that made it complicated?' asked Emily. Jess bit down on her bottom lip.

Amanda peered at her, there was something she wasn't saying. She was censoring herself, Amanda could see that. It reminded her of the months after Emily left, when Jess changed. They didn't fall out, but neither Amanda or Lolly could work out what was different, or how to get Jess back.

'I remember you changed,' said Amanda, carefully. 'When Emily left, you sort of went into yourself. I was never sure if it was the pressure of exams, or stuff at home. You wouldn't talk... talking helps. Talking is good for us. Talking helps us to unpack things.'

'I don't know if I can,' said Jess.

They fell silent. Jess shook her head, still gazing out of the window.

'Well, look, you can't talk on an empty stomach. If nobody wants roast chicken, I'm getting crisps. Gather your thoughts, Jess. Trust us.'

Amanda pulled a couple of bowls out of the kitchen cupboard, grabbing bags of onion rings and kettle chips, whatever she could find. The awkwardness of having Lolly in the house was being suitably masked by a chance to help Jess. For now at least.

She dropped the snacks onto the coffee table in front of them. Lolly went straight for the onion rings, Emily pulled the kettle chips closer, peering, but not actually taking any. Had she been able to eat stuff like that in the last few years? Probably not, which made Amanda feel sorry for her because no amount of money and fame could get in the way of her and a bag of synthetic crisps. Jess didn't move.

'You can trust us,' said Amanda to Jess.

'I know. I know I can. It's just not that simple.'

'Nothing is simple. But Amanda's right,' said Lolly, crunching on her crisps. 'This is us, Jess. Me, you, Amanda and Emily. There is nothing we can't talk about. Like, do you remember back when we were on study leave for our GCSEs?' she asked.

Amanda thought back to what felt like months and months of red-hot summers in which they would sit on the beach, talking about life and the universe. Sharing their hopes for the future. Watching the surfers. Putting herself back there reminded her that she'd always dreamed about opening her own floristry. Dreaming.

'I remember how low I felt back then,' Lolly continued. 'Stuff was going off with Dad and Jo. He'd met someone, Jo didn't like her. It was all hushed tones and closed doors. Lowered voices on the telephone to his girlfriend, trying not let me hear them talk. It was weird, she kept coming round. I remember feeling removed from home. Replaced. I remember missing Mum more than I ever had before… or maybe since. And I remember how sitting with you girls was the thing that got me through. You were my survival. You were the reason I'm still here now, sitting here.'

'Shovelling onion rings,' said Amanda, grabbing a handful before passing it back to Lolly.

'You girls were everything to me,' she said.

'Ditto,' agreed Emily.

'We still can be everything to each other,' said Lolly. 'You still can talk to us, Jess.'

Jess let out a sigh. She crossed her legs into the chair, hugging her knees. 'Things change. We changed. Emily left. Lolly, you'd decided you were going to go into nursing, you went off to college after our GCSEs. You got new friends. Amanda was obsessed with boys.'

Amanda felt a nostalgic pang for those days. The days that taught her about life and love and sex. The days that led to the months to the year she met Pete. They still saw each other, just not as often. For her, Pete was the beginning of the end for their friendship. She was obsessed; she was free with Pete on the back of his bike. She could still feel how it felt to spend hours on the beach whilst he surfed, before drinking pints down the pub with all his mates. That part of her life was in technicolour, faded only by getting pregnant with Zennor when life got suddenly terrifying, and small, and a little bit claustrophobic. And the girls were too far apart to help by then.

'We all changed,' said Amanda, sadly.

'We did. Which I guess was inevitable. And it meant I couldn't talk. I was stuck. That's all I remember. I was stuck. I needed to escape…'

Jess

'From what?' asked Amanda.

Jess shifted uncomfortably in her seat, her eyes flicked up towards the girls. Jess didn't want to go back over it all, she didn't want to relive any moment, and yet, as the girls sat around her, patiently waiting for her to talk, she knew she needed to move on. This stuff with Jay, did it bring everything back? Or did it just highlight the fact that none of it had gone away, just been buried, deep?

'What were you escaping from, Jess?' asked Emily.

Jess looked up at her. Her old mate. A girl whom she loved. A girl whom she'd hidden the biggest secret of her life from. 'Just... stuff,' she said. 'I can't... but life got harder, foggy even. I was functioning, the days came and went, I lived, but I don't know, maybe looking back I was living half-heartedly.'

'Where were we?' asked Lolly.

'To begin with, you were around, we were doing what we did. Revising for GCSEs, secret house parties, days down the beach, walks in the park. You guys were a sort of safety blanket, a place that I knew, I understood. I didn't have to think about it with you, I could be the kid I yearned to be. For a while.'

'Until you couldn't?' said Amanda.

Jess looked at her, unsurprised. 'Until I couldn't.'

'I remember how distant you grew. I thought it was us,' said Lolly.

Jess shook her head. 'No, no! It was never you. It could never have been you. I just needed to break all ties. I couldn't fake it any more.' Jess looked at Lolly, whose eyes glistened. 'Don't! Don't start, because *I* don't want to. Right?'

Lolly nodded, a tear escaping with the force. 'Sorry.'

Jess half smiled. 'I remember you both came to the Hub one day when I was working. Jay and I were flirting, I liked the innocence of it. It gave me a boost. I didn't want to pursue it though, the idea was too frightening and yet I remember Lolly, you told me to go for it. To make the most of being young.'

'I think I might have said something about getting a shag to loosen you up,' said Amanda, scrunching her face up. 'Sounds a bit crass now, on reflection.'

Jess laughed. 'You did say that, yes. And I don't know, I guess when the flirting progressed, it wasn't so frightening. He wasn't so frightening.'

'Why would he have been frightening?' asked Emily.

'I don't know, I was just in a weird place.' Jess smiled, weakly. 'But suddenly, with him, everything was different. He was kind, and gentle. He was funny, so funny. He could make me cry laughing with an off the cuff remark. He was tender, so very tender. He kind of swept me off my feet, I didn't know I could feel like that and before I knew it, I was head over heels.' Jess drifted off for a moment. 'But it was too much. He was too much, too kind, too supportive, too understanding.'

'How can any of those things be bad?' asked Amanda. 'He sounds great!'

'Yeah, but I don't think I felt I deserved it. I kept pushing him away, I kept setting him up to fail.'

'And did he?' asked Lolly.

'No. He never did. He just proved even more how great he was.'

'Sounds awful,' said Amanda, winking at Jess.

Jess half laughed. 'I was messed up. I'd already planned the trip away. I couldn't not go.'

'That's right. God, you went for so long. I fell pregnant with Zennor.'

'Right.'

'You know, I really needed you lot when I first fell pregnant,' said Amanda, wistfully.

'Until you didn't,' said Jess, carefully, their meeting at the garden centre in mind.

Amanda nodded. 'Until I didn't.' Amanda sipped at her wine, thoughtfully. 'I remember thinking it odd that you stayed away so long, out of all of us, I didn't have you down as the travelling type.'

'I don't think I was. But it was the only way I could escape. Matt had been all over, America, Europe, China, Australia. He'd done stuff, seen stuff. He'd come back all tanned and full of life and I don't know, maybe wisdom too. He knew stuff. About other cultures, about life. He seemed so calm and in control of his own destiny. I felt like maybe that's what I needed. To get away and experience life outside of Cornwall. It felt claustrophobic and I was falling for Jay, which made me feel more so. Mum and Dad thought I was too young for a serious relationship anyway, told me I'd be mad to miss out. I told Jay I was going, that I needed to do it on my own and I think I'd really wanted him to tell me to stay but he was so encouraging, so supportive of me. He told me I had to go, that he wouldn't be the one to hold me back from realising my dreams and I don't know... I couldn't tell him they weren't my dreams.'

'Shit,' said Lolly, wiping her eyes. 'I'm sorry, I can't help it,' she said, reaching for a tissue. 'I can't believe we missed all this.'

'Did you miss it, or did I hide it?' said Jess, smiling sadly at Lolly. 'You couldn't have known. I didn't talk. I didn't have a voice somehow. I just sort of floated from one point to the next, blown on the wind of whatever direction life took me.'

'Seems strange to think of you like that,' said Emily. 'I always saw you as the strong one of us all. Quietly so, not like Amanda's fierce strength. Yours was always steady. Self-controlled.'

'Yes!' agreed Amanda. 'You were the one to get shit done.'

'I don't think that was strength, though. Back then. I think it was fear. It was lack of knowing who I was in a house where I was supposed to be clear and free and independent. Mum and Dad believed in me, in my personality, in giving me the space to own me and for years that was great, empowering as a kid, but things changed and I didn't know what to do with the freedom, it sort of locked me up.'

Amanda

A phone rang in the kitchen. 'Do you need to get that?' asked Jess, seemingly jumping on a chance to change the subject.

'No, no, it's fine,' said Amanda. Irritated by the subsequent text message sound.

'So, if he carried on waiting, and you were unhappy, why didn't you go home and be together?' asked Emily.

Jess laughed to herself, then wiped her eyes with the back of her hand. Amanda passed the tissues. 'I met some girls whilst travelling. They seemed wise and strong. I think I was trying to replace you guys, but you know…'

'We're irre-fucking-placeable!' said Amanda, and the girls paused, smiling at one another.

'I'd talk to Jay often, anytime I had the cash and could find a phone. I must have been really subdued after each call 'cause as time went on, they started taking the mick. They told me he must be a sap for waiting. That he couldn't have any ambition. They couldn't believe he hadn't just jumped on a plane to follow me out there and I'd tell them it was because he wanted me to have my journey, my experience, that he didn't want to interrupt that or take over. They said I was being naive and though it hurt to be apart, like physically ached, I felt like I had to stay. I had to see out my travel, finish what I planned. So I told Jay everything the girls had said to me.'

'Oh no…' Lolly blew her nose.

'I told him he had no ambition. That I couldn't love someone who hadn't lived. I told him it was pointless him waiting for me if he was doing nothing else with his life.' Jess stopped talking. Amanda didn't remember her ever crying before. Lolly was the crier in the group, maybe followed by Emily. But Jess, just no. Amanda wanted to wrap her up and fix it all for her. 'Do you know that saying, if you love someone enough, set them free.'

'Wasn't that *Jonathan Livingston Seagull* or some shit?' asked Amanda.

'Blimey, you do read!' nudged Lolly.

Amanda stuck her tongue out, moving the crisps just out of her reach.

'I don't know where it came from. All I know is that it was exactly that. Jay loved me. And he set me free. And after time had passed, I didn't come back and, of course, he fell in love with someone else. He had every right.'

'It's so sad,' said Lolly. 'The idea of what could have been.'

'I thought I'd moved on,' whispered Jess.

Lolly

'Urgh, girls, I think I might have gone too hard too fast. My head is banging,' Lolly said, eventually, rubbing at her temples, peering into the now empty bowl of crisps for something to line her stomach with.

'There's more in the kitchen, go fetch them if you like. Along with another bottle,' said Amanda, throwing another log on the fire, poking at it until it raged and danced.

'I should probably opt for a tea, if you don't mind.'

'I don't mind, you can have whatever you can find.'

Emily held her mug up. 'Do you fancy putting some water on this teabag?'

Amanda recoiled. 'You are allowed more than one teabag you know… if you can find another herbal one!'

'It's fine, water's fine. Thanks.'

Lolly shivered as she left the warmth of the lounge. She looked out of the window on a sprawling garden as she topped up the kettle. She peered at photos on the fridge as she reached for the milk. She saw Amanda's phone light up with a text message.

Amanda. She hadn't opened up much yet, not like she had about Kitt and the boys. Not like Jess just had about Jay. As the kettle boiled, Lolly idly wondered what life was really like for Amanda these days, at the other end of the parenting timeline. Single in this big old house. Was she lonely? Did she miss having Zennor around? Did she meet people, other than young lads in bars or whatever it was she mentioned before?

Emily had been quiet too, reserved almost. Was she regretting getting back in touch? Lolly thought it possible given that they'd all been so bloody earnest in their storytelling. What had happened to them? To the light and the fun they used to have? Reaching into a cupboard above the kettle, Lolly found a mug and teabag. The cupboard door had a host of photos Blu-tacked to the inside, stuff from over the years. And there, in amongst them all, was a photo of the four of them. All grainy and old. Lolly stared at it, picking it from the cupboard door. She could remember the exact moment it was taken, they were kids. So young. Her dad had taken them all to see Wet Wet Wet at the Coliseum in St Austell and this was taken whilst they were waiting for the band to come on. They'd been so giddy to be at their first concert, Lolly was obsessed with Marti Pellow. She'd scoured her back catalogue of *Smash Hits* magazines for interviews in which he'd been asked important details like his favourite colour, his favourite food and whether he preferred cats or dogs.

'Oh my god!' she shouted through to the lounge. 'Girls, you are not gonna believe this!' She picked up the bag of crisps to take back through, throwing them on the table for Amanda to top up the bowls. 'Look what I just found!' She passed the photo to Jess.

'Wet Wet Wet? Jesus, how long ago was that? We look like children!'

Amanda grinned. 'We were children.'

Emily took the photo from Jess. 'Wow, how long ago! That was my first concert. I couldn't talk for days after from all the screaming.'

Lolly laughed. 'Dad was so irritated by the screaming, he swore he'd never take us again.'

'Is that why he only dropped us off when it was Simply Red?' Jess laughed.

'Exactly! And wouldn't come near the Radio One Roadshow at St Ives Rugby Club!'

Emily let out an uncharacteristic belly laugh. 'Radio One did not play St Ives Rugby Club.'

'They did! Ocean Colour Scene played the year we went,' said Lolly.

'Yes! I remember. God, that was a fun day out!' said Emily.

Lolly left the girls giggling over the photo and some story about Amanda copping off with a roadie round the back of the rugby club. As she went back to the kitchen to make the tea, she felt dizzy with drink and memories and a warmth that came from being around them all. She could almost forget the crap going off at home and the guilt she was now beginning to feel over it all. She hated fighting with Kitt. She needed him, however independent she liked to believe she was, he was her mate, her right arm. He was the one she turned to when she needed a prop and them being at odds was awful. It all felt so wrong. Things weren't perfect for them, it was tough since the boys came along. She was focussed on them, Kitt was focussed on work. But they'd been together forever, they just needed to work through it. She wasn't naive enough to think that a baby would solve all that, but it wouldn't break them. The first two hadn't. They just had to find a way to sort things. She vowed to head home after the tea had sobered her up a bit. As she moved to leave the kitchen with two mugs in hand, Amanda's phone rang out. She reached for it, glancing at the screen. 'Amanda, you're a wanted woman!' she shouted.

Amanda

'You've a text message too,' said Lolly, with a wink as she handed over the phone. 'Looks like someone needs to speak to you.'

Amanda's breath caught in her throat as she saw a familiar number flashing up.

'Go on, answer it. We can be really quiet, can't we, girls!' Lolly said. Jess laughed with her. Emily smiled. Lolly's eyebrows were practically at the back of her head and Amanda fumbled to cancel the call. 'If it's the same person their text said they *had* to talk to you. They practically begged!' she said, blowing on her drink. 'Oooh, oh… maybe it's that guy that Zennor caught you talking with? Did you exchange numbers?'

'Nah, he doesn't have my number. It's probably nothing.' Amanda put her phone on the coffee table. Her hands shook.

'Nothing?' Lolly laughed. 'Nothing that's turned you all wobbly!' she said, nudging Jess, delighting in an opportunity to wind Amanda up. 'Since when have you been embarrassed? Come on, who is it? Tell us? Tell us everything!'

'Tell us *everything*? Christ, Lolly, we're not kids any more!' Amanda barked.

The girls went quiet and the mood shifted in the room. Amanda stood up feeling a bit faint and a bit bad because Lolly looked stung and it was no bloody wonder. 'Logs, we need more logs.' Amanda hurried out, no doubt leaving them wondering what the hell had just happened. How on earth could she erase the last few minutes because whatever the reunion had been unfolding into, she had likely just put the kibosh on it. She fussed around in the understairs cupboard trying to regain composure.

There was a pause before she sensed someone behind her. 'I was just kidding, Amanda. Sorry… I didn't think…' Lolly's voice was small.

'No, no it's fine. It's nothing.' Amanda waved her away. 'Ignore me. I don't know where it came from. Hormones probably. Have you found them getting worse? Like in the last couple of years, I've definitely noticed…'

Lolly peered at Amanda who was half talking to her and half rustling around in the cupboard. Only when she saw her take a sniff did Amanda realise the cupboard held a pair of those stinky trainers she was working on and the smell was creeping out from behind her. She shut the door quickly, ushering Lolly back into the lounge.

'Logs?' Jess reminded her and Amanda wondered if her tone was a bit protective somehow. Was she defending Lolly? Who now looked like a lost lamb as she sat nursing her tea on the sofa.

'Yes! Logs. I think I have some in the back.' Her phone started ringing again and she could tell the girls tried not to look at who was calling. Well, apart from Lolly, who just stared at her feet. Amanda reached for her phone, cancelling the call and turning it off. If that was him, what the hell was he playing at? Did he want Lolly to find out? Had he been worried about what Amanda might say? Maybe Amanda should be more worried? And yet with them all here, in her room, the last thing she wanted was to lose them all over again. 'Back in a minute.'

She went through the kitchen into her back room, shutting the door behind her. She looked at her phone. Three text messages in the last hour. Plus a voicemail. She threw it on the bed they'd had sex in only a few days ago. She looked around the room, a room she was usually proud of. She had supported herself and had a bit of fun in the process. She had acted out her own fantasies and those of other people. She wasn't just someone sleeping with other people's husbands, which is all it would look like to Lolly if she found out now, under these circumstances. Though maybe there was no way Amanda could present this that made it look any better. Because people didn't see the good that she did. The men who'd got to forty, still virgins. Men with disabilities, men who found it difficult to connect with women. She'd lain there with men who just wanted to feel connected, no physical exchange other than a cuddle and a talk and the understanding that that was all that was needed. It wasn't always like that, there were the men who took advantage and the men who messed her around. The men who thought it was okay to push on when she'd told them no and the men who'd take what they wanted then abuse her in a fit of post-orgasm guilt or anger. But it was a job, her job. And fundamentally, it was a job she loved. Amanda knew what people thought of women like her, and the men who used her services, but they weren't all like Kitt, that was for sure. And she wasn't going to be dragged into the stereotype by a client with his own agenda.

She had to recompose. She had to gather herself and focus. She needed to get the girls to leave because the mood had changed and if Kitt was going to keep ringing, who was to say he wouldn't just turn up on her doorstep. She took a deep breath and headed back into the lounge.

'Girls, I'm really sorry. This is awful, but... that phone call. It was... well, I need to sort something. I'm so sorry, I just... I can't explain right now. I hope you don't mind, this has been so lovely. Seeing you all after all of this time.'

It was Lolly who got up first, Jess passed her coat. Emily gave her arm a squeeze.

'Can we do this again?' asked Amanda as the girls gathered their things and headed for the front door. There were murmurs of agreement but she couldn't help thinking they sounded polite more than committed. She'd blown it. No question.

Emily

By the time Emily and Jess had walked her up to the taxi rank, Lolly was smiling. They had all agreed that Amanda had always had her moments. Just as she could bring the party, she could end it too. And they all knew that sometimes she'd been one to keep things from them so why would it be any different now. It had been a source of frustration in the past but given that Emily hadn't come entirely clean about her own life right now, she didn't feel in much position to judge.

'Bless, Lolly,' said Jess, waving her off in a cab. 'She's not changed much, has she?'

Emily smiled. 'No, not at all. It makes me wonder if any of us have, deep down, I mean.'

Jess looked at Emily, almost studied her, which made Emily feel uncomfortable. Exposed somehow. She was used to being looked at, but usually people were scrutinising her hair and make-up, her chosen outfit. Jess though, Jess seemed to be looking into her soul almost. 'You were quieter than I remember,' she said.

'You think?' Emily started walking, though she wasn't sure in what direction.

'Definitely. You were never that quiet when we were younger.'

'Oh, I don't know about that. Besides, I enjoyed watching, learning about you all, you know. I was the one to leave. Maybe I'm a bit of an outsider.'

Jess grabbed Emily's arm. 'Wait on, I don't think any of us look at you that way. Is that really what you feel?'

'I don't know. It's been quite nice not to be the one getting all the attention… is that a bit humble braggy?'

'Not at all. I can imagine it gets tiresome, being in the public eye.'

Jess had no idea. Emily wasn't one of the super-famous but even she grew irritated by the assumption that she was public property, just because she did a job that occasionally pushed her in the public gaze. 'I shouldn't complain, not really. I'm walking this way, what about you?'

'Yeah, me too.'

Jess and Emily wandered toward the bottom of Pydar Street in a comfortable silence. Emily replayed the reunion, considering what it might be like to raise a child with three brilliant women as godmothers. Because the more she thought about this baby and her new life back in Cornwall, the more the idea appealed.

Eventually, Jess asked, 'Is life good for you, Emily?'

Emily peered into Waterstones' window. She'd not read a book in ages, she missed things like that. 'Yeah. I guess so. Life's… okay,' she said. 'I mean, I'm back here to make some changes, so you know…'

She walked on. She wondered what the bean in her belly was doing. Did it move as she moved, or was it rooted to her insides? How tiny was it? Did it hear her yet? She knew nothing about babies, about pregnancy. Perhaps she should start looking it up. Except the more she thought, the more she warmed to the idea, the more real it became, and she knew she was going to have to face up to the reality that, probably, Jackson had a right to know.

Before the silence forced her to expand, she heard a voice behind her. 'Hey, Emily, how are you doing?'

She spun around to see Mac standing before her and Jess. He was grinning widely. 'Oh! Hi!' They stood, smiling, and Emily noted what a joy it was to see a familiar face, someone who didn't want to air kiss and feign interest like back in New York. 'What are you up to?'

'It's Mum's birthday in a couple of weeks. Popped in to find a present.' He paused, looking at them both. 'Yeah… well, I've not been in town for ages. Do you know my mum's aunty was born in the houses up Walsingham Place? I remember going there as a kid to visit. All wonky floors. Just been past now on the way to Mallets and they're all offices, it's bonkers. That cafe's good though, behind the car park. Apparently if your name is Richard you get free coffee today.'

Emily smiled at Mac's chat. He had much more to say today than he had the other two times they'd bumped into each other. 'Great day for Richards.' She laughed. 'I was just meeting up with old friends.' Mac looked at Jess. 'This is Jess, an old school friend. Jess, Mac, he lives in the village.'

They each nodded a hello.

'Hey, I've got some more fish if you want it? I'll bring it already filleted this time, eh. Wouldn't want you turning green again!'

'Oh, ha! No, it's fine. I'm… I've still got some left.'

'Poor Emily, I was trying to do her a favour, help her out. Mum had said she was trying to lay low for a while.' Emily noticed Jess's eyes flick back to her when he said that. 'So I took a load of mackerel up to hers, nice bit of fresh out the briny. But the second I cut them open, I lost her to the downstairs loo!'

'Ahhh, that's just feeble.' Jess laughed.

'Yeah, well… you know… I guess I'll never make a fisherman's wife,' Emily joked, then noticed Mac turn pink. 'Well, anyway, nice seeing you, Mac.'

'Uhm, yeah, and you. Jess.' He nodded politely in her direction.

'Mac.' She smiled in polite response.

The three of them paused in the middle of Truro. Mac eventually made to move before turning back. 'Erm, I'm headed home now, if you need a lift back, Emily?'

'Oh, no, thanks. No, don't worry, I wouldn't want to put you out.'

'Well… I'm just going back to Gorran so it's not exactly putting me out. Unless I can give you a lift too, Jess? Where are you headed?'

'Me, oh no, I'm Falmouth. No, you two head on. Emily, it's been lovely seeing you. Please, let's not leave it so long next time.'

'Oh, I don't mind staying on in town, for a bit longer. I mean, we could grab something to eat?'

Mac hovered but Jess shook her head. 'No, I need to get back. A few bits to sort before heading back into the office tomorrow.'

With the mention of the office, Emily was reminded of Jess's current predicament. 'You okay?' she asked, sort of wishing Mac wasn't still stood there.

'I'm fine, honestly.' Jess pulled her in for a hug. 'Look, let's talk in the week, see if you fancy catching up again.'

'I'd love to, Jess. I really would.'

'Great, go on. Get a lift from your man here.'

'Oh he's not… I mean…' This time it was Emily's turn to go pink and Mac looked to the ground. 'Well anyway, okay, it was lovely. See you soon.'

'See you!' And with that Jess wandered off, Mac looked expectantly, and Emily wondered why the butterflies had returned to her stomach.

Lolly

Lolly made the taxi swing by McDonald's on her way back. A Big Mac and large fries had gone a long way to sorting her wine induced wonk and by the time she pushed open her front door, she felt almost back to normal. 'Hello!' she shouted out. The house was quiet. There were no lights on in the lounge or the hallway. 'Boys?' she shouted.

'Down here,' called Kitt. 'But you can't come in yet.'

She pulled off her coat, hanging that and her bag in the downstairs loo. 'What are you doing?'

'Wait a minute!' he called.

Lolly wasn't sure whether to be intrigued or nervous. 'Where are the boys?' she asked, peering upstairs to see if somehow he'd managed to get them to play in their rooms. They didn't normally play in their rooms and given that both lights were off, they obviously weren't there now. 'What's going on?' she asked, opening the kitchen door just as Kitt finished lighting a candle on the table.

'I didn't know what time you were going to be back so dinner's not quite ready.'

Lolly looked at the plates and the wine glasses, the roast chicken cooking in the oven. Gary Barlow songs were playing in the background, which set Lolly on suspicious because Kitt hated Gary Barlow. 'What's going on?' she asked.

'I've been thinking about you. About us. About what you said the other day.' He pulled a chair out for her, motioning that she should sit down. 'I've been distracted lately, I know I have. And I know you're finding things hard, and I guess I just realised I needed to try harder. Do my bit, you know?'

'Right…'

'So Mum came and took the boys. She has them overnight.'

'What about school?' She sat down, gazing at the table, impeccably laid out. Then she felt bad for assuming he probably got his mum to sort it all out before she took the boys.

'She said she'd take them in. Agreed that we needed a bit of time for each other. So, we've got the night to ourselves. The house. I've cooked a roast, I opened a bottle of wine. I thought we could have a nice evening together, talk, reconnect, you know?' He stood behind her, bending down to move his arms around her waist, kissing her neck. 'I thought we could see how things unfolded…'

'Kitt…' Lolly let herself lean into his kiss. She reached behind her, running her fingers through his hair.

'I'm sorry. I've been a dick,' he said, nuzzling into her.

'I'm sorry too, I just… I don't know, I've been preoccupied, focussed on the wrong things maybe.'

'It's fine, I understand. I get why it's important to you.' He carried on kissing her neck in-between his words. 'And I want to do my bit, I want us to try,' he said, letting his hands run up her sides, cupping her breast. He turned her around to face him, running his thumb over her nipple and Lolly's breath caught in her throat.

'How long will tea be?' she asked.

'Long enough,' he answered, pulling her into him. 'Shall we go upstairs?' he asked, pushing himself into her hip, kissing her lips and her cheek and her neck.

'Or shall we do it here?' she suggested.

Kitt pulled back to look at her. Even in the last few weeks of trying for a baby, it had been a long time since they'd done it anywhere other than the marital bed. Lolly pushed him to sit at the dinner table, straddling him. She kissed him, appreciating the sound of him enjoying her taking control. She moved against him, the traces of alcohol taking away any notion of uncertainty she might have had before. And in that moment, for the first time in months, she didn't care if she got pregnant or not, she just needed to be close to her husband. Right there. In the kitchen.

Emily

Apparently it wasn't butterflies at the prospect of getting in Mac's car, it was actually morning sickness. At 4.30 p.m. on a Sunday afternoon. Mac seemed totally forgiving of the fact that she grabbed the first thing that came to hand, which happened to be a jumper his sister had bought him the year before last. She offered to replace it. He told her it was fine, that he didn't really like it anyway. She wished – for the second, or maybe third time since they'd met – that the ground would open and swallow her whole. Right there in the layby he'd pulled in at on the St Austell Road.

'Are you okay though? Did you eat something whilst you were out?'

'No, no I didn't eat anything.'

'Maybe there's a bug going around. Mind you, you weren't well when I popped round, were you? I mean… I don't want to pry, but are you sure you're okay? Is there anything I can do? Or Mum, Mum likes to help. Please do let us know if there's anything—'

'No, no, it's nothing. I'm fine. Last time was definitely the mackerel, this time… I don't know – car sickness?'

'My driving's that bad?'

'No, no. I don't know… maybe I do have a bug. I was feeling a little off this morning. I just really wanted to see my old mates so came out anyway.'

'Right.'

There was a pause. Mac looked around. Cars whizzed past. Emily realised she really wanted to tell someone about the fact she was pregnant. She hadn't said it out loud once and stood here now, in a lay-by with an all but stranger, she really wanted to tell him. But why now? Why him? Was it just because she'd been sick into his jumper or was it because she realised she really wished she'd mentioned it to the girls this afternoon but her moment passed and never really came back. Hearing Lolly talk about her boys made Emily imagine being a mum. Hearing Amanda talk about Zennor was a glimpse into the future with a grown-up child and even though things were clearly tough for them at the moment, Emily imagined having her own grown-up child and really liked the idea. Jess proclaiming her disinterest in children made Emily all the clearer, she had always imagined herself a mum, perhaps not in this way quite. She might have preferred it to be with someone who actually wanted to be a father. She'd have liked to settle with a home and a dog and a baby who was loved by both parents. But it was what it was. And if she was ready to step away from the acting, which it was clear to her was a no brainer, then becoming a mother... well, maybe that was a gift that would be the making of her next phase in life. She hadn't been sure what made her think twice, sat in the abortion clinic in New York. Or what made her tell Jackson she'd gone through with it, but now, here, she was grateful to her previous self.

'We should probably get you back to yours,' said Mac, checking his watch. 'We could swing by Mum's on the way, pick up some of her gingerbread. A friend of mine swore by it when she was pregnant. You know, for the sickness, I mean, not suggesting you're pregnant. I mean, you don't look it—'

'Oh! No. I mean…' Emily felt herself colour and a wave of nausea return. She buried her head in her bag, searching out a tissue for as long as it took to regain her composure. 'Don't worry. It's fine. I'll be alright soon enough. Yes, let's go.'

She climbed back into his truck and they set off steadily, Mac driving a steady pace, hands at ten to two.

'So, was it nice to meet up with old friends then?'

'Yes, I think it was.'

'You don't sound convinced.'

'No, it was, I just… I suppose a lot has happened in the years since we were really close. We were kids. We've changed.'

'So much that you've nothing in common any more?'

'No, I don't think so. I think we're still fundamentally the same people, I mean they all seemed great. I just… I think I felt guarded somehow. Like I couldn't totally be me.'

'Are you always like that?' Mac asked, eyes fixed forward on the road up ahead.

She thought for a moment. 'I didn't think so, but the more I'm back home, the more I wonder.' Emily opened the window, letting her head rest against the seat belt so air could brush past her face.

'You need to stop again?'

'No, no, I'm okay.'

'I haven't got any more jumpers,' he joked. Emily smiled. 'Jess seemed nice,' he said.

'Yeah, she is. She always was. She was the determined one of us all, the one who'd get stuff done, you know? She was different now though… I suppose you never really know what's going off in other people's heads, do you?'

'How so?'

Emily didn't want to gossip about Jess. If there was one thing she knew better than most it was how painful people talking about you could be. The judgements, the assumptions, she hated it. 'I don't know, maybe she's not as in control as we'd all have believed. And maybe that makes me feel better.' Mac didn't respond and Emily immediately felt bad. 'That sounds awful, doesn't it? Oh god, what a horrible thing to say.'

Mac gave her a quick look and shake of his head, before fixing back on the road. 'Why is it horrible?'

'Suggesting that her situation makes me feel better, what a narcissist.'

'I think we probably all have the capacity to be a bit narcissistic. I wouldn't beat yourself up about it. Look, Mum's probably in the shop. Give me a second, I'll get you some of that cake. Hang on.'

But as Mac jumped out of the car, there was a tap on the passenger window. 'Emily!' said a familiar American voice.

She didn't need to look to know who it was.

Amanda

Amanda sat in her lounge, staring at the fire. It was nothing more than amber glowing ashes. The room was getting cold and the timer had thrown one of the corner lights on. Having heard Lolly talk about her hopes for another baby, it just made Amanda all the more torn. She'd never go back on her obligation to clients, but she was a friend to Lolly long before she'd been a service for Kitt and she couldn't bear the idea of Lolly being so desperate for another baby knowing what she knew about her husband. She picked up her phone to read his messages.

Just imagine what she'd think of you if she knew was one of them, as if Amanda should be ashamed of herself. She never really thought she was, but she had to accept that she must hold some sense of shame somewhere, otherwise she'd tell everyone without fear of retribution. *If you value your friendship, you'll say nothing* was another. Amanda resisted the urge to point out that if he valued his marriage, they wouldn't be in this situation. There was another three in which he grew increasingly foul in his language and description of her. She'd got abuse before now, men who thought that her career choice meant she was free rein for whatever hatred they wanted to spout. She was generally thick-skinned enough to ignore it but, on this occasion, his superiority made her angry.

She tapped out a text to him. *It's clear you have no respect for me, and I couldn't care less, but your wife? Perhaps it's time you told her the truth!* She clicked send then threw her phone across the sofa. Then her blood ran cold because she never texted clients, and this one in particular, she should be staying well clear of. What if Lolly saw it? What if she tracked her down? Or worse, realised the number was the same. Shit. Shit! Amanda jumped up and paced the room. Why had she just done that? What the hell would she say if Lolly connected the dots? She probably needed to know about what a shit of a husband she had, but not this way. Not through Amanda. When her phone rang, she practically leaped on to it. But instead of Lolly or Kitt, it was Pete.

'Amanda, it's Zennor. She's had an accident, we're on our way to A & E.'

'What! What's happened? Is she okay?'

'I… I don't know. I think she's taken something.'

'She's taken something! Taken what?'

'We're not sure. I'm going to try and call round her mates now. Just meet me up at Treliske, okay?'

'I've been drinking,' she said, digging out boots, coat and bag.

'Then you'd better get a taxi and mainline coffee on your way up.'

'Okay, okay. I'm coming.' She grabbed her keys from the side and flew out of the door. How many times had she told Zennor about drugs? About being careful what she drank and never putting her drink down in a bar. She'd given her the facts, she'd never been one to out and out tell her not to do them because she knew that would likely make Zennor go out and try more, but Christ, she'd hoped the facts would have been sufficient deterrent.

She looked up and down the road. Sunday. Where was the best place for a cab? Would there even be any? She fumbled in her bag, making sure she had her purse before heading for the nearest taxi rank.

'Amanda! Are you okay?' said a voice as Amanda ran past the chip shop. Amanda turned to see Jess carrying a bag of drenched chips.

'Jess! I thought you'd be gone by now.'

'I was wandering. Thinking. What's the matter?'

'It's Zennor. She's in A & E. Pete says they think she's taken something. I don't know, but my head is fucked and there's no buses and I can't drive and I don't know what to do.' Amanda put her hands on her hips, heavy breathing as realisation dawned. 'Shit, Jess. I don't know what to do.'

'Come on, let's get you up to the hospital. Here, have some chips. I don't know about you but I was feeling a bit fuzzy by the time I left yours. Ten minutes in the fresh air seeing the girls back off home, I needed these!'

Amanda hungrily grabbed several chips. 'Thank you,' she said, in-between each one.

'There weren't any cabs at the rank,' said Jess. 'I was going to wait for a bus but here, let me call one from our work account.'

'Are you sure you don't mind?'

'Of course not, hang on. Take these, you probably need them more than me.'

'I'm not hungry.'

'You can't turn up pissed. Eat.' She thrust the bag in Amanda's hands. 'Hello. I need a cab on account. Victoria Square up to Treliske, please.'

Amanda leant against the wall, shielding the chips from a hungry looking gull that squawked above her. 'Piss off!' she shouted to it.

'They'll be here in five,' Jess said, nicking a chip. 'Hang on.' Jess went back into the chip shop for a moment, coming back out with a polystyrene cup of steaming black liquid. 'I can't promise it's decent, but it'll help. Come on, we can wait by Malletts.'

'I can't believe this, Jess,' said Amanda, navigating the snicket. 'What a fucking day.'

'Well, it was okay, wasn't it? When it was just us lot.'

Amanda nodded but hadn't forgotten Kitt's text messages. 'It was nice, it was lovely in fact…'

'But?' asked Jess, watching up and down the road for their ride.

'Oh, look. It's nothing. It was lovely.'

The cab pulled up and Jess opened the door for Amanda. 'Come on, in you get. I'll come up with you, then get it to take me home, if you don't mind?'

'Of course not, if that's okay with you?'

'Totally. Come on.' She took the empty chip cone from Amanda, launching it in a bin before climbing in the back beside her. 'Treliske, please.'

They travelled in silence. Up the hill, past the train station. Past Sainsbury's. They hit a bottleneck of traffic by the Aldi and Amanda stared out of the window, biting her lip.

'Are you sure you're gonna be okay?' asked Jess, when they pulled into the hospital drop off zone. 'I can come in with you, if you like.'

'No, don't worry. I'll be fine.' Amanda climbed out of the taxi, bobbing down to talk to Jess through the open window. 'Look, thanks, and for today too. I know I went a bit… weird earlier. It's complicated. But it's been nice to see you. I'd love to stay in touch. If that's okay?'

'Of course, you've got my number now. Let me know how Zennor is, okay?'

'Okay.'

Amanda waved the cab off as it pulled away, took a deep breath, then went off in search of Zennor and Pete.

Emily

'Are you sure you're okay? I don't mind waiting outside, or coming in, or whatever you need,' said Mac, eyeing Jackson suspiciously. He'd reluctantly agreed to give Jackson a lift up to her house but kept watching him through the rear-view mirror. Emily wasn't sure whether to be irritated or relieved by his sudden brotherly concern.

'It's fine. Don't worry,' she said as Jackson grappled with his bags, climbing out of the car. 'I can handle him.'

'Okay. If you're sure.' Mac looked at Jackson again. 'You've got my number. If you need anything, anything at all, just call.'

'Thanks, Mac.'

'And don't forget your ginger cake. Maybe book in with the docs if things don't improve. And make sure to drink plenty, replenish the waters, you know?'

Emily smiled at him. 'Of course. Thank you. And thanks for the lift… sorry again about your jumper…' She patted the bag in which she had stuffed it. As he pulled away, down the hill and out of sight, she dropped it in the bin. She'd replace it rather than wash it.

'Who was that?' asked Jackson, watching Mac drive off, gritting his teeth so his jaw flexed.

'Just one of the guys from the village,' said Emily, unlocking the door. She opted not to expand because she didn't have to explain herself to Jackson or anybody. It irked her that he probably thought she was playing games. He made a noise that suggested he was suspicious and she ignored it, instead pausing before she opened her door because she really hadn't wanted Jackson to know where she was living, let alone have him come inside. 'Mind your head,' she instructed.

Jackson followed her in. She could see his reflection in the mirror, glancing around the entrance hall, peering down steps to the kitchen and over to the lounge. 'Quaint,' he said. Which was probably code for small, given that he was really more attuned to wide, open plan spaces with large chandeliers and marble worktops. 'You never said you wanted to live here,' he said, accusingly.

'I didn't know I would.'

'Never thought I might like to come too?'

'I didn't really think it was your kind of place.'

'It would have been nice to be in on it though. Maybe we could have gone in together, got somewhere bigger.'

Emily hadn't wanted bigger. Emily had never wanted bigger. Jackson had encouraged her to think she liked all that, but now she was home, she knew more than ever that quaint, or whatever patronising term he wanted to use, was exactly what she wanted. 'Tea?' she asked.

'Anything stronger?'

Emily dug around, finding a bottle of red in the back of a cupboard. She placed a glass in front of him, motioning for him to take one of the bar stools by the kitchen island. She poured him a glass, feeling faintly green at the smell.

'So,' said Jackson.

Emily flicked the kettle on. 'So.' She wasn't going to make this easy for him. That he had turned up unannounced had pissed her off almost as much as the fact that he had sent Mason the last time.

'How've you been?' he asked.

'Yeah, good. Fine.' She cut a slice of ginger cake, taking a large bite as she turned to face him. 'You?'

'Yeah. Good. Busy, you know. But fine.' He paused. 'I guess.'

'Right.' The cake was hitting the spot so Emily cut another slice. 'You want some?' she offered, waving her knife in his direction.

'You're having more?'

Emily looked at him. 'Yes. Would you like some before I finish the whole cake?'

He raised his eyebrows, disapproving. 'No. No, thanks.'

'Right.' She pulled up a stool, sat down opposite him and waited.

'I want you to come home,' he started.

'I am home.'

'You know what I mean.' He ran a finger up the stem of the glass and along the rim, ridding it of a smudge she hadn't noticed. He rubbed his fingers as if ridding himself of dust or germs or whatever else he might have picked up from her glassware. Had he always been like this and she just hadn't noticed? Or had she chosen to ignore? 'There's talk of a new show at Studio 54. You always wanted to play there.'

'I did.'

'I reckon I could definitely get you in without an audition. The producer loves you and owes me a favour.'

'A favour?' She laughed. 'Is that what I am now? A favour? I knew things were bad but…'

'Things aren't bad. You kept saying that, things aren't bad.'

'You suggested I get surgery on my face.'

'I suggested that for you, because you were unhappy with… things.'

Emily thought back to the day she'd stood before a mirror and picked at her hips, her sagging boobs, her jawline. All she'd needed was for Jackson to tell her he thought she was beautiful. Instead, he'd given her the name of a mate who might be able to help.

'I miss you, Emily.'

'Me or the pay cheques?' she said, immediately wishing she hadn't. She didn't want to spoil for a fight. She didn't need the negativity in her life, in her home.

'I miss you, Emily,' he said again, getting up from his seat and moving towards her. 'I miss us.' He pulled her face towards him. 'I don't understand why you just left? Was it the clinic? Did you feel guilt about what we did? It was the right decision, baby. We're just not in that place at the moment. You don't really want a child, you'd hate it. All the nappies and muck and grubby fingers.'

He'd hate that, she thought, moving from his touch.

'What changed? What made you just up and leave so suddenly. For you to go without talking to me, without even packing anything.'

'I didn't need anything. I have it all here.'

'But, I thought we had it good. We had dreams, things we'd not yet achieved.'

'People change. Dreams change.'

'Do they? Really?'

'Yes, Jackson. They do. I've changed. I don't want to live to work any more. I want truth, I want honesty.'

'I've never been anything other than honest.'

Emily looked away. He probably had always been honest, which was more than *she* was being right now. 'I want normality.'

'*This?*' he asked, incredulous.

'Yes! This! What's so wrong with this?' She moved to the sink, gazing out of the window at the grass that needed cutting and the rambling rose that was now in full bloom. 'This is everything I want. Well…

nearly everything.' She was under no illusion that becoming a mother would be hard, she'd seen enough women do it to know how difficult it could be, but she wanted the challenge. She wanted to see what she was really made of.

'How was it?' he asked, gently. Emily's shoulders dropped. 'I kept thinking about you having to go through with it on your own. I just … I couldn't get away, babe. I know that must have hurt, but I really couldn't. I called you.'

'I know.'

'You never called back. You didn't even answer my text messages. When Mason came, it was only because I couldn't leave straight away. I've had to sort a lot out to come now, it's not ideal…' Emily bit the inside of her lip. 'But for you to do something like this, I guess I knew you had to be desperate, and all I could think was how hard it must have been, how sad you must have felt. How empty…' Jackson moved beside her, slipping his arms around her waist, his hands resting on her stomach making her flinch and move away. 'We did the right thing, Emily. You know we did.'

'Jackson…' She turned to face him.

'You need me, Emily. We need each other.'

'Do we? Or was it habit? Was it just because it was comfortable to stay together? When I talked to you about the baby you just—'

'Maybe we can talk about it again, in a few years' time. Maybe things will change. Maybe there will be a better time.'

'Jackson.'

'Don't do this to us, Emily. Don't ruin everything—'

'I didn't go through with it,' she said, her voice low, frightened. Jackson froze, staring. 'I couldn't do it. I know I said I would, but I just couldn't. I needed more time. That's why I'm here…' Jackson said nothing and Emily's heart fractured. 'And now I know I want this baby, I need it. It's right for me. I know you don't want to be a father, I don't expect anything of you. I am not coming to you for support, you just have a right to know. And now you do.'

'But we agreed…' he said, stepping back away from her.

'I know. I know what we said…'

Jackson looked from her eyes to her belly. He glanced out of the window then down to his glass. He twisted the stem and wine swilled. He shook his head, he rubbed his hands through his hair.

'Jackson… say something…'

Jackson silently stood. He stared at her for what felt like an age. Then he turned and walked out of her front door without a single glance back.

Jess

Jess flung on the lights at home, catching sight of her reflection in the black of her kitchen window. She stared at the whitewashed walls and clutter free surfaces. Her home was the polar opposite of Amanda's, it was stripped back, bare. She had no photos or mementos from the past. She opened the cupboard to reach for a glass tumbler. She'd never been one to take photos, never mind stick them to the inside of her cupboard doors, maybe she should start. She pulled out a new bottle of her favourite Cornish gin, a gift from a client. Peeling the faux wax from the lid she felt a puff of pride at a job well done, before her heart dipped. These were her photos and mementos, gifts from clients… it was so one-dimensional, so basic.

Which was her all over.

What was she doing with her life? She was forty and she'd achieved nothing of significance, apart, perhaps, from buying her own home. Matt had a girlfriend. They had a life together, couple friends. They had kids and Jess marvelled at how he was with them, a brilliant, warm and funny dad. Her parents had completed steady but successful careers and were now enjoying retirement in their garden, or mini-cruises to places they'd never seen. She thought about Lolly and her little family. How desperate she was to expand and how important it was to her to experience the love from a mother to a daughter. Had Jess ever felt anything intense and life-affirming?

But she didn't need to answer because she knew she had. And she knew she'd walked away from it.

Was it time to make some changes and, if so, where should she start? Was leaving work running away from things or the chance to start something new? She didn't really think she wanted children, but that didn't mean she didn't want a family of sorts. A partner. Maybe a dog. Maybe friends who had family. People she could care for. Were the girls in her future? Emily? Could she be friends without telling her what happened when they were teenagers? Did she ever suspect anything? The party had been at her house, after all. Opening up to the girls today, Jess certainly felt they could be in her life, whether she told Emily everything or not. Did they feel the same? The way Amanda kicked them all out, she wondered. But what was it Amanda said? It was complicated. What was complicated?

Jess flipped open her laptop. Facebook stared back at her. People's lives splashed in the form of photos, updates, memes. Jess rarely posted anything, was always more of a lurker than a sharer. Maybe that's the first change she should make, update her status. She thought for a moment, then tapped out:

Met up with old friends today. Where does the time go? Was so great to see them.

She clicked post then sighed at how dull it was. Almost immediately Matt posted, *Fuck me. You have friends?*

She wanted to laugh because he always could poke fun and it did generally make her smile, but this time, somehow, it stung. With the exception of the girls – three women she'd not seen in twenty years – her friends were colleagues. Often colleagues that were significantly younger than her. People her own age had disappeared over time, usually as they got married, had children, moved their lives on from pickling in alcohol before passing out in front of *Sex and the City* reruns. Her hand rested on the gin stopper. Something had to change. She had to change. Not change because she wasn't good enough but change because the life she had was not the life she wanted any more. Maybe it had never been the one she wanted, maybe it had been the life she'd happened upon because she didn't know what else to do. She didn't remember having hopes and dreams as a teenager. Or in her twenties. She hadn't had dreams since she was fifteen. As a kid, she'd wanted to be a singer or a hairdresser or a nurse or a vet. As she got a bit older, she'd told her parents of a plan to have a small holding for all the dogs and horses and pandas she'd rescue. How quickly those dreams dissolved. Replaced with an emptiness. Not once had young Jess dreamed this life: at home with another bottle of alcohol and few plans for the coming weeks other than work, work and more work. Her phone rang, Matt's number flashed up.

'Hey, loser. How was it?'

'It was good. It was nice. I mean… they were all lovely and it was nice to catch up and I hope we'll stay in touch. I think you were right.'

'This is not news.'

'Don't be smug.'

'Come on then, what was I right about?'

'You were right that it's time I made some changes.'

'Like what?'

Jess thought for a moment. What *could* she change? What in her life had any capacity to be different? There was so little variation, so few options to choose from. 'I'm going to leave work.'

'Oh, Jess! We've talked about this. You can't walk away just because of Jay.'

But Jess realised, in that moment, that this wasn't about Jay. This was about her. Totally and utterly about her. Young her who'd had dreams. Teenage her who'd had them taken away. 'It's not because of him, it's because of me. Because I deserve better from my life. Because I want more from my life.'

'Christ, who are you and what have you done with my sister.'

'I mean it, Matt.'

'I believe you, I just wonder where it's all come from.'

'I don't know. Meeting the girls, it made me think. Maybe I should go travelling again.'

'You hated that.'

She flicked on the kettle, staring out of the kitchen window. 'True. Maybe I should retrain.'

'Better. What have you always wanted to do?'

'I don't know. I don't know what I've always wanted to do. And maybe that's all the more reason to sort this.'

A small voice mumbled in the background of Matt's phone line. 'Look, I need to get off, it's my turn to bath the kids. Do some research. Dream big, little sister. Just don't make any rash decisions until you've talked them through with a sensible grown-up.'

'Well, that can't mean you then!' she said as he put the phone down.

Jess sat down at her table, pulling her laptop round to face her. She pushed all the work papers out of reach before sitting with a Google search on her screen. *Finding yourself at 40* she typed. She scrolled and read, she clicked and clicked through pages and pages of advice. The only thing that stuck out was something on Psychologies that said she should sit and listen, be aware of all that was around her because the universe was speaking if she were only prepared to take note of the hints. The adverts, the people she met, songs on the radio. So she sat, and she listened. And it was silent, so she went over to the window ledge and switched on her radio, excited to hear what song might play, how it might determine her future, how it might inspire the next phase of her life… and as the music kicked in, Jess realised BBC Radio Cornwall were playing the worst of all Madonna songs ever recorded, 'La Isla Bonita'.

She was going to have to listen harder.

Lolly

Lolly stood in the shower, enjoying the sting of red-hot water. She ran her hands through her hair, tipping her head forward to massage her neck and shoulders. She missed that kind of sex, the kind where it was just about the two of them, living in the moment. No need to worry about the kids coming in, or one of them coming too loudly and waking them up. It felt good. She dried her hair with a towel, padding down past the framed family photos on the staircase. She paused on the one of them on their wedding day, stood before the window in the tiny hotel room they exchanged their vows in, his head bent down to kiss her full on the lips. The only wedding photo they had on view. How life had changed since they got married, and not just because of the arrival of the boys. Kitt's work had taken him away, then back home, then away again. Her own work had got more stressful as the department faced cutbacks and the number of patients per physio increased. Life was stressful, and that was before they'd got to the bit about paying the bills. The constant lurch from one month to the next, wondering if they had enough income to cover the outgoings. That had been one of the reasons Kitt had given as to why they shouldn't have any more children, back when they first started discussing it, she'd persuaded him it'd be fine, but she didn't really know for sure herself. She just knew she couldn't let something like that be a reason not to try.

And though that was still the case, she had to stop being so one-dimensional about a baby. If the last hour had taught her anything, aside from the fact that sex just was more comfortable in a bed these days, it was that she'd lost sight of what she and Kitt needed for a happy life together. Some balance. Some time for them. Some time when she wasn't just thinking about getting up the duff. She took a heavy breath in; the house was full of the smell of roast chicken and garlic. She could hear him clattering in the kitchen, bringing the last of their meal together. His infamous roast potatoes, garlic oil drizzled Mediterranean veg, the proper gravy that he was always so good at, no granules when he cooked. And she smiled because she loved that he cooked, she loved that he cared enough to try when things got too close to bad. She loved him, she always had. And she knew that he loved her, they were a team.

She went into the lounge to put some lights on, drawing the curtains on the dark skies. Kitt's phone lay on the coffee table, so she picked it up. He was still listening to Gary Barlow and she knew he'd prefer some of his own music. So she pressed her thumb on the home screen, trying to remember his password. And then her heart stopped at the sight of a message from a number not stored in his phone.

It's clear you have no respect for me, and I couldn't care less. But your wife? Perhaps it's time you told her the truth.

Amanda

Pete waited at the top of the stairs for Amanda. 'Don't panic, she's going to be okay.'

'Where is she? What did she take?'

He pulled her in for a hug, squeezing her tight. 'It sounds like she didn't take anything, more likely her drink was spiked.'

Amanda pulled back, her hair catching in Pete's beard leaving them connected for longer than either intended. 'Spiked! What the hell? Why do people do that sort of thing? In the middle of the day too. Jesus!' She followed him through the double doors and down the winding corridor to Zennor's ward. 'Oh god, did she… was she…'

'No! No, we don't think so. Becky found her slumped in a corner of the pub. She's just through here, sleeping it off.'

'I told her to keep an eye on her drink,' said Zennor's friend Becky, her face pale, her eyes red from crying. 'It happened to one of our mates, we know people do this. I can't believe she put it down.' Becky looked to her feet. 'I'm so sorry, I don't know what to say.'

Amanda sat down beside her. 'Don't worry. It's not your fault, nor your responsibility to keep an eye on her.'

'And she's going to be fine, they said so, didn't they?' said Pete, taking up the seat on her other side. 'It could have been so much worse, had you not been there. You did all the right things.'

Becky sniffed, then nodded.

'Look, get yourself home, love,' said Amanda, opening her purse to find some cash. 'Here, take this, get a taxi back. We'll take over from here, okay?' Becky looked up, unconvinced. 'Go on, go home. Her dad's here, I'm here. She's going to be fine.'

Becky sniffed again then pulled her coat around her, taking the money Amanda held out. 'Thank you, if you're sure you don't mind.'

'Course not.'

Amanda watched Becky wander off down the corridor, turning to face Pete who was watching her. 'Poor lass, she must have been terrified.'

'Dunno what she was more worried of, the fact it happened or the fact she had to tell us.

'Poor thing, I bet she was terrified. Shit, my head.' Amanda searched in her bag for painkillers, her head beginning to throb from a combination of stress and alcohol. Amanda stretched her arms, then scratched at her head and neck.

'You alright?' asked Pete, moving up to sit beside her.

'Nope.' Amanda knew there was no point pretending otherwise with Pete, he always knew, even when she did her very best hiding.

'Wanna talk about it?' he asked, taking the blister pack from her fumbling hand and popping two tablets into her palm.

'Nope.'

'That's what I always admired about you, your ability to really open up to your feelings.'

'Shut your face and don't be a dick.'

Amanda knocked the tablets back, swigging the last remnants of warm, flat Coke from a bottle in the bottom of her bag. She let out a sigh.

'She *is* going to be fine!'

'I know, I know. It's not that really...' The tablets were stuck in the back of her throat and she could taste the bitter, acidic chalk as they began to break down. 'It's just been one of those days. And this has topped it off nicely.'

'I know what you mean. I was just about to watch *Poldark*, imagine how pissed off I was to get the call.'

Amanda let out a laugh. 'You were not.'

'How do you know? Maybe Aidan Turner drives me wild with desire too?'

'I happen to know that he's lacking a few crucial accoutrements for your taste.'

'Oh but that stubble,' Pete said, with mock desire.

Amanda had always liked Pete's ability to shift her mood. It was never in that excruciating, *give us a smile love, it might never happen*, kind of way. More just gentle poking until she relented. He hadn't changed, in all the years they'd known one another. He barely looked any different either, which irritated her.

'The nurse said they'd keep her in overnight, just to be sure. You don't have to stay, if you don't want to.'

'No, I know. I guess I'm here now though, not sure I fancy going home either.'

'So what's up then?'

Amanda thought for a moment. 'If you knew something about someone that you thought they had to know, but you knew that telling them would really hurt them, would you still tell them?'

'You're sleeping with Aidan Turner?' Amanda shot him a look. 'Okay, okay. Sorry. Erm... would I tell them? I don't know. I guess it depends.'

'On what?'

'On if they really would be better for knowing or if I just thought they might.'

'They would definitely be better off for knowing. But it will completely ruin them.'

'Then I don't know I'd want to be the one to do it. Can't someone else tell them?'

'Someone else should!' she said, 'but someone else definitely won't have the bollocks to.'

'Ah, so it relates to a man.'

'Doesn't it always?'

'No. Not always.' Pete got out his tobacco tin and started rolling a cigarette.

'Crash us one, would you?'

He rolled his eyes, but she knew he would. She always loved his roll-ups. 'Come on, walk with me. I believe it's frowned upon to smoke in hospitals these days.'

She hooked her arm through his. 'Bloody smoking bans.'

Outside, they leant against the road sign facing onto the side of Home-base at the retail outlet. It was unusually quiet, only the occasional car leaving the hospital car park. Amanda yawned, exhausted.

'Long day?' asked Pete.

'I guess you could say that, a lot has happened, that's for sure.' Pete smoked quietly, one hand stuffed into his jean pocket. 'I met up with some old friends from school. Not seen them in years. Do you remember me talking about Jess, Emily and Lolly?'

'Course.'

'So, Emily's moved back here and it's been so bloody long since we saw each other, we had a catch up.'

'Nice.'

'It was. We had a good chat. I mean, life's moved on for us all, you know.'

'Well you're all old now, aren't you?'

'Thanks.'

'So, you had a nice time with them, but presumably know something that one of them needs to know?'

'Exactly.'

'So why can't you just tell them?'

'Because it would incriminate me too!'

'Ah…' Pete pushed off the road sign to turn and face her. 'And we don't like to incriminate ourselves now, do we?'

Amanda let out a groan because when he put it like that, it did sound pretty selfish. And she wanted to talk to Pete because she had told him loads of secrets in the past and he'd never once judged. But this was different. And if he judged her for this, she didn't know what she'd do. It wasn't like his opinion mattered to her… but his opinion mattered.

'Look, don't worry. I'll work it out. Now, why don't you go home and get some rest, I'll stay here with Zennor.' Pete looked at her, presumably wondering if it was a good idea to leave given their daughter's current opinion of her mother. 'Go, please. I'll be fine. She probably won't wake up until tomorrow now anyway and then you can be here and make like you never left her bedside.'

'I'd never do that.'

'I know. Go.'

Pete gave Amanda a kiss and went as if to leave. 'You know, I'm always here if you wanna talk.'

'I know you are. I don't want to. Not just yet.'

He shook his head. 'I will never work you out, Amanda Kenwyn.'

'If it's any consolation, I suspect I won't work me out, either.'

As Pete walked away, Amanda resisted the urge to call him back and tell him everything. This was her mess, she needed to sort it. No man had bailed her out before, she wasn't about to let them now.

Lolly

Kitt pulled the seat out for her as she came into the room. He shook out a linen serviette waiting for her to sit down, no doubt so that he could drape it artfully across her lap.

'You've got a message,' Lolly said, passing him his phone. 'I didn't mean to read it, but I was looking for some music and... well...'

Kitt took the phone, studying her face as he did. She fixed him with a look that she hoped would put the fear of god up him because though she'd stood for a few minutes in the lounge, trying to think of a rational reason why this message might not spell doom for the rest of their evening, she was really struggling to come up with a way that could be.

She didn't sit down, as he opened up his messages. She didn't breathe as something like fear flickered across his face. She didn't move as he paused, probably trying to come up with some reasonable excuse as to what the message meant.

'It's not...' he started, but stopped before he finished, presumably because he knew that was a pretty weak starting point. 'The thing is...'

Lolly folded her arms. Waiting. There was no way she was going to make this easy for him. He looked down at his phone again, deleting the message before throwing his phone down on the table. 'Well?' she said, eventually.

Kitt dropped into his chair, head in hands. 'I don't know how to tell you.' Lolly stiffened. 'I just… I couldn't tell you. I didn't want to let you down, I really tried to… It just didn't feel right…'

'What didn't feel right, Kitt? Hmm? What truth have you got to tell me?' In her head, she'd already packed his bags and kicked him out because if this truth was that he was having an affair she now operated a one strike and you're out position.

'I lost my job.'

'You what?'

'My job. I lost it. Weeks ago.'

Lolly dropped down into the chair. How could he have lost his job? He'd been working, she'd seen it. He'd been heading out of the house to the office. He negotiated working from home to try and be around a bit more… he said it was a trial run… he said they might let him do more hours at home if things worked out. 'Weeks ago?' she asked.

'It was all so sudden and… I didn't know what to do or say.' He stumbled over his words and Lolly sat aghast.

'So who's that message from?' she said, wanting to read the words again but she'd already seen him delete it.

'Katy.'

'Katy, Katy?' Kitt looked away. 'But her number's stored in your phone, Kitt. That wasn't her number.'

'I deleted it, when she let me go. I was so angry that she could do that to me. To us. I deleted her number.'

'But… how could she? She knows what your job means to us, why did it have to be you?' They'd both known his boss for years. They'd spent time together, she'd been round for barbecues. She knew Katy was his boss, but she sort of thought they were friends as well.

'That's what I said; there were other people that could have gone. Like John, he does nothing most of the time, why couldn't he go? She said her hands were tied, and I didn't know what to say, I didn't know how to tell you…' He broke off, his eyes filling with tears. 'I just couldn't let you down like that, Lolly. I didn't want to lie, but I didn't know what else to do and I knew you'd worry. I thought I'd be able to fix it before you found out.'

'But you've just been paid.'

'That was my last one. I don't know where my next pay cheque is coming from. I thought I had something sorted the other day and it fizzled out.'

'Where have you been going every day?'

'I've been all over, setting up in cafes for the day until it was my time to come back.'

'But what about the other day when you got held up at work and couldn't pick up the kids.'

'I… I…' He dropped his head, shaking it. 'I went for a trial with one of those door-to-door sales companies. I thought maybe I could hack it and get that to work in the short-term, but I couldn't bear it, Lolly, it was awful.'

Lolly moved around to him, 'Oh, love. Come here, oh my god, you must have been so frightened about it all. I mean, why didn't you just tell me? I can't understand why you didn't just say!'

'I didn't want you to feel under pressure with work and stuff, and I knew you were focussed on other things at the moment. I know how important another baby is to you, I really do.'

'Shhh, shhhh, we don't need to think about that now. It's fine, don't worry. Look, you've made this beautiful meal, let's have a breather, let's eat. Then let's work out how we can sort this.'

'I don't deserve you, Lolly. You are so good to me.'

'We're a team, Kitt. We always have been. When I'm down, you pick me up. Now it's my turn to do it for you. Come on. Let's eat.'

Emily

Sunday. That was when Jackson walked out on Emily without a word. It was now Wednesday and she had no idea where he was, what he was thinking or doing. His Facebook account had gone unusually quiet, nothing even from his interns who would usually take over when he couldn't be bothered. Emily had tried calling him, but the phone just rang out.

She thought about all the conversations they'd had about children. When they first got together and he told her he'd never wanted them before he met her, but that maybe she'd make him think again. When they'd been together a few years and a friend of theirs got pregnant, making her broody, he'd told her he thought he was getting too old, but 'never say never; maybe when there was a better time'. Or when she first told him she was pregnant and he accused her of doing it on purpose to trap him, which made no sense, they'd been together for years. And yet he was insistent. She knew full well he hadn't wanted kids. That he'd only ever said maybe because he wanted to like the idea but what if he ended up like his own, absent, dad; hadn't she thought about that? About bringing an unwanted child into the world. Had she considered his needs in it all?

She'd been so devastated by his reaction she'd reluctantly agreed to let him book the clinic. She wasn't sure she was ready for a baby. She didn't know if she could change her life to become a mother. Yet she'd been terrified when she arrived for her appointment. Was that his problem? Was he actually just frightened? Was it more fear of becoming a father than a dislike that he had? Had she just exposed him to the single biggest thing he feared, and that was why he needed to get away? Put time and space between them whilst he worked out what he wanted to do. Like she did. She left because it felt right, but this baby meant they were connected forever. Could he change his mind? Did she want him to? The longer they were apart, the more she reflected on the twists in their relationship. He had controlled everything in her life from the moment they met, she felt free to be apart from him, and yet... she couldn't ignore the tiny part of her that missed him. She'd loved him for years. Their lives were intertwined. Did she want to try and find a way to make it work, or were her hormones getting the better of her?

'Morning, love. How are you today?' Betty was stacking some shelves just inside the doorway. 'I saw you wandering down here, you're away with the fairies, my girl. What you thinking about?' she asked, shuffling tins to the back and front of her display with rapid action.

'Oh, I don't know. This and that.' Emily wasn't ready to tell her what the this and that was. Betty would probably be one of the first in the village to know, but she wanted to keep the secret a little longer. She was just about adjusting, the feeling she'd got with the girls hadn't gone away. She wanted this baby, she made the right choice not to go through with the abortion, but somehow seeing Jackson walk away so easily made her want to hide the fact a little longer. Could she cope with the questions about the father? If she told them he'd gone, then he decided to come back, would people judge him? 'Actually, one of the things I was thinking about was builders.'

'Builders?'

'Yeah. I think I want to do a bit of work at home, sort a couple of rooms out. Now that I'm staying, there are a few things I want to change around. Really put my mark on the place, you know?'

'Oh, I know.'

'Do you have any recommendations? I'd rather it was someone local.'

'Well, it depends what you want doing? I mean, I don't want to peddle my son out each time, but he is a dab hand and you know what it's like for people down here, we all do a bit of this and a bit of that. Just to keep the wolf from the door.'

'Oh! Well, I hadn't realised. I mean, he might not want to… it's just a bit of a stud wall that needs to come down. And some bits of built in furniture maybe. Nothing major, but I don't think I'd manage it on my own.'

'No, course not. I mean, he'd be doing it in-between other stuff, but if you're not in a tearing hurry.'

Emily thought about how long she had until the baby arrived. 'Well, I mean, I don't need it doing yesterday, but I dunno, I guess over the course of the next few months would be okay…'

'He's away on the boat. Not sure when he'll be back, when the conditions worsen, or he's caught enough I suppose. I'll send him up.'

'If you're sure?'

'Course! It'd be a pleasure. And besides, I reckon he has a twinkle for you.'

Emily coloured immediately. 'Betty! You can't say that…'

Betty let out a generous belly laugh, wiping her eyes with the back of her hand. 'Oh, I'm teasing. Reckon you need a bit of time on your own, don't you? Dunno what has gone off for you these last few years, my girl, but there's a distracted look in your eye. You're here, but not quite present and I'd like to bet that that's got something to do with that man you were hiding from. Now, if I can give you one piece of advice it would be that we're a long time dead, take your moment to focus on you. It's precious.'

Emily picked up the bits she needed, thanked Betty for the shopping and chat, and headed back up the hill home. She hadn't entirely expected the lecture on life from Betty, and she was more than a little disconcerted at her comment about Mac having a sparkle or whatever it was she said, but one thing she was now more certain of than ever, was that she was going to be a mother within six months. If she was going to make the most of this precious time to herself, she needed to get herself together and work out what her new priorities were. And without doubt, her new priorities included the girls. Friendship. She'd read all about how isolated single women can feel when they have children, and she was not about to let that happen to her. Lolly, Jess and Amanda were about to find out just how much she needed them.

Jess

Since Sunday, Jess had lurched from staying put to jacking it all in. Staying put was usually the decision she came to when she wanted to rebel against her heart's desperation to cut all ties with Jay. Leaving was generally the choice when her head was drowned out by hormones and gin. Matt had repeatedly told her not to leave, but the more she thought about it, the more appealing the idea became. And the more she scrutinised that, the more she realised this might not (just) be about Jay, but about her own future too. She hadn't stopped asking herself what she'd done with her life since seeing all the girls and her answers, whilst perfectly acceptable, just hadn't lit her belly with the fire of a colourful life. It was now Wednesday and she couldn't escape the fact that coming into the office every day was getting increasingly fraught with anxiety and discomfort. The work she did was, whilst interesting in the main, still the same sort of thing she'd done for years. She'd allowed herself to become one-dimensional and the realisation was beginning to gnaw away at her conscience.

She wanted to see if she could embrace colour and excitement, things she'd avoided for so long. What life was there to enjoy? What passion? Not sex passion… although she wasn't averse to that either, but passion about other things. Food. Art. Theatre. She'd always wanted to try paddleboarding, she lived in bloody Cornwall and barely saw the sea.

She wanted to visit different countries and – whilst Matt laughed for much longer than was necessary when she suggested this – she couldn't help but wonder what it might be like to experience other cultures now she was a proper, bona fide grown-up. She knew she wasn't the backpacker type, she could never go through that again, but she did love culture. Who's to say she couldn't do all that via Airbnb rooms or three-star hotels?

The longer she sat in this meeting about sales figures for a client's new product, the more she realised it was time to do something different.

'What do you think?' asked Jay, the room falling silent as they all looked to Jess, expectantly.

'Pardon?' Jess looked at her screen, which had gone blank because she'd stopped reading the detail ages ago. She surreptitiously woke it back up again, pretending her login to full screen was in fact a very important note about something she needed to remember for later.

Jay stared at her. 'I'm suggesting we push Cobber's social media back to the client with the advice they recruit an intern to manage it internally.'

'Right.' Jess read through the notes in front of her, realising they were for the previous client discussion. Not Cobber's, the start-up bakery that they'd recently taken on. 'And what's your main reason for that?' she asked, really hoping he'd not already explained it in too much detail beforehand.

'Well, like I said.' Oh. 'I just think that our own social media team are full on and we're missing opportunities for out of hours conversations. They need to take on an approach like Yorkshire Tea or some of the Waterstones' accounts, you know? Chatty, fun, engaging. On from morning 'til night, not just nine 'til five. We need to break the myth that sourdough is artisanal or elitist. They're making specialist products, but they're not specialist prices and I think it's important they're seen as accessible.'

'Yes. Yes. I agree. Okay. Do you want to have that conversation with them, or shall I?'

'We can do it together, later? They're coming in at four, aren't they?'

'Yes! Of course they are. Great. Let's do that then.'

Jess couldn't remember the last time she'd felt so out of touch in a meeting. When she got back to her desk she closed down all the open tabs on her internet browser, vowing to only look at top ten countries to visit information when she got home tonight. Instead, she idly clicked through her emails, deleting the spam. Responding to quick requests for thoughts or advice. She made herself a cuppa, working through the to do list she'd memorised. Her mind wandered to Amanda and Zennor. She'd texted on Monday to check that Zennor was okay and apparently she was going to be fine, but Jess couldn't help but wonder if Amanda was. The sudden pulling back from them all on Sunday set off alarm bells for Jess.

She could head into Truro early, her meeting with Jay wasn't until later. She could drop round, just check if Amanda was really okay.

As Jess was about to knock on Amanda's front door, it swooshed open. 'Lovely to see you, same time next week?' Amanda asked, talking up the hallway. A ruddy cheeked man was about to answer until he saw Jess at the gate to Amanda's house, at which point he did a weird nod then shake of his bowed head, scurrying down the path.

'Jess!' said Amanda, looking after the man as he disappeared down the street. 'What are you doing here?'

Jess felt suddenly weird, like she was somewhere she wasn't supposed to be. 'Oh! I just… well, I wanted to come and check you were okay. I didn't think… I'm sorry, am I interrupting?' she asked.

'No. No, he was leaving anyway. I was just… well… are you okay?'

'I am, I think. You?'

Amanda pulled her dressing gown around her. 'Yeah, yeah. I'm fine. That was… an emergency plumber. I was about to have a shower this morning and couldn't get the hot water to work.'

'Oh. Right.'

'It was the pilot light.'

'Oh, well that's easy to sort then.'

'Yes. He sorted it.' Amanda nodded in the direction of the man who was now nowhere to be seen.

There was an awkward pause, Amanda in her dressing gown, leaning against the door. Jess stood on the bottom step, wishing she had just called instead. 'I was worried about you,' she said in the end, because she'd nothing to lose. 'After Zennor. And Sunday.'

'Oh, it's fine. No… it's…'

Then Jess had a sudden realisation. 'Oh my god!' Her hands flew to her mouth. 'Was that the bloke that messaged? From Sunday. The complicated one?'

'What? No!' Amanda stepped back into the house. 'Christ, no. Come inside.' She pulled Jess in, shutting the door behind her. 'God, were you always this bloody nosy?' she asked, walking away from Jess down the corridor.

'I've been worried. You weren't right on Sunday when we all left, then there was the stuff with Zennor. I just wanted to check in on you.'

'Zennor is fine. Like I said the other day, she had a lucky escape. Tea?'

Jess nodded, pulling a bar stool up to the kitchen worktop. Amanda moved a fifty-pound note from the kitchen side into a tin that appeared to be overflowing with notes.

'Christ, drinks are on you!' said Jess, trying to lighten the mood.

'It's my wages. I'm always paid cash in hand.'

'I didn't realise cleaning pays so well?'

'It doesn't,' said Amanda, fixing Jess with a look. 'Sometimes I think it would make life a lot easier if it did, frankly.'

'What's going on, Amanda? I'm worried about you. What's the matter?'

Amanda looked at Jess, almost scrutinising her. She moved a few things around the kitchen, shut a photo-covered cupboard door. She looked back at Jess, almost a side glance. 'If I tell you something, it's because I need your help, not because I want your judgement.'

'Of course not,' said Jess. 'I'd never judge.'

Amanda laughed to herself. 'We'll see,' she said. Then she paused, before sitting down opposite Jess and saying, 'So, I do clean, here and there, just so I'm not lying to Zennor. But, that's not my only job...'

Amanda

'Right,' said Jess, uncertainly.

Amanda took a deep breath. 'I'm a sex worker.' She said it in the most matter of fact way she could. Jess didn't flinch at first. There was maybe a glimmer of surprise in her eyes, but nothing obvious. Amanda only noticed it really because she knew that some people tried to pretend they weren't shocked when she told them what she did. 'I've done it for a while now. It pays significantly better than hoovering up sand after holidaymakers.' She nodded in the way of her money tin, as if to prove it. 'I was finding it hard to pay the bills. I didn't want to lose this place, it's mine. My sanctuary. It's saved me every time life has got shit.'

Jess blinked.

'I'm not on drugs. Nobody is making me do it. I wasn't abused as a child and I really do like sex.'

'O-kay then...'

'I feel empowered. I'm the most confident I've ever been. It's nice giving people pleasure.'

'I see.'

'So there we are.'

'There we are.'

The two women looked at each other. Amanda was unusually desperate to know what Jess thought. It didn't normally bother her.

She didn't do this job for anyone else, technical specifics aside, she did this for her. But Jess's face was pretty much one of the best poker faces she'd seen.

'So… that guy earlier…'

'Was a client. I'm on a break technically at the moment, need a bit of space. He's someone that usually just wants to chat though, a regular. His wife has Alzheimer's, he's her main carer. I guess I'm his respite and I didn't want to let him down.'

'Right.' Amanda watched as Jess slowly nodded, processing. 'And that's the complication?'

Amanda prickled. 'Kind of.'

'Kind of?'

Amanda groaned into her tea. She'd thought about this pretty much non-stop since Zennor got out of Treliske and Pete promised her he'd try and get them to meet up and talk. Knowing Zennor was going to be okay had eased that worry but brought the whole Trev/Kitt/Lolly thing crashing right back to the forefront of her mind. Hence cancelling all her clients bar this morning's. She needed time away. She needed to think. It was throwing her choices into question. She'd never met a wife before, least of all known one. Karenza said it wasn't her place to tell Lolly but how was she supposed to let one of her oldest friends continue in a marriage that, it seemed to Amanda, functioned on lies. Jess had always been one for good advice, could Amanda trust her on this one too?

'Come on then, talk to me. I'm not judging, maybe I can help.'

Amanda looked down at her hands, wondering where to begin.

'Are you sure you're doing this of your own free will?' Jess asked, suddenly.

'I am! I am, I promise. I know people think that there has to be some dark secret to it all, but there really isn't. It's just a job. And I love it. Until…'

'Until things get complicated.'

'Exactly.'

Jess reached out her hand. 'You can trust me, you know.' She smiled at Amanda who immediately felt as though she wasn't alone. As though she could tell Jess anything and Jess would probably find a way to resolve it. 'Whatever it is, you can talk to me.'

'Okay.' Amanda took a deep breath. 'I have a new client. I've only seen him a few times. And I don't normally hear anything about their private lives, those things are left firmly at the door when they come in. Usually. I have a room down the corridor where I work. Or we go out and eat food, watch a film. Or we talk online, or whatever, you don't probably need the details.'

'Well… I can't help being mildly inquisitive,' said Jess, with a wry grin.

'Maybe some other time.'

'Probably best. Go on.'

'So, this new client is married. Which happens. I don't like it, but I take some comfort from the fact that mostly it's not actually because they don't love their wives. It's not black and white, you know, and I don't feel it's my place to judge.' A point of view she'd always stuck by. But then she hadn't had sex with the husband of a good friend before now. 'The problem is, I know this particular husband's wife.'

Jess's mouth dropped open and for the first time throughout the entire conversation, it was no longer impossible to guess what she was thinking.

'I know, I know. Well… I didn't know, at the time. I knew he was married, but I didn't know who to.'

'And now you do.'

'I do.'

Jess sipped at her tea, mulling over Amanda's revelation. Then her eyes widened, and slowly, she looked up at Amanda. 'Oh no,' she said, quietly. 'It's a friend, isn't it?'

Amanda nodded.

'And you hadn't realised because you'd not seen that friend for a long time.'

Amanda nodded again.

'Like… twenty years or so.'

Amanda put her head in her hands.

'You had sex with Lolly's husband.'

Amanda nodded. 'Shit, Jess, what do I do? I mean… she seems so happy!'

'Well, I guess you stop seeing him. I mean, now you know.'

'Well, of course I stop seeing him. That's not in question. I'm a sex worker not a heartless bitch. I can't see anyone at the moment, this morning excepted. I don't know if I can ever do this job again, in fact. I mean… Lolly!' Amanda's eyes filled with tears she'd been trying not to cry. 'What am I going to do?'

'Should you tell her?'

'By rights, no. I mean, morally, it's ambiguous, but professionally, his privacy was part of the deal. That's why he came to me. Or any other of the workers he's seen. He pays for sex, we don't tell anyone about it.'

'He does this a lot?'

'The way he was… I know that it wasn't his first time.'

'Right. I mean, I don't really understand the business.'

'No.'

'So, you can't tell her.'

'Not really.' Amanda got up out of her seat, slinging her tea down the sink. 'Christ, I need something a bit stronger. You want some?' she asked, offering a glass of wine up.

'I can't, I've got a meeting at three.'

'Benefits of self-employment. I've just declared it a bank holiday.'

'Bonk holiday.'

'Now is not the time for jokes, Jess.'

'You're right. Sorry.'

'What do I do, Jess? How do I get out of this mess?'

Jess thought. 'I'm not sure, love. I don't know.'

'This is A LOT harder than that time I found out Dad was having an affair by skipping school to go to the pub.' Jess gave Amanda a pitying look because no doubt she could remember how many weeks Amanda had played with the idea of getting herself into trouble to let her mum know her dad was being a shit. Again. For the fourth, or maybe fifth time that they knew of. She'd told her mum in the end and her mum, after an afternoon of sobbing and screaming in her general direction, had decided she would stay with her dad because she loved him. That was the day Amanda knew she had to move out as soon as she was able. That decision was hard, but this was somehow worse. Grown-ups were supposed to be able to cope with bad stuff, but this was Lolly. Lolly and Amanda. She didn't feel like a grown-up and she'd put money on the fact that Lolly didn't either.

So how would she cope to hear the news of her husband, and how on earth could Amanda tell her, without landing herself in it and losing someone she'd only just reconnected with. Someone she adored?

Jess

Amanda's bombshell lingered throughout the afternoon meeting. Jess had gazed distractedly out of the window at the river as the tide came in, filling the mucky, dank banks up with salty water that flowed in from the Falmouth Estuary. Boats bobbed and a swan glided past. Jay had nudged her beneath the table, dragging her back into the meeting in which she redeemed herself with a hashtag suggestion that they all loved. By the time their client left, she thought she'd pretty much got away with barely being present.

Well, she got away with it with the client. Jay, on the other hand, muttered something about how it would be useful if she could be there in mind as well as body, before giving her a curt nod after the client left, and heading straight off home. Things had begun to fracture since Sunday. Or maybe it was Jess that had fractured. She'd been wondering about taking a few last-minute days off. Give herself some headspace. She was always in trouble for not using up her holidays. And she had time in lieu available too. They had Jay, did they need her as well?

Post work, she'd gone to the local pub. She ordered a wine, glancing over the menu in case anything took her fancy. Except she wasn't really hungry. She thought about calling Lolly but didn't want Amanda to feel she was trying to stir anything up. She thought about inviting Amanda over to join her but by the time she'd left, Amanda had talked herself into something of a pickle and Jess suspected she maybe needed her own space too.

Jess wondered if any of the women had noticed life getting complicated. Or if they, like her, felt it had come all of a sudden. Perhaps over and above the usual complexities of life. Except it didn't appear that Lolly hadn't fully noticed it herself. Maybe she was in too deep with the baby stuff. How could Kitt do that to her? They'd been such a tight team over the years, or so Lolly suggested. How long had he been using women like Amanda?

Women like Amanda. That made it sound so bad to Jess when she thought about it. What did it even mean? When she told her what she did, Jess had fought back every urge in her body to question why the hell she would be doing that. Her feminist instinct was to immediately call Amanda out for selling herself short. For allowing herself to be objectified. For being taken advantage of. And yet, the more she'd talked about it, the more it seemed to genuinely be something she enjoyed doing. It seemed to be something that really did empower her and as much as Jess perhaps didn't understand how that might be, there was no denying that Amanda seemed happy in her own skin. She was paying her own bills. She was living life her way, using her body the way she wanted to. Wasn't that the epitome of being a feminist? Jess hadn't totally rectified it in her own mind, but perhaps it was the last thing to think about at the moment. The main thing to think about was how on earth they were going to tackle this with Lolly. Or even, should they? Was it their responsibility to tell truths that could break her? That could end her marriage? And if it was, how did they do that without it hurting Amanda too? She hadn't known Kitt was Lolly's husband, Jess one hundred per cent believed her in that respect. It's no wonder she went weird on them all if she was getting messages like the ones

Jess had seen this afternoon. And if he'd turned up at Amanda's house, that could have been… God, awful. Jess shuddered at the thought.

She pulled her phone out, calling Amanda's number.

'Hey, babe,' Amanda answered, her tone melancholic.

'Hey. You okay?'

'I guess.'

'Any clearer on what to do?'

'No.'

'What if I called Lolly, just to check in? I've not spoken to her since Emily and I packed her off in a cab. I could give her a call, see if she had a good time. Find out how things are. Just test the water a little so we know what we're dealing with, you know?'

'It's probably not a bad idea. Just, please, don't say anything to her.'

'Of course I won't. Not yet. I mean, really, the only person to tell her should be her husband.'

Amanda let out a low laugh. 'Yeah, okay. Somehow I don't think that's going to happen.'

'Well, no. But maybe he just needs time.' Amanda let out a noise that told Jess she was unconvinced. 'Look, I'll call her. I'll let you know how it goes. Let's catch up in a few days. I think I'm going to take some time off work anyway.'

'Oh? You okay?'

Jess took her wine from the waiter, mouthing a thank you. 'Yes, I'm fine. Well… maybe I'm having some kind of mid-life crisis. I don't know, seeing you lot has triggered all sorts of feelings I wasn't expecting.'

'Tell me about it.'

Jess smiled. 'Christ, I knew I shouldn't have met up with you all. Bloody pains in the arse. I was perfectly happy in my life before you all came back into it.'

'I can recommend a well-paid alternative if you fancy a career change,' said Amanda and Jess could well imagine the mischievous glint in her eye as she said it.

'No, thank you very much. You will not now, or ever for that matter, get the chance to be my pimp.'

'Shame. You'd make a bloody fortune.'

'I'm hanging up now.'

'And so domineering.'

'Amanda!'

'I'm going. Let me know how things go.'

'Will do.'

Jess pushed her phone across the table, letting it sit beside her laptop. She looked around at the people in the bar, a few people in for post-work drinks. A few others on a pre-theatre meal by the looks of it. If there was one thing Amanda had taught her, it was that you should never judge. As Jess looked around, she wondered if there were any other sex workers in the room. Men or women. Amanda was a normal looking woman. She didn't permanently dress in PVC or wear false eyelashes and plump up her bought and paid for boobs. She was no different to Jess, Lolly or Emily. She was no different to the woman over there, sipping her drink with a coquettish grin. She was no different to the girl behind the bar or the woman who'd just walked in with a newspaper under her arm and a dog by her side. She was normal. Yet, Jess couldn't help thinking Lolly wouldn't see it that way if she ever learned the truth.

Lolly

Lolly jumped off the bus outside the Museum, sneaking up Swifties Ope on her way to Boots up Pydar Street. She was part giggly and part terrified. Giggly because she just had that feeling in the pit of her belly that this test would be different. It was probably the wrong time of her cycle, but she hadn't been able to shake off the idea that it needed to be done and buying a test from the chemist at work was not an option. She was then terrified because she rarely came into Truro on her lunch break and didn't want anyone she knew to see her here either. She just wanted to nip in, get the test, eat one of their lunch deals down Victoria Gardens, then head back to work to lock herself in the toilets.

With a furtive glance over her shoulder, she grabbed two packs of the Early Detection kits along with a cheese and onion sandwich and a bag of Monster Munch because she couldn't remember the last time she'd had a bag of pickled onion crisps. Actually, she could. It was when she and Kitt went to celebrate their first wedding anniversary in Scotland, about a hundred years ago. She'd eaten pickled onion Monster Munch on the bank of Loch Ness and Kitt said they'd never spot Nessie if she thought Lolly was a monster eater. Or something. It was silly nonsense, back when they were silly. When they had time and space to talk waffle and get away with it. Back when they had no kids at all and... and he had a job.

She queued up, waiting her turn, remembering how he looked this morning as he left home. She'd told him he didn't have to pretend any more. That he should take the day off, stay in his PJs, watch some crap on Netflix with his hand down his pants, should the mood take him. He wasn't having it though. He said something about needing to stay in the game, to keep connected. He had meetings set up. His CV to update again. Lolly hated to see him so skittish about it, so uncertain. And the guilt, she could still sense that even though she'd told him not to feel that way. But he'd always been that way, she could see that now. He always seemed to feel guilt or responsibility for something, and she knew it was because he was brought up to support and provide for his family, but it wasn't necessary.

'Lolly?' A hand touched her arm and her heart stopped. She tried to hide the test as she turned around to see Kitt's former boss.

'Katy!'

'Hey lovely, how are you?' She leaned in to kiss her on both cheeks and Lolly wondered at what point she might show any kind of remorse for firing her husband. 'It's been so long, how are you?'

'I'm okay. I guess. I mean, you know, all things considered.' Since my husband is out of work and depressed is what she really wanted to say, but Lolly wasn't up for making a scene.

'I said to your other half a few days back, it's been ages since we've seen you. We should have you over again, it'd be lovely to catch up.'

'Would it?' asked Lolly, staggered by how brazen Katy was being. 'Wouldn't it be a tad awkward, I mean… considering…'

Katy looked at Lolly confused. 'I don't understand, what do you—'

'Next, please.'

The cashier looked at Lolly expectantly. Lolly's palms itched with the pregnancy test clenched within. Katy looked bright and totally normal and Lolly didn't want to cause a scene. Not here. Not now.

The automated cashier call played out. 'Cashier number four.'

Lolly made her excuses. 'Oh look, sorry, I'd better…'

'Of course, yes. Okay. Well, maybe we'll see you sometime, I'll talk to your hubby.'

'Really! Don't you think you'd be better off leaving him alone right now?' Katy's mouth dropped open. Lolly shook her head in disgust, turning on her heel.

Shaking, she handed her money over, apologising for needing to buy a bag. She rammed her stuff in the bag and scuttled out of the shop without a backwards glance at Katy. How dare she? How dare she sack Kitt then behave like nothing had happened? Lolly half wanted to turn back round and give her a piece of her mind but she didn't want to embarrass Kitt and she didn't have masses of time in any case. Sitting in Victoria Gardens was probably for the best. Let herself calm down. Anxiety and anger wouldn't be good for this baby… if she was indeed as pregnant as she felt she just might be. That had to be her focus now, her priority.

Taking a breath to adjust her composure, she opened the pack of sandwiches on her lap and scrolled through her phone as a message came through.

How are you? Did you get home okay? It was SO lovely to see you!

Lovely Jess. How good it had been to get the girls back together. How connected did she feel to them? It surprised her. Even Amanda, despite her cutting the afternoon short. It was like she'd found her tribe. The women she could rely on. She had friends, of course she did. She loved Beth at work. She had the mums from school, but these women were different. They were old souls to her, people who, she now realised, she had missed. She took a bite of her sandwich, giddy to be able to message back. *I'm okay ta, just snatching five minutes peace in town before heading back to work. How are you? It was great to see you too, thanks for making sure I got back.*

The bubbles of Jess typing back gave Lolly a warm feeling. The bite of pickled onion Monster Munch, however, did not. They may have been a mistake. Did they always get caught up in your teeth like that? She rooted her tongue around the side of her mouth wishing she'd stuck to a French fry.

We should do it again. Maybe dinner one night? Do you like curry?

Lolly loved curry but now was probably not the time to be spending cash on meals out. *Things a bit tight at the moment. Cash wise. It seems Kitt has lost his job. I didn't know, poor bloke admitted it when I got back the other night. I saw a text, thought it was something awful and it turned out he'd been pretending to still be in work because he was so worried about letting me down. Can you imagine? So, curry might have to wait until he's got sorted, but you could all come round to mine one night? He'd hide himself away, no problem. Let's do that. A cheese night. And wine.* As she typed, she grew more excited. Kitt would be fine to keep the kids away, watch a film up in their bed. Lolly could get a bit of cheese in; the girls could bring a few bits too; it would be cheap and they could talk all night, she'd love to have them round. *What do you think? Would you all come?*

The dots of Jess's response didn't come straight away. She was probably at work. Lolly finished her sandwich. She unenthusiastically ate the last of her Monster Munch. She took a sip of water from the bottle she carried everywhere and brushed down her clothes. Still no response. Had she been too eager? Oh god, what if Jess was being polite? What if they never wanted to get together again? Lolly couldn't bear the idea of not seeing them for another twenty years. *I'll message the others, set up a group. It's no problem if you can't make it. I know how busy we all are. Better get back to work. Talk soon! X* She hovered over send, unsure if it was a bit much. She flicked back through her messages, it was fine, wasn't it? She'd not said anything stupid or offensive. Jess was probably just busy. That's all. And Lolly was being needy. One of her least favourite traits. She clicked send, dropped her phone in her bag and headed back to work. She had a pregnancy test (or two) to take.

Jess

Jess walked into her boss's office with what she hoped would come over as respectful but not to be messed with. She was well aware that what she was about to say would come as a surprise, but her gut was telling her this was important and, having ignored her instincts for most of her adult life, Jess felt now was the time to stop.

'Hi, Susan. Can we talk?'

Susan looked up from her screen, flicking her glasses off onto the desk in front of her. 'Of course. What can I do for you? How did you get on with Cobber's? Did they go for the intern idea? I think it's great, will really free us up to focus on the detail of their expansion.'

'Yes, they're fine. Actually, we managed to land them a piece in *The Times* this morning so they're not questioning anything.'

'Nice work. Come on then, what is it?'

'Well, I know this is not going to be ideal, but I need to take some time off.'

Susan pulled her diary in front of her, pen poised. 'You're allowed time off, when would you like?'

'Well... I could really do with tomorrow and next week too. I've shifted things around, the team have got it all in hand. I know it's last minute but I just... I have some thinking to do.' Susan put her pen down. 'A few things have happened recently, I need to take stock. I need space to think.'

'Are you okay?'

'Yeah, I am.' Jess wasn't sure that was entirely true. She didn't feel okay, but then she didn't feel ill. If anything, she felt confused. 'I don't know how to explain it other than maybe it's a mid-life thing. Maybe it's hormones. Maybe it's just that I've not had much of a break and I feel I need to sleep, but I promise, if you can let me go, I'll be back, full up and raring to go.'

Susan looked at her, narrowing her eyes just enough to suggest that she was trying to work out what was really going on. Jess stood tall, zipping up like her Pilates instructor had always advised. She kept eye contact and she hoped, above all else, that Susan wouldn't detect any of the self-doubt she was having right at this moment. Not least because Jess wasn't sure where the self-doubt was founded. Did she really know what she wanted to do for the next few days? Aside from trying to work out how to help Lolly and Jess and writing pros and cons for all the alternative career ideas she'd come up with. She'd realised in the last twenty-four hours that her past was catching up with her. Stuff left undealt with. Seeing the girls had triggered it and now she just needed to work out how to stop burying the things that hurt the most. And for that, she needed not to be in an office with Jay.

'You sure you're okay?' Susan asked.

'Positive.'

'And the team have got it covered?'

'Million per cent.'

'I guess that's one of the benefits of having Jay here now, there's two of you to shoulder the overall responsibility.'

'Yes. Definitely a benefit.' Jess tried not to let the words stick in her throat.

'You can never go on holiday together!' Susan said, laughing. And Jess had to remind herself that she didn't mean together, together. 'Go on, no problem. Have a few days. Can we call if we need you?'

'Sure. No problem,' lied Jess, because actually she had already decided to turn her phone off the second she walked out of the door.

'Go on then, get out of here. See you a week on Monday. Have fun.'

Jess thanked Susan and walked out of the door feeling an odd mixture of relief and trepidation. Did she really want time to think? Or was thinking about to make life more difficult? Thinking could unravel her; it's why she had always avoided it. Thinking set her off down a path of lost loves and missed opportunities. Thinking made her revisit stuff that changed the course of her life forever. Space and time she needed, no doubt. But thinking… that might be a very different matter.

As Jess left the building, Jay jumped out of a cab, taking a receipt from the driver and stuffing it into his back pocket. It was probably polite to let him know what was going on, though his face dropped when he saw her waiting.

Ignoring the fact, she said, 'I'm heading off. Taking a few days away. And all of next week.'

'You're what?'

'Heading off.'

'I didn't realise you had leave booked?'

'No, I didn't.' Jess pulled her bag into her chest, clasping her fingers across its bulk. 'A last-minute thing really.'

'Oh, right. Nice.' His tone did not suggest he thought this was nice at all.

'The team are fine, they know what I was on with. They can pick stuff up until I'm back.'

'Right. I was rather hoping we could catch up, I wanted to chat about a few things. Jess.' He looked over his shoulder, pulling her into the doorway of an empty shop. 'This isn't how I wanted to do this, Jess, but we need to talk. We need to sort this out.' He sighed, checking again that there was nobody in earshot. His hand fell from her arm to her hand, their fingers lightly touched. He looked at her like he used to look at her, back when they first got together. 'I didn't come here to cause problems for you but—'

'But what? Huh? What did you come here for? You're a married man, Jay. You've a beautiful wife. What the hell are you doing, playing with fire? Playing with my emotions.'

'That's not… it isn't like that.'

'Isn't it? Because with you holding my hand, with you looking at me the way you're looking at me right now, that is how it feels.' She flicked his hand from hers. 'I can't do this, Jay. I can't. I thought I could, but I'd be lying to myself and I don't deserve that.' He stared at her, fracturing her resolve. 'Go. Go and get on with your job. Leave me alone.'

'What about work stuff?'

'It'll have to wait until I get back, won't it? You'll survive. You've coped perfectly well without me before, we both know that.'

Jay looked injured. 'Right. Well. That told me.'

'What do you mean?'

'No, nothing. When you're back. Fine.'

'Jay!'

'No, no. I get it. It's fine. Maybe it's a good thing you're not here for a few days. Might give me a chance to get my feet under the table without feeling like your subordinate.'

'What on earth makes you feel that?' Jess said, lowering her voice as one of the girls came out and jogged down to the bakers.

'Oh, I don't know. Your tone in meetings. Your superiority. Your heading off on annual leave that you hadn't booked, without even talking to me about it.'

'Why do I have to talk to you about it?'

'Because we're a team? Because as your opposite number, we need to communicate. Christ, Jess, I thought we could be adult about this but it feels like you've done nothing but put obstacles up since I got here.'

'Obstacles! I didn't ask for you to start work here.'

Jay looked at her, eyes wide.

'Sorry. I'm sorry, that was… I don't mean it. I just… this is harder than I was expecting.'

'Isn't it.' He was deadpan. Frustrated. He looked at her as though he held her in the lowest possible esteem and now she couldn't work out whether he'd come back to be closer to her or because there was a job he wanted to do and either way, he was married. And she deserved better than all of this. That much she did know.

'I once knew someone, a girl, many years ago. She was brilliant, but she had no clue. She was smart, but didn't realise. She was the love of my life and losing her was the hardest thing I ever lived through. But I did live through it. And I learned to love again. But what I took from her was the importance of living your best life. Of pushing yourself, of finding things that challenge you. And whilst now I wonder if that's really why she went away, or if she was even that person I believe I knew, I will never forget what she taught me.' Jess held her breath, not daring to speak. 'And I don't know, maybe in another life things would have been different.'

'Jay…'

'But we are where we are. And life moves on. And we all have to as well. I just hope that one day, the girl I fell in love with can find the person I know deep down she is. Because she deserves to be happy. She deserves to smile. It's just a shame I was not the person to make that happen.'

'Jay…'

'Have a good break, I'll handle things here.' He took her hand again, he gave it the smallest squeeze that was so full of a love she used to know that Jess almost lost control of her heart.

Then Amanda called.

Amanda

Amanda padded around her kitchen until the line connected. 'Jess, it's me.'

'Hey, how are you?'

Did she sound weary? Amanda wasn't certain but if she didn't now, she would in a moment. 'So, guess who I got a message from.'

'His lordship.'

'Yup. And guess what he's done now?'

'I don't need to guess.'

'You've spoken to Lolly?' Amanda braced herself against the kitchen worktop, the only place she could steady her anger at this point.

'I messaged her, like we agreed. Turns out—'

'He's lost his job,' Amanda finished her sentence, still shaking in disbelief at his manipulation both of Lolly and of the situation. 'Or that's what he's told her. And if Lolly mentions anything, I'm to go along with it.'

'Of course you are.'

'Yup. She saw a text I sent him saying that I thought he should tell her and he managed to turn that into "I've lost my job and you need to feel sorry for me" instead.'

'But as far as we know, he hasn't lost his job at all. It's just a lie to cover up the fact he was seeing you?'

'As far as we know.'

'Wow. He's really something.'

'He also thinks I should put some distance between us again. Thinks it's unhealthy for his wife.'

'Maybe him fucking other people is unhealthy for his wife.'

Amanda stayed quiet, she knew Jess wasn't judging her, but the venom in her tone made Amanda feel part way responsible.

'Sorry, that wasn't directed at you.'

'I know, I know.'

'This isn't your fault,' said Jess and though Amanda knew it wasn't, she appreciated Jess saying it out loud. 'God, what do we do now? We can't just let her think that, can we? Is it our place to get involved? I don't know how these things work any more.'

'No, me neither.'

Amanda could hear cars in the background, seagulls cawing. 'Where are you? You got a meeting?'

'No, no. Actually, I've taken some time off.'

'Because of this? Oh god, I feel so bad.'

'No! No, not you. Not this. Just… everything. Life. A sudden realisation that I've been avoiding dealing with some shit for most of my adult life and maybe it's time I stopped. But it's big, and I don't know where to start so actually, if anything, this is a useful distraction but I don't suppose that's a nice thing to say about a crisis in Lolly's marriage.'

'Do you want to talk about it?'

'Maybe. No. Not yet. I don't know.'

'Okay…' Amanda rubbed her eyes with thumb and forefinger. 'Lolly then. Should we tell her? Should I be the one? I mean, I sort of feel like I should, but I don't think I can bear to see how it will hurt her.'

'Do you remember when we were kids, when one of you saw Martin Harris kissing Liz Major in French that day.'

Amanda could remember it as if it was yesterday. They'd been mid GCSEs. It was back in the days when they finished school at Easter or some such, using the time to revise ahead of their exams. It was like one long summer of skiving from the books and pretending she really cared about what results she might get. 'I remember.' It was Lolly who saw Martin, Jess's boyfriend at the time. He and Liz were huddled in a corner of the room where they thought nobody could see.

'Didn't you three get together? Didn't you talk through how to deal with it?'

'We did!' Amanda had been against the idea at first, the idea that they should take Jess for a walk and a picnic and break the news to her somewhere she couldn't immediately storm off and try and find either Martin or Liz. Which was wise because as Amanda recalled, Jess had the capacity to be pretty fiery back then. That plus exam stress and teen angst hormones, it could have gone wildly wrong. It also made her realise how much Jess had changed.

'When I think back now, I was so glad you took time to get it right. It's stupid, we were young, it shouldn't have mattered really, but it did. And I felt safe with you all. I felt that my feelings mattered, you cared. Let's get together with Emily. Let's talk through the best way to do things. This is bigger than me and Martin, this is Lolly's life, her marriage. He's the father of her children, he's the future she planned.'

'That doesn't mean he won't still be. After she finds out.'

'Of course not, and so we need to navigate that too, if we want our friendship to stand the test of another twenty years.'

'I really do,' said Amanda, feeling a sudden, overwhelming sense of need for these women in her life. 'I really do.'

'Me too. I'll call Emily. Have you got time today?'

'Absolutely.'

'Stand by, I'll call you when I've spoken to her.'

Lolly

If she went to the toilet downstairs, near the main entrance, Lolly decided she was probably most likely to get a bit of privacy. If any colleagues were using those ones, they weren't likely to be colleagues from physio since they mostly used toilets in their own building, round the corner. She tried to act as nonchalant as possible whilst butterflies formed in the pit of her belly. This could be it. This could be it. She felt differently this time, tired, a little bit sick, but mostly… intuitive. It was strange, she felt like she already knew, without having to take the test. She felt like she had already formed a bond with the tiny person that had to be growing in her belly because how else would she have suspected. She felt like she had the heart and soul of another human just sleeping within her. With clumsy fingers, she ripped first box, then packaging, pulling out the paddle she needed to pee on. She'd done it so many times over the years, she'd got it down to a fine art.

She put the cap over the fibres, resting it on the toilet roll dispenser as she nervously waited. She remembered this would be the longest three minutes. She breathed deeply, using the yoga count on her fingers to slow her thoughts down. She closed her eyes and imagined what their daughter would look like. Blonde hair, green eyes, bright, wide smile. She'd laugh and play and run. She'd be smart and fierce. She'd have confidence. She'd know all there was to know about her rights, about her choices. Lolly was ready to pass down every last drop of knowledge she'd picked up in this life, the things she wished she'd been told. The things she wished her mother had been around to talk about. For so many years, Lolly would have imaginary conversations with her mum, and now she could have those conversations with a daughter too. She just knew it. Her mother was called Valerie. It wasn't a modern name, but it was a name Lolly loved and she had every intention of passing on the name to her own daughter. Kitt didn't like it much, but he'd already said she could name their daughter anything she felt was right. He was invested, he knew how important this all was. He was prepared to take Lolly's lead, and she loved him for it. And as the timer counted down, twenty seconds, fifteen, she realised just how much she loved Kitt. How much he had been there for her. How much she had expected of him and how much he tried, even though he didn't always get it right. In fact, he so often got it wrong, but he tried. And that was everything to Lolly.

Five. Four. Three. This was it. Two. She reached for the test. One. She closed her eyes, blinking away the salty tears invited by anticipation. And she looked. And she looked harder. And she checked her watch. And she looked again and she scrutinised the test for the faintest of marks because she knew it was early but it had to be there. And she remembered when she was pregnant with Stan how it had been such a surprise because she was sure the test couldn't have picked it up straight away and yet it had. It had. Just a faint line. The subtlest indication. So why wasn't it there this time? She waited longer. She bit down hard on her bottom lip. She checked again and she checked and she held it up to a different light, shone her phone light on it. But it wasn't there. And it felt like a sucker punch. Like something had whipped her of breath. It was like a ton of bricks landed on her hopes and dreams and she barely had the strength to stand.

The next time she looked at her watch, ten minutes had passed quicker than the two that spelled her heartbreak. She took a deep breath, she had work to do. She had patients that relied on her, colleagues who would wonder where she'd been for the last nearly two hours. She'd tell them she had come over unwell, she'd say something to explain away the redness in her eyes and the shake of her hand. And later, she'd try again. Just in case.

Except this time, she felt empty. And numb. From pregnant to barren in a matter of minutes. The pain never getting easier.

By the time Lolly got home, she was on her knees. She'd spent so many hours being the most upbeat version of herself, she was exhausted. Beth had asked if she was okay when she got back into the office and Lolly felt bad that she'd shrugged her off then whipped out to an appointment but needs must.

She had hoped that when she got back, Kitt might be home, since there was no need for him to keep up the pretence of a job any more. Her mother-in-law, singing along to Radio Two, was the only indication she needed to know he'd not picked the kids up and her heart dropped because the only person she wanted to see now, needed to see in fact, was him. She wanted to cry with him, she wanted him to tell her how he was. She wanted them to share their disappointments of the day and relax into one another's arms, knowing that tomorrow, things might be different. For him at least.

'Hi, Jean, you okay?'

'Yeah, fine. You? Good day?'

Lolly hung up her coat, checking her face in the mirror in the downstairs loo. 'Yeah. Fine thanks. Same old. Where's Kitt?' she asked as innocently as she could muster.

'Oh, he called. Said he'd got caught up at the office and would be home late. Something about a big meeting or a new client. I don't know, I wasn't really listening.'

Home late? It didn't make sense. How could he be home late if he didn't have a job?

Jean pottered about the kitchen, putting pots away and generally tidying up from the boys' tea.

'Don't worry about that, I'll sort it. You get yourself off.' Lolly nestled her phone between ear and shoulder as she took a pile of plates from her, waiting for the line to connect.

'Did he say how late?'

'No, just late, and I didn't ask. Sorry,' said Jean, taking off the apron she always put on when she arrived to help out. It matched the slippers she kept in the hallway.

Lolly smiled, shoving the plates into the cupboard, wondering how he could lie so easily when he no longer had to. Then she realised, he probably didn't want his mum to know yet. She'd only worry or offer to give them money. She tended to worry. He wouldn't want that. 'Hmmm, bless him.'

'You two both work so hard,' said Jean.

Lolly half-heartedly agreed whilst reaching for Jean's coat and bag. 'Go on, you go. Thank you for getting the boys. I'll take over. Think I'm gonna put them in the bath and then have one myself.'

'I can stay longer, help with that. You look shattered, sweetie.'

Lolly let Jean pause with hand cupped to her cheek. It felt like the hand of a mother supporting her child and yet Lolly could never totally let herself relax into it. Jean had asked her to call her Mum, back when she and Kitt first got engaged. Lolly had agreed, and yet somehow it never felt right. It never stuck. She loved Jean, wholeheartedly, but she wasn't Mum. Which was a shame, because today, Lolly felt like she needed her more than ever. And yet... 'No, no. Don't worry, we'll be fine. You go.'

The door closed and the house fell almost silent, with the exception of the muffled sound of the TV coming from the lounge. The boys would be transfixed, glassy eyed over *CBeebies* no doubt. She should go in, she should gather them up and be grateful for them. There were women all across the world who would give anything and everything to have these boys, and as her guilt piqued, she looked to her handbag where the remainder test was tucked away.

It was gone nine before Kitt got home. Lolly had fallen asleep in their bedroom watching *Real Housewives*, anything trivial to help her forget the fact that tonight's tests had also been negative. He smelled of beer and fags and something she couldn't put her finger on. And as he fumbled out of his clothes and into the shower, Lolly realised how desperate he must feel and vowed not to make what was left of their evening all about her. They had each other, and that was something she was grateful for.

Emily

'Oh my god, Emily, your house is so gorgeous!' said Jess, peering around the hallway into the lounge and over to the kitchen.

Emily looked around, trying to use the fresh eyes that Jess had, realising all over again how much she loved her home. 'Thank you. I do love it here.'

'It's so peaceful,' said Amanda. 'Like, in Truro it's all cars and buses and gulls and people and here it's…' as if on cue, one of the sheep from the back field declared its presence '… sheep! Like, who has sheep in their back garden?'

'Come on, come in. Who's driven?'

'Me,' announced Amanda, putting her keys on the side. 'I'll have a tea, please.'

'Cool.' Emily flicked on the kettle. 'Jess? Tea? Coffee? Something stronger?'

'Gin. Do you have any gin? I could really go a gin.'

Emily reached to the back of one of the cupboards to pull out a half bottle of gin she'd left behind the last time she visited. 'Does it go off?' she asked the girls, sniffing the bottle. 'It smells okay!' she said, offering it up for Jess to sniff. She didn't pull a face so that was a good start, until Emily realised she had no tonic. 'I could go down the shop for you?'

'No, no! Don't be silly. Let's open this wine I brought instead. I should have brought my own if I'd wanted it so badly.' Emily felt bad as Jess opened the bottle, pouring into the glass she'd passed her. 'You drinking?' she asked.

'Oh no. Not today.'

'Not today? It's Friday! What better day for a cheeky, ice cold, Sauvignon Blanc.'

Emily felt bad. She was keeping this from them and it seemed silly, she should just tell them. She also really wanted a cheeky Sauvignon Blanc. Would one hurt?

'Well, I shall pour it and leave it there, just in case you wish to join in.'

'Thanks. Come on, let's sit through here.'

The girls followed, each dropping into one of the three feather filled sofas that surrounded a small coffee table. 'Oh my god, Emily… is that…?' On the coffee table, the photo of all four of them sat in a gilt frame, the image slightly faded in colour with age. 'I can't believe you've got this photo!'

'It was always on my bedside, after we moved.' The girls stared at her. 'I missed you!' she admitted.

Amanda stared at the picture, Jess sat back in the chair, crossing her arms.

'Why did you have to go?' moaned Amanda. 'It was never the same without you, was it, Jess?'

'No, no. It wasn't,' said Jess, quietly.

'It was Dad, he just uprooted us all. I don't know, something to do with work. It all happened so quickly.'

'You're telling us! Do you remember, Jess? Emily had that big party, didn't she? For her sixteenth. Jesus, I got so drunk that night.'

'Were you the one to raid Dad's drinks cabinet?'

'Yes! Yes I was. Well, me and Jess, isn't that right?'

Jess nodded.

'Oh my god, I got into so much trouble for that.'

'It was hilarious. We hid out in the garden, necking a bottle of some kind of whiskey, don't remember what, never touched the stuff since. I think I passed out. Jess, you just disappeared.'

'We should focus on what we came here for,' said Jess, suddenly.

'I always thought there was a bit of a story there, you disappearing. It was long before you met Jay, wasn't it, so couldn't have had anything to do with him. And after Martin whatshisface, so not him. Who dragged you away from me that night, Jessica Morton? Huh? When I was shitfaced in a garden. I'm sure I was sick in the daffodils, you could have saved me from it. Instead of doing whatever you were doing—'

'For god's sake, Amanda! Not now,' Jess shouted. She adjusted herself on the chair. 'We've got things to sort,' she finished and Emily wondered why her hands shook.

Amanda stared and Emily's heart raced. Did they know about the baby? And if so, why would they make a deal of it like this? Jess looked distressed, Amanda folded her arms.

'Sorry, but please,' said Jess. 'Let's just talk about Lolly.'

Emily breathed out, relief washing over her. 'What about Lolly?' she asked.

'Well...' Amanda placed the photo back on the table, leaning forward, her elbows resting on her knees. 'It's complicated.'

Emily stared at them both. 'What is?' she asked. 'What's going on?' She tucked her feet deeper into the cushions beside her, nerves jangling with the awkward energy in the air.

Jess adjusted herself, almost as if regaining composure after her outburst, but she looked hurt, and suddenly vulnerable. 'Sorry, Amanda, that wasn't called for. Sorry.'

'It's okay. Look, we're both worried. It's fine.' Amanda didn't look fine.

'Shall I?' asked Jess, sheepishly. Amanda nodded. 'Okay,' began Jess. 'Amanda and I have reason to believe that Kitt may not be telling Lolly the truth about a few things.'

'Right…'

'And we're not sure how best to tackle it all. Like… we've only just all got back together and it would be awful to lose her now.'

'So, maybe we don't get involved,' said Emily. It seemed quite simple to her, she hated how people always seemed to want to stick their oar in things and was quite surprised that either Jess or Amanda were inclined to do so. Besides, looking at the pair of them, it seemed there might be more pressing matters to talk about. Something wasn't right. 'There's nothing worse than people sticking their oar into stuff that's not their business. We should just be there for Lolly if things implode, after all, it's nothing to do with us,' she reasoned.

There was a pause. 'Except it kind of is,' said Amanda, carefully. Emily looked at her, she put her mug down and fidgeted with her clothes. 'Christ, I wish I'd had a drink now,' she said.

When Amanda finished talking, Emily wasn't quite sure what to say. No matter which way Amanda framed it, Emily felt that she was the kind of woman who slept with other people's boyfriends and husbands. And even if they weren't with anyone, she was the kind of woman who took money for sex and everything about that sat awkwardly for Emily. Weren't the men taking advantage? Did it perpetuate the imbalance between men and women? Surely things like this took objectification to a whole new level. Emily wasn't sure where to begin, or whether to, in fact. Because she loved Amanda, she always had. It seemed so odd to imagine feeling about her any other way, and yet she couldn't help but look at her differently. 'So,' began Emily, uncertainly. 'Are you still seeing him?' she asked.

'Of course not!' said Amanda, clearly shocked. 'Blimey, Emily, what do you take me for?'

'Well, I don't know how these things work…'

'Neither do I, that's why I'm here. To try and work out what we do about it.'

'What *we* do?' asked Emily. '*We* aren't sleeping with Lolly's husband.'

'Neither am I, now. As soon as I realised, I have tried to distance myself from him, despite the texts and calls he's made because he's so bloody scared that I'll say something and land him in it.'

'So why don't you?'

'Because I can't bear the idea of hurting Lolly.'

'But she needs to know, right?' said Emily.

'Of course she does,' agreed Amanda.

'Oh, and he's told her he lost his job and has been hiding the fact from her but he is still totally and utterly employed,' finished Jess.

'He's saying he's been made redundant?' Emily shook her head in disbelief.

'Yes.'

'But he's not?'

'Well, the last time I saw him he was very much still working. There was no hint that he was about to lose his job. I mean, normally people lie about having a job when they haven't got one, not the other way around. What's it all about?'

A knock at the door interrupted them and both Emily and Jess practically jumped out of their skin. Emily looked up towards the door, confused. She wasn't expecting anyone. 'Give me a minute.' She peered through the window by the door to see Mac throw her a wave. 'Oh! Hi!' she said, pulling the door open.

'Mum said I was to swing by when I got the chance, something about a price for some work. Look, I don't mind if you want to go elsewhere, I know she can be a bit forthright with things like that.'

'Oh no, it's fine. Come in. Sorry, I've got some friends here.'

Mac stood awkwardly in the hallway, smiling.

'Come through, come through. This is Amanda, and this is Jess.'

'Jess, yes. We met the other day? In Truro? You were with Emily when I bumped into her.'

'Yes, hi!' Jess jumped to shake his hand then realised Amanda had stayed in her seat and she sort of hovered with a wave. Mac let out a weird sort of laugh and waved at her again.

'Girls, will you give me a minute. I know Mac sometimes disappears on the boats so if I can just show him what I want, I can leave him to price it up before he heads off again.'

'You're a fisherman?' said Jess.

'Yeah.'

'And builder… presumably,' said Amanda.

'Yeah, And I have been known to do a bit of gardening too.'

'Jack of all trades,' said Amanda.

'Master of none.' Mac smiled, he seemed to try and focus on all three but Emily couldn't help notice he generally focussed on Jess. He seemed nervous, almost shy. Nothing like how he'd been the last few times she'd seen him. Jess dropped back into her chair, picking up a magazine from the rack beside her.

'This way,' said Emily, heading upstairs.

Mac nodded a smile in the girls' direction and followed her up the stairs.

Jess

Jess's heart continued to race. Talking about Lolly hadn't quite consumed the flashbacks and her hands shook. Could she ever tell them the truth? Should she, even? What if it was a catalyst for something else, like the real end of their friendship? What if speaking up meant she never saw these girls again? They were the reason she'd found a strength to take stock of her life, she didn't want to compromise that, and yet… she was in Emily's house. Withholding the truth.

'Would,' said Amanda, staring at the space Mac had briefly stood in.

'Would what?' asked Jess, distractedly.

'Him. I would.'

She had a look on her face that made Jess realise she was talking about sex and she couldn't help but colour up a little. 'He seems nice,' she agreed.

'*Nice*? Is that all you can say? Christ, has Jay completely drained you of wanton lust?'

'Give it up!' said Jess, in no mood to feign lusting.

'Anyway, what was that all about?'

'What?' Jess didn't want to do this, not here, not now.

'Just now, you went weird. What did I say?'

'It's nothing.'

'Jess, it doesn't look like nothing. It doesn't feel like nothing. If I upset you, I am so sorry, please know I wouldn't do that on purpose.'

'I know. I know you wouldn't.'

'So what's the matter?'

Jess looked at Amanda. She looked around Emily's lounge. 'It's nothing I want to talk about, okay? I mean it.' Jess looked at Amanda and hoped she got the urgency. She was going to have to deal with this at some point, somehow, but now wasn't the time. And she knew for certain that she wasn't protecting anybody but herself, this time. Just like she always should have.

Ten minutes later, Emily and Mac reappeared, Mac with a paper of notes in his hand. 'Well, I'll price it all up, shouldn't be too expensive. Or take too long. All fairly simple, I'd say.'

'Great, thank you.'

'Mum said you wanted it doing in a specific timescale?' His eyes flicked to Jess who looked away, hoping he hadn't noticed she'd been staring at him since he came back downstairs. There was something about him. Amanda was right, he was attractive, but there was more to him than that. Something she didn't think she'd noticed before. She was drawn to him.

'Oh, no. No. Well… I mean, ideally before… well, maybe in the next six months or so?' said Emily and Jess noticed her uncertainty around him. Did Emily like Mac?

'That'll be fine. No problem. Leave it with me.' He turned to face Jess and Amanda. 'Bye then… nice to see you again,' he said to Jess.

'Yeah… you too.' He held her gaze and she searched for something interesting on her trouser leg.

'Right. I'll be in touch. Bye then.'

'Yeah… bye. Thanks for popping round.' Emily waved him off down the lane.

There was a pause before Amanda jumped up. 'Oh. My. God!'

Emily spun around, closing the door behind her. 'What?'

'What? Him! Mac. Fitty McFitface or should I say Fitty MacFitface!'

'Amanda!' she said, with a tone that Jess thought sounded a bit protective. Jess pushed a nudge of disappointment to the back of her mind wondering why she felt it in the first place. Emily and Mac would be gorgeous together. She deserved someone as lovely as he seemed.

'Never mind him,' Jess said, meaning entirely the opposite. 'What are we going to do about Lolly?'

Amanda groaned, dropping back into the sofa. Emily raised her eyebrows, cynically. Jess couldn't help notice that Emily hadn't taken the news of Amanda's career path entirely well. She seemed spiky, sort of distanced. Was she judging Amanda? It didn't seem like something Emily would do, but how well did they all really know each other?

'So, what are we going to do?'

'Well, I think we have to give him the chance to say something first,' said Amanda.

'But what if he tells her about you?' said Jess.

'I don't know, I mean, it doesn't help him, does it. It probably makes things worse. It wouldn't surprise me if he didn't say anything at all about me.'

'I guess that's something,' said Emily.

Amanda looked at her for a moment, then carried on. 'So, maybe I just need to apply some pressure. Tell him that if he doesn't, we will.'

'We?' asked Emily.

'Well… I mean, I guess I could but…'

'We can do it together, Amanda. If you'd prefer,' said Jess. 'You know, if you want back up.' Emily muttered an agreement but Jess wasn't convinced by it.

'So what, do I text him? I don't want her to see it again.'

'I don't think you've any choice, have you?' said Jess.

'Maybe not.'

'Perhaps don't text him when he's likely to be at home, this time?' said Emily.

'Right.'

The women fell silent. It was uncomfortable. The warmth of friendship seemed to have cooled during the last hour and Jess was fairly certain it was because of Amanda's confession. Eventually, Amanda asked. 'Emily, you seem a bit… I don't know. I feel like maybe you're not impressed with me, with what I do.'

'It's your business, Amanda.'

Jess held her breath.

'It is, but I guess your opinion matters to me.'

'Mine? Why should mine matter?'

'Because it does.'

Emily got up, adjusting the curtains by the window, staring out into her garden. 'Look, what you do is your business, it's nothing to do with me.'

'True. But still… I don't want us to fall out about it,' said Amanda, sadly.

'Look, come on, girls,' said Jess. 'Of course we won't fall out about it, will we, Emily? We need to stick together if we're going to help Lolly. That's why we're here. That's who we're talking about.'

Emily nodded, turning to face them, leaning against the radiator. 'Fine. Just… bear with me, okay. I guess it goes against what I believe in, it feels… I don't know, maybe it feels anti-women.'

'But it's my choice, Emily. How can that be anti-women?'

'And what about all the women who do it whose choice it isn't?'

'But that's not my fault. I can't be responsible for anybody but myself, me and my choices.'

Emily nodded, unconvinced. 'I guess, I just don't understand it.'

Amanda stood, slowly. 'I don't need you to understand it, Em. I just want you not to hate me.'

Emily folded her arms. 'I don't hate you, Amanda.'

The room fell flat, silent, uncomfortable. Amanda nodded. 'We should probably get off, leave you to it, Emily,' said Jess, carefully.

Emily nodded and Jess finished off the wine left in her glass. 'Come on, Amanda.'

Amanda nodded, taking her cup through to the kitchen. 'Thanks for the drink.'

'No worries,' said Emily, flatly, hovering by the front door. 'Keep me posted. Hopefully it'll all get sorted without too much upset for Lolly.'

'She'll come round,' Jess said to Amanda as she dropped her off.

'Not everybody does,' said Amanda, sadly. 'And normally I wouldn't care, but this time, I do. It's different with you lot.'

Jess nodded. She knew. She got it. 'Look, I'm sorry about earlier.'

'It's okay.' Amanda sought out eye contact. 'Is there anything you want to talk about?'

'Honestly? No. Not yet. Maybe never. Sorry. But let me know when you've texted Kitt, and if you get a response. Okay?'

'Okay. And I'm here, any time. If you need me.'

'I know. Thank you.'

Amanda nodded then pulled away from the kerb.

Was meeting a turning point for them all? Was it about to unpick the lives they'd built for themselves? Maybe their friendship hadn't really survived the almost twenty-year hiatus. Perhaps it was naive for any of them to think it had. They'd drifted apart before, what made them think this time would be any different?

Amanda

Locking up the car, Amanda reached into her bag for her house keys, head down on her way to the front door.

'Mum,' said a voice as she made her way up the short path.

'Zennor!' Amanda wanted to throw her arms around her and give her a big hug, but she wasn't so sure it was going to be welcome and she couldn't deal with another bout of rejection today. 'How are you feeling? Are you fully recovered? You could have let yourself in you know,' she said, pushing open the door.

'I don't think so.'

'Oh, right.'

'I came around to see you. To let you know I was okay. Dad said you'd been really worried about me and I started to think maybe we should just sort this out.'

'Oh, love.' Amanda's heart lifted.

'But that's probably not going to happen now,' she said, reaching into her pocket.

Amanda's heart sank as quickly as it had lifted and she looked at Zennor whose lip curled, her eyes cold.

'I found this. Online. Well, I say I did. Billy found it actually. Couldn't wait to show me, could he?' Amanda took Zennor's phone from her but she didn't really need to look at it to know this was bad. This was worse than bad. In fact, it made no difference now what Emily thought, or how Lolly would feel if she found out. 'You fucking slag,' Zennor spat as Amanda scrolled through her own Twitter feed.

'Zennor. Please. Can we talk about this?' She stepped inside the house. 'Please, come in.'

'Come in? In there? Where you do this? Not bloody likely! You disgust me, Mum. I always knew there was something weird about you. Something that didn't quite sit right. I never imagined you'd sink this low though!'

'I don't see it that way. I love my job. Zennor, please. I know it probably seems strange to you…'

'Strange! It's disgusting, Mum. Look at the state of you, here.' She pointed to photos Amanda had posted. 'And here. I mean what the fuck even is that?'

Amanda looked at the pictures she'd posted, things she did to tempt people to pay for more images, or to watch her online. The hashtags made her cringe now. Why hadn't she taken more time to cover her identity? She had to begin with, lately though, maybe she'd got lazy. Or maybe she didn't feel the shame expected of her. The shame Zennor clearly felt now. 'Nobody needs to know, love. If you're embarrassed. You don't need to tell anyone, I'm very careful about how I present myself in the street.'

'Nobody needs to know? Everyone knows, Mum!' Zennor laughed one of those angry, bitter laughs. 'The lads were scrolling Twitter for this kind of filth and Billy said he recognised you. Said if he'd known he could have paid you he'd have been first in line.'

Amanda wanted to die. 'I thought you two weren't seeing each other any more.'

'Yeah, well. He came to see me when I got out of hospital. Brought me flowers. Told me that he hadn't realised how strong his feelings were for me until that happened.'

'They can't be that strong if he was talking about paying to sleep with me!'

'Don't you dare turn this on him. This is not his fault, Mum.' Of course. Of course she'd side with him. 'I don't know how you can do it. Are you on drugs or something? I mean, how little do you think of yourself to let men use you that way?'

'It's not like that, Zennor. Not for me at least.'

'Of course it's like that. It's shameful. It's abusive. It's disgusting.'

'It can be, for some women, absolutely it can. But it's none of those things for other women, Zennor, including me. If you'd listen, I can explain. Please. But not here, come inside. Please.'

'What? Are you embarrassed?' She stood, eyes fixed on Amanda, before raising her voice even louder. 'Are you embarrassed at being a prostitute, Mum? Would you hate for anyone to know that you let dirty old men fuck you for money?'

'Zennor!'

'Yeah, what else do you do? Eh? What other sordid shit are you doing? You should be ashamed of yourself. I was right to cut you out, Mum. We are done.'

'Zennor, please!'

But Zennor spun on her heel and stormed off down the street. No shouting was going to bring her back. No calling her would get her to pick up. Amanda noticed George from next door's curtain twitching and she sunk down into her boots, shame creeping. She'd not told Zennor because she was waiting for the right time to explain. When she thought Zennor might be mature enough to hear her. This wasn't the way she was supposed to find out and Amanda couldn't imagine how they could possibly reverse the damage. Oh god, she was going to go off and talk to all her friends. She'd talk to Pete. Pete. Amanda hadn't told him because they just didn't talk about stuff like that. And now he'd be hearing Zennor's version. Amanda sat on the step and pulled out her phone. She needed to call him. He had to hear this from her, not their daughter.

'Hey you, have you seen Zennor? She said she was on her way over.'

'I have.'

'Oh, you sound like it didn't go well?'

'Pete, I need to tell you something. Something that Zennor's just found out about.'

'Right... Are you okay, Amanda? Do you need me? Do you need help?'

'No, no... I'm fine it's just...' Amanda wasn't sure she could cope if Pete decided to judge her the way Zennor had. She'd always known he was important to her, even if they were no longer together, but the idea of him cutting ties on hearing this made her almost as upset as the thought she'd never see Zennor again. 'Zennor just found out that... oh god, I don't know how to say this.'

'You can tell me anything, Amanda. Come on.'

Amanda hoped he was being truthful. 'Zennor just found out that I'm a sex worker.' The phone went quiet. Amanda couldn't bear to wait until Pete found words. 'I do it for my own reasons. I'm safe. I get tested. I have a support network. I enjoy my job. I'm not doing it under duress.' Pete still said nothing. 'Please don't be mad with me, Pete, I couldn't bear it if you were.'

'Why would I be mad with you?' he asked, his voice quieter than before.

'I don't know.'

'What you do is your business, not mine.'

'I know but…'

'I mean… I can't say it's not a shock.' Amanda dropped down onto the top step of her home. 'I guess… I mean… it's whatever, isn't it.'

Was he convinced of that? Amanda wasn't sure. 'I wish Zennor felt that way.'

'Maybe she just needs time?'

'I wish it was just that, you didn't see how she looked at me. Like I'm a scumbag. The lowest of the low.'

'She's young. She's probably just shocked. Embarrassed even.' Amanda hurt at that idea, that she would be embarrassed. That Pete would suggest it. 'I meant it's not a normal job, is it?'

'You'd be surprised, Pete. If you knew what I knew, you'd be amazed at how many do it. How many normal women like me.'

'Well, I'm sure but… look. Don't stress, okay. Leave Zennor to me. Just… leave her to me.'

'Okay. Thank you. Sorry.'

'What for?'

'Bringing this to your door.'

Pete laughed a little. 'Amanda, you are something else.'

'Don't hate me, Pete.'

He paused. 'I never could…'

Amanda hung up. When she started this job, it was fun. It was exciting. It was something she'd even fantasised about, never imagining she'd do it herself. And when she'd done it the first time, when the nerves had gone and she got into her stride, she realised how much it suited her. How she loved the money. The sex. The flexibility. The fact she was master of her own destiny, paying her own bills, wanting for nothing from anyone. She'd never looked ahead at what could go wrong because she was enjoying living in the moment.

Would she have still done it if she could have foreseen hurting Lolly and Zennor? Amanda hiccupped a cry, wiping her eyes. How the hell was she going to make any of this right?

'Are you alright, love?' asked a frail voice. George stood above her. 'I heard shouting. And you're crying, what's happened?'

Amanda jumped up, taking George by the arm. 'Oh, it's nothing. Don't worry about me.' She wiped her eyes. 'It's cold out here, come on, get back inside.' She steered him towards his house. 'Do you need anything? I've got to pop to the shops, you must be ready for some milk again. What about bread? I've a casserole on for this evening, I'll plate you some up.'

'Don't *you* worry about *me*,' George echoed her words, using the rail to help him up to his doorway.

'As if I wouldn't worry about you, we're neighbours. That's what we do.'

'Well, I know. That's why I'm asking. Are you sure you're alright, love? It's not like you to be sad.'

Amanda took a deep breath. 'I'll be fine, George. Honestly. It's something and nothing. Now come on, get in the warmth, don't let the heat out. I'll see you in a bit.'

Jess

A lazy spring sunshine shone through Jess's curtains. It didn't wake her up, she'd been lying in bed, eyes open, mind whirring, since about five o'clock that morning. This was her first Monday off work in months. The start to her first week's holiday since at least last summer. Only she could wake before her alarm clock would normally go off. She'd groaned, tossed and turned for the first half an hour after waking before finally picking up her phone and scrolling Instagram, Twitter, then Facebook, before reaching for a book which she couldn't focus on because none of these things were enough distraction from her thoughts. Thoughts that had no structure or connection. They lurched from a vision of Amanda's face when she dropped her off on Friday, to the face she imagined Lolly would have when she found out about Kitt. She thought about work and the team. She thought about Jay. She thought about Emily and her quiet judgement of Amanda. She thought about the young girl she was before the night of the party. She thought about Mac.

She launched herself out of bed. She could not waste this week as she had wasted the last twenty years of her life. She could not let one man's actions steal any more of herself. Lolly's situation was making her realise that as much as anything, Lolly deserved better than Kitt and she deserved better than the one-dimensional life she had created.

In the bathroom, she pulled the shower on to red hot, letting the needles of water spike her neck and back, turning it up further still each time it cooled a little. How did people deal with this kind of thing? How could she face her demons? Was it time for therapy? Matt had always suggested it. The more she looked at travel options, the more it felt like she was running away. Again.

Downstairs, wrapped in a towel, she flicked the kettle on, staring at the world map on her kitchen wall. She'd seen it on Pinterest one day, a map in the kitchen surrounded by fairy lights and little red flags to mark all the places the owner had been to. She'd never bothered with the flags, but she loved to see the world splayed out in front of her. This time though, she looked at it differently. Her eyes fell on L.A. Maybe it wasn't about running away, rather facing up to her demons. Confronting them even. Confronting him… Her phone rang out as she pondered the idea.

'Hello?'

'Jess, it's Emily.'

'Emily! How are you?'

'Erm, I'm not okay. I need help.'

'What's the matter?'

'I'm in Treliske Hospital.'

'Oh no, what's happened?'

'I… I'll explain when you get here. They say I can go home if there's someone to help when I get there. I don't know who else to ask and I don't want to put you out but—'

'It's fine, it's fine. Which ward are you on? I'm on my way.'

'I'll wait at the main entrance. Are you sure you don't mind?'

'Of course not! I'll be there as soon as I can. Are you sure you're okay?'

Emily sniffed down the phone. 'I will be, I should be. Thanks, Jess.'

Casting L.A. to the back of her mind, Jess took the stairs two at a time, she pulled her hair into a ponytail, then brushed her teeth as she picked out clothes to wear. She flew back downstairs, grabbing her bag, phone and keys as she shut the door behind her.

Twenty-five minutes later, she pulled up at the hospital collection point. She could see a very pale Emily just inside the doorway.

'Hey, love. Are you okay?' As soon as Emily saw Jess, she burst into tears and Jess couldn't hear what she was saying through the sobs. 'Hey, calm down. Ssshhhh. Come on, let's get you home. No need to explain, just get in the car.'

It took five minutes of calm breathing and staring out of the window for Emily to finally explain what had happened. 'I was so scared, Jess. I was just getting things ready for Mac, he said he'd come this afternoon and start doing some work because the conditions weren't right for fishing. I went up in the loft to get boxes to pack a few bits away. I just lost my footing and fell.'

'Right.'

'And then I went to the toilet and there was a tiny bit of blood and…' Jess pulled up at the lights by Waitrose. 'I just… I've only just got used to the idea.' Jess turned to look at Emily as her eyes filled again and her hands nursed her belly. 'I'm pregnant, Jess.'

'Oh my god, Emily! Oh…' The lights changed and somebody behind Jess pipped their horn. 'Oh, Emily, congratulations!' Emily nodded her head, but the tears flowed once again. 'Hey, hey. It's okay. Is the baby okay?' Emily nodded. 'It's fine then, isn't it? It's fine!'

'Except that now I've realised I'm doing this on my own and I don't think I can, Jess.'

'Of course you can, hey.' She reached out to squeeze Emily's knee. 'Of course you can! Women do this all the time on their own. And you're not on your own anyway, are you! You've got me. You've got the girls.'

'I know, but you have your own lives. You won't want to be fussing with me when I've had it. You'll be off doing whatever you do. Working, living life!' She sniffed.

'Living life? Christ, I should be so lucky. I've just taken an emergency holiday from work because I realised I've done the very opposite of living life. Maybe I should just move in with you and we can raise the baby together.' Emily stared at Jess, open-mouthed. 'I was kidding. I'm just trying to make the point that whatever it looks like to you, my life really isn't all that.'

'But you seem so in control of everything, so sorted.'

'*Me*? Sorted!' Jess laughed out loud before the funny side disappeared and she was left with an empty feeling in her stomach. Then she realised that her bottom lip was wobbling and shit, she was about to cry too. 'Oh god, look at the state of us!'

Emily

'I can't believe it. When we all did drinks I was in awe of these brilliant, brave women you'd all turned into and I couldn't work out how I'd missed becoming one of those.'

'Are you kidding me? You've travelled the world, you've achieved status and money and things some people only dream of.'

'But it wasn't real. I was faking it the whole way through.'

'Maybe everyone fakes it? Maybe that's the point.'

'I suspect Amanda isn't faking it...' Emily looked down at her fingers, fiddling with her skirt. 'God, I was a bit shitty, wasn't I?'

Jess focussed on the road up ahead. 'Well, it was probably just a bit of a shock, that's all.'

'Yeah, but... she didn't need the judgement, did she?'

Jess pulled into a petrol station, pulling on the handbrake. 'Erm... no, she probably didn't need it. But you know, she'll have come across it before. And she will again.' She flipped the visor down to check the mirror, wiping her eyes clear of tears. 'Jesus, I don't know what is up with me. Realising life is not what you thought it was really does throw a whole load of questions up, doesn't it?'

'It does. Christ. I never thought I'd be here. Back in Cornwall. With a baby on the way. Alone.'

Jess turned to face her. 'But you're happy, aren't you? I mean, this small person is a version of you.'

'And a version of his or her dad.'

'Will he be coming over?' Jess asked, tentatively.

Emily shook her head. She'd heard nothing from him since he walked out after she'd told him. She could feel the tears return again.

'Oh, love, come on. You've got this. You're going to be an amazing mum, I just know it. Look, hang fire. I need fuel. Do you need anything picking up? Milk, bread?'

'Chocolate and crisps.'

'Chocolate and crisps it is. I'll be two minutes.'

As Jess filled the car up with fuel, Emily pulled out her phone. *I'm sorry about yesterday* she texted Amanda. *If I came across as judgemental, please know that I didn't mean to make you feel bad. There's no excuse. I'm just really sorry.* She clicked send, then dropped her phone back in her bag.

She pushed the small of her back into the chair and looked down at the delicate swell of her pregnant belly. In her bag was a scan. This tiny, grainy peanut of a baby was fine. The bleed was nothing to worry about. She just had to rest up and relax and stop climbing stepladders. She needed to focus on the future for her and her baby now. It wasn't just her any more. She was going to be a mother and with all the fear that filled her with, there was also a sense of focus. She hadn't envisaged doing it this way, this wasn't in her teenage life plan. But this is what she was faced with and she was going to do everything in her power to embrace it.

Amanda

Pete had promised Amanda that he would keep talking to Zennor and do his best to get her to agree to meet up. Amanda couldn't work out if she could detect a note of pity in his voice since he found out what she did. They hadn't discussed it again and he'd been a bit different, but not to the point that he wouldn't return calls or messages. And he hadn't stopped messaging her either, just a couple of times over the weekend to check in with her and make sure she was okay after Zennor walked off. All Amanda could do was distract herself, making the most of the fact that when she dropped the food and shopping off for George, it was clear he needed a bit of help around the house and she got stuck right in. Cleaning, washing his clothes, listening to his stories about boats and the war and his wife, Edie, who'd passed away long before.

It helped. As had the message from Emily. It shouldn't matter what the girls thought of her, she'd stepped back from them once before, back when she couldn't cope with the weight of being a new mum. They had lives ahead of them: Jess was off travelling; Lolly was training; Emily had long gone. She'd survived without them then, she could survive without them now. Except now, she didn't want to.

She finished packing up a bag full of clothes for charity, placing them by the front door to drop off later on. She just had one thing to do before she went out. Call Kitt. It was daytime. Lolly should be at work and wherever he was, whatever he was pretending to do, Amanda knew she had to try and get him to listen to her. Maybe she could help him, salvage something. Not for his sake, but for Lolly's.

'Hello, this is Kitt.'

'Kitt, it's Amanda.'

'Yup.' He didn't hang up, but his voice shifted to stony and cold.

'Have you spoken to Lolly?'

'I'm at work right now, this isn't a good time.'

'It is a good time because I've decided it is. So unless you want me to pop round your house this evening, you'll talk to me.' When she'd imagined this conversation, she hadn't seen herself getting shitty with him so early in the call. He told her to hang on, it sounded like he was moving about, presumably to somewhere a bit more private? 'So, does Lolly know you're at work or does she still think you're job hunting?'

'What does it matter to you?'

'It matters because she's my friend and you're lying to her.'

'So are you,' he hissed. 'Have you told her what a dirty whore you are?'

Amanda bit the inside of her mouth, she was not giving him the satisfaction of knowing how hurtful his words were. 'I've said nothing about what I do. Yet. But I will. And for the record, you didn't have too much problem with my line of work when you were directly benefitting from it.'

'Yeah, well. Let's call it a moment of weakness.'

'Weakness! Weakness? What are you talking about?'

'Things weren't great at home. A man has needs.'

'You were trying for a baby, Kitt. She is desperate. How could you do that to her?'

'Alright, okay. Maybe so. But she isn't interested in me, just making a baby. Which isn't going to happen anyway, since I never went for the reversal.'

'What do you mean?'

'I don't want another child. Why would I bother? I figured she'd go off the idea when it didn't happen. It's like the opposite has happened, it's all she thinks about. Maybe that's why I came to you. Either way, it's not your business to get involved in my life. Isn't there some kind of whore code?'

'Yes. But it doesn't cover servicing a friend's husband, funnily enough. I can't stand by and see you do this to her. It's not just you lying about your job, or the fact that you pay women like me, more importantly, it's the fact she so desperately wants a baby and Jesus, Kitt, I can't believe you know full well it's not going to happen!'

'She'll go off the idea eventually.'

'Will she? You really think it's a passing fad? This is about her mother, you piece of shit! This is about putting some ghosts to rest. This is about forging a new relationship like the one she never had.'

'It's not exactly a healthy reason to have a child. It's an obsession. She can't think of anything else. Do you know how hard it is being nothing more than a sperm donor? Because that's all I feel like I am,' he hissed.

'Oh, give me a moment while I weep for you. You wouldn't have to feel like that if you'd had an honest discussion with her. If you'd talked about how you felt. If you gave her enough credit that she'd listen and consider how you felt.'

'She's not interested in me! She doesn't care about my feelings. She's made that patently clear.'

'And so have you with hers. Stalemate.'

'I have to get back to work. If you've got a point to make, make it quick.'

'Tell Lolly about what's going on. Or at the very least, tell her about the reversal.' Amanda was raging, fuelled by utter hatred for the man who was torturing her friend. 'And if you don't, I will. And then she'll want to know how I know…'

'You wouldn't.'

Amanda stood up, her heart racing with determination and focus. 'Watch me,' she said, hanging up. Now, it was up to him.

Jess

'You don't have to do this,' said Emily as Jess put a bowl full of granola in front of her. 'I can manage.'

'Of course you can manage. But you don't have to is the thing.' Jess sat in the chair opposite nursing her own bowl. Upstairs, she could hear Mac hammering stuff and generally being all builder-y. Every now and then he'd come downstairs with a length of wood to cut out on the lane before heading back upstairs, clear eye protectors still covering his face. Jess found herself looking forward to the sound of him clattering down the stairs. 'So how are you feeling today?' she asked, mixing the crunch with the berries and yoghurt.

'So much better for the sleep.'

'Yeah, you zonked!' she said, smiling. Not long after they got back yesterday afternoon, Emily took herself off to bed for a nap and didn't wake until first thing this morning. 'I hope you don't mind that I nicked a T-shirt to sleep in. Or that I stayed over, I just didn't want to leave you on your own.'

'Of course not. I'm really grateful!'

The part of Jess that was pleased she could help was being picked apart as she watched Emily, wondering if she ever thought about that night at her party. If she ever wondered what had happened to change everything Jess knew about herself.

They fell silent as they ate. Jess imagined that, were it not for the thunder of Mac coming down the stairs and out the front door again, it would be lovely and peaceful in the house. It had a calming feel to the place. Almost nurturing. A safe haven. 'Does he know what he's building?' she asked, innocently.

'No. No. God, what would he care? No, I just said I wanted to rework things now I was staying.'

'What's he doing exactly?'

'Putting in another door from the front bedroom to the en suite so that baby and I can share. Jack and Jill, is it?'

'Ahhh, that's sweet.'

'And wardrobes, I'm gonna need a load of wardrobes for storage, so he's building some of them.'

'Lovely.'

'Yeah.' Emily put her empty bowl on the coffee table, reaching for her mug of tea instead.

'He seems nice,' said Jess, quietly so he wouldn't hear above the banging.

'He does. Yeah.'

'Maybe you two could…'

Jess moved her fingers as if to suggest there might be something between him and Emily and was surprised at how relieved she was to see Emily vehemently shake her head. 'God no! No! He's lovely, but really not my type. And I think I should probably focus on me and this little one for the foreseeable.'

'Yeah, I guess so.' Mac came back in, a length of wood in one hand as he dropped his tape measure into a tool belt. He caught sight of Jess's eye and she blushed. When he got back upstairs, Emily fixed her with a look. 'What?' asked Jess.

'You!'

'What?' Was it too cold to open a window? Jess was suddenly feeling very hot.

'The state of you!' The hammering began again and Emily raised her voice just enough for Jess to hear. 'You like my builder!'

'No! I do not!'

'You totally do!' She moved to sit cross-legged on the sofa.

'Don't sit like that. It'll open your hips too wide or something. I'm sure I read about it once.'

Emily moved, but didn't stop her line of questioning. 'You like him! Why don't you ask him out?'

'Emily! As if I'd do that!'

'Why not? You've spent all these years lusting after a man you thought you loved, maybe now is the time to realise you didn't.'

'Who says I didn't?'

'Okay, nobody does, but there is definitely something going on with Mac.'

Jess knew Emily had a point, but she didn't know what to do with the information. She hadn't been interested in anyone for years. She thought that part of her life had been a write off. She'd resigned herself to the fact a long time ago and had been fine about it. She missed having company sometimes, she wished she'd never left Jay behind, but over the years, she really thought she'd made peace with her choice. 'Anyway, there's no point starting anything, even if I were in the market to. Which…' Mac came back downstairs again, forcing Jess to whisper '…which I am very much not. But even if I was. Now isn't the time.'

'There's never a good time. Just like children!' Emily pointed to her belly, eyebrows raised.

'Yes, well…'

'So what is it time for? You said you'd taken a few days off work to think things through. What are you thinking?'

Jess put her own bowl down, noticing the atlas on the bottom shelf of Emily's coffee table. 'I think I've got some things to sort. To face up to.'

'Like what?'

Jess looked away. She'd had time to think, sat in Emily's house. Conversations played out in her mind, confrontations. And with each one, there had been fall out, consequences. There'd been a knock-on effect and in no scenario did their friendship come out well.

'Facing up to stuff is hard. Take it from me,' said Emily. Jess nodded. 'But it's necessary. However you do it. It's needed, so you can move on.'

'I know you're right. I just don't know how to go about it.' Jess had never felt so conflicted. Sat before a friend she trusted implicitly, unable to explain what was going off. 'Maybe I just need a bit more time to think. I can do that here, it's no problem.'

'Here? I mean, you're welcome, always... but I don't need you to babysit me?'

'You don't *need* me to. But maybe you'd like me to. Maybe it would be good for you to have me around for a couple more days whilst you get fully back on your feet. Like you say, that baby needs looking after. I can cook. I can clean up after Mac.' Emily raised her eyebrows at Jess but she chose to ignore that. 'I can get a few bits of shopping in for you. Help you plan what you need to do for baby. And when I'm not doing that I can walk on the beach and think. I think looking out to sea would be good for me, and it's too far away from where I live.'

'Well...' Emily sipped at her drink, thinking.

'I mean, if you really don't want me to stay, it's fine. I wouldn't want to impose but come on... it could be nice. We could have fun. It'd be like when we went to Hayling Island with school that time.'

'We stayed in a timber chalet that was freezing cold and sang karaoke to Kylie's "I Should Be So Lucky".'

Jess snorted. 'We did! I remember! And Tiffany!'

'"I Think We're Alone Now!"' shouted Emily and the girls fell about laughing.

Mac appeared in the hallway. 'Christ, are you two on the gin already?'

'She'd better not be in her state,' howled Jess. 'Oh shit! Sorry.'

'Some bloody help you are,' said Emily, still laughing. 'Ignore her. I'm pregnant,' announced Emily to a somewhat perplexed Mac.

'Oh! Congratulations.'

'So I'm gonna stay and help her for a few days,' said Jess.

'Lovely,' he said, smiling at her.

He disappeared out of the front door and after a pause, Jess and Emily fell about laughing again. 'Oh Christ, this is going to be interesting,' said Emily.

'Hush now,' said Jess, standing to catch a glance of Mac out of the window. 'Like I say. I am totally focussing on me right now. What do I want to do in life? What do I need to let go of?'

'Who do you want to—' but before Emily could finish whatever she was about to say, Mac walked back in and Jess froze. He smiled. Jess stared at Emily and the girls silently fist bumped. This was what she'd been missing for the last few decades, thought Jess. Camaraderie. Friendship. Something that wasn't spreadsheets and creatives and demanding clients. Maybe it was time to look at the future like it felt good, like it had hope, like she had once upon a time, back when she wasn't much more than a kid. Maybe it was time to stop blaming herself for who she was and how life had unfurled.

Lolly

'We need to talk,' said Kitt as Lolly walked in the door. He was sat in his office, hunched over his laptop and his tone suggested she probably couldn't drop her bags off, get changed and go to the loo first.

'What's up?'

He sighed. He pushed his laptop away from him. He flung his glasses on the table, wiping his eyes with thumb and forefinger.

'Hey, babe. What's the matter? Have you had a tough day?'

He laughed to himself this time. Then pushed papers around his desk.

'Come on, you can talk to me. We're in this together. I was checking our spreadsheets earlier, I think we can manage for a few months on just my wage if we make a few changes. You don't have to jump at the first job that comes up, you know, if you don't want to.'

'It's not that…'

Lolly slipped her coat off, throwing it over the bannister. She moved towards him, pushing her hands down his chest, resting her chin on his head. 'What is it then?' He took her hands from his chest, moving her away. 'Hey, what's the matter?'

'I don't want you coming in being all touchy feely with me, we need to talk.'

'What? I wasn't meaning to be, I was trying to be supportive,' she said, stung by his accusation.

'Supportive doesn't require you to come on to me.'

'I wasn't! I was just…' Lolly bit her tongue because it was clear from his tone that he wasn't in the mood for her to try and correct him on anything. She knew better than to bother arguing with him if he was in this kind of mood. She moved back to the doorway, folding her arms.

'The thing is…' He paused, he couldn't look her in the eye and Lolly didn't like the energy in the room. 'I don't know where to start, I don't know how to say it…'

'Say what? Kitt, you're worrying me now. What's happened?'

'Sometimes it's hard, when one person really wants something and the other goes along with it because a happy wife is a happy life but…'

Lolly's heart seemed to pause, she felt suspended, held by his words.

'I just don't know that I'm happy,' he said, eventually. Was now the time to tell him that she didn't exactly feel happy herself? 'And I've tried to be, I really have, but I just feel that we want different things.'

'What are you saying?' Lolly's heart hadn't paused now. It had pretty much stopped. Her breath was shallow because if she didn't breathe properly, she could slow down time. She could put the brakes on whatever was happening. 'Kitt, you're frightening me.' He looked up at her. 'Kitt…'

'I'm not saying anything… I'm just… I don't know. I'm confused. I'm…' He let out a growl, putting his head in his hands before looking back up at her. 'Work called me today. They told me they had a different job for me. In a different department.'

'They did what?'

'So I took it.'

'But—'

'We need the money. I need the work. If I don't like it, I can look elsewhere. It's easier to get a job when you have one.'

'Is this what you mean? About not being happy?'

'Yeah, I guess so.'

'But… what about us wanting different things?'

'Oh, Lolly, I don't know. I don't know what I mean. I'm stressed out, I'm confused.'

Lolly stepped back over the threshold into his office but resisted touching him again. 'Of course you are, this has been such a stressful time for you. Look, let's get your mum to have the boys for the weekend. We could go away, take some time to be together. Just me and you. Not Mummy and Daddy.'

'Is that your answer? A dirty weekend away?'

'I didn't say that, that's not—'

'Of course it is! That's all you're interested in at the moment. I sit here, trying to pour my heart out and you're not bothered. You're just focussed on getting pregnant.'

'That didn't even come into my head.' Lolly looked at the stranger stood before her. He had an anger she didn't recognise, a bitterness. 'I just meant—'

'I'm away this weekend. Some of the lads from work are on a golfing weekend. It's the new department I'll be working for and I'm going with them.'

'Right,' she said, biting down on her bottom lip.

'The boys'll be back soon, I've not started tea.'

'That's okay, I'll—'

'I've got work to do. The office sent me some papers to read through, a bit of familiarisation before I start back.'

'Right. I mean, that's great. I'm pleased for you. I knew you wouldn't be out of work long.' Kitt stared at Lolly, his eyes cold. 'I'll go sort tea.'

*

When they went to bed that night, Lolly edged herself as far away from Kitt as she could, just to make sure that they didn't accidentally touch and she wasn't accused of trying to jump him or something equally as insane. He'd been like a bear with a sore head for the rest of the evening, snapping at the boys, ignoring her. Something else was going on, Lolly was almost certain of that. She just couldn't figure out what it was.

Emily

Jess had decided to head home that morning. Emily was glad, not because she hadn't loved having her around, but because she was ready for some quiet time. Some time to work out what to do about Jackson. Some time to work out how long her savings would last without her working. Practical things like that. The tides were good so there was no Mac either, the first time all week in which she'd had total peace in the house. She sank into the bathwater, gazing out of the window across the sheep filled fields, out to sea. A large ship crossed the horizon, a couple of fishing boats bobbed closer to land. She briefly wondered if Mac might be on one of those, before her mind wandered to ways in which she could hook him and Jess up. She couldn't be certain, but she suspected he liked Jess too. Several times, she caught him sort of hovering in the hallway, or outside when she was unpacking her car with some shopping she'd picked up, trying to make polite chit-chat as she carried on about her 'jobs'. Jess definitely liked him but had made it clear to Emily that she was not about to ruin the moment to focus on her by getting into something that would most probably amount to nothing. 'Rebound romance,' she had described it at one point, to which Emily had pointed out that she had barely spoken to him and could not be on the rebound over twenty years after splitting up from someone.

Emily pulled herself up in the bath, wiping her hands dry to reach for her iPad. She balanced it on a wooden bath tidy that spanned the width of her roll top. She took a deep breath and opened Jackson's Facebook page. She hadn't stopped thinking about her feelings for him. Whether what she felt was grief about how things ended, or sadness at what she missed. She wasn't even sure she really missed him, or just the life they had that had grown normal, comfortable even, despite how difficult it could be with him sometimes. She was confused, uncertain about him, about herself, about what she'd walked away from. And yet, she felt peace at being back home. And maybe even excited at the prospect of becoming a mother. All she knew with any certainty was that she had to make it clear to Jackson that she wanted nothing from him. If he was so against it, that was his call. That was fine. He could walk away, and she could embrace this new life. She would let him know out of respect. No more, no less. It seemed strange to be planning a future with a tiny person that was half of him and yet have nothing to do with him, but he made his feelings clear when he walked out of her house last week. He'd not said a thing then, he'd not been in touch since. He'd posted a couple of things on Facebook she could see, some links to a new project he was working on. A review for a film he'd supported and the dates for the return of a theatre show that he'd got a few clients in. There was rarely ever anything personal to him on social media so Emily was surprised that she expected anything else, and yet she couldn't help but feel a pang of sadness that he could be so cold and dismissive. He'd never been clear about children. Whatever he wanted to tell himself about it, there had always been ambiguity. And he'd wanted her, hadn't he? Once upon a time? Could his feelings really be switched off that quickly? Could hers?

She typed his name into an email. She let her hands hover over the iPad keyboard for a moment, then she wrote:

Jackson,

I feel I should let you know that despite your disinterest in me or our baby, I am obviously going ahead with this pregnancy. By the end of this year, you will have a child who carries your DNA, a child who is part of you. I'm sorry if I ever misunderstood your feelings on children. I can see now that you have no interest in children or becoming a parent. And I accept that my leaving, and my decision to keep this baby, took any love you may have still had for me. I'm not asking you to be part of this. I don't need your financial support. I intend to do this alone like the millions of other warrior women there are around the world. I'm sorry that I lied. But I'm not sorry I changed my mind.

She paused. She felt like she wanted to tell him she'd loved him. She felt this was a pivotal moment in her now, her future. And yet, there were no words to describe how she really felt about that. It was a combination of so many emotions that if she tried to convey them, he'd no doubt tell her she was being over dramatic or unnecessarily complex. He hated her need to put a name to how she felt about things, he'd always tell her to let things go, to live in the moment. Which is all fine, but he didn't mean it from the point of view of mental health and acceptance of that which we have no control of. He meant it from the point of view that her scrutiny was irritating and wasn't there something more interesting to do like drink, or party. Like network or work. She had spent so many years censoring her emotions that there was a sense of freedom to no longer having to do that, which meant that now she was sat in a cold bath, crying, her heart breaking for the her of yesterday that boxed away who she really was in order to fit in to a world she didn't love because being with Jackson seemed to make life easier. All the years lived like that. She didn't trap him, no matter what he wanted to say, but maybe he trapped her. All those years ago. Now, this baby was a chance to live, to reclaim herself, her body, her future. And the fear that she felt was matched by the excitement. She looked back out to the sea, the ship had gone. The fishing boats too. There was nothing in view but a denim blue sea and pastel skies. And hope. The gentlest glimmer of hope in her future. She had to grasp it with both hands now, she wasn't going to let it go with doubts and second guesses.

Thanks for everything you gave me, I can take it from here,
   Emily.

Amanda

Pete knocked on Amanda's front door. She recognised the pattern and for a brief moment she really hoped he'd have Zennor with him. If anybody could get her to talk calmly and without judgement it would be Pete. She didn't know what magic he had over their daughter, but Amanda was now utterly reliant on it if she hoped to reclaim anything of their relationship.

'What will you do for a tenner?' he asked as she opened the door, clutching a ten-pound note.

'Pete!' she said, taken aback.

'Alright, I'm kidding. Just wanted to lighten the mood from the outset.'

'Well, it's weird,' she said, grabbing her coat. 'Come on, walk with me.'

Pete shoved the money back in his pocket, then waited for her to lock up. 'Okay then, where do you want to walk to?'

'Let's go down the river. Watch the tide come in. Maybe we can sit and talk.'

They walked on in silence. It was past five in the evening and buses and cars filled the roads as commuters made their way home. The streets were busy until they made it out the other side of Truro, crossing to Malpass Road past BBC Radio Cornwall, a bunch of offices full of law firms, and then apartments. As they came to the path along the riverbank, Amanda felt herself let go of a little tension. Brown water

– starkly contrasting to Cornwall's usual crystal clear seas – meandered along the riverbed towards the city centre.

'So, how's Zennor?' she asked, eventually.

'Thinks the world is against her and that you're the root cause.' Amanda winced. 'Sorry, did you want me to sugarcoat it for you?'

'No, no. I get it.'

'It's a shock, before she was just angry at you because she's trying to find her way in the world and you were an embarrassing obstruction. Her opinion, not mine, for the record. Now though…'

'Now I'm a genuine embarrassment with something shameful to throw in the mix.'

'Do you think it's shameful?' he asked.

'No. But I know that's what people who don't understand think.'

'I have told her it's not as straight forward as she is making it and maybe I'd started to make some headway, but her mates are all talking about it and someone suggested I might have been a client and now she's back to square one.'

'Oh god.' Amanda felt her legs turn to stone and made her way to a bench to take the weight off. 'Shit.'

'Yeah. Not ideal.'

'Did you put her right?'

'I told her we were young and in love and made stupid choices. I told her I was not then, nor have I ever been a punter.' He reached in his pocket. 'Still got that tenner, mind.'

'Pete, please.'

'I know, I'm sorry.'

'Shit, what do I do? How do I fix this?'

Pete took in a deep breath, letting it out into the dusk night air. 'I don't think you can, Amanda. Short of telling her you'll never do it again—'

'If that's what it takes!'

'I don't know if it would be enough.'

'I'll do whatever she wants.'

'I know, but you also have to do it for you. Be you.'

'What do you mean?'

'I mean, just as you have no right to dictate her life, she has no right to dictate yours. We just need to work out how we get her to understand it as best she can.'

Amanda watched a bird digging in the clay sand as water surrounded it. Lifting its beak to feast on whatever animal it found in the bed. 'I'd thought about it for years, you know. Way before I started.'

'Which was when?' Pete asked.

'Well... I did a bit of video stuff, photos, years ago. When Zennor was small.'

'Woah, Amanda!'

'You'd gone, I was broke. I didn't want to move, I wanted to fend for myself and raise my daughter. Going out to work meant I'd spend all my income on childcare. It was harmless, she never knew, it never went any further. You weren't around to help, I needed money.'

'I left you in a mess, huh.'

'You did. And I survived. It all helped until Zennor went to school and I was terrified of being found out so I got a job in a shop. Part-time hours so I could do the school run, be there when she needed me.'

'So when did you go back to it? When did it move to what you do now?'

'A couple of years ago. Not long after you got back. When Zennor left and I had the house to myself. The bills were mounting up again. I was lonely, I was angry too. At being left, at you swanning back and taking over. I saw something online. An interview with a load of women who were doing it. They loved it. They earned good money. They were proud and took no shit. I admired how in control of their lives they were. I wanted that. I wanted to reclaim me, my finances. I wanted to stop scrubbing toilets for a pittance when I could be earning decent cash and having lots of sex.'

'I suppose, given your appetite, it's probably not a bad industry.'

'Like I said on the phone, I enjoy it. There are moments, the clients who don't wash so well, the rude blokes who think they can throw money at me and I'll do anything. But there are the ones truly grateful for the attention. There are the ones who want no strings and pleasuring you is as much a part of their enjoyment as whatever you do for them. There are the ones who pay for nails and hair and waxing. There are the women.' Pete looked up. 'Yes, a few women, women who are curious, women who want to spice things up with their husbands, there are the other girls who do this for a living. Many of whom I've never met but talk to every day on social media. Every single one of them I'd count as a friend.'

'Zennor was never going to take it well.'

'No. It's why I never told her.'

'Parents aren't supposed to have sex.'

'Let alone enjoy it.'

'And get paid.'

'Jeez… I've really done it this time, haven't I.' Amanda leaned forward, resting her elbows on her knees, allowing her head to drop. She felt Pete's hand, warm and comforting on the middle of her back. He didn't move it. He didn't say anything. He just let it rest there, as if letting her know that she wasn't alone. And that act of gentleness warmed her heart. 'Thank you,' she said, quietly.

'What for?'

'For not judging. For listening. For being here.'

'Who am I to judge? I walked out on my wife and daughter and didn't contact them for years.' Amanda shook her head. Those things stopped mattering a long time ago. 'And I listen because I care. How can I understand if I don't take the time to hear your side?' Amanda felt her throat strip raw. 'And I'm here because you are the mother of my incredible, if fragile, teenage daughter. You did it all on your own, and I am so proud of her for who she is and you for raising her that way.'

'She hates me. She's hated me for years.'

'She's angry. At you. At me. At life. She's a right to be. I know it wasn't always easy.'

Amanda remembered all the times she scrimped for enough money to pay the bills, when her shop wages just didn't quite cut it. The times she'd stay up late supergluing her own shoes back together so that Zennor could have new ones. The times she'd tell Zennor she wasn't hungry because she wanted her to have the last slice of bread. The times she went to work and then spent every last penny of her wages on petrol so that she could drive Zennor to the beach on a summer weekend. She remembered the years she hid that poverty from Zennor and the times, as she got older, when she confessed to it. When school wanted hundreds of pounds for a school trip to France and there was no way of her coming up with the cash. Her eyes stung at the memories and she was relieved to feel Pete's hand, still on her back.

'I think she was about eleven when I stopped being cool mum, when I started being an embarrassment.'

'Hormones.'

'Hormones. And me. Being me. Not preparing to apologise for it. Trying to be proud despite how shit things were.'

'And why should you apologise?'

'Because maybe she needed me to be somebody else, to at least pretend.'

'And you think pretending would have been better?'

'No,' said Amanda, quietly. 'No.'

'She needs time, Amanda. That's all. Time. And she may never like what you do for a job, but she will come round. She is her mother's daughter. Fierce and independent and fixed of mind.'

'That's what I'm afraid of.'

'And when she realises this is you, being happy and independent. She'll come round. I promise.'

Amanda laughed, sadly. 'If only it was that easy.'

'Hey. Come here.' Pete pulled Amanda in for a cuddle and for a moment, she let herself relax into his warm chest. It wasn't like the cuddles he gave her back when they were kids. He was older now, softer. He was calmer. More gentle. He was everything he'd never been before and she loved that.

Lolly

The girls had all agreed to coming round today. Lolly worked 'til late yesterday and Kitt's Mum had jumped at the chance to have the kids, what with him being away with work. 'Kitt can pick them up when he's on his way back,' she said with glee. 'We'll go to the Maritime Museum then have pizza or something after.' Lolly loved her mother-in-law's generosity of time and the clear joy she took out of spending time with her grandchildren. Would her own mother have been that way? She'd never know, not even having seen how she was with Lolly and Joanna.

When the doorbell went, she jumped up from the sofa, dropping her book on the side to answer the door. She was excited. If Kitt could disappear on long weekends with his new work colleagues, maybe it was time she did something for her. She fancied a retreat. Maybe a few days at Bedruthan Steps with the girls. They could celebrate their newly rekindled friendship with jacuzzis overlooking the ocean. They could drink gin and tonic as the sun went down. They could watch movies on a giant bed with room service.

'Come in, come in! Hi, hi, hi.' She planted each one with a kiss and a hug, pulling them through the door to her home. 'It's sooo nice to have you here, go on through there, let me put the kettle on. Are you hungry yet? I made soup, and some bread. I thought about cooking a roast, but I didn't want to be too focussed on that instead of you lot.'

'Soup sounds perfect,' said Emily, sniffing the air. 'It smells divine!'

'Oh it's just a sort of Thai bisque type thing. Light, but warming.'

'Perfect,' said Amanda, hanging her coat up on the hooks by the front door. 'How are you?' she asked, coming through to the kitchen.

'Oh, good. You know,' said Lolly, ignoring the fact that she'd spent all morning crying because she was now more certain than ever that something was up with Kitt and she just couldn't put her finger on what it was.

'No Kitt?' asked Jess, looking around.

'No. No. He's off somewhere. A weekend away. Work colleagues.'

'I thought he'd lost his job?' asked Emily.

'Yes, well, they called up. Apparently something came up in a different department. He starts officially on Monday.'

'Wow. Right.'

Jess glanced at Emily in a way that made Lolly wonder what she was really thinking.

'I know, I was surprised too, but it just sort of happened and I think he'd been so worried about not having any money and not providing for us, he just jumped straight into it.'

'Of course. I see.' Emily pulled a chair out, shifting herself into it. 'That's great news. Really good. Congratulations.'

'Thanks, thank you.' The girls fell quiet as the kettle boiled. 'So!' said Lolly, wondering where the weird energy had come from. 'What's going on with you three?' They looked at one another. 'What? What is it?'

'It's…' Amanda started.

'It's me. I have news,' interrupted Emily. Amanda looked to Emily, who nodded. 'So, you kept asking me why I wasn't drinking when we met up the other week and now that I've got my head around it, I think I can finally tell you…'

'Oh my god…' said Lolly.

'I'm pregnant. Fourteen weeks.'

'Oh my god!' she said again, forcing a smile whilst hating the fact that she wanted to cry.

'I had a bit of a near miss this last week, Jess ended up all but moving in with me, but I'm out the other side and baby is fine.' She reached into her handbag and Lolly felt sick. 'You want to see a picture?' she asked and Lolly wanted to shout *No!* 'Here is my baby bean.'

Amanda rushed to see the photo, Jess held back, presumably having seen it before.

Lolly forced herself to go over, taking a deep breath because she was happy for Emily, she really was. If this was what Emily wanted she was happy for her. It changed nothing about her own situation and she shouldn't suddenly make it all about her. She was happy. She was happy. She was… crying. Shit. She was crying.

'Hey, Lol, oh no! Please don't,' said Emily, hastily stuffing the picture in the bag and turning to hug her. 'I'm so sorry, I didn't think… well I just thought… I didn't expect you to react this way, I'm so sorry!'

'It's fine,' hiccupped Lolly. 'Really, I'm sorry. I don't know what's wrong with me. I'm being stupid!'

A rush of cold air came up the hallway and Lolly's boys charged into the kitchen, throwing their arms around her legs. She quickly wiped her face. 'Boys! What are you doing here?' she said, cuddling them into her, her eyes filling just as soon as she'd wiped them away. 'Gosh, I've missed you.' She sniffed. 'Where's Daddy?' she asked, looking down the hallway after him.

'Here,' he called out, dropping bags in the hallway as he slammed the front door shut. 'The weather caved in so golf was called off.'

'Right, I see,' she said, wiping her face again, painting on what she hoped was a reasonable attempt at a smile. But it couldn't have been, because as soon as Kitt saw her, his face changed. And then he looked to Emily, Jess and Amanda.

'What's the matter?' he asked, hovering in the doorway.

'Nothing, it's nothing. Not now,' she said, motioning to the boys as her bottom lip wobbled.

'Boys. Upstairs,' he instructed. The boys ignored him. 'Boys! Now!' he shouted and they scuttled away to the relative safety of their room. He paused. He walked closer to Amanda, then stopped, as if he couldn't break through the force field around her. 'You just had to, didn't you?' he spat. 'You just fucking had to, didn't you?'

Amanda shook her head and Jess moved to stand between them.

'What's the matter?' asked Lolly, suddenly made nervous by Kitt's tone.

'I should have known a low life scumbag like you couldn't keep it quiet. I should have known, that's what all this is about, isn't it? This friendship. It's nothing to do with her, you just want to bring me down, don't you?'

Lolly stared.

'I haven't said anything,' said Amanda, standing her ground though her voice wobbled.

'About what?' asked Lolly.

'Really? Why's she so upset then?' he asked, venomously.

'Emily just told her she is pregnant, I guess that hit a raw nerve right now,' said Amanda, fixing Kitt with a steely glare.

'What should she have told me about?' asked Lolly, stepping back to steady herself against the kitchen worktop. 'What are you talking about? Kitt, what's the matter?'

'I think it's time you left,' said Kitt, despite the fact he was now pretty much blocking Amanda's easiest exit route.

'They're staying for lunch,' said Lolly. 'I invited them.'

'*She's* not staying,' he hissed in Amanda's direction. 'We don't have people like that in our house.'

'What do you mean? People like that?' asked Lolly. But as she did, she felt the room go cold. She saw Kitt's face shift. She saw Emily look away. She saw Amanda swallow. She felt as if at any moment, her entire world was going to come crashing down…

Amanda

'He means sex workers,' Amanda said, with as much poise and self-respect as she could muster. 'He presumably thinks we're the lowest of the low and doesn't want my kind in his house.' Amanda watched Lolly's confusion grow. 'I think he thinks that I've told you about something he should probably have told you before.'

'It's got nothing to do with you,' said Kitt over his shoulder as he moved towards his wife. 'Lolly. Don't listen to her. Ignore her. She's clearly got issues.'

'Has she?' asked Jess, standing beside Amanda so their shoulders touched. Two against one. 'Or is it just that she knows something you don't want Lolly to know?'

'Baby, ignore them, they're obviously all in this together.'

Amanda felt Emily's shoulder to her other side. 'Lolly, I don't want to hurt you. It's the last thing I would ever want to do. I love you, but... you need to ask Kitt to be truthful with you.'

Lolly shifted her gaze from Amanda to Kitt. He reached his hand out to stroke her face but she visibly froze. He must have sensed it too because he dropped his hand. 'Lolly, it's not what it seems.'

'What isn't?' she asked, her voice now quiet but uncharacteristically strong. 'What isn't what it seems?'

'This. Them. Her!'

'So how is it, Kitt?'

'It's lies.'

'What are? She hasn't said anything. Or was she about to? Hmmm? Was she about to say something and you didn't want her to because you know it would spell the end of our marriage.'

'Lolly.'

'Because it's not the first time you've done it, is it?'

Amanda held her breath.

'And the last time, you said you'd never do it again, didn't you? That was a lie too, wasn't it? Because you *have* done it again. I should have known. In fact, I did know. I've known there was a problem for days, weeks even. I just didn't know exactly what. And is that it? Or is there more? Hmm? Or do you want to make up some stories, some excuses that you think I'm stupid enough to fall for.' Kitt said nothing. Lolly sought out his eye contact, forcing him to face her. 'So she's a sex worker. And you slept with her. You paid for it.' She paused, to Amanda it looked as though Lolly could taste the lies, the bitterness. 'Was she good? Did she do all the things I never have? Did she satisfy you? Did it feel exciting to hand over cash and have someone do whatever you wanted them to do?'

Amanda flinched because it wasn't like that. She wasn't a slave, she wasn't there for them to take advantage of in any way they chose. She retained control. The clients who abused that trust didn't come back.

'Go,' Lolly said, low but certain.

'Lolly, please, we have to talk about this.'

'Why bother? I've heard it before. I've forgiven you before.'

She stared at him for a moment and both Emily and Jess moved closer to Amanda, letting her know she was going to be okay, no matter what. And then a peace descended, a quiet. Lolly shook her head as if she pitied Kitt. She turned her back on him, reaching inside a cupboard for a bottle of champagne. She poured four glasses, handing them to each of the girls. She turned to Kitt, 'It's time you left. And this time, don't bother coming back.' Then she turned to the girls, raised her glass in Emily's direction and said, 'To Emily, to the baby, congratulations. I'm really happy for you.' She clinked each glass as the girls stood in silence and watched her sink the lot, before topping up her glass and sinking the second. Amanda's heart raced.

'Lolly, we should talk.'

'There is nothing to discuss.'

'It's not that straightforward.'

'We were trying for a baby, Kitt. It's not like you weren't getting it at home. The only other reason for you doing it must be compulsion and I can't live with a man who behaves that way.'

'Lolly!'

'LEAVE!' she shouted.

Kitt looked from her to Jess, Amanda and Emily. He went to the door, he looked back at Amanda as if she was the one to ruin his life and she bit down hard on her lip because he would not do that to her. A rush of air shifted the energy and the door slammed shut.

Jess

'So,' said Lolly, 'how far along are you, did you say? You must be so thrilled. Are you going to find out what you're having? And what about the father? I assume it's Jackson? What does he say? Oh my god, does this mean you're going back to America?'

'Lolly,' said Jess, reaching out to her. 'Are you okay?'

'Me? Of course. I just lost twelve stone of deadweight. I've never felt better.'

'Lolly,' said Emily.

'What? No, seriously. As you just heard, it's not the first time he's ever done it. I forgave him once, I don't have to forgive him again. I can't trust him. Simple as that.'

Lolly wasn't convincing any of them. Amanda was biting her bottom lip, clearly not okay. Jess wanted to reach out and let her know it was going to be alright but the dynamic in the room felt odd. She put her drink down and watched as Amanda seemed to search the ground for something to say. 'Lolly…'

Lolly stiffened. 'Don't.'

'Please, I need you to know—'

'I don't *need* to know anything. I don't *want* to know anything.' Lolly's voice was cold, detached. 'You slept with my husband. It's your job. It's fine.'

'It's not fine, Lol. I know it's not fine. But you need to know that—'

'Shall we move into the lounge? I've put out some crisps. The soup has burned to the bottom of the pan now so we should probably just order take out or something. If anyone's hungry. Not sure I have much of an appetite, but I bet the boys would be happy with pizza for tea.'

'It was before the reunion,' said Amanda. Lolly stood stock-still. 'I knew he was married, some of them are, but I didn't know he was married to you.'

Jess felt split loyalty, she wanted to go to Amanda and hold her hand, she wanted to wrap Lolly up in cotton wool and take away the pain she was so clearly feeling. She also felt for Amanda who was now white as a sheet and not anywhere near as confident as the woman she usually portrayed.

'When I realised, when you said who you were married to, I can't tell you how I felt, there are no words, I mean, I felt sick but it was more than that…'

Lolly let out a noise that suggested she knew what it was to feel full of mixed emotions. Emily put her hand on Amanda's arm with a gentle squeeze. Jess took Lolly by the shoulders and guided her to one of the bar stools.

'I didn't know what to do. I told him I couldn't see him any more as soon as I knew. Then he started texting, calling, he wouldn't leave me alone. After we all met, he told me to back off, to leave you alone. But I'd realised how nice it was to see you all again, to be reconnected and find that so little had changed. That life had moved on but we still had friendship.'

'You had sex with my husband.'

'Not after I knew who he was, Lolly. I promise,' Amanda pleaded. 'I only contacted him a couple of times after that and it was always because I was trying to get him to be truthful with you.'

'About seeing you?'

Jess looked up at Amanda. Amanda's eyes flicked to Jess.

'What? Was there something else?'

'Lolly, he should be the one telling you this,' said Jess.

'What? You know something too?'

'We all do,' said Emily, gently.

'What else is there? What else do you all fucking well know about my husband?' Lolly stood, moving herself away from them all. 'Come on, what dark secrets is he sharing with you?'

'Really, I think you need to talk to him,' said Jess.

'I don't want to talk to him. I don't get the truth from him. Fuck him! He can pack his bags when I'm not here. I don't want to see him or hear from him. I don't care, he can't hurt me. He can't hurt me any more...' but as she said it, Lolly unravelled, her body going limp. 'All I wanted was to be happy, to be married, to raise a family. It's all I ever wanted. Apart from a daughter. I really thought that would be it, that a girl would make our lives. That we would be complete, that I'd be complete.'

'I'm so sorry,' said Amanda, now letting silent tears stream down her face.

'Still, we had sex last night. So you know, it might still happen.' Emily caught Jess's eye. 'What? Come on! What!'

'He didn't have the vasectomy reversed,' said Jess, carefully. Lolly stared, not certain of what she was hearing. 'He told you he'd been, but he didn't.'

'He didn't want another child,' finished Amanda.

'But he knew...' said Lolly, breathless. 'He knew what that meant to me...' And that was it. That was the final detail to finish Lolly off. Jess moved to hold her as Lolly dissolved into the pain. She wrapped her arms around her, her own body moving each time Lolly sobbed. Emily took Amanda's hand in hers and they stood, waiting, for however long it would be until Lolly could look up again and breathe.

Lolly

'I need to sort the boys, I need to make them tea,' said Lolly, eventually, her throat raw and her head pounding.

'Don't worry, we'll sort it,' said Jess, scrolling her phone. 'I'll get them pizza, set them up with a film or something upstairs.' She disappeared up to find their room and Lolly was grateful for one less thing to think about.

Emily dug around in her bag. 'Here, use this on your face,' she said, handing over some kind of spritz spray that smelled of frankincense and bergamot. A fine spray landed on Lolly's face and for a second she could almost feel normal. 'Take these too, stave off the headache before it arrives and takes over,' she said, passing a blister pack of paracetamol and running cold water into the champagne flute.

Lolly was dazed, grateful for their kindness. She couldn't believe how quickly her life had changed. It hadn't been perfect, she knew that much. It had been difficult after she found out the first time, not long after Stan was born, but she blamed herself. It had been a difficult birth, it took a long time to recover, she had neglected Kitt's needs. But the difficulty was part of marriage, that's what she'd always told herself. However hurt she'd been, she was making it work because that's what she signed up for when they married. And when they agreed to be parents. And when they agreed to have another... another that she would likely never have. Emily leant against the worktop and Lolly was reminded of the new life growing inside her belly and her heart caved with a jealousy she didn't want.

'I should probably go,' said Amanda, interrupting her thoughts.

Lolly looked up to see her red-rimmed eyes. The confidence, the banter she normally offered in times of stress, it had all gone. Amanda was pale, tired – frightened? 'You don't have to go,' said Lolly, not yet sure how she really felt about her.

'I think it's probably for the best. The girls can look after you. I'll check in, in a few days maybe, when you've had some time.'

'To get used to the idea?' Lolly asked.

Amanda shook her head. 'That's not what I meant... I don't really know what I meant. Or what I expect, I just... I'd like to talk things through. When you're ready. If you want to.'

Lolly bowed her head then nodded. She loved Amanda, but she couldn't help that to look at her hurt right now. She wasn't sure what was more painful, what her husband had done, or that he'd done it with someone she trusted.

Amanda grabbed her bag, she kissed Emily. She moved towards Lolly who was relieved when she opted to give her arm a gentle squeeze instead. Amanda paused before walking down the hall. 'I stopped as soon as I knew he was your husband,' she said. 'I would never knowingly hurt you... ever.'

Amanda walked down the hallway, meeting Jess at the bottom of the stairs. They exchanged hushed words before Lolly saw Jess hug Amanda, then carefully close the door behind her. And as Jess came through to the kitchen, Lolly's tears returned. The four had become three and it felt incomplete.

'Hey, hey. Come on, come here,' she said, pulling Lolly into her chest.

'What am I going to do, Jess? I can't do this alone. The boys. Work. The house! I can't do this on my own.'

'You don't have to.'

'I can't have him back. Not this time. I can't do that to myself.'

'I don't mean that, I mean us. Your other friends. Work. People will help. You'll get all the support you need. Whatever you decide to do next, we're here for you, aren't we, Emily?'

'Of course, love. Of course we are.'

'You've got your own stuff to deal with,' said Lolly, not meaning to sound quite as bitter as she suspected she did.

'So we can work it out together,' said Emily. 'We can be there for each other. Support one another. You've done this before, you'll know what I'm about to face.'

Lolly wasn't sure she could. She wasn't sure she was selfless enough to support someone with a new baby. And, oh god, what if it was a girl? Lolly hated herself for thinking it, but she just didn't know if she could put aside her own wants to be there for anybody right now.

'Is that someone at the door?' asked Emily, straining to see down the hall.

Lolly hadn't heard anything. 'Tell him I don't want to see him,' she said. 'If it's him, tell him to go away.'

'It's probably the pizza I ordered.' Jess jogged down to open the door.

'Hi… is Lolly in?' asked a voice. And Lolly knew exactly who it was and lost it all over again.

'Hey, hey…. What's the matter?' said the woman making her way in and straight to Lolly. She looked up at Jess and Emily. 'What's happened,' she asked. The girls looked at Lolly's older sister. 'I thought I'd surprise her a few days early…'

'Kitt's been at it again,' said Lolly, the words snatched through broken sobs. 'We were trying for a baby and he hadn't even had his vasectomy reversed.' She buried her head in her sister's chest, her sister looked stunned, stroking her hair.

'How did you find out?' asked Joanna, which made Lolly let out another, loud sob. 'Hey… hey…'

'He was seeing a friend of mine. She has sex for a job.'

'Oh god.'

'She says she didn't know.'

'I believe her,' said Emily.

'I'm certain,' chimed in Jess. 'We met up and she told us everything. She was trying to get Kitt to tell Lolly herself and he wouldn't have it. He was getting more and more aggressive towards her.' Lolly sniffed, Joanna stared, stunned. 'Lolly, Amanda hates how this has hurt you,' she pleaded.

It was two hours later when Lolly closed the door to Jess and Emily. The boys had been fed and the leftover pizza sat congealed in the box on her kitchen top. She could hear Joanna bathing them, making them laugh, telling them outrageous stories and splashing water all over. Lolly stood by the patio doors looking out onto the garden she'd planted with Kitt. Plants were out of control, others were dead. A deflated football sat in the middle of the lawn and Lolly could remember the last time they all went out to play with it. It was Christmas, when Kitt had finally told her they could try for another child. When she thought that New Year was going to be their best yet. In that moment, the ups and downs they'd had through their marriage had paled because he'd finally agreed to something that meant everything to her. She remembered falling in love with him all over again. She remembered how close to him she felt, how lucky she felt to have a husband and a home and two healthy boys. She remembered that feeling of excitement about what was to come, and she remembered going to bed that night, them making love, and her drifting off to sleep imagining what their little girl might grow up to look like. To sound like. To be like.

It was the last dream in her life. The last thing she wanted to achieve. It was her only missing piece. And now, at forty years old, everything she hoped and dreamed for herself and her boys lay in tatters. And she had no clue if she would survive.

Jess

Jess and Emily were silent in the car. Jess didn't know about Emily, but for her, the last few hours had propelled life to the forefront. Just as Lolly was facing the reality of what Kitt's actions meant for her as a mum and a human being in her own right, Jess could feel her own baggage unfold. Something she'd hidden for so long, something she'd held shame for. Something that had set the tone for the rest of her life and something she now knew, without any doubt, she had no blame for.

Should she say something? Report her attacker? It had been so many years. Who would believe her now? Did she even believe herself? There were times when she relived what happened and wondered if she'd simply misread his advances.

Her best friend's father.

She'd relived it in recent days, she'd tried to remember if there was any innocence in his touch, in the ghost feel of him up against her. She could still taste stale whiskey and smell the stench of his cigar. She still felt the grip on her arm when she tried to leave and felt the fear, deep in the pit of her belly, as he told her to stay. It would be their secret, she didn't have to be frightened, he would be gentle. That it didn't matter if it was her first time because he was experienced, he'd show her how to enjoy herself.

'What happened to you?' asked Emily, out of the blue.

Jess stared out of the window. That Emily's father hadn't actually had sex with her was only because someone tried to get into his office and he lost his nerve. That she got away with her virginity intact didn't take away from the pain of knowing where and how he'd touched her. It didn't save her fear, it didn't stop the vivid memory of his touch.

'At the party. What happened to you?'

Would Jess always be able to feel him?

'Jess?'

She didn't respond, biting the inside of her cheek instead. She couldn't tell Emily what had happened without the rest of the story unfolding. And just as Amanda hadn't wanted to hurt Lolly, something it was clear after tonight she couldn't have avoided, Jess didn't want to hurt Emily. There was nothing in her bones that wanted their friendship to disintegrate. She was ready to make changes, she could see that now, but not ones that would affect anyone else.

She had told her parents that same night. Full of shame and regret and hurt. They hadn't fought for her, they let him escape. Let him run away with his family and start a new life in a new country. Maybe if they'd dealt with it then, it would have been different. Did he stop? Was she the only one? Or was this the way he was, a symptom of an era that had no respect for women, for young girls. An era that protected men and their delicate reputations above and beyond anything else. If she said nothing now, all these years on, did it make her complicit? Was she letting him get away with it?

Or was she protecting herself in the only way she knew how? By protecting the life and the people she needed to have around her in order to survive. In order to thrive. In order to stop him suffocating the rest of her life as he had from then until now. He'd taken enough of her life, hadn't he?

Emily stopped the car outside Jess's house. 'Did something happen to change you, Jess?' Emily's voice was soft, gentle. She didn't pose a threat, she was safe in so many ways and yet...

Jess nodded. 'Something did.'

'Oh, Jess,' Emily whispered. 'I'm so sorry...'

Jess took a deep breath, forcing herself not to give in to tears because she was tired of them. 'You don't have to be sorry any more than I do,' she said.

'When? I mean... how? Who? I thought we knew everyone there? Who did we know that could have done something like that?'

Jess pulled her bag into her, if ever there was a time to tell her it was now. And yet... 'Do you know what? The detail doesn't matter. It changes nothing.'

'I know, but... I just feel so bad for you. I mean, you were so bright, so full of life. It must have been so awful, to have sucked you away like that. Someone should pay, they shouldn't get away with it. You deserve better!'

Jess nodded. 'I do. But you know, I think I've realised something, just in these last few weeks of having you lot back in my life, I can't let it take any more of me. It's had too much, *he's* had too much. I won't allow him to take any more. I do deserve better. I deserve happiness. I deserve to find me.'

'We all do!'

Jess nodded. 'We all do.'

Emily pulled Jess in for a hug. 'How the hell did I get through life this far without you lot?'

Jess laughed. 'God knows, but we made it this far and we're doing okay, just imagine what the rest of our life will be like now. All four of us, taking on the world.'

'Yes!'

'And your little one. He or she is not going to go short on love and affection and guidance and wisdom… and maybe stories about you from when we were kids.'

'Thank god I moved away before any of the really embarrassing stories happened!' Emily laughed.

'Oh I don't know, we were sixteen. I reckon there's a few we can drag up, no problem. Look, go on. Thanks for the lift. Text me when you get home.'

'Will do. Love you, Jess.'

'Love you too, Emily.'

Jess stood on the street, waving Emily off before turning to let herself into the house. There were things she needed to do, without a doubt. Therapy to start with, get talking through things. Matt had been right about that too, not that she'd ever let on. He was already smug factor ten at her taking control of her destiny. It wasn't going to be easy, and she still wasn't sure how she felt about effectively letting Emily's dad get away with what he did, but one thing she did know was she was ready to make changes. Changes that applied to work too, and not to avoid Jay, but to welcome new opportunities. She could just about feel, in her heart, a determination to explore her dreams, something she'd buried years ago. Now she just had to work out what they looked like.

Emily

Exhausted, Emily threw her bag down and dropped into the sofa, face down before adjusting because her bump was not happy. She tried calling Amanda after leaving Jess but she hadn't picked up. Maybe time was needed there, time and patience. Lolly would come round, Emily was certain of that and it wouldn't take long before the four of them could pick things up properly. They'd have to, at the risk of selfish thought, Emily needed them. She couldn't help feel they probably needed her too.

She turned over, letting her legs cross on the chair arm as she put her hands, palms down, on her belly. Seeing Lolly in so much pain had really brought it home to her that she was lucky, as perverse as it felt. She was lucky that she could do this her way, alone, without distraction. She wanted to read up on every aspect of pregnancy, then motherhood. She wanted to read blogs and accounts, she wanted to plan for their future together. A tight team of two, with three fairy godmothers. She pictured the nursery all finished, her rocking in a chair, feeding her newborn. She thought about the school and the friends and the birthdays. She closed her eyes and imagined them wandering down to the shoreline to paddle. Tiny toes lost in the sand as the tide turned. She groaned at the knock on the door because she couldn't be bothered to get up but had dropped the latch so if it was Mac, he couldn't let himself in.

She suspected it probably was, he'd left some tools here the other day and might need them before he came back to hers.

'Hello, I'm coming,' she shouted, hauling herself up to standing. 'Woah, head rush. Hang on,' she said, giving herself a minute before padding across to answer the door. 'Maybe I just need to get you a key, then you can come and go as you— Oh!'

Where she'd expected Mac, Jackson was standing. 'Emily.'

'What are you doing here?'

'I've had time to think. I've decided I'd come and get you. We could do this together, raise our baby in New York. I know I've always said I didn't want children and I really didn't think I did, but the more I've thought about it since—'

'—since you walked out in silence when I told you I was pregnant.'

'Well... yes.' He ruffled his hair and she was glad he appeared to feel some kind of shame at the fact. 'But I didn't know what to do. The whole journey back to the airport, on the flight home, I kept telling myself it was best for us both if I left you to it. I've got a big new project on, I knew I needed to focus. But I can't focus... not without you by my side.'

Emily looked at him. She'd never seen him look vulnerable before. She'd never seen him look needy. Was he nervous, or scared? 'You'd better come in,' she said, standing back.

Jackson stood in the hallway looking around again. 'It really is lovely here,' he said.

'That's not what you said last time.'

'I was being a jerk. I thought you would want to feel like I was fighting for you. I thought I could just come back and collect you, I didn't realise...'

'What? That I had my own mind.'

'No. Well... maybe. I don't know. I guess—'

'You underestimated me. Just like you always have done.'

'Do you really think that?'

'I know that, Jackson. You thought I'd do what you said when you booked that termination. You certainly didn't expect me to leave you. And I don't think you imagined for one minute that I'd stay here. You have *always* underestimated me and, for a while, it didn't matter, but you know what, it does now. It does matter.'

'So, I've learned my lesson. Christ, Em, I will never underestimate you again. You are so much stronger than I ever realised, and I know you could do this on your own, this whole...' He circled in the direction of her belly, which irked Emily slightly. 'But you don't have to. Let's go home. Let's do it together. Let's be the best parents we can be.'

'I am home.'

Jackson looked around. 'Okay... so we'll stay here.'

Emily was stunned. 'What?'

'We'll stay here,' he said, swallowing. 'We'll stay here. Start a new life. Cornwall seems... nice.'

'It is. But it's also not New York.'

'No, I know but... look, that's how much you mean to me, Emily. I would be prepared to move, to change my life. For you.'

'For me? And the baby.'

'Of course, and the baby. I just need you to believe in me, to give me a chance. Emily, I love you. I have always loved you. I will always love you. If that means loving you comes with an extra one, here in Cornwall, then so be it. I'm prepared to work at this, for you...'

Emily looked at him. He held his arm out, gently taking her hand in his. His touch was familiar, his hands soft. 'I love you, Emily...'

Three Months Later

Amanda

'I'll pop round later,' shouted Amanda to George, closing the door behind her. He'd spotted she was nervous as she poured milk into his teacup. He patted her hand, told her to relax. That whatever was making her anxious might not be worth it. And if it was worth it, not to panic, because she was brilliant. He had no idea what she was about to face, but she appreciated his words of encouragement all the same. It didn't stop the nerves though.

She'd been nervous since Zennor texted asking for a meet up. It had been so long, she was desperate to resolve things. In the shower that morning, she'd finally let herself imagine the conversation, she'd thought what it might be like to be friends again, she'd let the water run across her face 'til she could barely breathe, stepping out of its flow to gulp at fresh air before diving back under. Anything to take away the feeling of being out of control of her destiny, because that's what this felt like.

She waited on the swings at Boscawen Park, somewhere she'd spent so much time when Zennor was young. The sun was just beginning to gain strength as they approached summer and Amanda turned her face to feel its gentle warmth. The number of times she'd sat here in years gone by, the time Zennor took her first steps over by the slide, just as a toddler came flying down and wiped her out. Or the time she'd brought a load of Zennor's school pals down for a birthday picnic because she couldn't afford to take them to Burger King or wherever it was that Zennor actually wanted to go. Or before that, when she was a teenager herself, she remembered that GCSE year, the long summer, spending a couple of days here with the girls because they'd wanted to come into town shopping but got distracted by some boys who walked in this direction, even though it was further out of town than they had planned to be. The illicit excitement of flirtation with boys probably a lot older than her when she'd managed to get the girls to follow her lead. She could still feel those brief moments of teenage giddiness. She took a deep breath, allowing her memories to come and go as a way to settle the nerves. Then the sun disappeared behind a shadow and Amanda instinctively knew she was here. It was time to face up to however this conversation was going to play out.

'Hey,' she said.

Zennor didn't say anything, but she didn't scowl, as was the look on her face so many times before.

'You cut your hair.'

Zennor nodded.

'It looks nice. *You* look nice.'

Three months wasn't all that long in the grand scheme of things and yet it was forever for Amanda, waiting for Zennor to decide if and when she would talk to her mother again. And in that time, it seemed to Amanda that she had changed somehow, she held herself differently, she held eye contact, she was beautiful.

'I missed you,' said Amanda, daring herself to stand and hold out her arms for Zennor. Her heart leapt when Zennor met her gesture halfway and they embraced. It wasn't like the hugs she'd got in this park when Zennor was a child, running at her mum for her to scoop her up in her arms and squeeze as tight as she could. But it was contact, something she'd barely allowed Amanda to make since she hit her teenage years. 'Funny, being back here…' said Amanda.

Zennor looked around. 'Yeah, I figured it was neutral. And it's a nice day.'

'It is.'

Zennor sat on the swing beside Amanda. A young mum arrived with a toddler on a scooter who whizzed past them heading straight for the slide, abandoning his ride to run up the steps and shout to his mum that he was the king of the castle. It made Zennor smile and Amanda could see the little girl in her, the one hiding behind the young woman who was beginning to emerge.

'I've thought a lot about this. Us meeting,' said Amanda. 'I've tried to think of all the things I need to tell you to try and help you to understand who I am and what I do.' Zennor swung gently as she spoke. 'And I don't think there is anything I can say that makes it okay with you, if you're not okay with the idea of it in the first place. I mean, I can well imagine it's weird for you to think of me as anything other than your mum and I know I never did that in quite the way you wanted.'

Zennor's face stayed poker straight but that she was listening gave Amanda hope.

'I don't think I'm this way because I was young when I had you… I think this is just who I am. And maybe that means that I could never have been the type of mum who did the whole sensible, grown up persona thing, but…'

'You did the best you could.'

Amanda's breath caught in her throat. 'I did. Zennor, I really tried.'

Zennor nodded, though watched the toddler as he ran from slide to sand pit to seesaw back to sand pit.

'It took me a long time to be okay with me. To accept that the things I was happiest doing were not the things that society expected of me. And I wrestled with it, I felt guilty. I felt like I'd let you down, or maybe even womanhood down. But I realised something, probably after I'd started the sex work.' Zennor flinched at the mention but Amanda knew that if she was to get through this, they were just going to have to be transparent about it. 'It was after you went to live with your dad, I'd never done it whilst you were at home. I remember that first client. I was terrified. I wondered what the hell I'd set myself up for. God, I was almost sick with nerves but he was so gentle, so in need of care that we sort of saw each other through it.' Amanda paused, giving Zennor a breather. 'And when he paid me, he thanked me. He hugged me and I knew that what I'd done was made him feel something special, for just a short time. It was something he needed and that made me feel good. I wanted to shout it from the rooftops because I felt proud.'

'Proud?'

'Yes. It felt right. And the more clients I saw, the more confident I became. In my body, in me. It felt like I'd been wasting my time all the years I'd jobbed in pubs, the shop and cleaning. Not because there's anything wrong with those jobs, but because I loved my new career. I could pick and choose when I wanted to work. I could select clients. I was never doing anything I didn't want to do.'

'But isn't it dangerous? Don't you get men who take advantage?'

'Yes. It happens. Just as it happened in many other jobs I had. And I don't want to play that down, sometimes I've been scared. Sometimes they've assumed they can treat me badly because of what I do, but

I've got stronger. In many cases, I can spot which ones are likely to be that way and don't entertain it. And if it does happen, I know I have a support network to get me through it. Maybe I take a few days off for some self-care. Report them if needs be. Give my friends and peers a heads up that there's someone like that doing the rounds.'

Zennor shifted to straddle the swing, looking at Amanda. 'Are you safe?'

'Of course. This is my body, my livelihood. Safety is paramount. I go for regular testing, I always use condoms. There are certain acts I refuse to do and if they want that kind of service there are other women they can see.'

'But aren't they exploiting you?'

'I don't happen to believe so. I know there are women who are exploited. There are women who aren't able to keep safe. And there are men who don't care about rules or boundaries, but that's not generally my experience of it.'

'I was so embarrassed,' said Zennor, fixing her mum with a glare. 'Billy was fascinated. Each time we met he kept asking me questions.'

'I told you to steer clear of him.'

'I didn't want to. I liked him…' She looked down to the ground. 'Turns out, he only liked me because of you.'

Amanda's heart sank for her baby. 'I'm sorry. That's…'

'Men for you?'

'Some of them. Not all of them.'

They sat in silence for a while. Amanda wanted to ask all of the questions of her daughter, desperate to know how things were, what she'd been up to. She sensed, however, that time and patience was needed.

'Dad and I talked, when he first came back. I was really angry with him, I was bitter. I wanted to scream at him, when he first came up and introduced himself. I couldn't believe he had the audacity to be so brazen. And I did get angry, on one particular day, I did scream at him.'

'And how did he take that?' Amanda was genuinely curious. They hadn't really talked about Pete coming back, or Zennor opting to move out to be with him.

'He waited until I stopped being angry. Then he told me he couldn't turn back time. That he made bad choices. That he wished he could do things differently, better. He told me he wanted to build a relationship with me, that he loved me, that he would give me all the time I needed and that he would never do anything to hurt me again.'

'I don't know that I can stop doing what I do, Zennor. I'm happy. It earns me good money. I mean… I suppose if our future were to depend on it, maybe I'd have to—'

'I'm not asking you to.' Amanda felt a pang of guilt at the relief. 'I guess I'm just saying that he had to tell me all of those things when he came back because he'd not been around to tell me them when I was growing up. He never showed me how he felt. You though… you've always been around. You've always told me how you felt and you've always shown it… just in your way.'

'You are the most important person in the world to me.'

'I know.'

Zennor stood, blocking the sunshine from Amanda's eyes again. 'I don't like what you do, Mum, but I don't like being angry with you.' Amanda held her breath. 'And I want you in my life, just… maybe… don't talk to me about it.'

'Of course I won't. If that's what it takes, if that's what you want.'

'I want to take it slowly and see what happens. I want to learn how we do us again.'

'On new terms. As two women.'

'But you're still my mum, we're not mates.'

'I know. I'm your mum. I get it.'

Zennor half smiled. 'I have to get back. I've got an interview this afternoon. For a college course. Photography.'

'Oh, Zennor, wow! That's… that's brilliant.'

'I'll call you.'

'Okay. I'll wait, I guess… unless…'

'I'll call you.'

'Okay.' Zennor started walking away and the overwhelming surge of love for her daughter took Amanda's breath away. 'I love you,' she shouted after her.

'I know you do,' she answered, and Amanda thought she could hear her say I love you too.

Emily

Jackson busied about the nursery, finishing off the paint job that he'd taken off Mac because what was the point in spending money on someone to do something he could do equally as well. Emily was downstairs making them tea. She studied the twenty week scan of their daughter, taken weeks ago and now pinned to the inside of her cupboard door along with the twelve week and a card from Lolly that said how thrilled she was for her.

Jackson's phone rang. It hadn't rung for days. The first few days after he'd moved himself in, it would ring constantly. Day and Night. People wanting to know where he was, when he was due back. To begin with, he'd made grand gestures of solidarity. 'I'm staying here. I'll be back to sort out a few things, but then I'm moving to Cornwall permanently.' 'You'll have to find somebody else.' 'I'm so sorry to let you down, but this is important. I need to be here.'

Emily couldn't work out quite why she felt the way she did about these declarations. It felt weird, uncomfortable. She figured it was probably because she had never known him to dedicate his life to her in the way he was apparently doing, but even still, it was strange.

He stayed for two weeks then went home for two. He packed up a load of things and when he arrived back, he had a whole host of things that he'd organised to be shipped over. Emily had ignored the niggle, the irritation at his return. Mac had finished building the wardrobes for the baby and Jackson promptly filled them all up with his stuff. He was noisy. Just his presence, after a couple of weeks on her own, save for Jess's occasional visits – which she now knew was only slightly to do with seeing her and a lot more to do with hanging around to see Mac – he took up space. He loomed large. She figured she'd get used to it. At least, she hoped.

And then he'd get the calls that he took outside. Or upstairs behind a closed door. The pings on his iPhone of emails that he had to tend to straight away. That was when she'd realised that no matter what he had said when he arrived on her doorstep – in fact, no matter what he wanted to try and become – he just couldn't leave the hustle. Agenting. New York. L.A. Work. It was all in his blood, he was showbiz. He pretended that wasn't the case. She'd let him get close but told him it would take a little longer for her to trust him fully, to be with him, to let him hold her. She'd caught sight of him studying her body one morning in the bathroom and she felt shame at the stretch marks knitting a web across her pregnant belly, shame at the new flabbiness of her bum and hips. How her boobs had begun to swell beyond what she knew he liked. It wasn't his fault, she'd told herself at the time. He was a product of an industry that desired airbrushed perfection, not pregnant reality. But still, the scrutiny hurt.

So this morning's phone call, in which she blatantly heard him say that he wouldn't be too much longer, was the end. It was the moment she realised he couldn't be the man he was presenting. And even if he could, she wasn't sure he was the man that she wanted. In fact, she wasn't sure she wanted any man at all. The more time she'd spent with Amanda, the more she'd realised that it was possible to raise a child alone. That it was going to be hard, but parenting was in any case. She was privileged, she had money. She had friends. She had a community that spread from Cakebreads Village Stores across the whole village. Betty had checked in with her weekly since she found out the news and was giddy. There were plenty of kids up at the top of the village, but somehow Betty told her she felt this one was special. She said she couldn't imagine a time when Mac would have children so if Emily didn't mind, she might quite like to take on the role of surrogate grandmother. She'd said it when she'd just baked scones and Emily would have agreed to anything at that point in time, but the more she thought about it, the more love Emily felt for both Betty and the village as a whole. They'd embraced her once again when they knew she was to become a mother, and they'd done their very best to embrace Jackson too.

But he couldn't embrace Cornwall. And he couldn't embrace Emily's choices in life. And he seemed to have a real problem with Mac despite the fact that it was obvious Mac had eyes for nobody except Jess.

Emily climbed the stairs to the nursery.

'Hey, baby,' Jackson said, loading up the roller for another patch of baby blue wall. 'Are you sure you don't want to do this pink?' he said, for what was probably something like the fifteenth time and Emily wondered how she'd ever fallen for a man with such simplistic gender assumptions.

'Blue's fine. It's calming. It matches the sea and the sky out of her window.'

He shrugged, applying the paint to the wall, pressing on as he rolled.

'We need to talk,' said Emily, sitting on the stool he'd been using to reach the corners.

'Oh dear. That sounds ominous,' he joked. 'Hang on.' He picked out his phone, which had rung in his pocket. 'I'll call them back,' he said, as if doing her a favour, just as he had several times in this last month or so. 'What's up?'

'This,' she began. 'This is what's up.'

'I thought you liked the blue?' He looked around the room, confused.

'I do. It's not the paint. It's us. I don't like us.'

Jackson froze.

'I've tried to give it a go, when you came back, you seemed so certain you could make things work, make things right and, I don't know, I didn't have the heart to tell you I didn't think it was possible. But I've tried. You've tried. And it's not going to work.'

'But I've moved to Cornwall.'

'Have you?'

He went to open the cupboard doors. 'My stuff is in your cupboards. My apartment is on the market!'

'Is it?'

'Well, it will be. Very soon.'

'But that's just it. Yes, you have some stuff in the baby's wardrobe, but you don't want to be here.' He went to disagree, but Emily knew there was nothing he could say. 'I left because I didn't want that life any more. And I know you can't just leave it behind. I left because I was getting old and the industry didn't want me to be anything other than a twenty-something yes-girl. That's not me…'

'You could have pretended. You still can.'

'But I don't want to. I've pretended for too long. I've compromised since before I realised what compromise was. I've gone along with whatever anybody wanted, and it was usually a man—'

'Oh right! This is some feminist shit, is it?'

'No, it's not feminist shit. It's life. It's my life. And I don't want it to be dictated to me any more. I want to define it. I want to live it my way.'

'Which is why I'm trying to adjust to living in a village full of idiots.'

His sudden drop of facade should have stunned Emily, but she'd been waiting for it. 'It's time you left.'

He muttered something, shaking his head. He threw the roller into the paint tray and blue splashed onto the carpet. 'Just like that? Eh? No discussion. I should just leave, should I?'

'I think it's best for both of us.'

'And what about that?' he said, pointing at Emily's swollen belly.

She placed her hand protectively over her bump. 'You don't really want her.'

'How do you know?' he spat.

'Well, do you?'

He put his hands on his hips. He stared at her.

'And that's fine. I'm not asking you to be here for her.'

'But I want you.'

'You want who I was before I left. You want the compliant me that goes along with whatever it is you need. Whoever you need me to be. The one who stands beside you until you tell me I can walk ahead.'

'I want the you I fell in love with.'

'She went, a long time ago. She's fierce now. She's going to be a mother. She has no interest in playing games. She just wants to live by the sea and walk on the beach. She wants to bake and see friends. She wants to tend to her garden and raise her daughter. She wants to volunteer. Maybe paint. Who knows, maybe she wants to write. She wants to see who she can be without the expectation of others.'

'Right. And she doesn't want a father for her child.'

'She doesn't *need* a father for her child. Especially not one who's playing for time.'

'And that's why I never put the apartment on the market.'

'I know.'

Jackson's eyes narrowed. 'If you don't want me, I don't want you. I don't want anything to do with that baby.'

'That's up to you. You can see her, if you change your mind. I can visit with her. You can come here.'

'Come here! I don't think I'll bother.'

'So you'll have to wait until I come to you then. On my terms.'

'Of course. Of course it's on your terms. And what about money? You wanna haul me through the courts for maintenance?'

'I want nothing from you.'

'Yeah, right.'

She stood. 'Jackson, I want nothing from you. I never have. I never will.' She looked around the room. 'I'll let you get yourself organised, get your things together. Take as long as you need. Leave whatever you'd like me to ship back.'

And with that, Emily left the nursery feeling lighter than she'd ever felt. And more excited for her and her baby's future than she could ever have imagined.

Jess

'So I toyed with travelling. I did a bit when I was a kid, but I don't know, I just didn't love it, you know? And I don't have anything to prove any more.'

'Have you ever had something to prove?' asked Mac, who'd been happily listening to her nervous rambling.

'I think so, though I don't know to who, if I'm honest. But it doesn't matter. The upshot is that I'm not going away now.'

'I'm glad,' said Mac, glancing over quickly before fixing his eyes back on the road.

'I'm glad too,' she said, her stomach flipping, which made her wonder why she'd avoided this feeling for so many years. Whatever this feeling was, she wasn't sure, but she was excited. She was giddy. She couldn't stop thinking about him. She barely slept last night, running over the sort of things they might talk about. Wondering where they'd go. Wondering if he'd kiss her. Stopping wondering if he would kiss her because she wouldn't sleep if she kept on thinking about his lips on hers. The thought again made her a bit weak so she changed the subject. 'So, where are we going then?' she asked.

'It's a surprise.' He grinned.

'I'm terrible with surprises. I just want to know straight away.'

'Do you need to learn about delayed gratification?' he asked, holding her gaze for longer than her butterflies could cope with.

'Maybe. Or not. I don't know. Give me a clue.'

'Okay.' He thought for a moment. 'It's somewhere I love.'

'Well, that's no use, I hardly know you.'

'Okay, it's somewhere outdoors.'

'Okay, that doesn't come as a huge surprise.'

'It's somewhere that you can just sit.'

'Nice. I like sitting.'

'It's somewhere that relates to something you said, ages ago.'

'Right…'

'It's somewhere you can hug lots of furry things…' he said, grinning.

'Furry things. What sort of furry things?'

'Big ones. Small ones. Friendly ones. Timid ones.'

Jess laughed. 'Where the hell are you taking me?' she asked, as he indicated left off the main road opposite a field of llamas or alpacas, she couldn't quite tell the difference.

'It's somewhere that I'd love to help out at, if I had more time. And lived closer.'

'Right…'

He indicated right again, heading down a tiny lane between two houses, just outside Falmouth. 'You're lucky, they're basically all on your doorstep.'

'What are?' she asked, now laughing.

'Donkeys!' he announced, pulling into a driveway.

'What?' She giggled.

'Donkeys. Rescue donkeys. I've brought you to one of my favourite places in Cornwall. Flicka Donkey Sanctuary.'

Jess belly laughed. 'Donkeys! I mean… I could never have guessed donkeys. This may be the strangest place for a first date.'

'Not in my book. First dates are for falling in love, right?'

Jess swallowed because she wasn't sure what first dates were for but quite liked his view of them.

'So here you get to fall in love with these amazing rescue creatures.' He pulled the handbrake on and jumped out of the car, jogging round to open her door. 'They have a cafe for lunch and look, down there, you can see the sea.'

It was the first red-hot day of the year, when the sun really had started to get up a bit of warmth and the skies were bright blue and never ending. As she climbed out of the car, she heard the sound of a donkey bray in the field opposite the car park.

'That'll be Walter,' he said, craning his neck to see. 'I saw him when he first came in. He'd been kept in a storage unit without windows. When they came to rescue him, opening the doors made him blink because the light was so bright.'

'Oh no!' Jess said as Mac took her by the hand and led her over to the paddock. 'Oh look, look at him.'

'I know, right, he's so handsome. And so gentle, come here, Walter.' The small patchwork donkey heard his name and trotted over to see them. Mac held his hand out, letting Walter sniff then push into it for a fuss. 'There's a good boy. You've got some friends now, eh? See, he was like that the first time I saw him. How can such a gentle animal be treated so badly?'

Jess's heart melted. Walter let Mac tickle and scratch his cheek and neck, watching Jess all the while.

'You said something about volunteering, or animal rescue. It was weeks ago at Emily's. That day we were there and Jackson kept subtly asking when we were leaving but you and Emily were talking about work and the fact you wanted to make a change.'

'Oh, god, yes. I remember that day. You were building the shed and I had to shift my chair because you looked…' Jess trailed off because she realised she was suddenly overwhelmed with embarrassment at the memory of her thoughts that day.

'I looked what?' he asked, leaning closer to her.

'Well… you know.'

He held her gaze again, his deep brown eyes twinkling. 'Well, anyway,' he said, returning his focus to Walter, much to Jess's heart's relief. 'I just thought that maybe, if I plucked up the courage to ask you out, that I could bring you here. That maybe it would inspire you somehow. And also because I love it. I mean, look at them! Come on, put your hand out.'

Mac took hold of her hand and placed it on Walter's neck beneath his. She wasn't sure if her heart racing was with love for the donkey or lust for Mac, either way, she could barely breathe. This was the most perfect place. The most perfect, ridiculous, date.

'I can't believe you brought me to see the donkeys,' she said, beaming.

Mac nudged her gently. 'Just wait until you see Bertie,' he said, leaving his hand on hers before taking it. 'Come on!'

And oh, he was right about Bertie. A massive French donkey. Some fifteen plus hands. He looked like Chewbacca, or a man in a dreadlocked donkey suit. He had giant ears that flopped as he shook his head. And in another field there was a smaller version of him, not a rescue but one brought over to raise the awareness of this rare breed. Mac told her everything, all about them. He pointed out donkeys, reeling off their names.

'That's Paddington, he's cheeky. He chases Penny all over and when she's had enough, she'll give him a little nip on the bum. That's

Annabelle, she's a total sweetheart. Look at those ears, her hair waterfalls from the tips. She loves cuddles when you can get her over to see you.'

'How do you know all these donkeys?'

'I've been quite often over the years. I love it here.'

Jess could tell why, it had something about it. A strange peace. A gentleness. The collection of pigeons in the courtyard. The twilight herd. The volunteers cleaning, grooming, telling stories of the donkeys, working the tea room.

'Lunch?' Mac asked, pointing to a cabin called Bray-k Time.

'Yes!' she said, realising that as well as feeling quite giddy, she was also feeling hungry.

Jess and Mac sat on a bench outside the tea room, paddocks surrounding them, the occasional bray from donkeys interrupting the otherwise peaceful environment. They talked about their childhood, their families. She told him about her work and he told her about his numerous jobs. He loved being on the sea, the freedom, the connection to nature. He loved to stand on the beach looking out at the horizon just breathing. Jess had admitted she rarely got to the beach, apart from when visiting Emily.

'Have you been to Vault Beach, just behind her place?'

'Yes, it's stunning!'

'I often park up at the National Trust car park and walk the dog. So often I go there and see nobody.'

'Maybe we could go together sometime.'

'I'd like that.'

*

Later that evening, after they'd spent hours outside The Ferry Boat Inn, overlooking the Helford River, he pulled up to her house. He got out of the car to open her door and she could barely breathe with the anticipation, the need to kiss him. For him to kiss her. To feel him close. They'd held hands. They'd sat beside each other, close enough to just be touching. She'd felt his thigh press against hers as they sat silently watching the river. She'd felt his arm behind her as he leant back, resting it on the bench. That was as close as they'd been and all she could think of was what it might feel like to kiss him. To close her eyes and lean in and for their lips to touch. And as they stood on the top step, him telling her what a gorgeous time he'd had, she took his hand. And as he leaned into her, asking her when he could see her again, she pulled him in closer and said, 'When are you free?' and he took her face in his hand, a small smile spreading across his as he told her he'd never met anybody like her and she said, 'Me too.' And he slipped his arm around her waist as she leant her cheek into his hand. And then her heart almost stopped as he leant in closer, and she reached up, and their lips brushed and she had to stop herself from letting out a sigh because it felt so gentle, and so perfect and so exactly what she had been missing out on for so many years and perhaps, just perhaps, it had been entirely worth the wait.

Lolly

'Are you sure you're okay?' asked Joanna down the phone. Since Lolly and Kitt had split up, she was on the phone most days, visiting whenever she could. It had definitely drawn them closer. 'I can come with you if you'd prefer, I really don't mind. I can just take a few days off work again.'

'You've done enough,' said Lolly, rinsing her coffee cup clean and laying it on the drainer. These were the tiny wins since Kitt had gone. He used to hate reusing a mug and as a consequence they'd get through all their mugs and cups on the days he'd been at home. She'd always asked him why he couldn't just rinse them and he'd told her that was disgusting. She took a certain sense of pride in not giving a damn now. 'Anyway, Emily said she'd meet me for lunch afterwards so I'll be fine. I've got back up.'

'If you're sure.'

'I'm sure.'

The meeting with the solicitor took less than an hour. She explained Kitt's adultery, avoiding reference to sex workers because each time she thought about it she thought about Amanda and she hated how it made her judge her. After a few weeks reeling from the reality of the state of her marriage, she and Amanda had met up. Lolly had shouted at her, told her she was disgusting and perverted and everything that was wrong with the world. Then she'd broken down in tears and Amanda said nothing but reached out her hand and held it with such dignity and generosity, given what Lolly had just said, that it extinguished any anger she had about her having slept with Kitt. She believed her when she said it happened before the reunion. Amanda also explained why she did the job in the first place and whilst Lolly could never claim to understand, or even like it, she did have to acknowledge that Amanda was making her own choice, paying her own bills. And she loved her. Just like she always had. She just preferred not to really talk to her about it.

She pushed open the door to Mannings, where Emily had booked them in for a special lunch. She promised it wasn't about celebrating what Lolly had just been and done because let's face it, what was there to celebrate, it was the end of her life as she'd planned it, but Emily wanted to do something special. To support Lolly. Lolly loved a nice lunch and needed the cold glass of Sauvignon that was waiting for her.

'So how'd it go?' Emily asked.

'I don't know really. I mean, I guess it's fine. I explained the situation, gave her the details. Gave her Kitt's contact details.'

'He still living in that bedsit in Penryn?'

'Yup. Probably thoroughly enjoying the student life.' Emily shook her head in disbelief. 'It's fine. He comes round on the weekends to take the boys out. I can just about be civil with him for their sake. The house is on the market as of this weekend.'

'Oh no!'

'It's fine. Honestly. I thought I'd be devastated but I want a fresh start. I'm going to try and get one of the new places up by the hospital. I don't need much space, somewhere smaller and cheaper will be better for me and the boys. I can walk to work so no parking costs. The boys can move to the school up there and I think it'll be fine.'

Emily smiled. 'I think you're amazing,' she said, holding up her glass of mineral water.

'Hey, we're in this together now, single parents. We're gonna need each other, I reckon.'

'Damn right!'

'Enough about me. Did Jackson go?'

Emily nodded. 'He went. Yes. Took a suitcase full of stuff and told me to sell or burn the rest. He wasn't bothered about any of it. Dunno why he bothered bringing it over in the first place, except to make a show of moving his life to Cornwall.'

'Do you think that was all that it was then? A show?'

'Totally. His entire life is a show. Always has been. Always will be. I think I knew that, but I guess I felt I should at least try and see if it could work. Given that he's the father and all that.'

Lolly nodded. She felt for Emily but couldn't help be pleased that Jackson had gone. She'd never really taken to him. 'So what happens next?'

'Well, the room is painted. I finished it off with Mac the other day.' She pulled out her phone to show Lolly pictures of a Pinterest-perfect nursery, ready and waiting for baby's arrival. 'Mac is hoping to clear the cupboards at the weekend, when he gets back from his current fishing trip. Then that's it. Jackson has gone. It's just me and this little one.' She stroked what was now quite a generous baby bump.

'Did they go out, Mac and Jess?'

'Oh my god, they did. I've heard it from both sides and all I can say is you may want to consider buying a hat.'

'Ahhh, that is sooo lovely.' Lolly was genuinely pleased although wished it wasn't tinged with a hint of envy. She knew she'd survive alone and she had made the right choice to start divorce proceedings, but she couldn't help the fact that she had always wanted to be married. And she loved being with someone. And she wanted to one day have that again.

'I bought you something.' Emily passed a small box and a card across the table.

'What's this?' asked Lolly, taking it, confused.

'It's just a little something, I hope… well… open it. See what you think.'

Lolly unwrapped the box, lifting the lid and peeling open creamy tissue paper. Nestled within it was a gold bangle with a single star on it. 'What's this? It's… it's beautiful!' She took it out, stunned.

'Try it on.'

She opened the clasp and placed it on her wrist. 'It's gorgeous, Emily, thank you!'

'Well. You can't thank me yet.'

'What do you mean?'

'It comes with a request. You need to read the card.'

Lolly ripped open the envelope, admiring her bracelet all the while. On the front were two women propping each other up with a bottle of gin and big hearts between them. It said *Friends are my lifeblood, but Gin definitely helps!* beneath it, which made Lolly laugh since she didn't drink gin and Emily drank nothing at the moment.

'I'm counting the days down until my first G&T,' said Emily.

'Mother's Ruin,' warned Lolly as she started reading.

And then she bit down on her bottom lip because she couldn't say anything. And then her eyes filled and she could barely read the words. And then Emily's hand reached out to hold hers and she said, 'Please say yes.' And Lolly nodded, a tear spilling on the card. 'I so wanted to ask you and then I worried it was a bit insensitive, but I can't think of anybody else I'd rather ask.'

Lolly sniffed a big snotty sniff then laughed and hiccupped. 'I can't believe you asked me.'

'She needs a brilliant, smart, kind, inspiring woman and whilst she's going to have a couple of those in her life, I just thought you and she could make a real team.'

'Thank you, Emily. Thank you so much! I can't tell you what it means.'

'I think it means that until you get your own, you have a little girl to form a bond with.'

'I think it means I don't need my own.' Lolly sniffed. 'I have my boys and I have my friends and now, I have this,' said Lolly, pulling Emily up to give her a big hug. 'You are going to be such an amazing mum and I'd love to be her godmother. I've got the little girl after all.'

Epilogue

The setting sun sent the sky into a mad pink frenzy of wonder and all the women could do was sit and stare. 'This is the life,' said Jess, not daring to peel her eyes away in case she missed the moment the sun dipped down behind the horizon.

Lolly sighed. 'I know, right. I mean, where else can you sit in a jacuzzi, sipping champagne—'

'Well, sit on the edge and drink sparkling mineral water,' interjected Emily.

'Yes, well, some of us have to just wait a little longer before they can appreciate the dizzy heights of jacuzzi and alcohol at sunset,' said Jess. 'You don't want to boil baby.'

'What she said. We can come back, just as soon as you're ready. Though I've a few stories I could tell about jacuzzis!' said Amanda.

'Eeeuuuw! Don't! Not whilst we're in one,' said Emily, recoiling.

'Not here, these are very lovely jacuzzis. I'm sure we've nothing to worry about here, it's a high-end establishment, don't you know!'

Lolly said nothing. The more time she spent with Amanda, the more used to things she got. And some of the stories of what she got up to had, she had to admit, opened her eyes to her own somewhat vanilla sexual desires. She was quite happy to keep them that way, as and when the opportunity arose. Maybe when the boys were older.

'So I just wanted to toast us,' said Lolly. 'I wanted to say a massive thank you for being there for me. For holding my hand through all of this shit. For being incredible women who I never want to not have in my life again.'

'That's good. Since we're not going anywhere,' said Jess, sipping at her fizz.

'You can't. I need to live vicariously. Tell me everything about Mac and don't leave a single thing out.'

'Ha!' Jess laughed. 'You should be so lucky! Let's just say that he makes me a very happy woman and whilst I can't believe what I missed out on for all the years I thought I was in love with Jay Trewellan, if I hadn't missed out, I might never have met Mac.'

'Cheers to that!' said Amanda, clinking her glass.

'So you two are getting on better at work then now?'

'We are, yeah. For now. I still think I'm going to leave. I fancy fundraising. Charity work. I need to do some research but for now, I'll stick it out until I've made a plan. Although, I now realise how much Niamh has to put up with in him. I mean, seriously, he can be a real pain in the arse. I had totally and utterly built him up to be this perfect man and I can tell you, he is—'

'Not that much different from most other men?' asked Lolly.

'Well, Mac excluded,' said Jess.

'Mac will irritate you in time. It's a thing they do. It doesn't mean you won't still love him, but you know… living with them can really get on your nerves,' said Lolly, with a hint of sadness in her tone.

'I think, if I were to ever live with anyone again, it would definitely be a woman,' said Amanda.

'What?' said Emily. 'Has all this sex work turned you off men?'

'God no! Don't be ridiculous! I don't want to stop sleeping with men any more than I want to start sleeping with women... unless I'm getting paid for it. No, I just think women must be easier to live with.'

'I lived with Emily for three days and can tell you that even she had her moments!' Jess replied.

'What do you mean?' shrieked Emily, before saying 'Oooh, ouch.'

'What?' Lolly sat up, pouring herself a top up.

'Nothing, just Braxton Hicks.'

'You said that earlier. Are they getting worse?'

'Well, I don't know. I mean, maybe. They're more frequent.'

Lolly stopped pouring. 'What do you mean? They're getting more frequent?'

'Well, I don't know do I... ouch... ooooh...' Emily breathed deeply, placing her hand on her stomach.

'Have you had a show yet, Em?' asked Lolly, climbing out of the jacuzzi.

'Is that the vile bloody clot thing?'

'Yes.'

'Yes then. A few days ago.'

'Right...'

'Shit, it really hurts. Maybe I could just get in, let the warmth ease my back.'

'No, no, no, you're not allowed,' said Lolly, reaching to stop her. 'In fact, I think it's time we got you out altogether.'

Amanda looked at Jess, whose mouth opened in realisation.

'But it's lovely and warm, I could just have a second.' She allowed herself to slip in for a moment, breathing deeper, disappearing into herself as the sun dropped and a cool breeze whipped up.

Lolly placed her hand on Emily's shoulder, making her open her eyes. 'Emily, I think this might be it…'

'What?'

'This. Now. The Braxton Hicks. I'm not sure they're Braxton Hicks.'

'But I've got another week to go yet.'

'Yes, and babies will make their appearance when they're good and ready, not when you are.'

Emily's eyes widened. Then she tried to stand, the girls helping her. She paused to let another contraction wash over her before looking at Lolly. 'Shit… shit…' she said.

'It's fine,' said Lolly, calmly. 'It's fine. We're all here. Come on, get her out, girls, I think we have a little diversion to make.'

'But I want to stay in the hot tub,' said Emily, climbing out.

'If we're not allowed to have sex in it, you can sure as hell bet you're not allowed to birth in it,' said Amanda, wrapping her in a towel and guiding her back into their bedroom suite.

And as Emily began to breathe and then panic and then breathe, the girls rallied round, getting dressed, organising the birthing bag, loading up the car, buckling Emily in, and heading off to the maternity ward. This time, they would all be in it together.

The End.

A Letter from Anna

Hi! Lovely to see you here. And thank you for reading! If you enjoyed it, and want to keep up-to-date with all my latest releases, just sign up at the following link. Your email address will never be shared and you can unsubscribe at any time.

www.bookouture.com/anna-mansell

Looking back on previous author letters, normally at this point I tell you how the book was a long time coming etcetera, etcetera, but in fact, with this one, I had the idea at the start of 2018 and sit here at the end of November 2018, having just finished reading through the copy edits. So by my standards, this was a quick book to write. That said, I've felt quite passionate about the theme, so maybe that's why?

You see, I don't know about you, but I feel that everywhere I look and turn, women are judged for everything they do. From what they wear, to how they look. Choices to have children, choices not to. Choices to have a career, choices to not. Whether it's magazines scrutinising our bodies, or certain TV presenters on breakfast telly who like to judge the every move and thought of women they have and haven't interviewed. I suppose, my point is that I am exhausted by it.

I am tired of the judgement and I am over feeling the need to comply or conform. I'm forty-one, maybe that's why!

The other thing we get judged for, in my opinion at least, is how feminist are we? Too feminist and we're damaging the cause. Not feminist enough and we're a let-down, a disappointment to womankind. And if we are a little bit feminist but also like a door held open for us, WOE BETIDE!

We are, each and every one of us, complex, brilliant, flawed, funny, difficult, and inspiring human beings and I wish to celebrate that. This is a novel about four incredible women living very different lives. It's about the power of friendships and the difficulty of judgement. It is not a novel about a sex worker, or a woman in love with someone else's husband. It's not about a woman yearning for another child when she's got two already, it is not about a woman who can't decide whether to keep her baby or not; this is a novel about how women are judged in society. It's about our freedom to choose the lives we want to live. It's about the importance of friendship and, above all, maybe, it's about forgiveness. Forgiveness because we don't always get things right, and, if we're honest, we probably do all judge, but how we choose to live by those choices, or how we allow our judgement to manifest, says more to me about a person than any choice they made in the first place.

I hope you enjoyed reading *Her Best Friend's Secret* as much as I enjoyed writing it. If you did, I'd be very grateful for a review as they really do make a difference to the success or otherwise of our work and more importantly, I just love to hear from those of you that have taken your precious time and spent some hours in my imaginary world.

You can also message me via my Facebook page, through Twitter, on Goodreads, Insta or my website.

Thank you!

Anna x

      AnnaMansellAuthor

      @annamansell

      MrsAnnaM

      www.feelthefearandwriteitanyway.com

Acknowledgements

Here we are once again, my fourth novel. Which wouldn't have happened were it not for you, dear reader. So thank you. You really are making my dreams come true and if I could, I'd pop round and thank every one of you... except that might seem a bit weird. But know that I really do appreciate you!

There's a special group of readers who I am also indebted to. The readers who also blog about what they've read and champion our books. These are the women and men of the internet who read book after book after book, all in their own spare time, in order to tell the world what they think of them and that really helps to launch our novels into the real world. Bloggers I'd particularly like to name check are @choconwaffles @kaishajayneh, and @stefloz. In particular, @TishyLou warrants a thank you not just for blogging and reviewing my work, but for checking in on me when she knew things were particularly tough. More on that in a moment but for now, Trish and all the aforementioned, thank you for thoughtful reviews and passionate championing.

The team at Bookouture are an incredible bunch and I feel very fortunate to be part of the family. Kim and Noelle work tirelessly for us authors, shouting from the rooftops. They are amazing! I have to say a huge thank you to Isobel for her support of this novel, even before she entirely knew what it might shape up to be. She has trusted me to write these women and has guided me to shape their story. I don't know how she does what she does but I am very glad to be one of her authors.

Who else? Well, I write friends in all of my books because I would not be who I am today were it not for my own tribe. I chose a group of four women in this novel specifically because I am part of a four whom I adore. We've known each other for over twenty years… in fact, crikey, it must be twenty-five or twenty-six… and they are amazing and we are very definitely stronger as a team, especially when life happens and one of us needs the group. Ellen, Cas, and Claire, this year has been the hardest of my life and you have been there every step of the way – regardless of the distance between us. Thank you!

On that note, if I may be indulged for a moment, I want to say this. This novel proved to be a world I could escape to when my own was just too much. I'm not quite sure how I managed to write it given that I spent much of my time caring for my poorly mum during this year. Many hospital visits, many hours at her home, many trips to the docs or the chemist or the local shops or wherever it was she needed to be. It wasn't so much the time that made it challenging, but the emotional impact of it all. I somehow managed to finish the first draft sat by her bedside in hospital. The edits came in as she died. That I had something to focus on during the hardest time of my life was surely one of the reasons I survived. Genuine, heartfelt thank you to Bookouture – and in particular Isobel and Kim – for respecting and supporting me throughout that time.

Some other brilliant women should also be namechecked, in fact I wonder if I'd ever get out of bed if it weren't for knowing they've got my back: Lian, Clare, Maria, Ness, Lou, Crocker. Not to mention the beautiful friends who left flowers on my doorstep or sent cards through school bags this past year. Thank you for keeping me (and therefore this book!) afloat.

Of course, I would get out of bed, and do, every day, for my precious family. As ever, H, M and Him in Doors – you amaze me every day. You love me despite my own, innumerable flaws and complexities. I just hope that you know I love and appreciate you in return.

I've probably missed someone. That's the danger of writing these things. If I have, accept my profound apologies. It is not that you are not important to me, it is that my brain doesn't always remember every detail that it could. Sorry. But thank you. Truly.

Anna x

Printed in Great Britain
by Amazon